I0716574

TETHERS OF WAR

THE LUMINANCE SAGA

BOOK THREE

STEVEN RUDY

MYSTICHAWK
PRESS

The book is a work of fiction. Names, characters, places, and incidents are the product of the author's imagination and are used fictitiously. Any resemblance to actual events, locales, or persons, living or dead, is coincidental.

TETHERS OF WAR

Copyright © 2023 by Steven Rudy

All rights reserved.

No part of this book may be reproduced in any form or by any electronic or mechanical means, including information storage and retrieval systems, without written permission from the author, except for the use of brief quotations in a book review.

Edited by Tammy Salyer

Cover Design by Franziska Stern - www.coverdungeon.com

– Instagram: @coverdungeonrabbit

See Illustrations List

Map Illustrations by Steven Rudy, using (Wonderdraft and Adobe Suite)

* Illustration by Kateryna Vitkovska

Published by MysticHawk Press LLC

ISBN- 978-1-7370652-8-9 (paperback)

ISBN- 978-1-7370652-7-2 (hardcover)

ISBN- 978-1-7370652-6-5 (ebook)

First Edition: October 2023

TETHERS OF WAR

BY
STEVEN RUDY

MYSTICHAWK
PRESS

For

My Parents

Acknowledgements

My wife is amazing, her tireless efforts and sacrifices have provided so much for our family and for me. Because of her, I'm able to pursue these writing endeavors.

Thank you, D, for all that you do. I love you and know that none of this would be possible without you. Your support gets me through, and I appreciate you. Also, thank you for providing the in-depth beta read and never pulling punches.

I'm so very grateful for everyone who contributed to this project, but I wanted to thank my editor, for jumping into the middle of a book series and providing excellent feedback while guiding me to the best version possible for this book. I'm so very grateful for your help and contribution to this project.

I also wanted to thank children for always showing interest in "Dad's book". I will never be able to explain how dear, each of you are to me. You are a brightness to my world that glows like starlight.

"Accept the things to which fate binds you, and love the people with whom fate brings you together, but do so with all your heart."

— Marcus Aurelius

CONTENTS

ILLUSTRATIONS

*Art by Kateryna Vitkovska

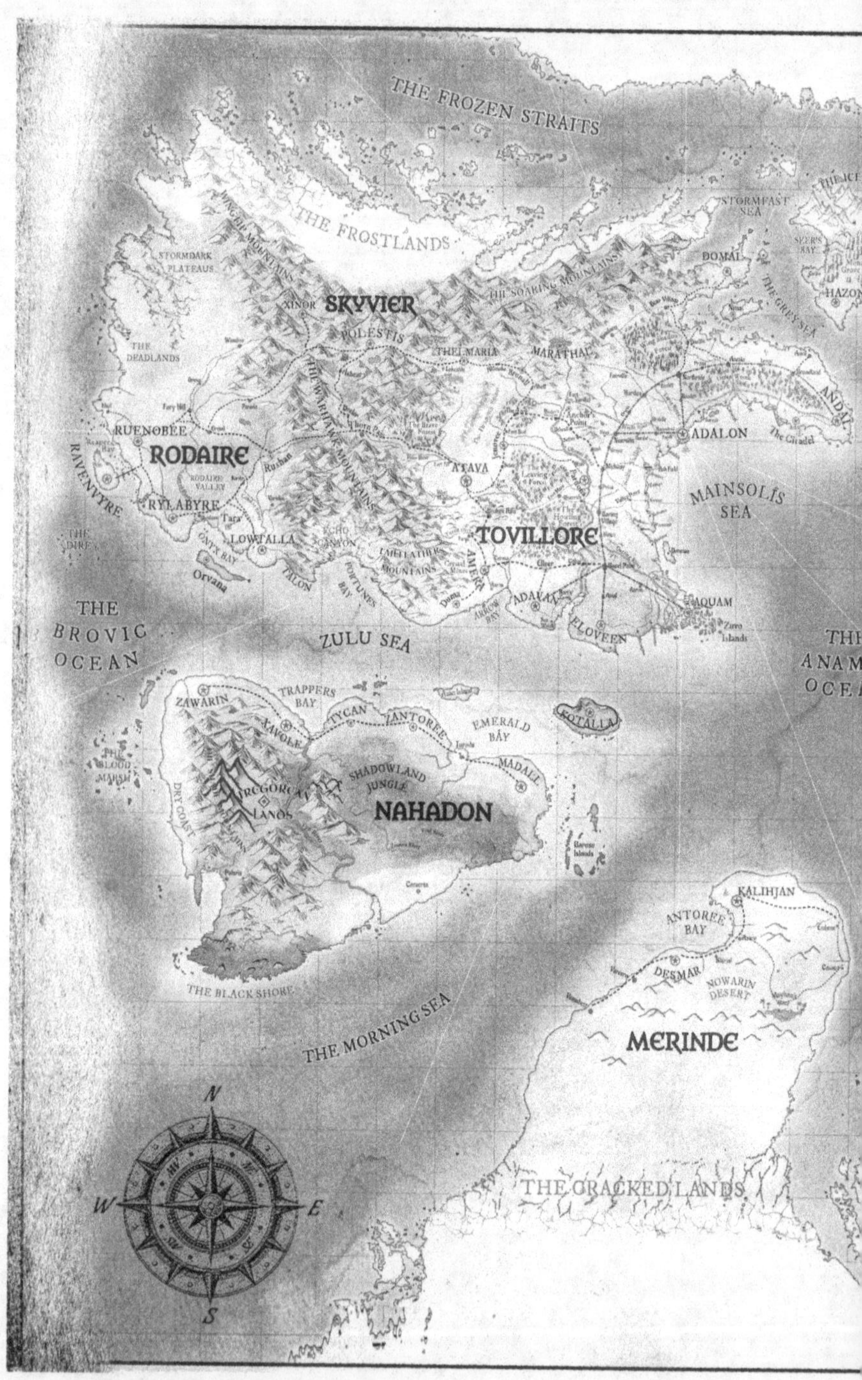

THE FROZEN STRAITS
THE FROSTLANDS
THE ICE
STORMFAST SEA
SYER'S BAY
DOMAI
HAZON
STORMDARK PLATEAUS
WINGFELL MOUNTAINS
XINOR
SKYVIER
THE SOARING MOUNTAINS
POLESTIS
THEL MARIA
MARATHAL
THE DEADLANDS
ANDAI
Fairy Hill
RUENOBEE
THE WARHAWK MOUNTAINS
Thorn
ADALON
The Citadel
RODAIRE
RODAIRE VALLEY
Rushan
ATAVA
RAVENVYRE
RYLABYRE
MAINSOLIS SEA
Tara
ECHO CANYON
THE DIRE
LOWTALLA
THEFLATHE MOUNTAINS
AMERIA
TOVILLORE
ONYX BAY
Orvana
TALON
FORTUNES BAY
Duma
ADAVAX
AQUAM
ARROW BAY
ELOVEEN
Zarro Islands
THE BROVIC OCEAN
ZULU SEA
THE ANAM OCEA
ZAWARIN
TRAPPERS BAY
TYCAN
ANTOREE
EMERALD BAY
KOTALLA
XAVOLE
THE BLOOD MARSH
SHADOWLAND JUNGLE
MADALI
DRY COAST
URGGOROA
LANOS
NAHADON
Rarone Islands
THE BLACK SHORE
KALIHJAN
ANTOREE BAY
DESMAR
NOWARIN DESERT
THE MORNING SEA
MERINDE
N
W
E
S
THE CRACKED LANDS

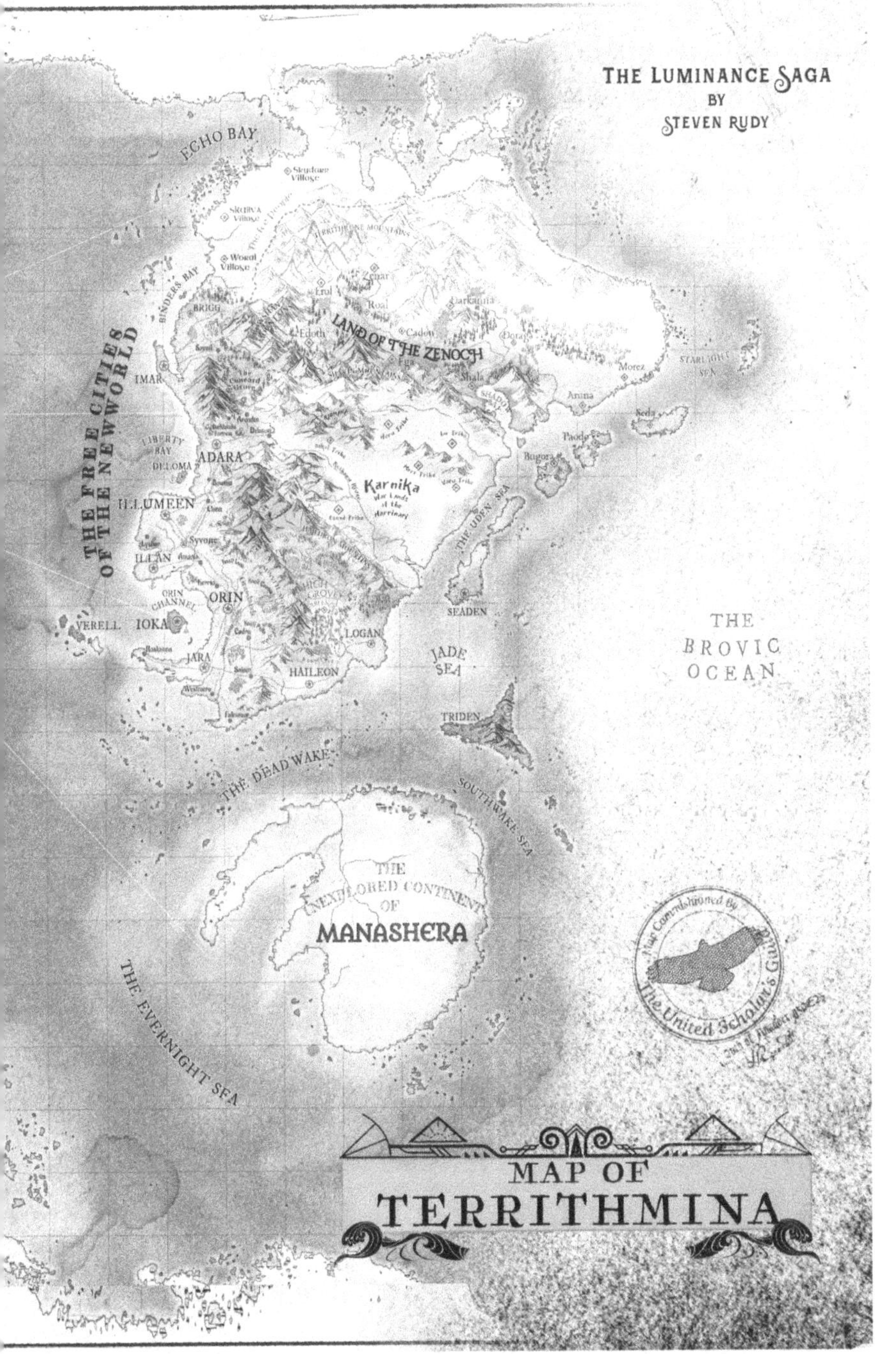

THE LUMINANCE SAGA
BY
STEVEN RUDY

ECHO BAY

THE FREE CITIES OF THE NEWWORLD

LAND OF THE ZENOCH

Skudow Village
Skurva Village
Woral Village
TERRITHUNE MOUNTAINS
BINDERS BAY
BRIGG
Zenar
Erol
Roal
Darkania
Doral
Edoth
Cadon
Ega
DeMos
Morez
STARLIGHT SEA
Shala
SHADO
Aruna
Seda
Paodo
IMAR
Bugora
LIBERTY BAY
DELOMA
ADARA
Karnika
War Lands of the Harriners
ILLUMEEN
Syvone
THE UDEN SEA
ILLAN
ORIN CHANNEL
ORIN
HIGH GROVE
VERELL
IOKA
SEADEN
THE BROVIC OCEAN
Roakona
JARA
LOGAN
JADE SEA
HAILEON
Westmere
TRIDEN
THE DEAD WAKE
SOUTHWAKE SEA
THE UNEXPLORED CONTINENT OF
MANASHERA
Not Commissioned By
The United Scholar's Guild
THE EVERNIGHT SEA

MAP OF
TERRITHMINA

PROLOGUE

THE RODAIREAN LEGION ANCHORED THEIR GALLEY SHIPS NEAR THE last pier, at the last island of the Dire, in their search for the remaining Sea-rippers. They expected to find monsters and no survivors. On approach, it became obvious, the Sea-rippers, the very monsters they had come to the Dire to hunt, had already been gruesomely dispatched. Bits of the dead creatures were decomposing all around, with some of the corpses slipping back into the sea with the tide. However, the evidence of their terror and destruction was all around.

The crews of the *Steadfast* and the *Moonfall* landed and filed out on the stone pier. Dorian walked with his men among the wreckage. Ship fragments and splintered wood were scattered on the shore. Rolling waves splashed over dead bodies, and the rubble of a town destroyed loomed on the rise.

"What happened here?" Dorian muttered.

"What killed the monsters?" Teego asked, his hand tightening on his sword and sweat beading on his brow.

Dorian shook his head, trying to understand what had taken place. *How is everything dead, and more curious, how were the Sea-rippers killed?*

"Keep your eyes wide, Tee. There must be more monsters here, hiding on the island. The people put up a good fight though," Dorian said.

The further onto shore they walked, the more wreckage they found. The monsters had laid waste to the structures and inhabitants with the same havoc and horrors they had seen before. The sea-scorpion creatures were terrifying and lethal. The Rodairean army defeated the swarm that crawled out of the sea near Lowtalla, but fighting still raged on in Orvana.

Dorian scanned around and noticed that the pattern of sand below his boots had started to change. There was a shape among the array of debris, circular in nature. The scattering suggested an explosion from the heart of the town.

The men slowed as they became aware of the scene, their Meiyoma blades drawn.

Dorian was the first to see her.

Alone on the road was a small dark-haired girl. Her brown eyes wide with shock, she stood trembling in a depression of the terrain at the center of the blast.

"Go retrieve the captain, we have a survivor," Dorian told Teego. He cautiously approached the girl. She looked like she couldn't be more than four years old. She was soaked head to foot with water and blood, and a substantial amount of sand and dirt was caked on her as well. Her sopping dark hair hung over her face, which bore a look of shock and fury.

"What's your name, little girl?" he asked softly, crouching down to her.

She clung to her necklace, and she peered up at him, confused. She either didn't know or was too traumatized to speak. Her head jerked up to see the captain coming over.

When more of the legion came into the area with the steel of their swords gleaming, her eyes bulged, as though she was about to be caught in the jaws of the monsters. She dashed away deeper into the island's interior.

"Wait, stop!" Dorian called.

"Find her," the captain yelled, watching her run away.

Some of the men circled around to the various paths, while Dorian ran directly after her, his friend Teego sprinting behind him.

In the thick island fora of trees and bushes, the girl disappeared. Through the foliage, Dorian spotted an old stone watchtower and headed toward it. When the trees cleared, they found the girl crossing a crest of jagged rocks leading out of the tower, the crash of the ocean spraying up around her as she jumped from rock to rock. They approached the riprap embankment, and the small child spun around at them, as if she felt them coming. Her wet hair flung around her in the turn, and her eyes glared with equal parts daring and fear. The color of them seemed to swirl.

"Ovardyn's black eyes," Teego cursed under his breath.

With each swell of the tide came random bits of rubble and wood. Some of it was hurtled back ashore, like the sea was rejecting the foreign objects. Dorian pressed in and closed the distance to grab the girl. With impossible agility, she dove for a larger piece afloat on the waves—a small platform on the water. She used it to jump to another larger partially submerged craft. Off that piece, she jumped to the crossway to sprint further down the coastline, free of Dorian's grasp.

They doubled back and caught up with her further up the tiny island, along with a small group of soldiers. She stood motionless amid a small mass of collapsed houses, with palm branches from the thatched roofs littered all over the ground. A man that Dorian didn't recognize from the second boat tried to grab her, but the girl spun through his arms and pulled a long stick from the dirt. She spun the stick and smashed one of the ends into her attacker's face, then she backed away. He toppled to the ground.

The other soldiers who had surrounded her hesitated, and took a moment to reassess this small exceptional person.

With coordinating effort, the group of five men closed in on her, pulling and grabbing for her arms. One of the men abruptly convulsed in pain, as though injured by an invisible phantom. He screamed, staring at his hands, his eyes wide with disbelief. The skin on his palms was charred black and blistered. More men cried out in pain. Whenever the girl put her hands on someone's skin, they were instantly burned. The men backed away, but some fell where they stood and passed out from some unknown force, without her touching them at all.

The little girl was shaking now. She appeared cold and her eyes blinked and darted all around like she was as frightened as the men around her. Underneath it all, Dorian saw a look of pure determination to survive.

Dorian decided on a different approach. Among the ruins, he spotted a dark green woolen blanket, and he tore it free of the wreckage. The men were angry enough to hurt the girl now and panicked. One of the men started to charge in to kill her, but Dorian ran past him and arrived first. He wrapped her exhausted body up in the blanket and moved her swiftly down the road, away from the mob as fast as he could.

Almost as if she was waiting to be protected, her body sagged in his arms, with small tremors reverberating through her as he ambled back to his ship.

"You're all right. I promise," Dorian told her.

Teego followed behind them. Holding his Sagean-eye necklace tightly, he kissed it and whispered scripture about omens.

"Teego, help me with her. Leave your prayers for the dead," Dorian said.

"That's what I'm doing, Dorian," he explained.

Together they brought the girl back to their ship while most of the other crews covered the rest of the island looking for more survivors. By then the rumor had spread that the little girl had somehow killed the swarm of Sea-rippers by herself. Dorian tried to take her below deck, but she shuddered with fear, and he led her to the top deck instead. The captain wandered over as more men arrived from their searches.

"How is she? Has she said anything yet?" the captain asked.

"She's still in shock," Dorian answered.

"Keep an eye her. She's under your charge, Lieutenant Dorian, until we get back to the mainland. I don't want anyone talking to her either. I don't want anyone to see her, understand?"

"Aye, aye, Captain."

With that, the captain turned to Teego. "Teego, go tell the master navigator, Morrowmaki, that I want the fastest course he can find."

"Yes, Captain." Teego jumped into action, sprinting down to the captain's quarters.

Dorian stood beside the girl, watching the soldiers return to the ships, their search coming up empty. This was the last island of the Dire they had left to search. The only survivors they had found were on the big island that still had ancient fortifications in place, and the girl. Many of the towers built by the Sagean Empire had been destroyed by the creatures.

When Teego came back, he was still whispering scripture to himself. He sat back with them, but distinctly kept his distance from the girl, still outwardly bothered by her presence.

"She's calmed down, Teego. You don't have to be frightened," Dorian said.

"The Ancients knew all, my friend," Teego replied, gazing out to the ocean. He continued, "In the fourth book of the Sages, it says, 'When the shadow awakens, and the termination line rolls over the world, none but the fingers of God will stand against the storm.'"

Teego shifted against the rail and pulled his necklace free of his broadcloth vest.

"I'm not scared, Dorian, I'm in awe. I read a book once, it belonged to my great grandfather. It was more sacred and rarer than all the volumes of the Sages. It was a book of the Fates. Inside, it spoke of many horrifying things, but one passage that has always stayed with me said,

You will know when the Last Dawn has come
When the hands of God touch the Territh
The Source-born will awaken.
And their eyes will swirl, and they will clutch lightning like a feather
And burn the flesh of heathens
And they will drink the sun,
And all will know that once again
the tethers of war have come.
And the world shall reap the whirlwind.

PART ONE

Ioka
To Illumeen
To Orin
To Roskanna
Jara
The Orin Channel
Ioka
Crimson Delta
Wildwood Shores
Herring River
Azel Bay
Cedar Point
Jewel River
King's Palace
Airstation
Ioka Docks
Ioka University
Rhema Harbor
Old Lighthouse
Omero Bay
Moonlight Coast
Adra Chain
Vacarden Cove
Rainbow Bay
Commissioned by United Scholars Guild

ONE

WAITING - ELLARIA

THE OCEAN IS A PARAGON OF INFINITY, ELLARIA THOUGHT. HER ARMS rested on the stone balustrade of her balcony as she gazed to the west. She had always found the ocean waves a wonder to behold, as though they were the closest thing to the abyss of time in motion. Time for her was moving slow. At that moment, she felt like a single drop of water flowing in the high tide, abandoned beneath a darkening sky threatening a perilous repose.

It was early morning, and the bay was clear from the Orin Channel, where the waters encircled Ioka, all the way out to the horizon line, where the New World armada was anchored in defense. The Sagean's blockade, established by the now dead Prime Commander Dunne, was still locked in place. The Sagean's naval force had strangled the New World for nearly nine months. Over that time, the extent of the blockade had expanded. In eight months, the enemy fleet had grown to over two hundred warships that stretched from the southern point of Verell all the way north and across Liberty Bay.

Just beyond the line of battle-ready ships of wood and steel, storm clouds were building. *Both real and imagined.* The winter had come early and been harsh, but the storm, she feared, was the start of the new world war. Ellaria and the New World leaders expected any day now for the Sagean's patience to lose out to his rage and the battle to begin.

Ellaria's gaze settled on a group of smaller steam-powered scout ships pulling a barge back to land for supplies. It was a continual effort to resupply the ships and the men at the front line. Already the Sagean had pressed the line significantly. This morning marked two months that Ellaria had been watching the tension build, and almost three months since the night in the Genesis Chamber.

Ellaria stared out at the tide and the majestic sky, waiting for any sign of Kovan. He had been far too long in getting to her, and her concern increased with each passing day.

The original plan had been to meet up in the Baruse Islands, but Kovan had been sidetracked. Unable to sail through the Zulu Sea, he had redirected his crew to the Tregoreans' harbor in Wuri Bay on the western coast of Nahadon. Kovan's new plan had been to find the aeronaut Bazlyn and fly the winddrifter to the New World.

In her last communications with Wade, he told her they were near Wuri Bay and only days from meeting up with Bazlyn. Ellaria knew they would have to wait for clear skies before the winddrifter might risk flying, but that had been ten days ago. By her estimation, it had been eight days since they could have taken off, and the airship should have been able to cross the ocean in four. Bazlyn's winddrifter was one of the fastest around and probably capable of doing it in three. However, ever since the night of the Genesis Chamber, airships now shared the clouds with Dragons, and there was no telling how dangerous the trip would be.

Either way it was a good plan. Her own voyage to the New World had been lucky to navigate the blockade and the Sagean Spear ships near Kotalla. The fleet of New World ships stationed on the Baruse Islands was forced to travel south near the boundary of the Anamic Ocean and the Evernight Sea. Kovan and the winddrifter would have to fly a similar path to avoid being brought down by the Sagean's warships. She had told them as much, sending them her travel coordinates to avoid an assault; but without word of their whereabouts, she worried something had gone wrong. Even the best winddrifter, piloted by the best aeronaut, can go off course. She desperately needed that ship to make it over the ocean. *Maybe the whole world needs that ship to make it,* she thought.

Ellaria opened her communicator watch and brushed the bronze dial with her thumb—as though she might will the thing to life—but the bells in the Aethon Towers rang out instead. When the bells ceased, she found she had company on the balcony overlooking the waters far below.

Elias's cat Merphi sat beside her, staring out at the same horizon. The mystcat was a lovely companion that reminded her of Elias, sometimes too much, and the cat too had been obsessively watching the ocean, sitting tall and statuesque, her white-and-gold fur cleaned and smooth. Merphi glared out toward the west as though she too waited for someone.

A rhythmic knock of three raps came at her door, which was opened from the outside. Palace guards swung the door aside, and the king's daughter, Dalliana, was escorted in. Ellaria's personal guard stood with head bowed at the door, and Dalliana's own guardsmen waited in the hall. The young queen-in-training glided in, with her delicate clothes moving as she walked. Dalliana's arrival meant it was time for their daily meeting with the governors.

The young woman's striking black hair was pulled up from her face. Her pristine dark skin was always accented by gold jewelry befitting her station, and was again today, as she wore a necklace of gold flower petals.

Dalliana approached the balcony, but Ellaria put out her hand to halt her and came back inside to meet her charge in the entry. She passed her unmade bed, where the blankets were cast to the floor in a heap as proof of her sleeplessness from the repeating nightmares she couldn't shake. It was not something she needed the princess of the New World looking at. Ellaria was here to provide a sense of comfort and control, to guide Dalliana. She couldn't herself be seen for what she was—a complete mess.

Nightmares of the Genesis Chamber from her subconscious replayed in her sleep for months. Though her eyes hadn't witnessed the horrors, her mind couldn't shake the screams from the temple.

"Morning, General," Dalliana greeted her. Always formally first and with the best posture of anyone Ellaria could remember. This time Dalliana greeted her with a letter in her hand.

"Good morning. Is that for me?" Ellaria asked.

"It is." Dalliana handed it to her.

Ellaria gave it a cursory review to determine who it was from before focusing her attention back on Dalliana.

"It's from Professor Arlene Kent, I believe," Dalliana commented.

"Screening my letters?" Ellaria asked, with a slight grin.

"No. I know who delivered the letter, and I can tell by Miss Kent's handwriting."

"I see. Any word from your father?"

"Not since his arrival in Adara," Dalliana huffed.

Ellaria shared the girl's frustration and worry. Danehin had departed for the fortifications in Adara soon after their arrival from the west. Danehin's recovery following his capture had been slow. Ellaria thought he had signs of dementia but had kept that to herself. To hide his health from the governors in the city, Ellaria proposed a cover story that the king's first order of business was to oversee the Darkhawks for strategic purposes and preparation for war. Ellaria expected the governors would request that their own doctors examine him, and they couldn't risk the political upheaval. Of course, everyone suspected something was amiss, but no one could prove it.

"Are the governors still asking questions?" Ellaria had Dalliana issue a statement that her father had accompanied the Darkhawk hero, Semo, back to the military base, where he would be honored for his service. After losing his leg in the battle in Nahadon, Semo was a shell of his former self. The mission to protect his King was the only solace Ellaria could offer the maimed warrior.

"No, they keep their suspicions between themselves. I did hear from Semo. The tinkersmiths in Deloma fashioned a mechanical leg for him," Dalliana said.

"That's great news," Ellaria said. If he couldn't fight in the war, at least the leg would allow Semo to be a training Sargent.

"How about your band of rogues?" Dalliana asked. "Any word from them?"

"If they found clear sailing, they could be here any day now," Ellaria said for the sixth day in a row. Still, she struggled to mask the solemnness that shrouded her thoughts. She knew Kovan, she knew him better than he knew himself. He would be fitful to stay in one place long. Which meant when their reunion came, it would only be a precursor to their parting.

Ellaria lingered, looking around the room for her hat.

"We can make the governors wait if you're not ready," Dalliana said.

Ellaria smiled. Dalliana had come a long way in the last three months. She now held her own with the governors and conducted the meetings on her own terms. In the battles of politics, it was a win. Still, the two of them had yet to impress upon the governors the precarious position the New World was in. The governors were foolishly convinced that the Sagean would wait for winter to end before invading. Ellaria knew better.

She found her hat and slipped a knife under her sleeve. "I'm ready," she said, heading for the door.

TREGOREAN LANDS
The Kaze Valley
Trappers Bay
To Xavole
To Tycan
To The Dry Coast
Moorlon
North Tangle
The East Bounds
The Western Wall
Sualden
Tarensky
Lake Azcerall
The Brayers
The Helix Glades
The Reskare Hills
Cadrin Mound
Tyn River
Twin Lakes
The Averient
Tarhallen
Saber's End
Polaris
The Wall of Nagari
Wuri Bay
The Shadow Field

Two

Ruins - Learon

Learon's fingertips brushed over the chiseled inscription again while he tried to puzzle out its meaning. He stood inside one of the few accessible halls among the partially collapsed temple. From the floor, a soft flickering light cast his shadow into the depths of the halls yet to be inspected. Two hundred feet in the other direction was the opening to the dark passageways, and it framed a field of destruction bathed in bright sunlight. The scattered semblance of the glorious structure that had toppled in the night, now a small sea of stone rubble, nestled in mud and a tangle of vines.

Further still, on the outer edge of the site, their canvas field tents were anchored in the clearing before the jungle, and among those, a collection of Renja guards on patrol at the hillside beneath the trees.

Tracing the inscription over and over as though the act itself would produce the translation he sought, Learon shrugged and retrieved the now tattered roll of parchment and made yet another shading. Something else to decipher later, he supposed. There had been so many similar inscriptions now that he had lost count—twenty or so on that roll alone, and Echoryn had three rolls in her pack already.

This was the second time they had searched the back colonnade of the temple complex. The first time, the rangers had only given them an hour or so to look, and they wanted to evacuate the area after the green Dragon had appeared overhead. Learon was determined to discover where Elias had disappeared that night.

In the months following the temple's destruction, Learon had spent most of his time with the Kihan people, learning more about their culture. Ellaria had left a month ago with a group of soldiers, heading out to the Baruse Islands. Since then, the soldiers accompanying her group had come back. Ellaria should have arrived in the New World by now. Her parting gave Learon the uneasy feeling that he was wasting his time here.

A sigh of frustration escaped his lips as he scratched the etching into the paper.

"You found another one?" Echoryn asked, approaching from an adjacent passage.

"Yes."

"Is it more drawings of the chamber?"

"No, it's writing this time."

"An inscription?" Echoryn said with surprise, and lifted her own lantern for a closer inspection. "So why are you mad? This is amazing."

"I'm annoyed. Ellaria, Elias, even Tali, they were the experts at deciphering this ancient language. I'm…" He let his sentence die.

"At least it's text instead of more drawings. Maybe we'll find it in one of the texts we brought with us."

"Maybe," Learon admitted.

Learon knew she was right. While they had found symbols, drawings, even single phrases, they hadn't discovered text like the one on the wall before them. This being one of the few structures still standing was a miracle in itself, but Learon wasn't out there to catalog the remaining art and texts of the ancient structure. He was searching for answers.

Still, the excitement of finding Elias's satchel that Learon had dropped that night had worn off. Most of the ancient complex was destroyed, and the grim reality that it was the only thing substantial they were going to find started to set in. Except for the blue crystal he had found their first day—the day they pulled Elias's body from the wreckage—which he had promptly hidden inside Echoryn's study.

Learon finished his sketching and lifted his lantern to peer into the darker depths of columns, stone corners, and dead ends.

Echoryn placed her hand on his shoulder. "Learon, just wait for the engineers to inspect the deeper passages. It's not safe with the tremors still shaking the ground. I promise we'll find everything there is to find before we go back to the city."

Learon agreed and they picked up their supplies before retreating to their tents. Inside Learon's tent, a bag lay open with a collection of books spilling out. They had brought a small library of different texts from the prophet's library to go through. Some were obscure and spoke about Nahadon, and some were history books for Learon to learn about the Kihan people. There were a few about the Trinity Guard and the various abilities of the warriors, but most of those read like folktales and fiction. Learon wasn't sure what to believe. He especially hated the passages about the Nimbus Warrior. They were always accompanied by statements that he was some kind of harbinger of death, that death followed in his footsteps, or that Nimbus Warriors grew so sick of blood that their own would turn blue. One book said they spoke to animals because they shared animal senses, and they were one with the wind. *It is nonsense.* Learon felt no different than any other man.

Besides a few mentions here and there, in all the collection, only one text existed about Dragons. It had some anatomy drawings of the noble beasts and a page of notations, but all of it was in a language Learon couldn't read. That book wasn't allowed to leave the city. It was so old they didn't let it out of a glass case. There was a small drawing of a sword inside that had caught his attention, as it appeared to be an Elum blade at first glance. Based on the drawing, the crystal blade was bonded with the dust of Dragon bones or blood. He wasn't sure.

Learon threw his things to the side and grabbed a book he had taken a liking to about the Fates. The tales of unseen hands guiding the heroic guardians in the ancient world before the Luminary Wars was epic and full of adventure. The Kihan believed in the Fates, but their religious texts were too dogmatic for Learon. Whereas this book, *The Seven Immortal Watchers*, talked about the Fates as the Watchers of the world and told of their trials through the ancient lands. Many of the Kihan believed it to be a kid's book, with its tales of the Watchers navigating the Brovic or riding Dragons. For kids or not, there was an exceedingly hopeful tone that Learon liked to escape into.

Echoryn came in a short time later after conversing with her head guardsmen and the engineer. She placed her things down and grabbed a shawl and flung it over her back.

"It's too cold," she said, fixing the strands of her red hair out of her face.

"Yeah, it's been windy since we've been down here," Learon commented, turning a page in his book.

"No, I mean it's not right. It never gets this cold here. Not for this long."

Learon thought about it. It had been windy and cold, with nearly nonstop rain, since the night the temple fell and the volcanoes erupted.

"Did the Kihan scouts confirm that the Dragons came out of the volcanoes at the Black Shore?" he asked.

"They never got far enough to adequately investigate. Rockslides barricaded their routes and they returned, but that's the prevailing opinion. Why?" Echoryn asked.

"Nothing. It's almost like the entire territh has gone cold giving life to the Dragons…" Learon paused.

"What? What's wrong?" Echoryn prompted.

"I was going to say, if Elias was here, I would ask him."

"Oh. I'm sorry, Learon. I know he meant a lot to you."

Learon turned his eyes back to his book, not wanting to say any more. This line of conversation always got back to how he hadn't visited the grave site in the Emerald Grove yet. In truth, he couldn't explain why he had avoided the area.

"Speaking of Elias, the engineer said they will have another portion of the structure investigated by tonight, and we can go through it tomorrow if it's safe. Also, the Renja told me they will spar with you again if you're restless," Echoryn said.

Learon smiled at her. "Will they take it easy on me this time?" he asked, touching at his ribs where a patch of purple skin marked the last sparring session he'd had with the Kihan rangers.

"Absolutely not. Learon, you're a Nimbus Warrior. They would see not giving their best as an insult to you and damaging to their pride."

"They are crushing me every time. How is that not damaging?"

"Damaging what?"

"The Kihan's legend of a Nimbus Warrior, that's what."

Echoryn waved him off. "They think you're just hardening yourself for battle."

"They would be wrong."

Echoryn nodded and rolled her eyes at the same time, as though she didn't believe something he said.

"I can't explain it. I don't have the skills to battle them."

"Learon, I've seen you do impossible things before. Multiple times."

"I know, but it's almost like I can't tap into those things when I want to, only when I have to."

"Is that what we're searching for? You think Elias left you an answer to all your questions?" Echoryn asked.

"Something like that."

"It's possible he never found anything, Learon. Besides, if he wanted you to have something, why didn't he give it to you? You said that you thought he acted strange, like he was preparing for death."

Learon didn't have a comeback for that. Elias had been acting strange, including sending Meroha on some assignment she refused to tell Learon about. What Learon really wanted to find was Elias's small notebook. Learon had seen him writing in it all the time. When they found the satchel, Learon thought it would be inside, but it wasn't.

As the war became reality, Learon couldn't fathom how they would defeat the Wrythen without Elias. To combat an evil none of them understood would take Luminaries that could wield energy, not a Nimbus Warrior who was only a mediocre a swordsman and whose instincts felt bound to disappoint when he needed them most.

Although war had begun on the north coast, there was very little fear among the Kihan that the fighting would progress deeper into the jungle. Learon believed it was a safe assumption, as the jungle was treacherous to navigate and probably impossible to march an army through.

As the cascade of insects and animal noises in the fauna scored the evening, Learon considered how absolutely terrifying this place was. Knowing what he knew now about the jungle, he had been a fool to wander off when he had been told about his parentage.

Given the presence of Echoryn, the Kihan's royal daughter, their research party was well equipped for the jungle and all their needs. Despite this, the relentless rain had plagued the expedition with persistent troubles. The rain washed out roads, besieged the camp with sinkholes, and made the network of ruins more unstable. Even breaks in the weather brought only momentary relief. A cool night was shortly followed by insects swarming the air or crawling out of the mud.

"Echoryn?"

"Squirrel?" she answered, her lips still sipping her clay mug of tea.

"I'm not sure I ever truly thanked you for coming to get me."

Her eyebrows went up. "What are you talking about?"

"When I crossed the boundary, and we were attacked by Ravinors."

"You're welcome, squirrel."

"I hate to think what would have happened if Tali would have run after me."

"She… Tali would have died, I think…" Echoryn paused and shivered slightly like a cold breeze had suddenly chilled her to the bone and passed. Whatever it was, she shook it off and continued, "Maybe stop running off like an eight-year-old throwing a fit." She grinned.

"Fair," he acknowledged. Though he felt justified in his petulance, it seemed like a childish thing to do when looking back on it. Like all surprising news, often the reaction to the surprise is more emotional than the logical understanding of the information. Still, her remark about Tali rattled in his head. It was the sincerity with which the comment was made that was haunting. "Why did you say that about Tali?"

A small grunt escaped Echoryn's lips. "Squirrel, you never let anything be. If you must know, I had a vision of it, of you and of her."

"What?" Learon said.

"It doesn't matter. I went instead of her, and she lived."

"I hope so."

"She's not dead, Learon. Whatever Elias did that night to make her disappear, she's alive somewhere. Even Ellaria believed that."

"I'm sure you're right."

In the lingering silence, his communicator watch lit up. Kovan's group had arrived in the province.

"They made it," Echoryn said.

"Yeah."

"It appears our time here is up," Learon said, but he sensed she grasped that already.

Echoryn hid her face in her cup of tea, and, as though something bugged her, she lowered it and glanced back over at him. "I have to ask you a question."

"All right, shoot. I'm an honest man," Learon said, though the change in tone had him tentative.

"I know you are. Let me ask you. If you could learn when you were going to die, would you want to know?" Echoryn said.

"Are you messing with me?"

"I'm serious."

"Is that something you've seen?"

"Oh, not yours, but others'. I've seen others'," she said.

Learon knew her foresight abilities had been advancing daily, and sometimes what she saw frightened her. But neither she nor Learon shared their burdens with the other.

"I don't know," Learon said, hesitating to say more.

"Never mind."

"No, I want you to share with me what's going on, but I don't have answers for you."

"I know you don't, but I fear no one does." She stood up and left his tent. Pulling the opening back, she smiled at him. "Good night, Learon."

Learon's mind felt like a tangle of thorns as he tried to sleep. Kovan's arrival meant that the time had come for Learon to leave. He had a promise to keep to Elias to find the Shadowyn, but he also had made a promise to the Renegades fighting in the Old World, and he needed to find Tali. Her disappearance weighed on him more than all of it.

Learon rolled over, staring at the opening to his tent. He had an unmistakable sense there were mysteries here he still needed to solve. There's a special sort of torment when you are caught between feeling like you're wasting your time and the sense that you have something yet to do. *What exactly happened? Where did Elias go that night and where is his notebook?* A new world war was starting, and Learon's services were probably more helpful to the Renegades fighting to survive in the New World at the front lines, or maybe with the Kihan. Having just learned that he was one of the Kihan, he was unsure what he owed these people, his people. The Kihan army currently skirmishing in the north with the Viper Lords were probably cursing his name for not bleeding by their side. No matter what he chose to do, he was letting someone he cared about down.

There was the small matter of figuring out who his parents were, which he hadn't wanted to give much thought to, as he knew it might consume him. Then there was Tali. It always came back to her, as she was ever present on his mind. He closed his eyes and could see her. He could hear her voice in his sleep, and their bond was so frayed that he felt cold when thinking about her. It was long past time he started searching for her.

Too restless for sleep, Learon abandoned his attempt and crept out of the tent. The guards outside Echoryn's tent perked up, and Learon raised his hand to wave. They eyed him with suspicion but let him be.

He scanned the sky above the canopy of jungle, and the sun had begun to lift the shroud of night on the horizon. Determined to search the remains of the site, Learon retrieved his supplies and crossed the field down to the ancient temple.

He slipped around the first rows of collapsed pillars and into the depths of the temple. Beyond the first set of walls and tunnels, he ducked under a series of precariously wedged stone blocks and proceeded deeper into the structure than before. After a few turns around nondescript stone walls and empty chambers, the hall opened into a larger expanse of stone columns.

Row upon row of carved posts covered the area like tree trunks in the mist, where fine dust particles hung thick in the air and visible in the farthest reaches of Learon's lamplight.

Learon entered the arena of posts with an eerie feeling of having been there before—something was familiar. Learon's hopes were dashed when at the reaches of the room he found nothing but walls. When he reached the last wall, he turned around and shined the light back across the desolate space, slightly dumbfounded. Something was here, he was sure of it.

As he scanned the darkness, a tremor rumbled below his feet. Somewhere far off in another part of the temple something crashed, and a thick layer of dust fell from the ceiling like a blanket of ash. A recollection of the Dragons drawn on the dome of the Genesis Chamber sparked in his mind, and Learon searched the ceiling, giving it a closer inspection.

Above him was a series of grooves neatly cut into the stone ceiling like a pattern of lines racing around dull gems placed in a series of arrangements that vaguely resembled stars.

His heart raced, and he began to follow the racing lines from the entrance to the far wall where they should have terminated, but they looked like they continued beyond.

Anxiously, Learon's hands scrabbled over the wall, looking for a lever or switch that might part the wall before him. When his searching came up empty, he moved on to the nearest columns. The second column he tried shifted at his touch, and one of the segmented coins started to rotate.

A series of foreign sounds emanated, but the wall remained in place. Learon dashed to the adjacent column and found a similar spot to manipulate. A burst of air puffed free, and the wall parted with a mix of a hiss and grind of stone.

Learon moved into the chamber. He immediately registered that the height of the ceiling was twice that of the spaces before and there was a mugginess to the room. After the moving wall had stopped, Learon heard a low hum. A hum he recognized.

In the darkness he found the symbol-inlaid dais and stepped up, walking slowly until the full archway of the ancient gate was in view of his lantern.

A Wave Gate here in the jungles of Nahadon. *Had Elias used the gate that night and returned?* Standing beneath the towering machine of magic, he felt frustration set in. That one answer had produced more questions, and in his daze of thought, he almost missed the small bundle of cloth lying on the ground covered with a coat of dust. Learon picked it up. It was light, and the thin piece of cloth was tied together with rope. He blew the dust away from the package, pulled the knot free, and unfurled the wrapping to find four letters written in Elias's handwriting, addressed to Ellaria, Kovan, Tali, and Learon.

THREE

STRANGE LANDS - TALI

SOMETHING WAS WRONG. THE SORENESS IN TALI'S MUSCLES HAD faded with rest, and while she still felt exhausted, something else was wrong. She felt empty and hollow.

The wind continued to wail outside the peculiar hut, and a loneliness had overcome her. It didn't help that her apparent caretaker, a blue-skinned Zenoch man, had spoken but a few words to her, and other than on the first night, she hadn't seen Mia again. Tali was beginning to think she'd imagined her and the mythical ice-panther by her side.

Tali had tried to ascertain answers from the man, but all her attempts went nowhere. She had yet to even learn his name.

He looked to be in his early thirties, but his face was stonelike, and his dark eyes always focused on something. He seemed a quizzical man, and she had heard him grumble about the season changing and bad omens, but he'd not said a word about where she was.

On the third morning, Tali awoke in the bed draped with furs, feeling depleted, when the Zenoch man entered again. He brought in a bag of supplies, food, and water and turned to leave.

"Thank you," Tali said hurriedly.

The man paused, perhaps startled that she was awake. But he only nodded and pushed aside the door flap to leave.

"Wait," Tali called after him. "What's your name?"

"His name is Tyzo," a gentle voice answered from across the room.

Tali sat up and found Mia sitting on the far side. She had apparently been there the whole time, watching her. Tali hadn't known anyone else was in the room, and an unease came over her.

"He never speaks to me," Tali said.

"He is a solemn man. Most Zenoch are serious and weary of strangers," Mia said. She crossed the room and came to her side. Her auburn hair was long and full, with stray locks of white.

Tali tried to maintain eye contact, but a dark shadow passed behind Mia. The giant white-and-black Torakuma prowled within the tight confines of the hut. Tali shifted back into her sheets.

"Is that what I think it is?"

"This is Koda. Yes, he's a Torakuma panther. He won't hurt you as long as I'm around," Mia said confidently.

"You're friends?"

"Something like that."

"I thought they were extinct."

"They're scarce, but not extinct."

The stunning animal was a combination of sleek fur and muscle. His size alone was foreboding, but his stripes, strong jawline, and the small twisted horns angled behind his short rounded ears created a menacing look like no other. Tali was mesmerized by him, but he was restless in the small space, and Mia waved him out.

"Wait outside please, Koda," she said.

Koda's dark emerald eyes looked at both Mia and Tali with intensity before he meandered back out into the snow. When he was gone, Mia turned her attention back to Tali.

"You have some story to tell, I'm sure. One I need to hear, but I must go into the village and calm the Duskmen. There are tales going around of demons and curses. Between this weather and whatever miracle they believe they saw in the sky when you arrived, the Zenoch are in a state of panic."

"Tyzo said something about the weather. What's wrong with the weather?" Tali asked, looking toward the door and the snowdrifts beyond. "It's just snow," she remarked.

"The snow is one thing here in the north reach, months early as it is, but the Eagle's Neck has frozen solid, and that has the elders unnerved."

"Eagle's Neck?"

"It's a pass through the Bowshan Mountains that you can see from the valley that collects snow in the winter. It eventually thaws and melts by midsummer. The Zenoch use it to measure the seasons for traveling and hunting in the mountains. It typically doesn't freeze until the first day of winter, but this year it froze a month early, the day after you arrived."

After Mia left, Tali paced around her small confines, barely picking at the food Tyzo had left. Her stomach screamed at her that she was hungry, but anxiety prevented her from devouring the plate of food.

She put the fruit down and took a deep breath. It was only a week ago that she had been in the Genesis Chamber, and nightmares had filled her sleep every night since. There were ones where she remembered the Wrythen's tendrils of smoky essence wrapped around her and stripping her energy. In others, she watched as Elias pleaded with Edward to take the long-dead emperor's soul from him, only for that evil Sagean soul to take over Edward and murder some of his own acolytes. The worst dream was the Wrythen slamming Learon into the wall. The image of Learon pinned lifelessly against the stone and falling to a crumpled heap as she stood helpless lingered long after she woke up. All these horrifying scenes played out every night in her mind, and she couldn't easily shake them. Maybe she was upset because she had survived, or that she had been cast away by Elias and had no way of knowing what had happened. *Perhaps it's a simple case of cabin fever,* she told herself, and she walked outside.

The sun set on the hilltop behind her and the mountain beyond. The air was crisp and cooling off by the minute. Tali took a few steps when her hands started shaking. She understood what was wrong, and why the panther had frightened her, and Mia had startled her. Tali had never sensed her; she couldn't feel the sun. She couldn't feel the energy around her.

Tali lingered outside until the tempests of energy came back to her. Her senses still felt dull, and while the signatures of energy were all around her, she couldn't pull on any of them without exhausting herself. She retreated to the hut, defeated but not totally disheartened. Moments later Tyzo entered, carrying firewood. Possibly because she sat in the side chair or because she was awake, but her presence somehow startled him. Tyzo stared at her for a longer stretch of time than she had seen him do before, other than the first few nights that she knew he had monitored her. She was still not used to seeing the blue skin of the Zenoch. He had a strong face, with angular cheekbones, hardened by a set of contemplative dark eyes.

"Are you going to talk to me this time?" she asked.

He stood stoically and just stared at her.

"I wanted to say thank you. Mia said you were the one who found me in the snow."

For a moment Tali didn't think he would respond. He continued into the hut and placed the firewood he carried in a stack near the lone small table.

"You're welcome," he said with his back to her. He had a deeper voice than she had expected, not terribly unkind, but his words came out with almost no emotion.

"Is this your, um, place?" she asked.

"No, it is only a hunting den."

"Mia told me to stay here until she comes back."

"Mianora is right, you should listen. Zenoch do not like outsiders."

"I don't know much about your people, honestly," Tali admitted.

"That is the way we like it," Tyzo replied.

"I really want to return to my friends; can you at least tell me how long it'll take me to get back?"

"It takes a day to reach the Genji Gap. If it is passable, it takes a week through the mountains. From there, you can go west to a city your people call Brigg. From the bay, you could sail anywhere you want."

"Well, not anywhere," Tali corrected him. "You realize there's a war on the horizon?"

"We have heard war is imminent with the Westlanders."

"You're not worried?"

"Conflicts outside our lands rarely concern me."

"I can understand that, but Tyzo, I am concerned for your people. There are very powerful Luminaries fighting in this war."

"Hmmm," Tyzo muttered.

Tali was unsure if he had just dismissed her words or not. His face was impossible to read.

"The old empire stayed out of our lands, and so have the Westlanders. Why would this war change things if the last one didn't?"

"Before, the people you call Westlanders were fleeing the persecution of the empire. By their very proclamation, they were inclined to have peace. But they have established many major cities now. They have gained their own great force. A nation to rival the previous one, in might and strength. You can't hope for them to stay out of here forever. Men live short lives, men in power shorter than most, and new leaders forget old treaties. But—"

"We are well protected here in the Zenon Valley," Tyzo cut her off.

"Maybe that was true, but a Sagean has risen from the dead. He will soon reclaim control of the old empire—if he hasn't already—and he'll want the people and the land he once lost. There will be war, and if the Sagean emperor wins, I can guarantee you, he will not stop at your border."

"How do you know all this?"

"It doesn't matter, and I'm not as up to speed as I should be. But my friends are fighting against this evil. They may be fighting it right now, which is why I must go."

"Mianora is working on it. If your presence here becomes known, getting out is going to be much more difficult. The entire region has a tenuous grasp on civility now."

"The Eagle's Neck thing?"

Tyzo squinted but answered, "There have been other things, not the least of which is the blinding glow from the hunting grounds just before dawn in autumn and the village awakens to find winter has arrived."

"I don't know what to say."

"Mianora said you wouldn't have much to say on that subject. Well, some of the elders have been warning of the end of ends, and this has fueled the panic."

Tali steeled herself. Was there nowhere on this planet not in an upheaval? She gazed out the flap as it moved with the breeze, thinking this was her life, her home. She was always buried in a conflict of desperation.

Something moved outside, and she shifted in her seat. Tyzo noticed her attention had been distracted, and he turned to investigate. Suddenly a little girl peeked her head around the opening.

"Uncle?" the girl called out, with big, bright wondrous eyes that grew bigger at seeing Tali.

"Saphree, what are you doing here?" Tyzo nearly lunged at her.

"Who's that, Uncle?" the girl asked with exuberance.

"Go back home, Pebble," Tyzo said.

"Uncle, I'm a Snowpine now, I'm old enough," the girl contended.

"I have to take her home," Tyzo said to Tali, pushing the girl gently back out of the hut.

Tali went to the door to watch them depart and could hear the kid arguing on the path.

"Who is she, Uncle? She's beautiful. Is she your girlfriend?"

"No. Keep moving."

An unexpected smile crested Tali's face. She receded to the side chair and waited for Mia to return.

It was another two days before Tali had a visitor, and it wasn't Mia, nor her brooding caretaker, but the little girl who'd peeked through the flap like a hummingbird, surprised by where her wings had brought her.

"Hello, I'm Tali," Tali introduced herself.

"Tali? That's a funny name."

"Is it?"

"Yeah."

Tali chuckled to herself. "Well my real name is Talhaleanna. Which I always thought was funny."

"Oh, it is. Yeah, that's much worse. You can't live with that kind of thing. My name is Saphree Eraw'Sa."

"It's nice to meet you, Saphree."

With the introductions done, Saphree must have thought the largest hurdle to their future friendship was surpassed, as she slipped onto the end of the bed and pulled a blanket over her lap before launching into more questions. "Do you have a hierarchy name?"

"What is that? Like 'Sa', in Eraw'Sa?"

"No. My clan's name is Sa. My age-rank is Snowpine."

"Where I come from, we don't have these age-rank or hierarchy names."

"You don't?"

"No. What does yours mean?"

"The words are for age and strength."

"So, it's based on your age?"

"Yes, but also your position among our people. Tyzo is a Sun-Spear."

"Is that good?"

"Oh yeah. He's part of the warrior classes, iron, spear, shield, and fire. But that's nothing, the elders are Twilight-Fire and Star-Crystal. And the High Elders, the Spirit Elders like Master Kena'Ko and Master Lor'Si, are said to be Spirit-Trees, but they retired to the temples in Darkanna, so who knows, really."

"So, it's like a numbering system for everyone?"

"Yes."

"It sounds confusing."

"I guess it can be to an outsider. What's really confusing is how your people know who's in charge at all."

"Well, at the moment..." She wanted to say that a war was being fought for exactly that right but decided to spare the little girl her last bit of innocence. "In the Free Cities, the people selected a king a long time ago and other leaders for each country in the nation."

"So, it's not determined on age and experience and wisdom."

"No. Probably more to do with wealth. So, tell me about your uncle," Tali said.

"What do you want to know?"

"You said he's a warrior?"

"Yes."

"Do the Zenoch fight wars?"

"Yes. Not as many as our ancestors, but the clans are always fighting."

"I see. Well, I'm grateful for your uncle."

Saphree leaned closer on the bed. "Is it true he found you in the snow?"

"Yes," Tali whispered back.

"So, you're a Morning-star or an Aurora-bird from the stars?"

Tali didn't know what the girl meant by that, so she hesitated to answer. She wasn't sure if it was a Zenoch myth or their words for a Luminary.

"And you can dream-weave?" Saphree asked.

"Ummm. No, my dreams are often nightmares."

"I'm sorry. My grandmother used to tell me that it's not good to be at war with your dreams. Can you fly, too?"

"Fly?" Tali chuckled, "No, I can't fly."

"You can't?" Saphree said, very disheartened. "Oh, I thought all Aurora-birds could fly like Luminaries?"

Her comment confused Tali. "I'm sorry, I don't know what an Aurora-bird is. Also, I don't think Luminaries can fly."

"Oh, they can. I heard a boy from Roal talking about it once."

"Well, I was brought here by someone else's magic."

"Was it an evil Luminary? A Sagean?"

"No. It was my friend. He is a Luminary though, but he's not evil."

"He's not?" Saphree asked, quietest of all.

"Nope."

Saphree leaned back and noticed that the sun was long out of the Blue. She hopped up and laced her boots back on.

"I have to go, or my uncle is going to kill me," she said.

"All right. Be careful going back."

"I'll be fine. I come out to the Gap all the time. Can I come back and visit you again?"

"Absolutely. I really enjoyed talking with you. As you can see, it's lonely out here."

"I bet, farewell friend," Saphree said, pulling her fur hood over her head as she bounded out of the hut with exuberance.

Over the next week, Saphree returned every day, always at the apex of the Blue sun and leaving soon after the yellowing. Tyzo would come at twilight, deliver food, and check on Tali's firewood and water before leaving. Never communicating more than a few comments and never bringing her word of Mia's whereabouts.

On the ninth night after Tali had awoken there, Mia returned, accompanied by her large animal friend. The ice-panther stalked in with its sharp teeth bared but made no noise of aggression. Its short twisted antlers appeared darker this time.

Tali was sitting at her small table, finishing soup Tyzo had left her. It still steamed from some vegetable inside that Tali didn't recognize, but it tasted a lot like a potato.

Mia had a red nose and cheeks but cast her jacket aside upon entering. The ice-panther sat near the entrance, and without warning, it groaned.

"She looks healed."

The voice surprised her. It was soft and old, and it took Tali a moment to figure out that what she had heard was the ice-panther talking to Mia. Tali's eye's widened, and Koda noticed the recognition.

"How do you feel?" Mia asked her.

Tali blinked and moved her eyes away from the ice-panther to Mia. "I feel better."

Mia crossed the room and approached her with a purposeful stride. "Do you mind?" she asked, placing her hands on Tali's face before she could answer. The first thing she inspected were Tali's scars at the sides of her eyes. Then Mia gently pulled Tali's eyelid low with her thumb.

"Look up," Mia said.

For a short uncomfortable moment, Mia looked her over like a doctor back home, lifting Tali's black hair away from her neck and feeling at the base of her skull.

"Your eyes look better. They were bloodshot before," Mia commented. Tali blinked just thinking about them.

"No more headaches?" Mia inquired.

"Umm…" Tali paused, she wanted to say no, but now that she thought about it, there was a small ache still behind her ears. "A little bit."

Mia nodded and retrieved something from her coat. She placed a small glass ampoule full of a fine pink powder on the table. "Take a spoonful of this tonight and tomorrow after you eat."

Tali served herself a dose, and heard the ice-panther groan again. *"Is that truly necessary. Mianora?"*

Tali paused, but quickly tried to cover it up. She didn't want Mia to know yet that she could understand Koda. Mia didn't notice as she cast the ice-panther a scowl.

Finally, Tali figured that if Mia wanted to hurt her, she would have already, and she took the medicine. It was bitter, almost rancid tasting, and Tali had to wash it down with a glass of water and some of the broth from her soup.

Mia sat and waited for her to finish.

"So, when can I go home?" Tali said.

"Tomorrow. But I warn you, it's not going to be easy. I couldn't find a smuggler willing to take you. Instead, we must make our way through the Erol village to the pass."

"That's it, it's been seven days since you left?"

"I had to visit with the Spirit Elders about the light in the sky to convince them it was probably only a meteorite. The Zenoch pay close attention to the skies at night. They believe in the power of the night auroras. They believe the lights are the blood of God that the Fates used to become immortal. Nevertheless, the Twilight Elder, a man named Ashrata Nea'Ko, has sent a team north of here to Zenar to find the meteorite and bring it back. Also, you weren't healthy enough to travel before. Tell me, have your powers fully returned?"

"Not fully," she admitted. She could sense energy just fine, but controlling it seemed to require strength she didn't have yet. "They're there, but my strength is slow to return."

"That's what I was afraid of."

"What do you mean? Elias told me a Luminary can't lose their powers?" Tali asked, her pulse quickening.

"Lose? No. But your powers can and certainly do wain, especially with age. They can also be blocked. It takes a very strong spell. There's also a yellow gemstone called a viper-eye."

"Oh," Tali said, biting the inside of her cheek.

"If we could wait until you were healed fully and your powers fully accessible, I would, but we can't. You need to leave here. We're pushing fate, as it is. You need to rejoin the fight."

"All right. I'll be ready. You said when you returned you would answer some of my questions," Tali said. It wasn't as much of a question as it was a statement.

"Yes. If you indulge some of my own?"

"Deal." Tali had questions about Koda, and about Elias, but decided to start with something forefront on her mind. "You are a prophet; did you know I was coming here?"

"Actually, I'm not a prophet. Not anymore. Not for a long time. It's not an ability that stays in your blood, thankfully, as I don't believe anyone can survive inflicted with it for longer than twenty years. To answer your question. Yes and no. There are many paths of fate, and the strands of time are woven once. The messy part of being a prophet, the turmoil of it, is in seeing the various paths in equal certainty, the same event with small changing details. Major turning points, vertex turns as they are called sometimes, are visceral to experience and bear witness to. It's a maze unlike anything you can imagine. I used to see it. Variations of every part and every maze incarnation," Mia said with a far-off look in her eyes. Her voice held a sense of awe.

"How do you sort the truth?" Tali asked.

"First, tell me something. You've made it here, so I assume Kovan didn't die in Marathal?"

"No, he lived. He was saved by a fisherman."

"And did he have all his memories back?"

"Not yet. Not all of them. He was given cubes to help him."

"Cubes? Are you sure?"

"Yes."

"So, the Vygoths are meddling this time."

"What or who are the Vygoths?"

"It doesn't matter. Let's hope he survived the final cube. And tell me, when Elias sent you, was the emperor's spirit out of him by then."

"Yes."

"Good," Mia said, and her eyes darted down to a silver ring on her finger. When her chin lifted, her eyes were full of tears. "To answer your question, you can never sort the truth of it. However, understanding that takes a long time and a wisdom of perspective that you don't have until much later. In the end, prophecy exacts a terrible toll."

"Is Elias dead?" Tali blurted, almost afraid to ask. When she last saw him he looked weakened and was facing the Wrythen by himself.

"I don't know. He's not in the realm anymore. I know that."

"Is..." She couldn't bring herself to ask her next question, recalling the moments before Elias had sent her away and the sudden appearance of the Wrythen. She kept seeing Learon's body flying in the air and crashing through the wall. She swallowed hard, and drank her tea slowly, letting the steam wash over her. Her hands trembled on the mug; she couldn't feel Learon any longer. Now that she knew what it was, once his presence was gone from her, it left an emptiness, a coldness like bathing in cold water instead of hot. Tali wasn't ready for the answer she feared, so she changed her question. "You know so much about what's supposed to happen, what will happen. What can you tell me that will help me defeat the Sagean or the Wrythen?" Tali asked.

"I can tell you that you're not the one who defeats the Sagean." Mia stood, and she bundled her coat and scarf. "I can also tell you that you must get your rest. For you to do what comes next, we need to be on the road out of Erol by tomorrow night. I will send Tyzo tomorrow to pick you up after the Blue, and I'll meet you both at the Fallen Grove outside the village," Mia said and waved Koda to leave.

Outside, in the field of pulverized snow, Tali heard the ice-panther speaking again.

"You are aware she can understand me?" Koda asked.

"I know," Mia said.

New World Map
N
W
E
S
ECHO BAY
Skydarr Village
Skulliva Village
The Ice People
TERRITHRUNE MOUNTAINS
Woral Village
Zenar
Erol
Roal
Darkanna
BINDERS BAY
BRIGG
Edoth
LAND OF THE ZENOCH
Cadora
Doraga
Ega
IMAR
The Concord Grove
Shayn Mountains
Shala
SHAPO BAY
Morez
STARLIGHT SEA
Anina
Seda
Arosden
Delano
Darklands Fortress
Sagean Blockade
LIBERTY BAY
DELOMA
ADARA
Bownas
Hara Tribe
Lir Tribe
Paodo
Bugora
ILLUMEEN
Elann
Karnika
War Lands of the Harrinari
Moor Tribe
Varu Tribe
THE UDEN SEA
Synder
Syvone
Eenad Tribe
ILLAN
Amaria
Kerrio
Kasil River
HAILDRON MOUNTAINS
VERELL
ORIN CHANNEL
ORIN
SHIWAL MOUNTAINS
HIGH GROVE
THE LINK
SEADEN
IOKA
Cadra
Roskanna
JARA
LOGAN
JADE SEA
Saleer
HAILEON
Westmere
Falenmor
TRIDEN
THE BROVIC OCEAN
THE DEAD WAKE
SOUTHWAKE SEA
Commissioned
United Scholar's Guild
THE UNEXPLORED CONTINENT OF
MANASHERA
THE EVERNIGHT SEA

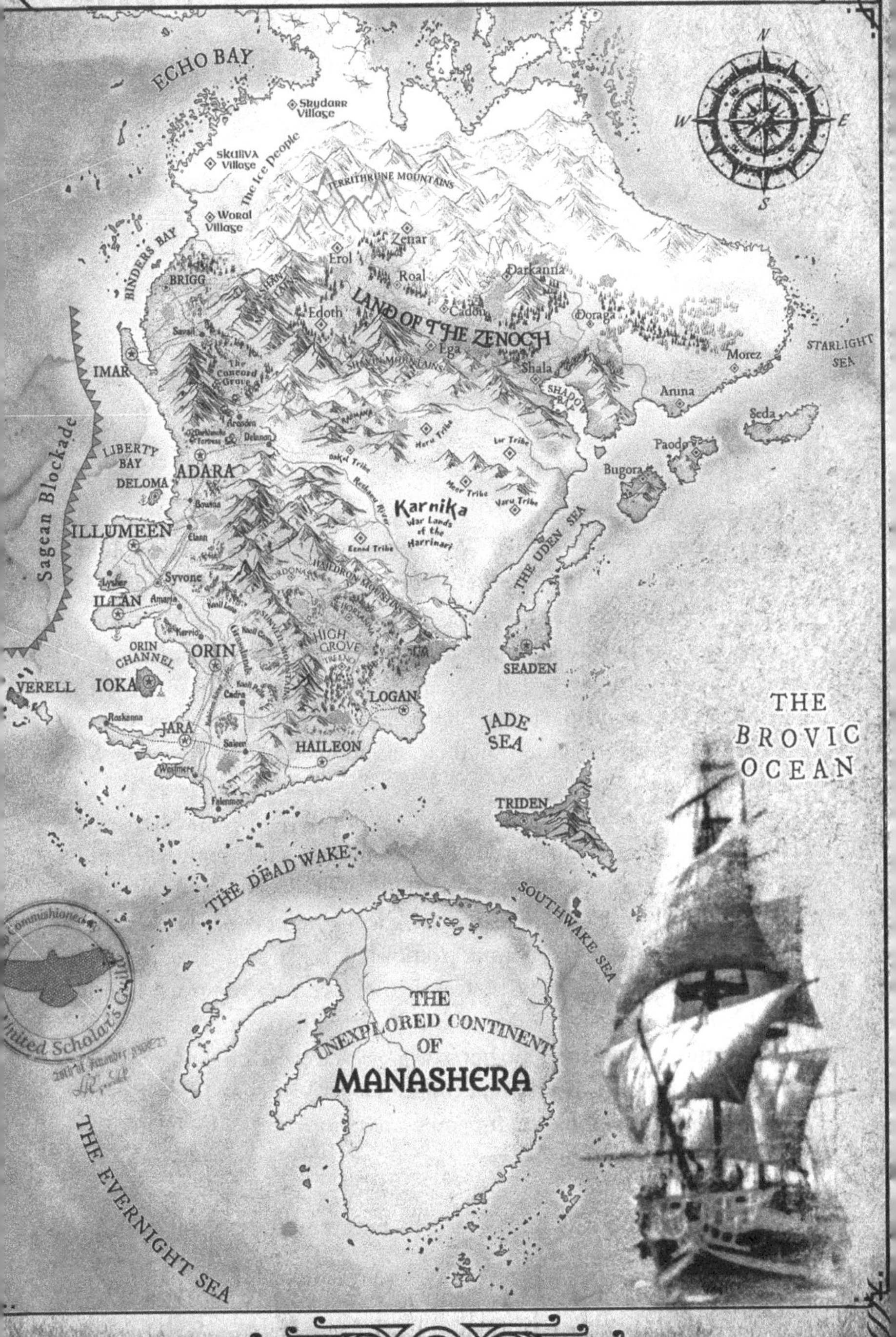

FOUR

EMISSARY - ELLARIA

"OUR PEOPLE ARE STARVING. TRADE BEING HALTED IS ONE THING, BUT our fishermen are grounded. We are running out of food in Illan. The way our laws are written, the regions don't fall under the Wartime Provisions Act until war has officially begun. This state of stagnation is suffocating," a governor named Atwood said, his hands in fists and his temples flexed.

After months of meetings, Ellaria had heard most of these tirades before. She had sympathy for their situations, but her patience was thin.

"Then let's attack. What are we waiting for?" Davro Shaw said. He was the representative from Illumeen and a snide man with short cut hair. Shaw was the worst type of know-it-all. He would listen to others only to profess his existing knowledge and deeper understanding, but he regurgitated common knowledge like it was sacred text. Shaw, probably more than the rest of the governors, despised Ellaria, but his hate was based on jealousy, which Ellaria was comfortable with. Someone jealous that her voice held weight or that her ideas were being listened to was one thing, but envy was another. Envy is always more dangerous when people are competing to be heard, and a few of the governors envied her, or at least her position as the princess's counsel.

"Most likely, we will have to attack, but we need to be on the same page about the best strategy. Either way I'll put our best options in front of my father for approval," Dalliana offered.

It was impressive how patient the young woman was with this group, especially considering Dalliana had been in charge of them for only eight months. Ellaria was sure that she herself would never have lasted as long. Not a single veteran of the Great War sat in the room with her, but they plotted and planned and strategized like self-proclaimed experts, impressed by their own ingenuity.

In total there were thirteen people in the room shouting over one another. Eleven governors were present, representing the eleven largest cities of the New World. Dalliana was there representing the king.

"I doubt there is any value in that. What's the point of his approval at this point?" Shaw complained, lifting his glasses and resetting them.

"I think, what my friend from Illumeen is saying, is that Dalliana, you have been the regent in charge since your father went missing. We trust your signature is enough to execute orders," Erole Burke said.

He was the governor of Orin, now the largest city of the New World and by proxy the second in command after Danehin. Two months ago, the daughter heir would have had final say over every-thing, but now that her father had returned from captivity, some of the governors demanded that orders receive Danehin's seal.

"Honestly, if she can't, then what are we doing here?" Atwood snapped. He was obviously at his wits' end. Ellaria tried to give him a break, as Atwood had been among several people in the New World to suffer under the effects of the Scree. While hordes of people had gone missing in the Old World, so too had some from the New World side of the ocean. A lot of them had not been as fortunate as Atwood to be recovered so soon. The exact number of Infected, as the New World referred to them, was unknown, but Ellaria suspected it was a number greater than the governors let on. Most still stuck on the other side of the ocean.

"I don't want to talk about Danehin. These meetings always turn to dust once that issue is brought up. Let's talk about the reality of what's going on and our defenses. Is the High Tide Program ready, Admiral Vaughn?" General Marr asked.

With his question, the room looked to Zeeland Vaughn from Deloma and the home of the largest force of navy ships in the New World.

"It is and its use is approved. The king approved the activation earlier this week. Don't worry, General, I have already sent word to Commander Pike to be ready. Pryor, our head engineer, could not be here today to explain everything, because he is busy with his team on Deloma. However, I would rather he be working to verify our defense system is operational than explaining the war machines to this room. Just know the machines are operational, or will be."

"That was the last piece I need to finalize my preparations," General Marr said. "Miss Moonstone, if you would, I have a deployment stratagem that I would like to run by you before I go back to Adara."

"I would be happy to look it over, General," Ellaria replied. What she didn't say was that she could offer better advice if they would be more forthcoming about the High Tide Program. The secret defenses were closely guarded, even from her.

"Anything else to report, Governor Ramell?" Dalliana asked the representative from Syvonne.

"Yes." Ramell cleared his throat. He was an older man, less prone to the typical political nonsense than the others were. Ellaria liked him.

"Three items; the Dragons, as we are all aware, have been spotted all over the world. We have all seen the red one flying over the southern cities. It is commonly spotted over the Sunveil Mountain Range," Ramell said, gesturing to the map spread out on the table. "A second one, a turquoise one, was spotted in the north at Binder's Bay. A third, yellow-colored one was spotted in Delanon flying in Karnika. Lastly, a fourth was seen over the Jade Sea. It was black, and it disappeared into the Brovic. We have conflicting reports from the Old World and Nahadon that say they know of at least three more. There are very few reports of any more attacks."

"Is it six Dragons, then?" Shaw asked.

Ellaria waited for someone to spout about the number six being cursed, but no one did.

"It may be as many as nine. We can't be sure, and it seems like each has claimed a territory, but it is curious that they don't seem to be dangerous," Dalliana commented.

"I wouldn't say that. The red one wiped out a village outside of Westmere," Shaw said.

"I think what Dalliana means," Burke interrupted, "is that they don't seem to be a threat. Our investigation confirmed that unless provoked the Dragons don't seem interested in the cities," Burke, the Orin representative, clarified.

"They don't for now, but there must be some impact to the natural order of things. They are gigantic and are constantly in flight, but I can't help but wonder what they are eating," Ellaria said.

"We've built thousands of new barns to house livestock along the plains, just in case, but so far, we think they're feeding in the south. We haven't committed enough resources to track them properly yet," Burke answered her.

"Well, until we're sure, it's best to keep the airships grounded," Marr suggested.

"Those barns won't help protect anything. What we need to do is start searching for this sword we have all heard about," Atwood suggested.

A few grumbles from the governors around the room, and a significantly loud sigh of annoyance from General Marr, erupted at the talk of the Desolation blade again.

"What?" Atwood exclaimed defensively.

"It's a myth, it's tavern talk," Marr complained. "A sword of crystal that can kill a Dragon," he muttered.

"Well, every tavern is talking of it. We have reports that groups from here to Orvana are out searching for it," Atwood said.

"In the Old World too. Our messages from agents from Adavan to Domal report the same story. Hunters of the blade scouring the land for a sword of lore," Ramell added.

"People are scared and people are stupid," Marr said.

"Point is that whether you think it's real or not, we can't afford for someone else to find it," Shaw said, then surprisingly, he turned to

Ellaria. "Back me up here, Ellaria. You researched it, I'm sure. What did you find?"

"I researched it with Miss Kent. We went through a lot of texts, and there is some substantial, albeit secondhand, evidence in the form of personal accounts and journals that suggest the sword held by Caleb Reaver, Avari Nova, and the Oakol king was a real sword. However, were talking about the oldest texts we have," Ellaria explained, but she tried to maintain impartiality. She had read enough to know the sword did exist, including detailed descriptions of the crystal and handle, but she didn't want the governors thinking there was a magical fix to winning the war and defeating the Sagean's army.

"And?" Marr asked to coax Ellaria to continue.

"Well, an object that has been lost for more than a thousand years probably is going to stay lost," Ellaria said.

"Who's to say? It could be found, and we could wipe out the Sagean and his army with it," Atwood said.

"It's very doubtful, Governor," Ellaria countered. "The Sagean Empire searched for it during the reign of the third Emperor Syler. We have more accounts on that than anything else, and they found nothing. People were offered land, riches, and titles if they found it." She cleared her throat. "All I'm saying is we should focus our attention and efforts on other things. If the governors vote for it, and the king wants to start an official search, I will support it."

"It may come to that, if the Dragons start attacking us, but for now I agree with Miss Moonstone and General Marr—we focus on the war," Admiral Vaughn said.

Dalliana nodded her head in agreement. "And the second bit of news, Ramell?" she asked.

"We've been informed of a meeting in Karnika between the Harrinari tribes and the Zenoch," Ramell announced.

At this Ellaria finally sat up and paid attention. Both native cultures had a long-standing truce with the New Worlder's, but while relations weren't hostile, they weren't exactly peaceful either.

"To what end?" Marr asked.

"They know about the impending war, and they're meeting to

decide what roles they will play. It's a summit. We believe it is to establish a peace treaty," Ramell said.

"Or just to argue over boundaries, again," Shaw said dismissively.

"Are we thinking we should send a delegation to meet with them? Did they request one?" Dalliana asked.

"They invited us to send people, but…" Ramell said.

Atwood scoffed. "By people you mean the king. These are both primitive people. What…"

Ellaria interrupted the man before his diatribe began. "We have to send someone."

"What, why? The Zenoch aren't going to help us. And the Harrinari are native tribes that are always at war with themselves. Neither is equipped to fight this war, and I for one don't want to owe another nation for anything," Neverin Zulhorn said. He was the governor of the northern city of Imar. A religious man who believed in the teachings of the Sagelight, yet not the emperor. Most of the governors had known him for a long enough time, they trusted him, but Ellaria found the line between faithful believers and zealots a thin one.

"Who sent the report, Ramell? Did it say if this is the Harrinari Witch Woman's doing?" General Marr asked.

"Gavin Miller, our emissary of the borderlands, sent the report. Within it, he again mentions the Harrinari Witch Woman, but nothing worrisome," Ramell said.

"Worrisome? We've been hearing about this Harrinari leader with magical blood for some time now. Uniting the tribes, but for what end? When do we start seeing the Harrinari as another threat?" Shaw asked, agitated.

"Those tribes will never leave their wind-blasted waste. It's some sort of penance for them, and one they're prideful about. It would be nice to have received this report in person," Marr said.

"Let's table that discussion for a moment," Burke suggested.

Ellaria clenched her fists below the table, and almost slammed her hand down. This summit between potential allies was quite possibly the most important thing she had heard come from these meetings, and it had garnered near disdain from the entire group.

"What else do you got, Ramell?" Dalliana asked, noticing Ellaria squirming.

"Well, news from the Old World is not good. Many of the cities are reporting some skirmishes, and the word is that the Bonemen are rounding people up that do not agree with their Sagean's sovereignty. The Sagean seems to have delayed the war with us, to subjugate his own people first," Ramell said.

"Good, maybe that's the edge we need," Atwood said.

"Good? How could you say that's good? It's horrible," Dalliana admonished.

"Atwood's right. This is on the people in the Old World to stop their Sagean from enslaving them again," Shaw retorted, twisting Atwood's sentiment, and leaving no doubt of his agreement.

"No," Ellaria cut in. "Don't be delusional, Emperor Mayock, the Sagean, already has complete control. And if our scouts can be believed, he has regained his powers, and with them he will undoubtably begin manipulating people en masse, refocusing their attention to another enemy. The oldest tactics of the empire's fascist regime, the ones they used for centuries, are in full steam. Cause chaos, complain about chaos, and blame others. Then maintain chaos, but promise to fix it, seize power, and exert power against those you've singled out as the opposition to a better life. A holy life. Don't forget this is wrapped up in the religion of the Old World. The emperor is a Luminary and therefore a Sagean, and in the eyes of many, the manifestation of God. His focus on his own lands will not be a burden to him."

"Is it possible the delay can be used to our advantage?" Dalliana asked, directing her question to General Marr.

"The High Tide Program is complete. Our focus is on the remaining war machines and fortifying the coast for invasion," Marr replied.

"Can we direct our power toward the Sagean's destruction? Because that's what we need to do," Shaw demanded.

It didn't take long for the entire council to break into more arguments back and forth. The military-minded governors of the northern regions of Imar, Adara, and Deloma were insistent on fortifying defenses and striking first. As though both actions could be done with precision. The coastal regions of Illumeen, Ilan, and Verell were the most vocal about the need to eliminate the blockade and attack. While the southern regions of Logan and Haileon remained quiet. Orin, the capital city of the New World, stayed neutral as always.

Ellaria rubbed the sides of her head with both hands and tried to tune the bickering out, but it was no use. Suddenly the attacks turned on her, but she missed the comment and only heard Dalliana's retort.

"Don't forget yourself and who you're talking to," Dalliana warned.

"All right, we know who she is. Or who she was. But this isn't the Resistance War. It's a new war," Shaw said.

"I hate to admit when Shaw is right, but we can't pretend this is going to play out anything like the Old War," Marr said.

Ellaria grumbled under her breath. *The Old War, is that their new term for it?* Instead of calling it the Great War, as it always had been, this felt like a sneaky way to undermine her position as an expert. When words like "old" got thrown around casually, the intention of the insult was hidden in plain sight. *There is always some way to cut a powerful woman down,* she thought. Even as early as her forties, Ellaria had suffered men trying to use her age to discredit her. Most often men in power and threatened by her standing. Those types of men liked to profess that only men grew wise with age. When the truth was that age brought many things. Sore bones, bad eyesight, stubbornness, but wisdom wasn't one of them. The growl under her breath must have been more audible than she thought, as the room finally quieted for a moment.

"Wasn't it you, Ellaria, who said a general should never mistakenly believe they can win any battle based on a previous one fought?" Burke asked.

"Something like that," Ellaria admitted. She grinned. At least one of them had read their history.

"Care to elaborate?" Burke asked.

"No, she obviously doesn't," Shaw jumped in. "How many of these meetings have we had already? She hasn't offered anything we don't know. We are all aware of her credentials, but so what? We just sit here and pretend she's not manipulating our young princess."

"You're out of line, Shaw," the representative from Logan said.

"Pleasantries be damned. War is at our doorstep. It's waiting offshore of my city. The old lady can either help or go to Overdyn to wait for the results, for all I care. All that really matters is that we…"

Governor Zulhorn recoiled at the devil's name.

General Marr snapped, "Watch your mouth."

Ellaria stood to calm the room.

"Shaw's not entirely wrong. He's an asshole, but he's not entirely wrong. I did defeat the emperor's armies a long time ago. In fact, I was sixteen when I won my first battle, and I'm fifty-six now. This is a different war, it's a different time, and we fight on different grounds, but they are led by the same man. The same devious and terrible Sagean lord I defeated. Somehow, he's back from the dead. If the rumors are true, and I believe they are, that man will have only become more bloodthirsty. I guarantee he's confident that his armies of Bonemen, automatons, beasts, and machines will overrun and crush who he wants crushed. You better believe he will send numbers at the problem, because he cares nothing for anyone, there's no land he will not burn, no innocent he will not slaughter. He cares nothing about your defenses, your sea vessels, your carefully devised plans, or your elite warriors. The Sagean will send whatever he has at his disposal to wipe the New World from the map."

"Then if you don't mind, how did you beat him last time?" Shaw said.

"Well, you see, ego is a weakness easily exploited in war. Unlike him and many other men I've thwarted in my lifetime, my ego stems from the reality of being right. When your strategies are sound and the art at which you wage war is thoughtfully sharp, it's no longer ego. It's truth, and truth is the fortitude that will see you through the darkness."

"That's all well and good, but how did you win?" Vaughn asked.

"Have you never read a book, boy? Haven't you all at least studied the events of the Great War?" She probably shouldn't have called the military man a boy, but she didn't care. She was at her wits' end with these types of people. She continued without easing her temper. "Even a cursory review of the accounts detailed in the tribunals could teach you something. Do you appreciate nothing of what came before? It was simple, we did the impossible. Everything the Sagean believed was impossible, we did. Most notably convincing the world, one town, one village, one city at a time, that it was time to fight for their freedom," Ellaria said.

"Of course, having Qudin Lightweaver helped," Atwood said.

"You got that right," Ellaria agreed.

"We should send forces north like you suggested, Vaughn, and flank them in the Anamic," Atwood said.

"We've been over this. Our scouts believe the Sagean has the bulk of his ships still at the citadel," Burke said.

Ellaria sat back down, with the bickering resuming.

"Then we land troops in Domal and attack from the north," Admiral Vaughn offered.

"Why do some of you insist on attacking the Old World, when the Sagean is already invading us?" Dalliana asked.

"Because they are out of breath and grasping for action. A counteroffensive can work, but so far there's nothing to counter. The Sagean's strategy has been to strangle us, to press a stalemate where the one who panics loses. When you blink in war, your enemy can lead you blindly," Ellaria said.

"If the Darkhawks don't want to attack, I will order my ships to break the barricade in two days' time. We are out of time," Atwood stated.

"You will do no such thing. I understand your urgency, Atwood. But you must wait," Dalliana said.

"Listen," Ellaria blurted out, "the only thing worse than a bad plan is an un-unified one. Right now, the real threat is within. The only thing that can take this place down is ourselves. Within the walls the threat is real, treachery and anarchy will be the undoing of us all," she warned. "You're all the same. Squabbling over the land and rules and titles—and amber, as though you can take it with you. As though it is a life force more powerful than the energy in your own bodies. But I will say this, at least you're open and honest about it. At least you're arguing in front of each other, instead of allowing matters to be manipulated by agents from the shadows. I've yet to see the blatant backstabbing I expected, but you're all still young, so give it time, I guess.

"But listen to me, as you have never listened to me before. Sagean Mayock is coming. His army will be on your shores soon. Maybe tonight, maybe next week, but he's coming. The ones who brought him back, they waited forty years to enact their plan, he will wait no longer. This time he has Luminaries by his side." *And Dragons, for the sake of the Blue, are in the skies again after more than a thousand years. If he controls them, we are doomed*, she thought, but she kept that fear to herself and continued.

"We do not stand a chance against any of it if we do not stand together. I was a general in the Great War, that's true. I have watched many men die, and the one thing I know for certain, they didn't do it because they wanted freedom. The war itself was the only freedom they would know. They fought because they believed in an ideal, in a future that would see them as ghosts. A whispered hope carrying them through, that one day they may be reborn to a world they helped shape. Dammit, I will not be a part of shaping its demise!"

"What do you recommend?" Marr said.

"There are two things we need more than anything: resources and fighters. This meeting between the Harrinari and the Zenoch— we must send representatives. I would like to go," Ellaria said.

"No way," Shaw said.

"Look at it this way, Shaw. If you send me with a small coalition, I'll be out of your hair, and you can carry on without me. If I fail to garner aid, there's no loss, as you don't expect any. We can pick up Danehin on our way to the region if they require the king's attendance." Ellaria looked to each of them and stood again. "Think on it, debate it. I will await your decision."

She started to leave the table, and some of the better men got out of their seats to recognize her departure. She waved them goodbye and headed for the door.

She exited the complex to the city square of Ioka. Crossing over the spacious courtyard, she avoided looking at the statues of marble placed all around and found a spot in a park near the Ioka University overlooking the city of Orin.

Ellaria sat on the bench and opened the letter from her friend. Arlene Kent was one of the finest scholars around and one of the few who had lived the last twenty years in the New World. No one was more versed in the history of the continent. So, when Ellaria landed, she sought Arlene out immediately to set her to researching the possibility of temples as old as the one in Nahadon. The letter simply stated that she was onto something and would explain more in person.

It wasn't long before Dalliana had joined her on the bench.

"They've agreed to your suggestion," Dalliana told her. "You leave in one week. Some of the representatives are traveling with you for part of the trip. Depending on the day you leave."

"Who?"

"General Marr is leaving right away, so I suspect it will be Atwood, Ramell, and Shaw with you until Syvonne on their trips back to their homelands. Vaughn will travel with you all the way to Deloma, and Zulhorn, from Imar, was selected to accompany you and my father to the summit in the wastes."

Great, the Sagelight-quoting grump, Ellaria thought. "You're not going?" she asked.

"No, they want me safe in Orin. So, what are you thinking?" Dalliana asked.

"I think I want our ship ready to go, so I can leave as soon as Kovan arrives. No matter what, I'll leave in a week's time. I'm also thinking the New Worlder's squabble like children, complaining of inequities. They're all mercenaries, misfit mercenaries or employees of mercenaries, remember that. Though I do want you to go back to them and request that they send a small company to protect the south. Eventually, I would like you to send a team, ideally headed by the Logan governor Irabell, to search Manashera. If the Menodarins are there, it's imperative that we gather as many allies as possible. Most likely, neither the Zenoch nor the Harrinari will be receptive to us. More than that, they might be mad about bringing war to their borders, but we're invited and that means something. They may be willing to trade."

"Trade what? Resources?" Dalliana said.

"Or knowledge," Ellaria said.

"One more thing, when you left, Burke brought up some rumors that the New World crime syndicate and the Old World bounty hunters, the Moonstalkers, are working together. Somebody named Targo Shine. Have you heard of him?"

"I have."

"I guess he asked about Kovan."

"Interesting. Well, I expected assassins and spies for the Sagean to be among us, but this sounds different."

"I thought so too," Dalliana said.

Together they sat in silence a moment before Dalliana got up to return to her duties. She stopped short and stared at the marble statues behind them, which Ellaria had chosen to sit facing away from.

"You don't like them, do you?" Dalliana said.

"The statues?" Ellaria asked.

"They're monuments, you know. They're reminders of history, but they are also symbols of honor and strength."

"All I see in them are ghosts and pain."

"I guess I understand that. For what it's worth, yours is my favorite. It's strong and flattering, and it's thoughtful. The sculptor really captured your spirit. I was never adept with alchemy, but there's a magic to that, right, to great art?"

"Anything that reflects real truth is magic."

After Dalliana departed, Ellaria decided to take a closer look at her statue. The stone figure was proud and beautiful and obstinate and almost embarrassing. She wished she felt anything but sadness at seeing the monument. Pride had never been an emotion easily accessed for her. The best sensation she could muster was a notion of resolve. She gazed at the stone face she once knew, steadfast and bold, and a new determination flooded her being.

She changed her mind, and instead of heading back to her balcony to watch the sky for Kovan, she headed to the university for answers. Before her own veins were truly stilled and sealed within stone.

FIVE

LAST WORDS - LEARON

LEARON PLACED THE LETTERS IN HIS PACK AND HEARD ECHORYN calling from the front chambers of the temple. He took a quick look around and scrambled out to meet her. Passing the field of columns and into smaller chambers, he was hoping to catch her before she found him. He turned a corner and found her with a small group trailing, a room away.

"Learon, you thickhead. There you are. Did you find it?"

Learon nodded his head yes, but answered, "No. It's not safe inside. That last tremor has destabilized the depths of this place."

She squinted at him, trying to understand what he was up to, then the group of soldiers and engineers came closer.

"It's too dangerous to go beyond this point. We should head back," Learon said.

"Your caravan awaits," the head guard stated.

They packed the remaining things and climbed into the cart heading for the river and the trip back to Sualden. Learon's mind raced at what the contents of the letters could be, but he wanted to wait until they were somewhere private to read his. It wasn't that he didn't trust the Kihan, but Elias had been secretive for a reason, so Learon thought it best for now to maintain that.

A day and a half later when they were back in the palace, they headed straight to the prophet's chamber.

Echoryn closed the door while he powered up the circulating lamplight.

"All right, out with it, bohoja," Echoryn said, calling him a word in Kihan that meant *protector*. Though the way Echoryn said it, to Learon it sounded more like she was calling him stubborn.

Learon pulled the letters from his pack and displayed them out for her to see. "I found a hidden room."

"You did?"

"These were on the floor in front of a Wave Gate."

"A Wave Gate? One of the Ancients' traveling gates?"

"Yes."

"Elias went to the gate that night?"

"More than that. Remember how I told you he was late getting into the chamber? I think he used the gate and came back."

"Why? For what, where did he go?"

Learon picked up his letter and waved it. "Let's find out," he said. He wanted to tear the letter open, but as hard as it was, he restrained himself to peel back the corners of the seal and started to unfold it carefully, but the weight of the contents stopped him short. He extended it to Echoryn.

"Me?" she said, aghast.

"I… I can't," Learon stammered.

"What's wrong?"

"I just… You read it."

Echoryn looked at him and nodded. She unfurled the page and slowly shifted her eyes from him to the letter. Learon's heart pounded, he was suddenly afraid of the contents and couldn't explain why exactly.

Echoryn stopped. "You haven't been out there yet, have you, to visit him?"

"What?" Learon said anxiously.

"Elias's tomb?"

Learon took a deep breath. "No. Why? Just read the letter," he pleaded.

"Fine."

Echoryn continued reading. "Huh, oh." She sighed and thrust the letter back at him. She had glossy eyes. "Read it, Learon."

He stared at her curiously, and then a knock came to the door.

Startled, Echoryn stood to receive their guest, and Learon placed the letters back in his bag.

Echoryn waited of him, then opened the door. Grace Derasi stood stoically in the darkened passageway. His robes were pressed, but from the glow of the passage lights, they could see he wore an exhausted expression and his pupils appeared edgy.

The Grace, Learon had learned, was the Kihan people's holy man. As such, he had many duties, including as a sort of records keeper for the Kihan's archives. His most important role was as an adviser to the kingdom. A prophet, like Echoryn, was a challenge to his authority and wisdom. However, Elias had trusted the man, so Learon did too, but only so far.

"Miss Echoryn Solhara, Kovan Rainer and his group have cleared our receiving team and will be arriving in Sualden within the hour. The ship they arrived in is still anchored in the bay, but we have kept them from leaving for the time being. The ship captain, a Captain Morales, expressed an eagerness to be off. It seems they plan to return to the mainland and Hazon."

"Thanks for the update, Grace Derasi."

"Also, I wanted to ask, was your trip successful?"

"We found a lot of interesting reliefs for the scholars to catalog and analyze. We brought back sketches. I already had them sent to the palace library."

"Anything of Elias's?" Derasi asked. It was a curious follow-up.

"Learon found Elias's satchel, but there wasn't much inside."

"Oh. Well, I'm glad you found something, Learon," Derasi said, but his tone seemed depressed, and with that he turned to go.

"Wait, my grace?" Echoryn said.

"Yes, young Solhara?"

"Can you ready a ship in Lake Azeerall for Learon? He wants to visit Tarensky before he departs for the New World."

"Yes, I will have one ready."

"Thank you."

Echoryn shut the door and readdressed Learon. "I don't want to hear your arguments. You're going."

"I can't, I still need to go get Bazlyn," Learon said. Bazlyn had made quite a few friends in the many taverns in Sualden. Being grounded had made the typically jovial man a recluse of strangers and a purveyor of all the Kihans' wines.

"I'll pack and then I'll go round him up," Echoryn said.

"Pack? The queen will never let you go with us to the New World."

"We'll see," she said, pushing him out the door.

LEARON SAT AT THE EDGE OF THE CLEARING, HOLDING HIS LETTER. The marble stone tomb was set up on a circular bed of crushed crystals in the middle of a lonely field. Learon had remained at the tree-lined edge for the past hour, not wanting to intrude into the space. The entire area felt like a sacred space.

Lost in his thoughts, he didn't notice someone had joined him in the meadow and was startled by the hand placed on his shoulder. He twitched to find Kovan standing above him. Learon started to stand, but Kovan pressed him down to stay where he was and sat next to him.

Kovan exhaled as he sat. "You know you're going to have to help me up," he grumbled. "How are you, kid?"

"I'm dealing." Learon fumbled for how to explain himself.

"I can imagine. We met Echoryn inside the palace. She filled us in."

"Here," Learon said, fishing out the letters. He handed Kovan the three that didn't belong to him. "Did Echoryn tell you about these?"

"She did. She's spirited, I like her. So, Elias left these, huh?"

"He found a Wave Gate deep inside the temple compound where he fought the emperor. I'm not sure if he used it that night, but he left these on the platform."

"That devious little…" Kovan grumbled and trailed off. "That's just like him to try and land the last word. You didn't read all these, did you?"

"No."

"I would have."

"No, you wouldn't have." Learon smirked.

"You're right," Kovan admitted. "So, that's it?" he asked, nodding his head in reference to the tomb. "And you're sure he's in there?" he said, unconvinced.

"I guess so."

"Didn't you go to the funeral? If I remember right, the Tregoreans give a pretty good send-off," Kovan said. His use of the word Tregorean, the mainland's common name for the Kihan, now sounded awkward to Learon after spending months among them.

"There wasn't a funeral," Learon answered.

"What? Why not?"

"I was told that was Elias's wishes."

For a moment Kovan stared at the tomb in silence, and he rubbed his chest and grimaced.

"Are you all right?" Learon asked, concerned.

"Fine. So, what answers did you come out here looking for?" Kovan said.

"I'm stuck wondering what I should do next. Should I keep my promise to Elias? Should I just go back home, find my mother, and help the Renegades? Or should I go looking for Tali?"

"Have you decided?"

"No," Learon replied.

"Well, if you're not coming with me, I'm sure Morales will sail you back to the mainland if you're intent on finding your mother or fighting with that group of Renegades. He's taking my friend Buroga back to Hazon. As for Tali, she's a survivor. Either we'll find her or she'll find us," Kovan remarked.

"What's the right answer, Kovan?" Learon asked, staring out at the fading light.

"There isn't one. The Renegades need help, but the New World needs our help too. The decision is yours, Learon. But if it's truth you seek, you may not find it where you think. The woman who raised you…"

"My mother," Learon corrected him.

"Your mother. If she's as sick as you said and in hiding, she might not be able to tell you the truth. I can assure you, kid, that the emperor knows of you now and your presence on the mainland will only endanger the ones you love."

"From what I've read about my abilities, where the Nimbus goes, death will follow."

"Then come with me. While I wasn't a Nimbus Warrior, I was one of the most infamous warriors in the Great War. I know how to navigate that life. Not well, admittedly, but I know that side of things. Ultimately, it's your call. I'm sure the Tregoreans will provide you with a ship and an army to go north, but tomorrow at dawn we're leaving for the black shore. The Tregoreans have already loaded Bazlyn's winddrifter onto a barge to sail the Tyn River to the south shores of Nahadon. From there we can sail the south winds to the New World," Kovan got off the ground and started back to the trail and out of the meadow. He stopped short and called back, "You know Ellaria messaged us about the Trinity and about your bond to Tali. It's possible that you can't feel her through the bond because she's a world away."

After Kovan left, Learon sat staring at the gravestone until the stars came out and finally opened his letter from Elias. Learon adjusted the lamp, unfurled the letter, and held the black inked script up to the light.

> *Learon,*
>
> *I trusted you would find these letters, as you have a seeker's heart. I'm sorry I'm not there to tell you these things in person. Mostly, I am sorry for what has happened to you and for what it is you still must do. In a lot of ways, the worst ways, yours is the hardest letter I have to write. It is a strange world indeed that sees such unfairness placed upon certain souls. Burdens of impossible weight and stakes destined to be carried by those with the broadest shoulders. Such is life, but always remember, in times like these, in hard*

times, in all times, always hold strong to the bonds of love. Love is a fragile energy of unequal power; it's the boldest of all of nature's things, and it can vanquish the darkest demons.

There have been many burdens thrust upon you, but do not fear. The Fates have seen to it that those that can succeed at the most difficult tasks are given the tools to persevere.

Whether by equal design or as a means of balance for your gifts, you have also been uniquely tested with the hardship of discovering who you are. This is the journey of all beings; yours is only more complicated. The path of life is vast and splintered, and while you're on it, remember it is more important to create yourself than to find yourself. A quest for the living is in the becoming; the quest for the dead flounders in the waiting.

After tonight I will be putting those two states in conflict myself, and testing the boundaries of both.

For your next steps, I will ask that you trust me. Trust that finding out who your parents are, or were, makes little difference to the man you are. Though the internal turmoil is real, the truth is not essential, nor is it immaterial. For this loss of time and love, I am eternally sorry. Suffering is never a solitary endeavor, even when the depths seem lonely.

Of your story, I know a significant amount, but what I want to tell you is that your separation was facilitated by the very evil you are now bound to fight and destroy.

I can also tell you that your birth mother is alive and living in the New World. I'm unsure exactly where, but I know you will find her. I'm sure that you have figured out by now that your birth mother is Mia, the last Kihan prophet. When I knew her, she was a magnificent being of honesty, courage, and unequal fortitude. Like all prophets, she was heavily haunted by the ghosts of tomorrow. I'm sure that the Kihan people have put this together as well, and that will make your departure from them more difficult, especially with as close of friends you have become to the new prophet. I can also tell you that when the story of what happened is finally brought to light, Kovan and Ellaria will be blinded by rage. I encourage you to remember that sacrifice is the nature of love, and that the ends to which we go to save the world require courage, and rarely constitute a level head.

I am trusting you to keep your promise and seek out the Shadowyn. Their hidden village lies in the north reaches of the Haildron Mountains. There are more than just fighting skills to discover there. Also, you must have Kovan accompany you. It is imperative that you both go, for there is something for him as well.

Lastly, you must know that the gates are unreliable and flawed. There were hints about this in some of my research, but having used them, I am now sure of it. They do not always take the traveler to the gate that was selected through the dais sigils. While the gates have a system of linking to other gates around the world, there is a curiosity in the system. The gates are somehow tied to the individual who passes through the portal. The strongest bonds can elicit a change of destination: love, revenge, blood, or pure need. I think if a squad of soldiers went through it, and one man in his company had second thoughts, the gate might take them to safety instead of the battlefield; or, for instance, if a father needed to discover a son he never knew he had, it might take him to a mountain peak he had never been to.

Learon, I spent the bulk of my life investigating the mysteries of this world, and everything I've found and studied suggests the greatest mysteries reside in the world we can't see—where the bonds of energy are derived. For we are all entwined forever in the cosmic order until the source calls us home.

As the saying goes, if your memory serves you well, we'll meet again.

Stay true,

Elias

Learon carefully folded the letter back up and held it while scanning the stars above. He sat there longer than he intended to, and when he finally left the meadow, he headed to Lake Azeerall to meet Kovan. It was dawn when he arrived, and Echoryn stood waiting for him on the stone embankment with his bag packed at her feet. She was dressed in her scout gear and heavily guarded by rangers surrounding her. The number of Kihan soldiers stretched down the lake shoreline and back to the columned entrance of the underground city of Sualden. Echoryn didn't have any bags of her own.

"I knew you would be here," she said. She had a sly grin and didn't seem as upset about his leaving as he thought she would be.

"I'm grateful," Learon replied.

She slid his bag over. "Be careful, squirrel."

Learon smiled and hugged his friend. His touch brought some grumbles from the soldiers, but the head guard waved them to stand down. Learon didn't have the right words to say goodbye or thank you. He wanted to thank her for her graciousness and her spirit, but didn't know how.

"Sorry," he said to her as he pulled away. He held her hand. "Thank you, for everything. You are and will always be one of my best friends."

Echoryn blinked rapidly and stood stunned for a moment. Then with her eyes glistening, she pushed him toward the rampart to board the boat. "You're welcome, squirrel."

Learon threw his bag on the deck and leaned against the sideboard to wave at her. "I'll return, I promise," he said, but inwardly he cringed at making another promise.

She waved back but said nothing else.

IT TOOK FOUR DAYS TO REACH THE SOUTHERN SHORE OF NAHADON. Following the river, they landed at an outpost to the port city of Cameria. Learon accompanied Wade and Stasia into the city to pick up supplies, leaving Kovan sleeping on deck and Bazlyn working on his airship.

They had kept a close eye on the skies for any sign of Dragons but hadn't spotted anything. The only thing troubling them was that their communications to Ellaria had all gone unanswered.

A day later, the airship was ready. At midday, when the Blue sun moved over the sky and slowly turned back to yellow, they began to take off. The *Regalia Savona* drifted into the air with a steady lift, and the land began to shrink away. Bazlyn turned gears to increase the steam and lift while angling the pullies to grab the wind. Learon spotted a small fleet of ships arrive on the river below. A group of

Kihan rangers gathered at the point they had launched from. They were pointing at the airship and shouting.

"What's their problem?" Wade asked.

Learon studied them from the diminishing vantage point. "I can't hear them, but they're mad at something," he remarked.

"I think they're mad at me," Echoryn's voice said from above them. Learon glanced up in shock to spot her head sticking over the edge of the ballast plank. "I sort of snuck on."

Kovan lifted the brim of his hat where he was sitting back on the bench. Learon thought he might order the ship back down, but he simply smiled and placed the hat back over his eyes.

"You're going to let her stay?" Stasia questioned Kovan.

"Sure. Why not? Maybe we need a prophet on this adventure."

Six

Mysteries - Ellaria

ELLARIA HAD SPENT THE GREATER PART OF THE WEEK WAITING TO leave on her journey holed up at the university, searching for information on all the mysteries still eluding her. They were piling up now, and each was nestling inside like a splinter embedded irretrievably deep. The back room of the Ioka University library was dark with the upper windows blacked out. The table before her was full of books about the Tempest Stone, the Wave Gates, prophets, Dragons, and the ancient swords that could kill them, and a new curiosity bugging her, the ancient race of beings called the Fates.

In her time with the Kihan, she had finagled her way into seeing their archives. One thing that kept coming up were references to the Fates. The followers of the Fates religion believed the Fates were immortals, always around, always tangentially responsible for the unfolding events of life. As the practiced faith of the Kihan, she could easily understand why there were so many references to them. What confused her were the frequent references to another similar group called the Watchers. In one of the oldest tomes from their collection, yet a third name was talked about. A group of ancient gods they called the Vygoths. A word translated in the ancient language to mean, *watchers from beyond* or *watchers from another world*. Again, the word Watchers showing itself. She had yet to determine if all three of these were one and the same, but it sure seemed that way.

Ellaria was no expert on the Fates or the religion in general. Some of the myths she knew said the Fates possessed knowledge of the future at their fingertips. That they couldn't be killed, and they could control time, because they were outside of its reach. Believers took comfort in the faith of these gods to orchestrate the future to the benefit of all humanity. Ellaria wanted to know the origin of these beings. The Sagean faction had established its own religion based around moral doctrines with a very real and powerful being at the heart of it: the Sagean Luminary. Ellaria couldn't help but wonder if the Fates too were based on something factual.

She set her book down and rubbed the bridge of her nose and eyes. The idea of a god or gods not only watching over the world but participating in the outcome was hard to fathom. However, the credence of life contained many unfathomable things. Prophets were real, Luminaries were real, the magic of symbols and crystals were real, so how could she deny the reality of immortal beings?

This curious line of thought hung over her as she sat in the library among the oldest books in the New World's collection. The smell of the books, the pebbled covers, parchment and ink in retrograde, old glue, and leather permeated the room. The remnants of history lost and pieced together. All the texts around her had been meticulously collected, salvaged, and curated from private collections over the years. It was the missing volumes, the lost works, that occupied her mind. The ghosts of what wasn't there haunted what was, *so how could she ever know the full truth?* She sighed.

The gas lamps overhead started to dim, but the sconces with capacitor gems were going strong. Their warm glow softly lit the passageways out of the private library to the main holding, where the sunlight streamed in. A flutter to the glow down the hall warned of someone approaching.

Arlene Kent strolled in moments later, holding a fresh stack of books, her dark hair on her shoulders and glasses always sliding down her nose. They had been meeting regularly since Ellaria's arrival, but something about leaving had made Ellaria stay longer each night. She couldn't sit any longer on her balcony, staring out at the sea.

Arlene was only six years younger than Ellaria, but it was enough to have avoided firsthand involvement in the war, and yet still be a significant witness. She was part of a unique generation that bridged the past of cart and carriage with the modern society of airships and electricity. Arlene, to her credit, carried the guilt of her age, and thus, the drive to document the war.

Arlene set another stack of books on the last available space on the table and sat across from Ellaria. With Arlene's help, she had slowly been unraveling the past one text at a time. Ellaria was training Arlene the decipher methods to read the Elegan language Elias had discovered, but nothing about it was quick. The oldest texts had barely survived the passage of time. Covers falling off, pages crumbling, and mites eating away at what remained, even the best preserved had smeared characters, water stains, discolored parchment, or faded script.

They found more secrets and gaps, then links. After seeing the archives in the Kihans' possession, Ellaria was sure that similar collections existed in the custody of other cultures. She feared that most likely the most important works were under lock and key by the Court of Dragons. The group of Sagean acolytes were in shambles with the Sagean's return, and their base of operations remained unknown to Ellaria.

As she held one of the oldest books in the collection in her hands, she couldn't help but be full of sadness and wonder, simultaneous feelings that conflicted with each other. It was one of the rare gems with no author and no real discernable title. At only forty-seven pages, the fact that it existed was amazing. The fact that it had survived a thousand years was unbelievable. It was small, almost pocket sized. The lower corner of the cover was torn away, the letters worn to nothing. The story of its life was maybe more interesting than the contents within. What books had it shared a cupboard with? What hands held the spine through time, and what had others gleaned from the words? The ancient text was still sharp, and by her translation was simply a collection of short stories or poetry—all random lines and unconnected images.

Arlene took the top two books off the top of her stack and handed them to Ellaria. "These are the two best books I have about Karnika. You can take them with you if want."

"Sure. My bags are already filled with books, what's two more?" Ellaria said.

"Well, the university in Adara has prints of both. If you don't have the room, your best bet is to meet up with the guides. Miller lived in Delanon for his whole life. He's quirky, but he knows the wastes. You'd like him. He has a real distrust of authority."

Ellaria turned the first book over in her hand. It had a nice weight to it. On the cover were three spears drawn at staggered lengths and the title embossed in a reddish hue: *The Wastelands of Karnika*. Inside, there was a subtitle: *The Tribes of War*. She turned to the first page and read the first few lines aloud.

"Karnika is the land of desolate plains and harsh wind. A name derived from the ancients meaning the Lost Ones. It is a land of lost cities, lost names, or peoples long gone..."

"I've never been out there. Are the winds as bad as they say?" Arlene asked.

"I only went as far as the valley once. We met a leader of the Oakol and sat with her for a time, but yes, they can be. The Oakol believe the winds are their punishment for a great sin they have forgotten. That's why they never leave the wastes."

"Is she the Oakol leader I have heard about?" Arlene inquired.

"No, the woman we met with was very old, in her nineties, and her..." She paused, remembering the old woman's tired, sun- and wind-burned skin. She could distinctly remember the old woman had a sort of seer's ability and had held Ellaria's hand briefly. The old woman's tiny frail fingers clasped Ellaria's right hand and turned it palm up as though she read Ellaria's veins. It was the skin of the woman's hand that Ellaria remembered most. It was incredibly soft skin, like it barely clung to the bone. Ellaria glanced at her own softening hands and closed the book.

"Anyway, I don't think that woman could be alive still. I'm sure whoever this Witch Woman is, she was probably trained by that old lady. The Harrinari are like the Zenoch in that they prize age in their leaders."

Ellaria tapped the books. "This covers the entire wastes? From Delanon to the Uden Sea?"

"Yes."

"Good. If there is more than one tribe gathering at this summit, I want some idea of what I'm walking into. These things can be more precarious than navigating the Brovic," she mused.

"That reminds me. I have a report from a science team out on Triden, about the Brovic mists," Arlene said excitedly.

"What about it. Is it spreading faster?" Ellaria asked.

"Actually, they've started to find data that it's retreating."

"What?" Ellaria's eyes went wide. "That's huge. I hadn't heard that yet in any of my briefings with the governors. It's more likely it was simply disregarded, but still, you would think they would be all over this."

"Maybe it hasn't reached their desks? I only read it a few days ago," Arlene said.

"I remember this study," Ellaria said, looking it over. "The Brovic mists' expansion was a contentious issue with the United Coalition of Nations. The Rodaireans refused to let anyone go to the Dire to investigate. That's why the science team was sent to Triden to study this side of it along the Uden Sea. This was years ago, and a lot of the apprehension was based on half the council believing it was a hoax and a waste of time and the other half warning Danehin not to meddle in the east. I can tell you, no one wanted to deal with it. Mainly because there wasn't any hard evidence of it having moved in a century. Do you have a copy of the report?"

"I do." Arlene left the small table of books and disappeared into the dark passageways. When she returned, she had a leather binder with a thick stack of papers bulging from the edges. "This is my records casebook. It's in here." Arlene handed the heavy book over.

Within it, Ellaria found the report along with new maps recently sent in by the Scholars Guild cartographer, reports on the High Grove tree species and new aquatic life found in the Jade Sea, and an interesting report on ruins under the Uden.

"Arlene, if this is true, it's a significant finding."

"I know. I hope it's true. That mist is frightening. I think everyone secretly held out hope that Qudin would fix it somehow."

"Evidence of the expansion of the Brovic mist was only in the last forty years, but our understanding of it is less than a hundred years old. The Sagean Empire didn't know what it was. What created it or why it existed. When the first explorers of the New World pushed east, they were surprised to find the mists at all. Our histories don't explain it. It is not referenced in the oldest tales, and the few texts and poems we have of the Luminary Wars don't mention it at all. It's not until after the empire was formed that the first mentions of the impassable Brovic and the 'Doomed' Ocean start to be talked about," Ellaria said.

Ellaria could only hope that Kovan would arrive soon. They were supposed to have a vast knowledge at their fingertips, with the Tempest Stone. All they needed was a way to use it, and Learon had told her that it could be activated through the small obsidian podiums like the one in Elias's vault. But hopefully they could find another in the New World and unlock the secrets plaguing her.

Resigned to finish up for the afterblue, Ellaria sat back in her chair, feeling her neck stiffen, having been there all morning.

"Are you heading back to your balcony for the afterblue?" Arlene asked.

"I think so. The ocean has always been comforting to me. Maybe I'll gain some rest before leaving for the north."

"The ocean, I thought you grew up in Tovillore?"

"I didn't live in Eloveen until I was ten, after my grandfather discovered capacitor gems and our family was elevated to the high order. Originally, I was raised in a small village by the sea in Rhodova. But my father was a military man with the Rodairean Legion, and he moved us to Ravenvyre when I was still very young to live with my grandfather."

"Your interest in the Brovic stems from your childhood?"

"You could say that," Ellaria replied while sorting the pile before her to select the books she was taking with her. Footsteps clattered in the hall. Arlene's assistant came rushing toward them with a letter. She handed it to her and retreated to the center stacks.

"She was told it's urgent," Arlene said, handing over a small letter.

Ellaria took it with a quizzical look and read it. It was from Dalliana. Ellaria's ship was leaving for Illan at midnight. Which meant there was movement at the sea front.

"Arlene, listen. You should leave the city. Ioka isn't safe any longer. Fighting is going to start any day now. Conceivably tonight," she said, waving the letter, "and I fear that the Sagean will be out for annihilation."

"I'll be all right."

Ellaria gathered her things and gave her friend a worried gaze. "Make sure you are. Go to the High Grove if you must."

"Don't worry about me, old friend. Lead the envoy and convince the Zenoch and Harrinari to join forces with us."

"I will," Ellaria said, and she rushed out of the library and back to the palace.

SEVEN

CROSSING THE ANAMIC - KOVAN

KOVAN HELD THE LETTER FOLDED IN HIS HAND, HIS EYES TOWARD THE clearing of clouds. Bazlyn descended beneath the cloud-deck to see the ocean below. They were hoping that the expanded field of vision could help them navigate away from the Sagean battleships in the water below as they approached the New World in the next few hours. They had yet to spot a Dragon, but the night before they were sure they had shared the sky with other airships.

Kovan assumed they were Sagean ships and had all the lights aboard extinguished and told Bazlyn to drift further south.

Coming out of the clouds felt risky.

"If we're spotted, can you get us out of here?" Kovan asked Bazlyn.

"Sure thing. I'll climb back up and out, and I'll do my best to steer her out of danger," Bazlyn answered, rolling a small gear to shift the sails.

"Do you think they have anything capable of taking us down, Kovan?" Wade asked.

"I'm sure they would have to. If the ships are war ready, the Sagean has thought of air attacks and certainly has some of his own planned. However, they won't be expecting something coming at them from the west," Kovan answered.

The cold mist of the cloud begun to part, and the expanse of the sea was coming into view below. "All the same, everyone hold on to something solid, in case Bazlyn is forced to do some quick maneuvers," he announced.

Everyone on board stationed themselves around the winddrifter, some of them gripping the side rail with white-knuckle anticipation. If they had the misfortune to appear above the Sagean's battlements, their long flight would see a swift and destructive end. The ship dipped below and free of the final mists to reveal the turbulent waters of the Dead Wake Sea. It was a welcome sight, and Kovan exhaled.

"Clear?" Kovan asked aloud.

"All clear," Wade called from the bow.

"Clear," Stasia said.

"Clear," Echoryn said from the ballast plank above.

Kovan, having not heard from Learon, turned and approached the stern to stand next to the kid. Learon stood quietly.

"All clear, Learon?" Kovan asked. Learon didn't answer, but Kovan followed the young man's eyes, squinting and rapidly blinking. Kovan looked out over the empty ocean behind them. "Did you see something?"

Learon nodded but continued to scan.

"In the sky or on the sea?" Kovan confirmed.

"Not sure, like something reflected on the surface," Learon said.

In short order, Wade had come over to look too.

"There," Learon called out in hushed tone.

"Where?" I don't see anything," Wade said.

"I don't either…" Kovan stopped midsentence as something on the waves seemed to shadow and disappear. "What is that?"

Learon's eyes grew big. "Dragon," he said, and accessed one of the cargo holds and pulled out the inflatable pontoon the Tregoreans had given them. He called up to Echoryn, "Echo, hold on up there. Don't come down until someone can help." Then he scrambled back to stand on the back bench, grasping a main line to steady his balance.

Wade appeared panicked and lifted a rifle to a ready position. Learon lowered the barrel of it with his free hand. "Guns only make them angry. Just be ready to start inflating that boat," Learon said calmly.

Still unsure he believed Learon, Kovan leaned over the edge to look below, when suddenly the entire winddrifter was plunged into shadow. A massive Dragon soared over them, close enough to count its dark-red scales, and it lifted up into the clouds. Everyone on board had instinctively cowered or crouched for cover. The beat of its wings pushed a rush of air into the ship, and the *Savona* swayed and faltered. A few of them on board were taken off their feet, from either the gust or the sudden tilt of the ship. Loose supplies on the deck slid into the sideboard.

Kovan found his feet and looked around. Stasia clamped her hand over her mouth. Kovan supposed it was to keep her scream in. The only one on board that had seen the Dragons up close before was Learon. He was right; the gun wouldn't do a thing to it.

Kovan rushed back to Learon's side. He had held strong, though he was precariously perched on the ship's edge.

"You've seen them attack, Learon. Is it coming back?" Kovan urged.

"This one's different? I'm not sure."

"Different how?"

"The one I saw over the temple was black," Learon replied.

"Who cares what color it is?" Wade said.

"I don't know if it makes a difference. But the Dragon the Kihan have been tracking off the western wall is green. The Kihan rangers told me it only attacked in defense. That makes at least three of them. Who's to say whether they're different in other ways or not?"

The red Dragon appeared again further away from them and just as quickly disappeared above.

"Did you see it act like this?" Kovan asked.

"No, I… There it is again," Learon said.

A darkness grew in the cloud, like an ink spill spreading on paper, until the full form broke out of the clouds two hundred feet from them. A rattling next to them caught both Kovan's and Learon's attention. Wade's hand gripped his rifle, but he was shaking so badly the buttons of his coat were rattling against the metal power cylinder. Kovan snatched the gun from him before the kid accidentally fired at the thing.

"I think, like the others if it wanted to attack us, it would have," Learon said.

Kovan nodded.

"What should I do?" Bazlyn managed to ask. The pilot's voice was unsteady, his hands at the wheel.

"Keep the ship on course and steady. No sudden movements. I don't want to draw attention," Kovan said.

"Kovan," Stasia called.

Kovan turned around to see the Dragon falling from the sky at incredible speed. The giant creature had put its wings angled back, and it sped toward the ocean. In an unbelievable maneuver, the Dragon's wings unfolded above the surface and the front legs plunged first into the waves. The ocean walloped against the intrusion, and the Dragon lifted off into the air once more.

It was no more than a few hundred feet up when it swooped back and soared in a circle until it was diving again. This time the entire Dragon went beneath the water, and the ocean pulsed where the Dragon was submerged and ejected a blast of salty spray up into the air. After a long pause, the Dragon burst out of the ocean with a whale in its claws. An incredible amount of water spilled back to the ocean as the two massive monsters flew away into the distance.

The awestruck ship of fools was speechless. Dumbfounded, Kovan shook his head as if trying to reconcile the reality of what they had witnessed. He patted Learon on the back and sat down. Now realizing that when the Dragon had flown over them, it was trying to determine if they were competition for its food. It was obvious, it could have destroyed them with ease, but the Dragon hadn't attacked them, because it had no fear of them or the airship. What Kovan found profoundly unsettling, was the thought that one day the Dragons would attack.

The winddrifter sailed over the southern city of Jara, with their destination two hours away. They had yet to see another airship in the sky. Kovan sat down and pulled out his letter from Elias.

Kovan,

I hope this letter finds you and finds you well.

I'm waiting in a small room before I head out to my

demise, and I can't help but remember a great many similar nights during the Great War. Most of those, I had you by my side, and I wish you were here now. I still don't know how we made it through some of those.

Thankfully the Kihan have done their best to heal me, and at least I'll fight one last time, but the truth is that this shadow has been bound to me for too long. I think I know how things will go when we reach the temple, and what I may have to do to survive. Having come face to face with the cause of my disease, I now know the solution to eradicate it. Regretfully, it involves bringing back an evil we know very well. Please know I'm torn by my decision, but believe there is no other way. I'll never be able to live with the Sagean's soul feeding off my own. If I can convince Edward to take it out of me, then I might have a chance to survive and fight at the last battle against the Wrythen.

When the Kihan healed me this time, I had a significant clearing of my mind. A huge cloud had been put there, and I now see the truth of the past.

I was told you were given a great gift of reliving your memories. By the time you read this, I'm sure you will have discovered the truth about your daughter. Kovan, my brother, I am terribly sorry. Please understand that I did not remember what really happened until today, when I awoke from my haunting. I can only speculate, but I believe Mia must have had a good reason to hide her from you and Ellaria. What that could be, I don't know. Life is a maze, and a great many paths will see us united. I understand your path will take you on a search for you daughter, but I have something for you to do on the way, something that will help you. I have set a task for Learon to travel to the lands of the Shadowyn. You must help him find their hidden village, as there is something for you there as well.

I was taken to the Shadowyn when I was very young by my grandfather and mentor. I didn't know until I was there that it was the home of my ancestors. When my grandfather brought me to the village, he also carried with him objects he stole from the Sagean's vault. One of those things was a special compass. When you find it, you will know what to do with it. I hope it helps you in your search.

I believe there's one last fight for us, and my aim is to be beside you in that moment, but first there's a trial ahead of me. One in the spiritual realm. I'll spare you the details, because I can hear your groaning as if you're right next to me. Beware of the reach of evil things. Trust yourself, unite the Trinity Guard, and when the final battle comes, I'll be there.

And don't despair, you will find your daughter.

Your friend and brother,
Elias Qudin

EIGHT

SIRENS - ELLARIA

THE PLAN HAD BEEN TO LEAVE IN TWO DAYS, SO THE NEWS OF HER departure that night was a surprise. However, Ellaria had already been packed and ready to go. She returned to her room and waited to be called on, and told the ship was boarding. She spent the waning hours of the afternoon light sitting at her balcony, trying to craft a letter to leave for Kovan. A letter she had yet to find the words for.

The breeze from the ocean had picked up, and she moved inside to grab her long sweater. It was draped on a chair near her entry door, with the last of her luggage and the pulsator gun Learon had sent with her when she'd left Nahadon.

As she reached for her coat, Elias's mystcat, Merphi, suddenly hissed at her. Ellaria sharply inhaled and jerked away, having missed that the cat was there.

But the cat didn't stay angry for long. It quickly spun around and started scratching insistently at the door to leave. The grey and gold and white cat seemed adamant that it wanted out of the room, and something about the fervor of her scratching made the hair on the back of Ellaria's neck stand up. It was curious behavior for a curious breed of cat, and Ellaria knew better than to dismiss it. Mystcats were notorious for their intuition, their connection and understanding of forces beyond human senses.

Ellaria placed her inking pen into her pocket, grabbed her gun by the belt, and reached for the silver door handle. The instant the doorway was cracked open, the cat dashed out and was gone in a flash. Ellaria jogged after it down the hall to find where the cat had run off to. In the corridor, she found Dalliana instead. The daughter heir sprinted toward her.

"What's wrong?" Ellaria asked.

Dalliana arrived out of breath and spoke between gulps for air. "The winddrifter you described, it's here."

"Kovan?" Ellaria said, an energy rising at her spine.

"Yes. The *Savona* was seen by our spotters in the south an hour ago," Dalliana said, pulling Ellaria by the sleeve to follow.

Ellaria's smile faltered at Dalliana's obvious concern for the situation. They briskly walked toward the main stairs. "What do you mean an hour ago? Why wasn't I informed?"

"I only learned about it from the head of my special guard. The better question is, Why wasn't I told about it? I came as soon as I heard."

Ellaria registered her understanding with a slight nod of her head, and they scrambled down the stairs. In the grand hall a group of palace guards rushed toward them, their arms out and waving for her and Dalliana to stop.

Ellaria scowled and huffed her displeasure. "What's this now?"

"You shouldn't run through the palace halls, Lady Danehin," the guard said, with another three of his men filing in beside him.

Ellaria thought his tone sounded too close to a scolding, and it was completely out of line, but she was more annoyed about their progress being held up. Whatever squad this was, Ellaria did not recognize any of them. She leaned into Dalliana in a passive shuffling of her feet.

"Where are your guards?" Ellaria asked softly.

"I don't know," she whispered back and then addressed the man. "Thank you for your concern, Special Guard. But we are in a hurry. So, we'll be on our way."

"Just wait a minute, Lady Danehin," the guard said, but his voice was insincere, and Ellaria felt like the large hall was suddenly closing in.

"Special Guard Durro." The loud voice of Dalliana's head guard boomed in the high-ceilinged space. The princess's guards were filing in with speed and efficiency. Jynor, the head guard, was furious, and he bit his words through gritted teeth. "Why are you in the palace at all? You're stationed at the Governors Hall. Return to your post, and If I see you speak to Her Highness again for any reason, I'll have you thrown out of the ranks. Am I understood?"

The guard Durro grimaced, but complied. "Yes, sir," he replied and stepped away with his men in tow.

"Dalliana, I don't know what's going on, but I have to get out to the sky port," Ellaria said.

"I know. Go. I'll catch up."

Ellaria didn't wait to hear the head guard's explanation and raced out to the sky port station to meet the winddrifter. Her grey-streaked hair bouncing on her shoulders, Dalliana and her guards followed a few paces behind, walking at a brisk pace. At the gatehouse the attendant held Ellaria up until they noticed a palace guard signal them to let her pass.

The sky port in Ioka was a giant three-tiered structure, where the ships landed on the top platform and passengers filed in through the bottom two levels. Each level was packed, as ships had recently been given the go-ahead to start sailing the short jump to the east where the Dragon's hadn't been seen.

Ellaria found a group on the stairs heading toward their departure, and she squeezed into their ranks and bounded up to the third level. She emerged at the top in a sea of giant ships towering above her. Lost among the confusion, Ellaria spun in all directions, scanning for one of her friends or the faded maroon sails of the *Savona*.

In her frantic search, she heard her name.

"Ellaria," Kovan called out.

She jerked around to see Kovan, and her breath caught at the sight of him. She hadn't seen him since the night in the Sagean tomb. Unbelievably, he was running toward her. Always so smooth and calm, it was almost out of character. When he reached her, he threw his arms around her and lifted her off her feet. The moment her feet touched back down to the floor, she started to say something, but her voice was silenced by a kiss. With his hands grasping gently at the sides of her face, she felt herself falling into him.

"Sorry," he said when he pulled away. "I've been thinking about that a long time."

Ellaria blinked and studied Kovan's face. She was speechless, which never happened to her. It was the kiss, but it was so much more. The man before her had a fire in his eyes, a liveliness like she hadn't seen in twenty years. A spark she remembered.

"Well?" Kovan asked in her moment of shock.

She swallowed and spoke. "Don't apologize."

Kovan smiled.

"Is everything all right? What's happened to you?"

"You wouldn't believe me if I told you," Kovan replied.

"I'm so glad you're here, I was preparing to leave."

Kovan pointed at the pulsator strapped to her hip. "I like how you're traveling nowadays. Where are you going?"

"There's a summit happening in Karnika, between the Harrinari tribes and the Zenoch. Someone must go for the New World."

"I'm glad it's you," he said. It was a surprising response; Kovan's typical instinct would have been to talk her out of it. His grin faltered. "I can't go with you."

"What, why not? Oh, torque it, Kovan, I knew you wouldn't be able to stick around here long, but by the Blue you literally just landed," she admonished him and punched his shoulder.

"It's not like that. Here," he said, handing her a letter with her name on it.

"What…" She started to ask what it was until she recognized Elias's handwriting. She looked at it and back to Kovan.

"I got one too. So did Learon. I need to find Tali, and Learon is supposed to go find the Shadowyn. Elias has asked me to take him."

She was aware of Learon's promise to Elias to be instructed by the Shadowyn, and she hadn't missed that Kovan had said he was going off to find Tali. *Does he think Learon's bond could help him find the young woman?* By this point, the others in Kovan's party had caught up to them, and Ellaria figured Dalliana and her escort would be there shortly. She smiled at the rest of them, her eyes stopping to register the two young women with them. Stasia's blonde hair stood out, but not as much as the other young woman's red hair. Ellaria almost choked when she realized the other woman was the Tregorean princess Echoryn. She would scold Learon and Kovan later for bringing her along, but for the moment, she gave Learon a quick hug and Wade a similar greeting, then waved for them to follow her. On the stairs back out to the main pavilion, she resumed her conversation with Kovan.

"Why? Why does Elias want you to take him?" she questioned Kovan.

"In the letter, Elias said there's something there for me. I don't know what it could be, but it must be important. Also, there's something else, I…" Kovan hesitated.

"What is it?" she asked. He seemed on the verge of telling her something but had held back.

"I just have to see it through. Don't I?" he said.

"Elias's request? I think so. But can you meet up with us after?"

"I will. I'm not sure how long it will take me, though."

"That's all right. We have to retrieve Danehin first in Adara, but we'll need to fix the watches."

"That thing I retrieved in Amera. Your last message said to keep it safe. Do you want it?" Kovan asked, referencing the Tempest Stone.

"No. I'm traveling with a large group, and I don't trust most of them."

"I'll hang on to it then until we need it. So, what happened to your watch?"

"I don't know," she admitted. "How do you know it's mine that's broken?"

"Ours are working fine between us. Since you stopped answering our messages, we assumed yours must have been damaged," Kovan explained.

"Not that I know of," she admitted. *If not damaged, had it been tampered with,* she thought. She opened the dial to inspect it. Dalliana approached, so she slid it closed again.

Kovan straightened at the arriving company but muttered to Ellaria, "Could it have been tampered with?"

"My thoughts exactly. I don't know," she said and grinned at Dalliana.

"General Moonstone," Dalliana said.

"Miss Dalliana Danehin, this is Kovan Rainer," Ellaria introduced the daughter heir.

Kovan removed his hat and clasped hands with the princess of the New World.

"It's amazing your winddrifter was able to make it here. Where is your aeronaut?" she asked, looking around.

"Bazlyn stayed on board. I'm afraid we are not staying long," Kovan said.

"I see. And how did you get past the Dragons and the Sagean's armada?" Dalliana asked.

"We sailed south and clear of the armada over the Dead Wake. We did run into a Dragon though, but it didn't attack us," Kovan explained.

"It didn't?" Ellaria asked.

"No, it was feeding off the Warol whales, right out of the ocean."

"Wow, really?" Dalliana said.

"Wait," Ellaria interrupted. "You encountered a Dragon in the sky? Was it red?"

Kovan nodded. "Yes. But it flew over us. Maybe it circled us too, but—"

"And it didn't attack?" Ellaria cut him off.

"No, why?" Kovan asked.

Ellaria's head was racing now. She turned to Dalliana. "Why is my ship leaving tonight? Were there signs of escalation on the ocean?"

"Yes, we think the Sagean is readying an attack."

"We need to raise the alarm, now," Ellaria said.

"What's going on?" Kovan asked.

"If Kovan's winddrifter can sail through, then so can the Sagean's airships. We've been under the assumption that the Dragons would destroy anything that joined it in the sky. The Sagean forces probably believed the same. I fear as soon as the Sagean's generals know they can make it through, they will try, and they would have known the instant any Sagean spy spotted the airship landing safely."

As though beckoned by thought, alarms started sounding throughout the city. Dalliana's face drained of color and her eyes grew wide. All of them looked up to the nearest bell tower, where the pipe-organ siren wailed. The massive crowd around them began to look at one another, confused. The volume of voices escalated with the heightened sense of the unknown, while dread settled into place in Ellaria's gut, where it frequently dwelled.

"Is that what I think it is?" Learon asked.

"The city alarm, the attack has started," Ellaria confirmed.

"Princess, we have to go," Dalliana's guard ordered. They had drawn their weapons and cast down their front shawls, a cape of blue and gold, signifying the guard in present danger.

Dalliana nodded and readdressed Ellaria. "Hurry to your ship while there's still time to escape off the island. We'll need all the help we can get. You must make it across the channel before the High Tide horns sound." The princess hugged Ellaria.

Ellaria held on a moment longer. "Dalliana, there are too many things happening at once. Something else is going here."

"What?" Dalliana asked.

"I don't know, but when you reach Orin, make preparations to head to the stronghold in the Valeer Mountains. In case something feels off there too, I won't be there to help you. Leave the city. Understand?"

"Understood. Bye, Ellaria, and may you stay in the Blue," Dalliana said, and she departed with her escort.

Moments later, the sunset painted clouds overhead were filled with a swarm of steel and sails. The Sagean's aircrafts appeared to come in slowly at first, but in a matter of a few heartbeats, a group of smaller front-propelled ships darted past. The fleet of massive cloud-parters trailed. Ellaria's eyes tracked the smaller ships as they passed, as the first explosion erupted.

The side of the palace was decimated with a ground-shaking thunderclap. Debris burst outward and chunks of stone fell, crashing in the courtyard. The entire facade was enveloped in a plume of fine dust that danced in the air.

Kovan grabbed ahold of Ellaria and brought her to the ground to huddle into a ball. A second explosion and a third erupted. Where those two hit, she couldn't see, but the first explosion looked like it had been aimed exactly at her room in the palace. When Kovan let her up again, she looked to the missing gap in the palace wall to verify her suspicion, and sure enough her corner balcony had taken much of the hit.

"Ellaria!" Kovan was shouting at her. Apparently, she had missed her name being called the first few times. She glanced at him, the stun of narrowly escaping the first strike clouded her mind. "Where to, where's your ship?" Kovan asked.

"It's docked at the east port," she answered and started down the road.

Together the six of them scrambled through the city streets. The docks were down a cobblestone road that wove through the eastern portion of the island.

They emerged from the paths onto a long pier full of panicked people shouting and arguing for passage. They waded into the mass of people, bumping into person after person. Ellaria could see that the number of strangers colliding shoulder to shoulder was having an effect on Echoryn.

When they slowed to check on her, two of the governors accompanying Ellaria on the trip came running her way. Both Atwood and Shaw raced forward and past them, each knocking into Echoryn in the process, Zulhorn following them. Nothing more than a passing glance of men rushing through a crowd, but Echoryn jerked and convulsed.

When she fell to her knees, Learon scrambled to her. "Are you all, right?" he asked.

Echoryn took a moment before opening her eyes, and when she did, she scanned toward the dock's end.

"Did they hurt you?" Ellaria asked.

The young woman shook her head and stood. "I'm fine."

"I don't think you should be around crowds like this," Learon commented.

"You might be right, squirrel," Echoryn answered him.

"Visions?" Ellaria asked.

"Yes. Let's hurry. We don't want to miss your ship."

Ellaria put her hand on Echoryn to help her along, but the girl jerked free and glared at Ellaria. A sparkling fleck of silver twinkled in the girl's eye.

"Sorry," Echoryn whimpered, and she turned to Learon and whispered something, then they were off again.

They found Ellaria's ship and readied to cross the gangway to board. The captain waved Ellaria on, but she put up her hand to stall.

Ellaria turned back and saw, to her surprise, Echoryn hugging Learon and boarding the ship with Wade and Stasia. Ellaria turned to face Kovan to say goodbye. She'd known their time together would be short lived, but this was too much, too fast. He stood scanning the docks with his piercing eyes. She could hear the sails of her ship climbing behind her shoulder, the chaos of people behind Kovan swirling.

"Where will you go, where will you start?" she asked him.

"I was thinking about going to Illumeen," Kovan said.

"Why not start in Elann or Bowma? How do you plan on finding the village, then?"

"Well, I figure we will need a pathfinder." Kovan winked.

"No," she replied, hoping he wasn't serious.

"Who else?"

"Not Valdimar?"

"Of course. If anyone knows a place to start, he will, or he'll know someone who does."

"Kovan, he's a drunk."

"Technically, yes. But he knows everybody. Don't worry, we'll send him back home once we have a route," Kovan said.

"Fine, tell him I said hello, and don't let him take Learon out for drinks or smoke."

"We'll be all right, I promise. I'll send Bazlyn to wait in Delanon. I'll meet you there in month. You know not to trust anyone, right?"

"Of course," she said, but she could tell he was lingering. His face wore trouble as obvious as anyone she had ever known, but you had to know him to see it. "You'll be all right?"

"Yes."

"Was there something else?" she asked, sensing like he was holding back.

He hesitated. "Not yet, but if I find what I'm looking for, I'll let you know." He took one step away but came back to her, embracing her in a tight, all-consuming hug and a final kiss. "Be safe. If you find trouble, tell Wade to message me. If I have to, I'll burn this world down to get to you."

"I know you would."

Then he dashed away with Learon, racing back up the winding paths. Ellaria watched them until she lost sight of them among the throng of frightened and aimless people.

There was an unexplainable relief to let him go as though holding him still and near was the equivalent to caging a panther or trapping the wind. But being away from him was torment, even when she knew they would be together again.

NINE

THE CHURNING WATERS - ELLARIA

THEY WERE ALMOST ACROSS THE ORIN CHANNEL WHEN THE WORLD turned upside down. The water should have been dark, but the explosions on Ioka and the surrounding cities had set a great many structures on fire. The violent orange glow coated the ocean-side, both from where they had departed and where they were headed.

Ellaria, ignoring the captain's orders, had stayed on deck to watch. Wade, Stasia, and Echoryn sat huddled in the first compartment near the captain's quarters, where the governors accompanying the voyage were waiting out the crossing.

The caterwaul of gunfire and cannons on the horizon continued with an endless cacophony of blasts. The primary battle was being waged at sea along the blockade line, but from her vantage point, it was impossible to tell how it was going.

Ellaria scanned all around, taking in the devastation when the warning call came from the ship's nest.

"They're retreating, Captain," the shipmate hollered down, and all eyes on board searched the east horizon, where the sea battle had suddenly shifted.

"Who's retreating?" the captain yelled in return. He was a lean, scrawny-looking man, with an unkempt, wiry beard that would have been more at home on a homeless man than on a lieutenant captain in the Republic of Free Cities.

"We are, sir. The Free City ships are charging back," the crewman responded.

Pulling out his spyglass, Captain Fryk turned the bronze threaded lens to his sight and studied the line. After a moment, and apparently unaffected, he slid his scope back beneath his jacket.

They had crossed the greater part of two leagues, with the onboard engine maintaining a steady pace and navigating the choppy waters with relative ease. The captain's eyebrow scrunched up, and a worried shadow came over his eyes, but he failed to call out any orders or change course in any way. Ellaria swiftly crossed the hull and headed up to the captain to see for herself what was happening.

At her appearance on the top deck, the captain let out a growl. "Miss Moonstone, if you will not stay below, you must stay out of my way," he barked and didn't make eye contact.

"What's happening?" she asked.

"Never mind and go below," Captain Fryk chided her.

Ellaria did not like him. She had met his sort before, master of his own destiny and all others could get torqued. "Give me the glass, Captain," she demanded, her hand out in front of her, waiting for his scope, her other hand on her hip.

He turned abruptly to face her, and she glared at him with an unwavering demeanor that dug away at his resolve like a chisel. With a grunt of announce, Fryk handed over his bronze scope, placing the wet metal into her palm.

She took it without blinking or thanking him and placed the scope to her eye.

On the dark, amber-laced horizon, the entire line of Free City ships was retreating back into the Orin Channel. The battered waves were dispelled across the sea, against a hundred ships charging inland as fast as they could. The sea splattered in chaos, but the ships were in unison.

"Captain, could it be some kind of maneuver?" she asked. "They're fleeing, but they're all together like it was planned."

Captain Fryk motioned to have the scope back. She handed it back, and he studied the retreat closer. With his eyes going wide, he wrenched a crew member walking nearby almost out of his shoes.

Gripping him at the collar, he ordered, "Tell Mavin to increase the speed, and tell everyone to hold on to something."

The man ran down the flight of steps in two leaps and continued to the depths of the ship.

"Full power!" Captain Fryk yelled out after the scab.

"Captain?" Ellaria asked, but he ignored her plea and scampered down the steps to give instructions to his first mate. "Captain, what's happening..." Ellaria's anger was silenced by a terrible grinding noise. All along the seawall, the largest lighthouses began to flash out an eerie green light that reflected off the waves. A horn wailed, and Ellaria went to the side rail to look toward the attack. In the wake of the retreating ships, something massive was emerging from the depths of the ocean. Past the Free City ships, the emperor's battleships that had pursued them deeper into the channel were now starting to turn away.

As the black mass rose, the waves around their ship swelled and dipped unexpectedly. The land appeared to be shaking. Whatever it was, she was now sure it was man-made and not some ancient leviathan. Then it stopped, the sound dissipated, and the waters settled, and for a fleeting moment Ellaria wondered if whatever was happening had failed.

A deafening crack broke the silence and echoed around the shoreline hills. It was followed by a roaring sound reminiscent of an airship engine, only much louder and accompanied by what sounded like a thunderous waterfall.

"Captain," the barrel-man in the nest above called out. His voice was trembling.

Everyone's eyes were fixed on the now abandoned blockade line. With the firelight reflecting off the lands and the high smoky clouds, and with the assault halted, she could see clearer than before. There were two distinct lines in the ocean, one beyond the other, which the emperor's vessels were charging as fast as they could to cross, but the sea was moving all around them.

Somehow the ocean was sinking rapidly in the space between the two lines. Ship after ship began to disappear, and without warning, the waters beneath Ellaria's ship started to hurtle their vessel and everyone on board toward the ever-growing black pit in the ocean.

The captain veered the ship away from the newly formed current. The sharp turnabout threw Ellaria off her feet, and she tumbled sideways into the starboard railing.

Behind them now, the ocean was being drained away. A few ships sat teetering on a precipice before tipping over and away into the abyss.

Captain Fryk screamed out coordinates, but it seemed no use—the ship couldn't make headway.

"Ready the anchor, but hold until my say," Captain Fryk ordered.

"The anchor?" Ellaria asked, climbing to her feet.

"Ellaria, for the love of the Great Blue, hold on to something."

With a jolt, the captain abandoned the head-on charge and angled them toward the shoreline and back again. One moment it looked like they might be swept away with the current, and the next she thought they were going to crash into the shore. Ellaria grabbed hold of the rail lines and braced for impact.

"Drop them," Fryk ordered.

A drastic halt abruptly rocked the ship, but their charge into the dead zone was stopped. They lingered in a state of stasis for a long moment, with the ocean charging around them. The roar of the ocean draining dissipated, and man-made seawalls had risen from the depths out of the tide. The waters in the channel rolled back against their ship and the rocky shoreline. With the natural order of the tide interrupted, a calm settled in for a moment, and the captain ordered everyone to abandon ship.

The drift had placed them only forty feet from shore. Some of the governors erupted from the cabin, cursing and agitated.

"What the under-death, Captain Fryk. You were warned about being on the channel," Shaw scolded.

To Captain Fryk's credit, he didn't submit to the fight and proceeded to usher the governors to a lifeboat without saying a word.

After it dropped them off on the shore, it returned for Ellaria and her crew of youngsters. Stepping down into the lifeboat, she looked up from the unsteady ladder to Fryk.

"Thank you, Captain. Don't listen to those gasbags," she said.

The captain smoothed his scraggly beard and nodded.

She stepped from the small boat to the shelf of rock and onto the shore and up to the nearest cliff, where the crowd was assembled. The gathering smoke from the island had clouded over the moon. Its rays of light now punched through in a scattering, and their part of the land was in darkness, with a forest looming behind them.

When everyone was ashore, another crack boomed, and the walls started to sink. Everyone stranded on the lower shore scrambled up to higher ground as the tide washed up. Then the rush of water and waves quickly overwhelmed the lifeboat, carrying it away and ultimately the main ship too. The captain sat on a small ledge overlooking the channel watching the last drift of his ship be stolen into the swirling pool beyond.

"Thank the Blue, we are on shore. *There be no better strength than solid ground before the vengeful light,*" Zulhorn quoted.

"Where are we even?" Atwood complained.

Admiral Vaughn stalked around in his long coat, his high collar shielding his face. He was a muscular man, but always stood stoically in the same smoldering mood as though everyone around him was his enemy. He tapped Shaw on the shoulder and whispered something Ellaria couldn't hear. Shaw straightened up and unfurled a cloak he held folded in his arm. He wrapped it around himself and pinned it at the front with his governors pin. With a scowl on his face, he followed Vaughn up the hill.

"I hate these people," Ellaria said to Wade after witnessing the exchange.

"It's a wonder you haven't hurt them, actually," Wade commented. "I'm rather impressed by your restraint."

"Don't congratulate me yet, Wade. It's a long way to Adara," Ellaria said, pulling her own coat tighter. They were stranded somewhere on the north coast of Orin, and the winter was cold and bleak with no signs of stopping.

AY
Skydarr Village
The Ice People
Kuliva Village
oral ge
TERRITHRUNE MOUNTAINS
Zenar
Erol
Roal
Darkanna
BOWSHAN MOUNTAINS
Edoth
LAND OF THE ZENOCH
Cadon
Doraga
STARLIG SEA
Ega
The eord rove
SHAVIN MOUNTAINS
Shala
Morez
SHADOW BAY
Aruna
Seda
arcoden
Delanon
RADMANA
Heru Tribe
Lor Tribe
Paodo
Dakel Tribe
Bugora
Maer Tribe
Karnika
War Lands of the Harriners
Varu Tribe
UDEN SEA

TEN

FUGITIVE - TALI

TALI SAT OUTSIDE UNDER THE BLUE SUN, TAKING IN THE FULL surroundings of the pocket of world she found herself in. An immaculate and overwhelming range of mountain peaks nearly surrounded her. Snow filled expanses of plateaus in the landscape, with a series of twenty huts like the one she had been staying in all subtly blending in. In the towering grove of pine trees positioned to the south, there was a crystal-clear stream winding inside, with frost and icicles in the slow shallows, where Tali got water every day.

Tali was ready to leave, ready to get back to the fight, but as she waited for Tyzo, she couldn't quite account for an upset feeling in her stomach. Her anxiousness had subsided when Saphree arrived for their daily chat.

The young, energetic Saphree sat with her, telling Tali all about the Zenoch lands and customs and about the great bears and the ice-panthers. The last of which Tali found most fascinating. She told her all about the five largest clans: the Ko, the Si, the Ri, the Lo, and her own, the Sa. Tali was overwhelmed by a culture and people she didn't understand.

In turn, Tali told Saphree about the magnificent cities of the mainland that she had been to. Mostly the young girl liked hearing about Ravenvyre, Tali's home, and the Amatori marketplace. It was a place Tali was surprised she could so easily speak of with fondness. *Homelands are funny that way.*

They were discussing boys when Tyzo emerged from the tree line, walking two horses into the field.

"Oh no, Ty is going to be mad I'm here," Saphree cried, seeing her uncle.

"You'll be fine, he already knows you've been coming out to see me," Tali reassured her.

"He does?"

"Yes. Trust me," Tali said. She had known for a few days that Tyzo was aware of their meetings, when he began leaving extra food for her.

Tyzo walked up to where they sat together on a fallen tree trunk with cracked grey bark.

"You should go back, Saphree," Tyzo said, stopping before them.

Tali jumped down to the ground and tried to help Saphree, but the young girl glared at her uncle, to the horses, and back to Tali.

"Are you going?" she asked Tali, her eyebrows drawing together.

"I'm afraid I am. I'm sorry. I only found out last night, and I didn't want to ruin our day."

"Why?" Saphree asked.

"I must find my friends. They need me," Tali said, reaching up for her again.

"I understand," Saphree said, taking the assistance and hopping down.

"Thank you for keeping me company. I'm sorry I have to go," Tali said, bending down to look her new friend in the eye.

"It's all right. Tyzo told me you would be leaving. I just didn't know it would be today. But I have something for you."

"You do?" Tali said.

The young girl smiled weakly, and her face reddened slightly. She reached into her coat pocket and pulled out a bracelet and gave it to Tali.

"Saphree, don't," Tyzo started to say but quieted with a stern look from the girl.

Tali smiled at the young girl's fortitude. Then turning her focus to her gift, Tali's breath caught.

It was a fine twin-braided band with gold flecks in the bindings, fixed to tarnished gold beads that held a crafted jade stone. The jade was shaped into a cloud on one end and a wave on the opposite, both clutching small circular gems, all no bigger than Tali's thumbnail.

Tali thrust it back. "I can't accept this."

"You have to," Tyzo answered.

Tali placed it on her wrist, and a pit settled inside. A sadness that she couldn't explain. "Did you make this?"

"I made the band; the pendant was my grandmother's. I thought you might need it. It will help you conquer your dreams," Saphree said.

With the overwhelming urge to give the girl something, Tali reached into her pack for the only thing she could think of. She found what she was looking for, and handed Saphree her feather earring, as it was all she had. "I lost the other one. But I bet you can make this into a necklace."

"Thank you, Tali. I will cherish it."

"Thank you, Saphree."

"Alright, Pebble, run home. We have to go," Tyzo said.

The young girl walked back through the woods on the path Tyzo had come from, arguing as she went that she wasn't a pebble anymore. Tyzo held the reins for Tali's horse and stood next to her until she was safely into the saddle, a simple act that reminded her of Learon. With a last gaze over the mystic land, they were off and heading toward the village-city of Erol.

Tyzo was not a talkative man, and Tali didn't want to annoy him, but she kept looking at her bracelet as they rode and had to know.

"Why would Saphree give me something so precious? It's obviously a family heirloom," she asked.

"It is our way," he said simply.

"But why wouldn't you let me refuse it? I can't accept it. It is too precious."

"It would have been very dangerous to refuse it. Protection stones cannot be possessed, and they cannot be turned down when offered. The stone and symbol have many properties, but it's the act of giving the stone that empowers it."

"How long had you known she was sneaking out to visit me?"

"After the very first day. She tried to walk out and back in the snow, using my tracks to hide her own, but I could tell."

"I wish I could give you something, to show my gratitude for helping me," Tali said.

"I want for nothing, except peace, and you will be giving me that once you are out of our lands," Tyzo said. It was harsh, but he said it without malice, and she respected him enough not to protest.

When they neared the grove of dead trees where Mia waited, a final question came to mind that she needed to ask Tyzo. "Do you trust Mia?" she asked as they dismounted inside the tangle of broken and frozen branches.

"I do, but she hides the truth."

"Then why does she have such standing among your people?"

"When she first came to our lands, our elders did not believe in her powers. But soon she proved her abilities. She came in the summer that year. I was a young man then, a Dawn-Root, and she told my people to prepare for a flood in the valley. She warned that if we didn't, the floods would devastate our sacred city of Cadon. I don't know what she did to convince the elders to act, but we spent a month digging new trenches for the valley and widening the river basin. At the end of the month, it began to rain, but not hard. For weeks the rain did not let up, and on the first day of autumn, the floodwaters came. In the winter of the next year, she again proved her abilities when she brought us peace with the ice-panthers. A sacred animal to my people, no human had communicated with them in generations. Her knowledge of events before they happened became invaluable to my Spirit Elders. We have relied on her for years to stay protected against the outside world," Tyzo explained.

"How long has she been here?"

"For almost sixteen years, but as the High Elders have retired to Darkanna and her powers waned, the new elders of the council of Hozahn-Natani—an ancient Zenoch word that means *wise leaders*— have become less reliant on her and more distrusting of her. Her position and standing has diminished."

"But you still trust her?"

"I'm partial to the words of the Spirit Elders over those of the Leading Council."

THEY MET MIA, AND TYZO DEPARTED ON HIS OWN WITH THE HORSES, leaving Tali and Mia to approach on foot. After an hour of walking through the hills parallel with the road, they reached the town of Erol as the sun set beyond the mountains. The village was sprawled along the mountain base, with smoke rising from chimneys all around. Entering the village was as simple as walking in among the wooden structures, as the defensive fortifications were all along the west and abutting the mountain to protect from outsiders.

When they got closer, Mia stopped them. "Here, put these on," she said, handing Tali a thick scarf to hide her mouth and nose and a pair of driftwood goggles to hide her eyes. The goggles were little more than a piece of wood shaped to her face with a single slit to see through.

"They're for snow blindness," Mia said. "The Harrinari use something almost identical to protect against the blowing dirt. Keep the hood of your coat tight over your head too and follow me. Once we're through the fortification, there are horses and supplies waiting for us on the pass. We just need to get there without being seen."

Deeper inside the village, there was a crowd gathered at the center of town. The circular field contained a stone-laden terrace and torches along the outskirts. Mia steered them around the edge before ducking into an adjacent alleyway.

"What are they gathered for?" Tali asked quietly.

"I told you; the village is very concerned about the star-burst on the hunting grounds and especially the sudden change of weather."

They kept to the alleyways to move through the village of Erol without being seen. Each building was a jumble of singularly pitched roofs, steeply sloped from front to back. In the alleys, where the roofs shed snow in heaps, they were forced to pass through by edging along the building walls.

Shouts from an angry crowd protesting at the town center sounded venomous, but also it was oddly orderly.

"Mia, why are they so afraid of the winter? Did they lose their harvest?" Tali whispered.

"It's not the weather, child. The farmers were able to save most of their crops. It's the signs."

"Signs?"

"They are big believers in signs, like the Harrinari. To the Zenoch, the Fates communicate through signs."

"What kind of signs?"

"It can be almost anything: lights in the sky, wind blowing snow off a mountain peak, the red hawk at dawn, even the synergies of stars, or the phases of the moon, all these things are important to the Zenoch."

"Then what do they make of your abilities?" Tali asked.

"My abilities abandoned me long ago. Now be quiet or they'll catch us."

In the gaps, Tali glimpsed the crowd again, and was astonished to see them sitting before a man, who, judging by his tailored uniform, was apparently some sort of official. He was accompanied by two other men that Tali had to assume were soldiers. The soldiers wore helmets or fur-lined steel, the charcoal-colored fur visibly protruding at the sides. The also held fine wood staffs to go along with bladed swords at their sides. The official's uniform lacked the helmet, but he wore a heavy fur cape and stood taking questions with his hands on his hips.

Making their way around the village, Tali started to feel that Mia had gotten them lost, until finally, two large columns to a gateway came into view. The opening led out of the village to the mountain pass, with a sentry posted at each column. When they were only twenty feet away, Mia held their position in the shadows.

"So, what now?" Tali asked, catching her breath.

"Shhh." Mia gestured for her to be quiet.

Mia kneeled to the ground and produced a stoppered glass of shimmering red sand. After shaking some dust into her hand, Mia began to draw a symbol on the tree next to them. Curious, Tali was about to ask what sort of spell Mia was casting when the shadow at their feet started to stretch as if it was liquid soaking into the ground. Soon, the shadow reached the guards and their pillars. When it did, the shadow creeped up the vertical surface and extinguished the flames inside the mounted lanterns.

Tali looked sideways at Mia, surprised by the woman's knowledge of an alchemy spell that could manipulate shadow—an uncommon skill.

"Let's go. The effect doesn't last that long," Mia urged and scampered forward, still crouching as she went.

Tali followed, and in the blackness, they snuck past two bewildered guards who were turning in all directions. The effects of the shadow apparently affected their eyesight more than Tali's or Mia's, who still could see the way, if only by moonlight.

"Mark, did you hear that?" a guard said. A leaf crunched under Tali's right boot, and the guard spun on his heels. He pointed the tip of his spear at Tali's face but looked right past her. He saw only darkness.

Tali exhaled when the guard moved on, and she swiftly moved further up the rise into the pass. Once clear, Tali and Mia raced for the underbrush of the trees lining the road. Fifteen minutes later, with the gate out of sight, Mia led them back to the road. Tali continued to glare at Mia. Something about the spell made her see Mia in a whole new light. Tali had seen spells and read of others but had never heard of anything like what Mia had done. She wanted to ask, but as evasive as Mia had been, she was starting to believe that secrets carried a lot of currency with Mia.

After another ten minutes on the road, a subtle glow ahead of them started to move in the distance. It was rushing toward them, and the sound of horses galloping on the hill accompanied the light. Dogs were barking amid the oncoming party. None of it sounded promising.

Tali looked to Mia for what to do, her pulse quickening.

The dogs charged toward the gap first, and then a squad of soldiers filed in around them from all sides, some dismounting and armed. Tali started to draw in what energy she could sense.

Suddenly the group of mounted men parted, and a tall, muscular man swiftly walked forward. He wore a large coat similar to the official she had seen in town.

"Ra-zar-si-on," the soldiers hollered in unison and pounded their staffs against their chests. The dismounted warriors stomped the ground, a clear sign of respect for the elder walking among them.

The leader, gilded in gold from head to toe, approached Tali and Mia unafraid. He held a long staff with bands of yellow and black, like a snake, and at the top a yellow gem gleamed.

Tali could feel the heat of energy at the sides of her face. She shook, afraid to lash out at these people and their leader. In a quick motion, the leader placed the tip of the staff over her head. The gem gently tapped her.

An immediate wave of nausea made Tali bend over. Her legs went as soft as soggy bread, and she stumbled to her knees. The torrent of energy evaporated, and she crumpled to the cold ground. As she blinked at the night sky, the stars above failed to penetrate the whisp of clouds, but the moon, peeking through the canopy of trees beyond, shined bright enough. It glimmered off the yellow viper-eye gem now glowing at the end of the leader's staff.

INTERLUDES I-IV

- Verro -

- Aylanna -

- Tavish -

- Ronick -

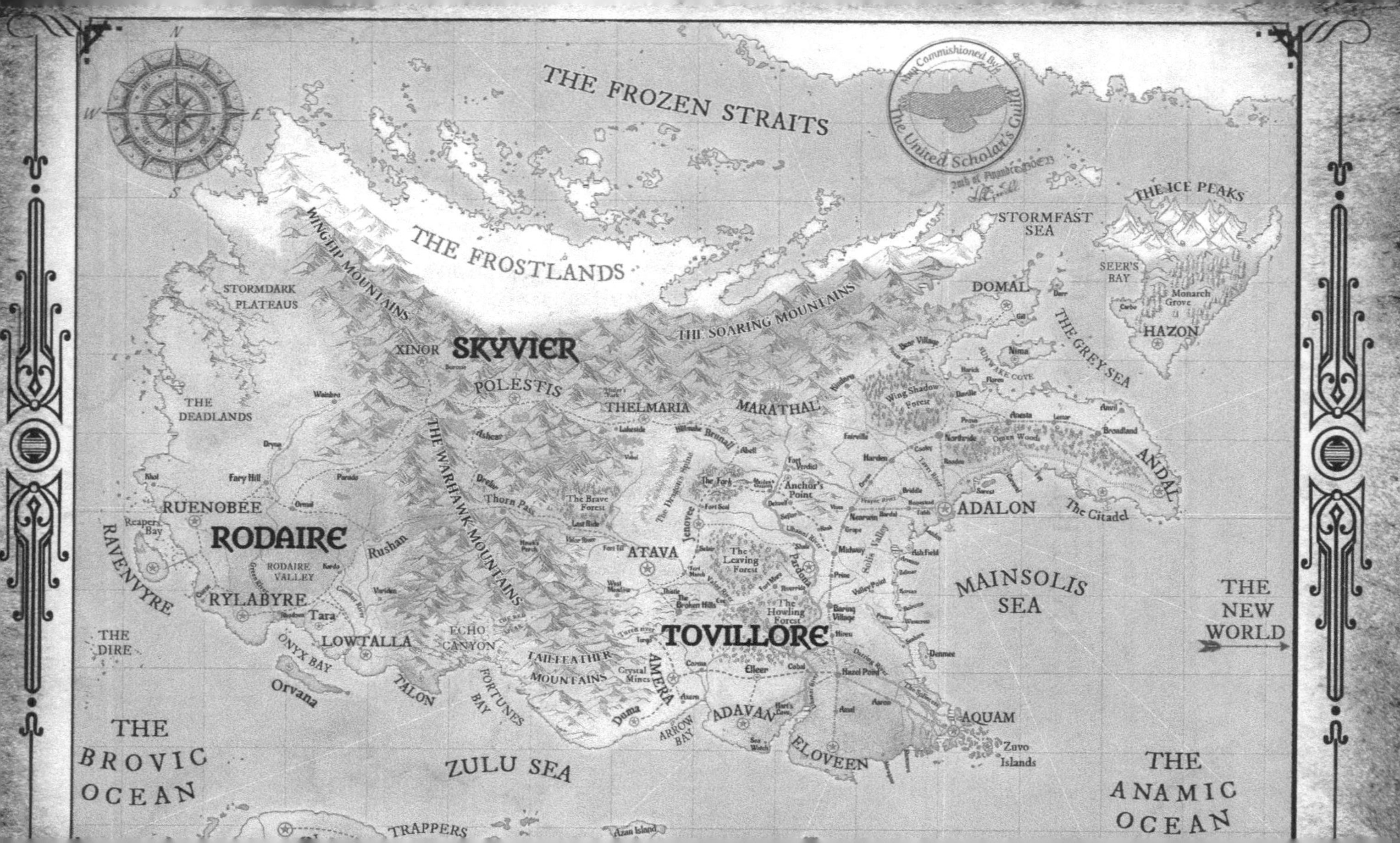

THE FROZEN STRAITS
Commissioned By: The United Scholar's Guild
THE ICE PEAKS
STORMFAST SEA
SEER'S BAY
Monarch Grove
Carbo
HAZON
DOMAL
THE GREY SEA
THE FROSTLANDS
WINGTIP MOUNTAINS
STORMDARK PLATEAUS
THE SOARING MOUNTAINS
SKYVIER
XINOR
POLESTIS
THE DEADLANDS
THELMARIA
MARATHAL
Wing Shadow Forest
SUNWAKE COVE
Nima
ANDAL
Broadland
Omen Wood
Northside
ADALON
The Citadel
THE WARHAWK MOUNTAINS
Fary Hill
Thorn Pass
The Brave Forest
Anchor's Point
RUENOBEE
Reapers Bay
RODAIRE
Rushan
ATAVA
The Leaving Forest
Pardon
MAINSOLIS SEA
RAVENVYRE
RODAIRE VALLEY
RYLABYRE
Tara
The Howling Forest
TOVILLORE
THE NEW WORLD
THE DIRE
LOWTALLA
ECHO CANYON
ONYX BAY
Orvana
TALON
FORTUNES BAY
TAILFEATHER MOUNTAINS
Crystal Mines
AMERA
Duma
ARROW BAY
ADAVAN
Elleer
Hazel Pond
AQUAM
Zuvo Islands
ELOVEEN
THE BROVIC OCEAN
ZULU SEA
THE ANAMIC OCEAN
TRAPPERS
Azan Island

INTERLUDE I
VERRO

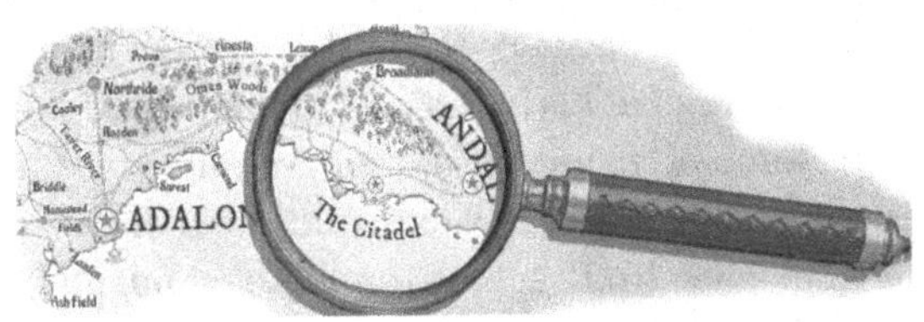

"TO MEDDLE WITH THE LUMINANCE IS BLASPHEMOUS. IT IS NOT A cloak you simply buy and don for fashion. There are repercussions for such arrogance," the Sagean Emperor told them, his voice like gears grinding on granite.

Verro didn't dare look the man in his eyes, but assumed they were as cold and dead black as always. He was scolding Verro and his fellow acolytes while he stalked along the open tables of gadgets and potions inside one of the Black Spire laboratories. The emperor's lead scientist, Victor Horn, had set out a display for review.

The emperor picked up a bronzed face shield, examined it, and continued, "The birth of these monstrous creatures that invade our skies, these Dragons, is a punishment for your transgressions," he snapped, and he spoke the word Dragon like the sound of it tasted foul in his mouth.

Sagean Mayock Kovall's spirit had returned somehow and now resided inside Edward's failing and mangled body, the consequence of his battle with Qudin Lightweaver two months prior. The scientists had saved the Sagean's life, and only they knew how truly close to death the man had been. He stood before them now, a ghostly being that was part machine and part monster.

The Sagean now wore a contraption that covered most of his face, except his mouth, which had yet to fully heal from the battle in Nahadon and remained swollen and purple. A tarnished metal was attached around his eyes and extended down the sides of his face, where two small tubes were connected at each side. The hoses looped back to a reservoir he carried on his back and maintained a continuous flow of liquid. Verro didn't know what the liquid was, but he knew the contraption was keeping the Sagean alive.

Verro Mancovi looked away and chose to fix his eyes on the tables in order to ignore the ghastlier things around the room. The biological experiments of the Sagean's scientists were terrifying. Horribly deformed beasts were floating in tanks of multicolored liquids. Most were dead, but some of them still moved even after death. Every so often, while the things slowly floated inside the thick substance, a twitch would emanate from a limb or bubbles might be expelled randomly. Every animation was revolting. Verro kept his head down, and his fellow acolytes, Delvar and Shirova, who stood beside him, did the same. All three had only recently recovered from the effects brought on by the Genesis Chamber device. Their efforts to transform themselves into Luminaries had been partially successful, but it had left all of them weakened and sick.

The sound of footsteps approaching from the hall interrupted the proceedings. General Alden Vic came in with the snake, Aramus Kayana, next to him. Both men were dressed in red military uniforms with white on their capes. Aramus, as unkempt as ever, still looked like the backstabbing weasel he was, no matter the clothes or jewels he wore. Jewels, Verro recalled, that had been Aramus's father's before he was murdered.

It was no secret that Verro had hated Theomar Kayana, but Aramus was only too happy to take up his father's position after the Sagean had killed him. At least, Delvar and Shirova still held some resentment toward the Sagean for killing their loved ones at the temple. Shirova's son Nathan was always rather spineless and was no great loss to them, but Delvar's father, Batak, would have been a true asset for Verro. In the years leading up to their takeover of the United Coalition, Verro had grown to rely on Batak's counsel. Given Verro's new position of being subjugated below a madman, he wished Batak had survived the temple so he had at least one person he trusted by his side. The Sagean's spirit may have survived by attaching himself to Qudin, and his new host body even survived the battle, but the Sagean was undoubtedly driven mad by all of it.

General Vic and Aramus kneeled before the Sagean. The Lord of Light appraised his subjects a moment before allowing them to stand.

"Your Excellency," General Vic began, "our spies have returned with reports of Moonstone's whereabouts. She was not killed as we hoped in the attack on Ioka. Our bombs destroyed the balcony, but she had left the city by the time the strike hit."

"I knew she wouldn't be bested so easily. You put too much faith in your spies," the Sagean said, his voice a rasp like sandpaper.

"There's more. Our spies report that Moonstone is only an advisor, she isn't the acting commander for the New World," General Vic said.

"Lies!" the Sagean shouted. "She is in charge, or they would not have pushed us back at the Orin Channel."

"As you say, Your Excellency. Reports now suggest Moonstone is part of a small convoy headed to Karnika to meet with the Harrinari."

"I expected as much, General."

"We have also learned that the convoy means to stop in Adara to pick up King Danehin."

General Vic had barely finished saying Danehin's name when the Sagean lashed out with a column of air constricting around the general's body. Verro now had the ability to see the air and the heat the Sagean pressed into the general, whose own shrieks were muted by the collapsing air around him. When the general's skin began to burn, the Sagean released him.

"There are no kings in my empire, General," the Sagean said.

General Vic fell to his knees, panting and desperately trying to breathe. "Yes, Your Excellency, Forgive me."

A wide grin spread across the Sagean's face, most of the sides contorted by the face plate. "Now, I will crush two of my enemies. Send the assassins to Adara to wait."

General Vic stood and waited to be dismissed.

"Stay a minute, General, and you too, Aramus. The good doctor was about to tell us what they've learned about the Mirthless," the Sagean ordered and wandered over in front of a Mirthless cadaver, stretched out on a steel table. The creature had been transported back to the Black Spire for dissection. The hideous nature of the creature's appearance of bone and skin was repulsive.

"Tell me about these creatures that protect the Mistress of Merinde, Dr. Horn," the Sagean inquired.

Dr. Horn shifted the inspecting glass strapped across his face like an eye patch until the right lens was in place. The inventor had been thought to be long dead when the Court of Dragons found him hiding in Aquom. He was old and cared nothing for people, only his creations. Verro had met very few people as devoid of empathy as Dr. Horn.

"They are humanoid, but based on my analysis of the nuclei of cells, my theory is that they were made from Ravinors," Dr. Horn said.

"Explain, Doctor. They look nothing like a Ravinor, and like the Dragons, I can't control them either," the Sagean demanded.

"We don't fully understand it. The facial structure is similar, but more of an exaggeration. While there is no tail, the bone, muscle, and skin are almost one, and somehow the creature's spine provides additional strength and agility like a Ravinor. The Ravinors were a spliced creation of the Nahadon swamp lizard, a human, and the bipedal Koogas from the Blood Marsh Islands. These things originate from some animal that lived in the Blood Marsh or a similar habitat," Dr. Horn said.

"The creatures are not native to Merinde?" the Sagean asked.

"No. Possibly Manashera, or even perhaps from somewhere inside the chaos-mists of the Brovic," the scientist answered.

The giant bone structure of the Mirthless face was horrifying, and Verro cringed and looked away.

"Verro, how did this Mistress of Merinde, come by these things?" the Sagean asked.

"I honestly don't know. No one on the Court of Dragons had ever heard of this mistress before our first meeting with her. She said the Mirthless were a gift from the Wrythen. I saw no evidence of any lab or equipment at her palace that could be used to create such a being," Verro explained. The mention of the Wrythen inflamed hatred in the emperor's eyes.

"A person doesn't just suddenly announce themselves as a ruler, gain followers willing to die for them, and conquer lands. I suspect she must be a being of power. A Luminary or a Fate has revealed themselves," the Sagean said.

He gave a final cursory look at the creature and moved to the back of the room, where a scientist was working a calculation. The man stood before ten different large drawing boards full of designs and sketches of machines for destruction.

"Mathematician, have you finished your calculations?" the Sagean asked.

The scientist took his eyes off his work to address the emperor. They were bloodshot and sunken, and the man looked like he hadn't slept in weeks. "I have, Your Excellency."

"Then please proceed to the next steps. Dr. Horn, make sure Mr. Mathis here has everything he needs."

"Yes, Your Excellency."

The Sagean touched the serpent ring at his finger, and a searing pain shot through Verro's body. He fell to his knees, along with Delvar and Shirova. All three suffered the sting of the emperor's power. Aramus grinned in the background.

The Sagean turned back to Verro and the others. "What was I saying before? Oh yes, I was talking about repercussions. The curse of meddling with powers beyond your understanding. The other curse, from your meddling with the Temple of Ama, is your weakened states and feeble powers. These powers you were gifted are so unremarkable I shall never call you Luminaries. You are merely leeches. A Luminary feels the charge of all forces at work, you 'leeches' feel fragments. You see only sparks and think that they are the light of God, but God is more vast than you know or will ever know. Your blood could never hold what mine does. Still, you three will be useful once you're strong enough to fight. So, 'leech,' what did the God of Light gift you?" the Sagean asked Verro.

His smokelike eyes curdled Verro's nerves, and Verro looked away to the floor.

"Verro, does your sensitive heart fear to look at my disfigurement? Would you prefer that I use my abilities to manipulate your minds so that you see your Edward as he was, or possibly my old self?" the Sagean asked.

"No matter your appearance, we are enlightened by your presence, Brightener," Verro answered, attempting to hide his fear. "I have a feel for the air, my Lord."

"Explain."

"I can sense the air pressure and the temperatures in the air and put them to work to heat or freeze, and in doing so, I can move the air with force," Verro said.

"You saw how I reprimanded the general?"

"Yes," Verro said.

"And how can your powers help my empire?"

"With practice, I believe I could sail a ship, when the wind has gone."

"Not good enough. I shall need you to power a whole fleet."

"Yes, my Lord."

"Could you bring down an airship?"

Verro thought about the idea and nodded. "Yes."

"Then you will be on the voyage with our main assault," the Sagean said, and he almost growled the last part like an animal. He picked up a big metal gauntlet off the table, examined it, and placed it back down before he continued his inspection of devices.

"Forgive me, Brightener Kovall, I thought the primary attack was on the Orin Channel and Illan?"

"It was a neat trick by Moonstone to thwart our navy at the channel. A momentary setback to the deployment, but one of no consequence. You and your fellow leeches will be traveling where I need you. I have a plan that will crush her. One she will not suspect."

"Yes, Brightener."

"And you, Shirova? What small, insignificant power did you receive?"

"I was gifted an ability with fire."

"Really. The manipulation of the flames or simply the heat?"

"The flames. Oddly I don't feel the heat at all. But the flames, they feel like living paint, and my hands are a brush."

"And your overall strength?"

"I don't know, but given a spark, I can turn it into a raging fire."

"Then you will go as well," the Sagean said, but her gift had made him happy. With his dead-man's eyes, when the Sagean smiled, it lifted his features and the contraption on his face unnaturally, as though the demon inside was happy against the will of the shell outside.

"And you, young Delvar Asheen?"

"I have a tie to the territh."

"You feel the energy beneath the ground?"

"Yes, the energy of the geology itself."

"What can you do to help the empire, my son?" the Sagean asked.

"I can bring destruction and death, Brightener."

* * *

Later, back in his room, Verro inspected the serpent ring at his finger. The tool they once used to subjugate Edward, and now the tool of their enslavement, was turning his finger black.

The room inside the Black Spire at the citadel was small and mostly barren of any extravagance, but there was a small window where he could look out on the citadel's training grounds and Navy Harbor.

The harbor was full beyond the citadel's tide-breakers, and the docks inside were alight in the night, with endless sparks and loud hammering as new ships continued to be constructed. The factories too were pumping out endless steam, and Verro could feel the massive amount of heat inside the buildings where the scientists were manufacturing more and more automatons. On a far field beyond the citadel, the lights of the gas lamps illuminated the land where the Sagean's secret project was being built.

Noises from the laboratories inside the Black Spire echoed through the halls. Everywhere Verro looked, the entire complex was hard at work creating the weapons and means for their Sagean lord to take control of the world. The Sagean had a singular focus on the total annihilation of the New World, but vengeance was the fire inside energizing the old spirit. The particular objects of his retribution were King Danehin and Ellaria Moonstone. Losing to Moonstone in the Great War, forty years ago, had fueled a hatred of her.

Verro rubbed the ache in his hand. The snake ring at his finger was always painful, even when the Sagean wasn't channeling energy into it, a pain that settled in his palm. Verro decided he needed fresh air and made his way through the winding corridors and the numerous stairways of the Spire. Choosing to avoid the floor lifts, he eventually emerged into the small gardens on the third level, outside the soldiers' quarters.

Verro found a spot overlooking the Mainsolis Sea and sat contemplating how he could be free of his imprisonment. But with each thought, a slight wave of nausea came over him, an effect of the Sagean's will—a power Sagean Kovall had over them that extinguished any negative thoughts against the emperor and slowly made anyone close to him willing to die for him.

Verro put his head in his hands and winced until the pain subsided. When it did and he finally looked up, a woman in a black cloak stood before him. She had approached so silently Verro had never heard her.

She stood in a way that the lamps of the garden couldn't penetrate the hood covering her face and the shadows upon it. She held out a small scroll. Verro took it and the courier left. Verro watched her go. She followed the paths until she didn't, and then the woman drifted into the darkness of the grounds and disappeared from his view.

He turned the scroll over in his hand, and the purple wax seal had a knot of string in the design of the Whisper Chain. He broke the seal and read; it was from Aylanna.

Verro,

I hope you are well and recovered from the sintering process. I have only just recovered my own strength and can pair it with my new abilities. Such a mysterious thing we embarked on to remake our blood. I feel the same, and yet I am a very different person. I hope you have not changed from the man I love.

I am ashamed of my cowardice in the temple. My escape was a last-minute safeguard I never meant to need or use. But use it I did. I am sorry for leaving you. My hope is to take over my home country and rescue you. To that end I am working diligently to reunite us.

As you can see, I have activated the Whisper Chain service again, and they are under my control. There are many battles to come, my love, both across the ocean and in our own lands. Prepare yourself for war. The Sagean may control Tovillore, but I now control all of Rodaire. With my advisors, I am making preparations to survive, and we will be the rulers of the Old World.

I should tell you; Batak is alive and serving as my aid. Our intention is to liberate both you and Delvar. The Sagean is powerful, but we were also visited by the Wrythen, and I have no doubt that the Old One will destroy the Sagean when the time comes.

I will send word again when time and matters dictate. Please stay strong and mindful.

Sincerely,

Aylanna Alvir

Verro examined the letter over again. At the bottom was a discolored line, and a small script said *tear here*. Verro tore the letter, and it sparked and turned to ash in his hands. He dusted his hands off and took a deep breath. His anger at being betrayed by Aylanna's escape had faded not long after he had returned inside the Black Spire. An ignited resentment had settled into grief for the woman he loved. Their affair had been a secret among the Court of Dragons—a secret alliance they kept a very close guard on to take control of the court. Hopes of such a future had vanished when Aylanna had escaped the temple and abandoned him. Her letter held hope for that future again. His feelings had somehow washed the nausea temporarily away. It was either his hope for salvation or his love for Aylanna, but something had temporarily alleviated the Sagean's grip on him, and the air was much easier to breathe.

RAVENVYRE
THE BROVIC OCEAN
PALACE OF REDVINE
JADE DISTRICT
REAPER'S BAY
BROKEN HILLS
BARGINER'S MARKET
THUNDERBREAK CLIFFS
CLOCKHEART DISTRICT
SUN BRIDGE
AMATORI MARKET

INTERLUDE II

AYLANNA

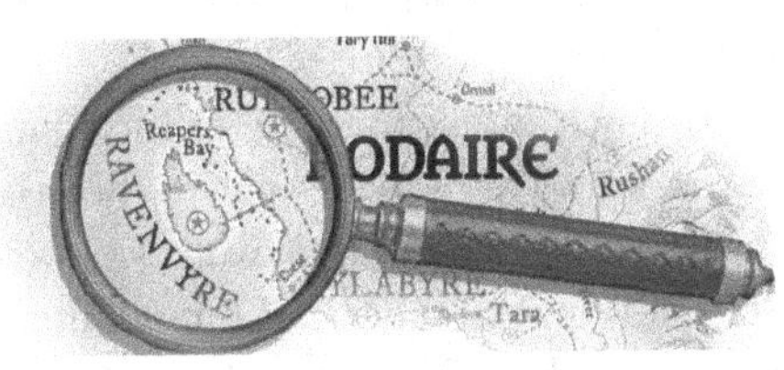

Aylanna Alvir stalked the underground passageways beneath the Palace of Redvine in Ravenvyre. Her best alchemist, from the jade district, had worked tirelessly to gain access to an old vault hidden in the depths of the castle. The ancient foundation of the palace was thought to have been built during the Luminary Wars, long before the Sagean Empire, making the structure over two thousand years old. The palace had been destroyed at least three times, but not since the ninth Emperor Saraxon made a treaty with the king of Rodaire, some five hundred years ago.

Aylanna grew up an heir to the Rodairean throne through an indirect linage. Alvir had been a prominent family for hundreds of years, living under the empire's rule in the Higher Order. She had learned long ago about the secret passages that supposedly stretched under the entire island—ways to escape to any port if needed, and containing small caches of supplies, crystals, and weapons.

All of it had to be mapped and subsequently searched for the Desolation blade. The Wrythen believed it resided in Rodaire, and Aylanna was determined to find it. Her greatest hope was to locate the blade and duplicate it before handing it over to the Old One. So far, they had covered over half of the tunnels and nearly all the small storage rooms they could access and found nothing. Her last hope rested on the one Luminary vault they'd discovered below the east markets.

Aylanna grew up hearing stories about the underground tunnels and the hidden vaults that required Luminary blood to enter. When they discovered this vault, they quickly found the truth of the old tales. On her first attempt, Aylanna's newly acquired powers had failed to pass through the entry. She was heading back there now because her alchemists had found a way around the safeguards, and she wanted to be the first to enter and examine the contents locked away inside.

She turned down the corner where the tunnel narrowed outside the vault entrance. There were places below where the tunnels became so small that she had to walk sideways or crouch to get through. Her team of searchers had hung lanterns every twenty feet, and lamplighters worked tirelessly to keep them lit all day and night. The air below the surface of Ravenvyre was stagnant and salty, but there was a ventilation system, more complex than she understood, that maintained the oxygen levels within the confined spaces.

Every lamp she passed, Aylanna could sense the light, like a vibration of energy. The light itself felt different to her now, a result of the bargain with the Sintering Fountain at the Temple of Ama.

What had come of the others, she had yet to learn, but given her own weakness in recovering and her limited Luminary abilities, she wondered if everyone had received similar powers.

She recalled the symbols inside the Genesis Chamber that night, but not clearly. Enough of a memory to wonder if each member probably received something unique. The thought of the pain during the procedure and the ancient masks clamped onto her head made vomit lurch to her throat. She placed her hand on the side wall and heaved the contents of her last meal.

"Mother, are you all right?" Her daughter Shaelea come running from the vault entrance to her side.

Initially angry with Aylanna, Shaelea had eventually forgiven her. Shaelea had tried to warn her that Edward had been searching for a way to remove the serpent ring that allowed the acolytes of the Court of Dragons to have control over him. What Shaelea hadn't known, what nobody had known, was that the scepter of Corinsura that powered the Sintering Fountain could also destroy Edwards Ring. The very object the court had manipulated Qudin into delivering to them so they could become Luminaries, was also the means for their own demise.

Later, when Shaelea had learned that after overtaking Edward's spirit, the Sagean had executed Theomar, Nathan, and others and reversed the pull of the serpent rings, Aylanna's actions seemed understandable, and she forgave Aylanna.

"I'm fine," Aylanna said, though in truth, she was unsure.

"Come. We have access now. The alchemists made a cloth that can cover the Caliber Stones, and it allows us to pass inside."

"Have you gone in already?"

"Only a few test subjects. I had two men go inside and sit for an hour and again for three hours to see if there were any effects."

"And?"

"They're fine. The man who stayed three hours reported a headache. That's all."

She passed the globes stationed on the wall covered with a shimmering cloth. The light beneath glowed against the rock. The entrance to the vault was pyramid shaped, but with a flat apex and a smooth header stone.

Aylanna took two lanterns off the poles, handed one to her daughter, and they entered together. The inside area of the vault was a voluminous space with a barrel ceiling of red brick. Similar glowing orbs inside the room had only a dim light. Aylanna supposed they were bypassing the security; otherwise, the orbs would have provided more luminosity. The room was lined with shelves, some still containing large and aged scrolls, some cubbies were picked clean, and a fine layer of dust was over most everything.

Aylanna's eyes caught the footsteps of the soldiers who came inside to test how secure their bypass was. The steps fairly mirrored each other's, and both men had sat only twenty feet inside, almost at the center of the room. As her eyes scanned around, she realized they had a problem.

"Shaelea, you're sure no one else came in before us?" Aylanna asked.

"Just the two soldiers I sent in. Why?"

"Because there are footsteps in the dust besides our own or the soldiers'."

Shaelea turned and spotted the steps immediately. Aylanna bent down to the tracks to look at them and compared them to her own.

"There's a trace amount of dust in these tracks. Whereas ours are freshly made, and they stamp the dust clear. These are older. How old I can't say, but by the looks of them, they are very old."

"There's more. Mother, come over here," Shaelea said.

Shaelea was standing in front of a painting and empty stone stand. In the shape of the outer walls, there were three small alcoves with marble altars and old paintings, faded and caked with dust but the images still discernable. Aylanna stopped at the two flanking Shaelea. The first was of a green Dragon flying over a rocky shore. Another depicted a Dragon of purple or black perched on the precipice of a cracked fissure. Below each was a name chiseled into stone: Folianori for the green, and Arukar for the purple. On the altars were single scales from the Dragons, placed in cracked eggs that looked like black molten rock. The eggs were long ago fossilized, but somehow the scales, while old, appeared intact and strong.

"Mother, look at this one."

Aylanna approached the third painting and found it was not a Dragon but a woman in scaled armor. She held a sword of green crystal before the moon, her black hair flowing behind her. Avari Nova, the queen warrior of Rodaire. She stood alone and the moon cast her shadow into a triangle that spiraled out of her feet on the ground. The image was familiar to Aylanna, but she couldn't recall where she had seen it before.

"Mother, look."

Aylanna tore her eyes away from the painting to the empty stand below. But it wasn't entirely empty; on it was a stand with glass legs with semicircle tops, like something that might be used to hold a sword.

"Avari Nova, what an amazing woman," a voice said behind them.

Aylanna turned around, startled by the intruder, and found her old confidant, Maki, standing there with his arms tucked inside his black cloak.

"It's not here, Maki," Aylanna said.

"I see."

"Do you know when it might have been taken from this vault?"

"The last ruler of Rodaire to use the palace died a hundred years ago. I would assume a Sagean lord must have taken the sword. But these crystalized fabrics to allow entry are easily made by clever thieves, so I suppose…"

"That it could have been anyone. That's what you are going to say?" Aylanna asked.

"Not anyone. There are treasure seekers and then there are thieves. Each has their talents."

"They would have to know it was down here."

"Have you considered the alternative?" Maki asked.

"Which is?"

"Maybe it was never down here."

"I think Maki is right. The vault was not so hard to find or impossible to enter. Could you use the Whisper Chain and ask around? Check in with the more widely known artifact collectors? Most died in their pursuits of treasure and glory. There can't be many still alive," Shaelea suggested.

"See if anyone has been acting funny?" Aylanna said.

"That, but also the word is out about the Desolation blade. A great many people are looking for it. From here to the New World, there are blade hunters. Could someone have found a trail we haven't thought of?"

"I will look into it for you," Maki offered.

"Thank you, Maki," Aylanna said. She feared what she would say to the Wrythen the next time it appeared.

"Are you all right Mother? You look pale." Shaelea asked.

Aylanna noticed she was gripping the fabric of her dress unconsciously, and let it go. She straightened the crease and looked around the room. She could only hope now that one of her agents would find the blade. Se looked back at her daughter and replied, "Catalog everything and then have it carefully brought up to the palace."

"Yes, Mother. I understand."

"Everything."

INTERLUDE III

TAVISH

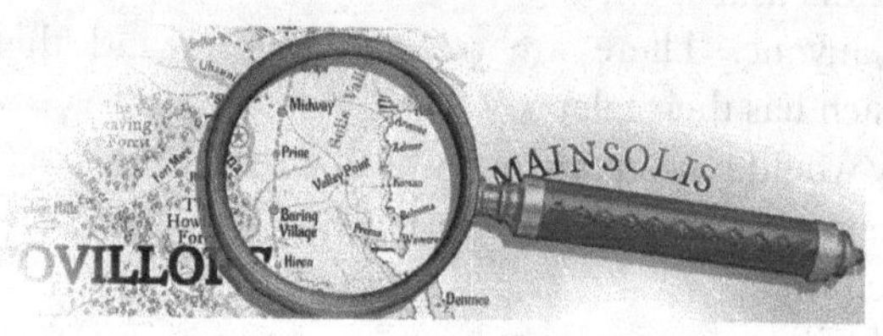

"Miguel, you here? I have something, and you won't want to let me leave without offering me a hefty sum," Tavish called out, entering the Waypoint Trading Post.

It was his last stop in Valley Pointe before he made his way to the coast. Most of the cities on the Imperial Road were under lockdown, and Bonemen were patrolling the streets. The return of the Sagean in Tovillore had halted travel and trade, but Tavish needed amber. Miguel's shop was a good vestige of trinkets and distinct commodities, and Miguel was an unusually honest trader.

"Miguel?" Tavish called out again.

"I'm here," Miguel said, emerging from the back room. He wiped his hands on a towel and smiled at his old friend.

"There you are. I have some pieces I think you'll be interested in."

"We'll see, Tavish. I hope you're not here to sell me stolen goods."

"No way." Tavish grinned and plopped his bag on the counter. He proceeded to go through a slew of small items, gauging Miguel's interest. Everything he showed him received a passing glance, but no more.

"Business is very slow, Tavish. I don't think I can make an offer on any of these," Miguel said.

"What about this piece?" Tavish said, sliding a brass spyglass across the counter. "You can't say this isn't worth something, Miguel."

Miguel lowered the double lens attached to the strap on his head and flipped a thin cloth in his hand as though expelling the dust from it before gently picking up the telescope for inspection. Tavish rolled his eyes. This was the same dance they always did. Miguel exaggerated his inspections of every item he was offered with his examining cloth and magnifying lens. The mere fact that he had picked up his tools told Tavish all he needed to know about his interest.

"Get on with it," Tavish said.

"The lens is out of alignment," Miguel commented.

"No, it's not."

"And there's a significant amount of dirt on the inside of the lens tube. Also, I wish it had a mount."

"A mount." Tavish choked out a laugh. "This is a nautical telescope, my friend. Hence the protective sling and strap that comes with it."

"It's missing the cap."

"It is missing the cap," Tavish admitted. "I'm sure you can find a cap around here that fits," he said, waving around at the mess surrounding them.

"I'll give you sixty marks."

"Sixty." Tavish gnashed his teeth. Miguel had always driven a hard bargain, but his shop had seen better days. After the valley had been plagued with the Scree, and now the takeover of the Bonemen, the shop was struggling to stay open. Tavish needed this sale if he was to make it back to Aquom before the Sagean's soldiers took over. "It's worth two hundred, Miguel, and you know it."

"I can put it on consignment for you for twenty, up front, with my usual take if it sells."

"Sixty and consignment."

"No way. I don't have the foot traffic, Tavish. And no one is spending what little they have. There's a war going on, in case you hadn't noticed."

"I'm aware. Forty-five."

"Thirty-five, but that's it. Thirty-five with a chance for more, or sixty and it's mine," Miguel offered.

"All right, you thief. Draw up the papers. I swear you're as stubborn as my brother Kovan," Tavish said. Thirty-five would have to be enough to get him home, and he knew there wouldn't be another opportunity to sell, unless he found some sucker near the coast.

Miguel smiled and reached below the counter. "Let me fill out this consignment agreement and—"

Abruptly, he went quiet, and Miguel's eyes glazed over in a swirl of red. It happened so fast that Tavish wasn't sure it had happened at all. Miguel stopped midspeech. His head cocked around almost mechanically like something had just occurred to him. Without a word to Tavish, Miguel walked to the back room.

"Miguel? Miguel, you all right?" Tavish asked.

When he reemerged, he held a long knife, and he came at Tavish in rush. Tavish jumped backward into the set of shelves behind him, making the contents crash to the floor.

Miguel barely registered the noise or mess. He scowled at Tavish like he was a stranger. He slashed the knife through the air, narrowly missing Tavish's arm. He growled like a wild animal and lunged, but Tavish kicked him back.

Suddenly a man with grey hair appeared, grabbing Tavish and pulling him away as another man sprinted in with two swords flashing. The second man wasted no time and attacked Miguel, brandishing his swords with a flourish of movements.

"Wait," Tavish called out, but it was no use. The newcomer had swiftly killed Miguel and stood panting over the body.

"Are there any more of them?" the man with grey hair asked.

But the older man's voice was drowned out, as Tavish's eyes were fixed on his dead friend across the floor from him,

"Hey, fella, are there more?" he asked again.

This time Tavish found his voice. "Any more?"

"Any more Redeyes?"

The word Redeyes made Tavish cringe. What he had seen of his friend had disappeared in an instant. Still mostly speechless, Tavish shook his head, but he had to know: "What are they?"

"Not all the Scree returned to normal," the man said.

"Gerald, there's a locked door in here. Come help me," the swordman called out.

"Coming," the man named Gerald said. He pulled Tavish's sleeve to go with him.

A loud bang shook the wall, and when they got to the back room, the man was rubbing his shoulder. He looked at Tavish in the face, locking eyes with him. "What's your name?"

"Tavish," Tavish muttered.

"Tavish. I'm Ronick, and this is Gerald. The store owner was your friend I take it?" Ronick asked and waited for Tavish to nod before continuing. "I'm sorry you had to see him cut down, but he was dead already, I promise you. Do you have any idea what's through this door?"

"It's the cellar. Um, a storage room," Tavish said.

"Gerald, go check the owner's pocket for a key," Ronick said.

"I can pick it," Tavish said. He grabbed some small tools off the nearby counter and kneeled to pick the lock.

"You know how to do that?" Ronick asked, but almost as soon as he had asked, the lock clicked home and Tavish turned the knob.

"I can pick most locks," Tavish said.

Ronick looked at him, on the verge of saying something, but as the door creaked open, the smell of death made both men recoil. When the sound of a muffled moan escaped from the cellar below, they rushed down the old wood steps to the small basement. The gruesome scene stopped Tavish in his tracks. Ronick jumped off the side, where the old rail was busted off. He landed on the dirt and went straight for a woman who was lying on her side with her arms and feet tied.

"Vera!" Ronick cried frantically.

The woman was moaning on the cold floor next to a set of tables covered with boxes full of clothing, weapons, and jewels. A dead body was crumpled in the corner. The ground was covered in blood, and empty chains hung from the wall. The woman was alive but appeared in bad shape. She threw her arms around Ronick as soon as he had cut her free, and tears streamed down her face. Ronick removed the cloth gag that wrapped tightly around her head.

"I didn't think you would find me," she wept.

"We almost didn't. This guy showed up at the store and bought you more time."

Outside the trading post, Tavish was still shaken by the moment. It had been a long time since the Great War, and he never did have the stomach for death. The sight of blood was enough to return old nightmares to him for a month.

"Where are you heading? Ronick asked.

"To the coast. I'm trying to get to Aquom," Tavish explained.

"Forget the coast. Those cities are crawling with Bonemen, and the Sagean already has a stranglehold on Aquom. You should ride with us," Ronick said.

If what the man said was true, then there was nowhere else to go. "Where to?" Tavish said.

"Me and a lot of other free folk have control over Fort Mare. We almost had Pardona, but those damned automatons pushed us out."

"It's a generous offer, but..." Tavish started to make an excuse to go his own way, but Ronick interrupted him.

"It's the only offer that will keep you alive, and it's not a free ride. We could use your skill with locks."

"Which kind of lock are we talking about?"

Ronick grinned and said, "I'll tell you on the way."

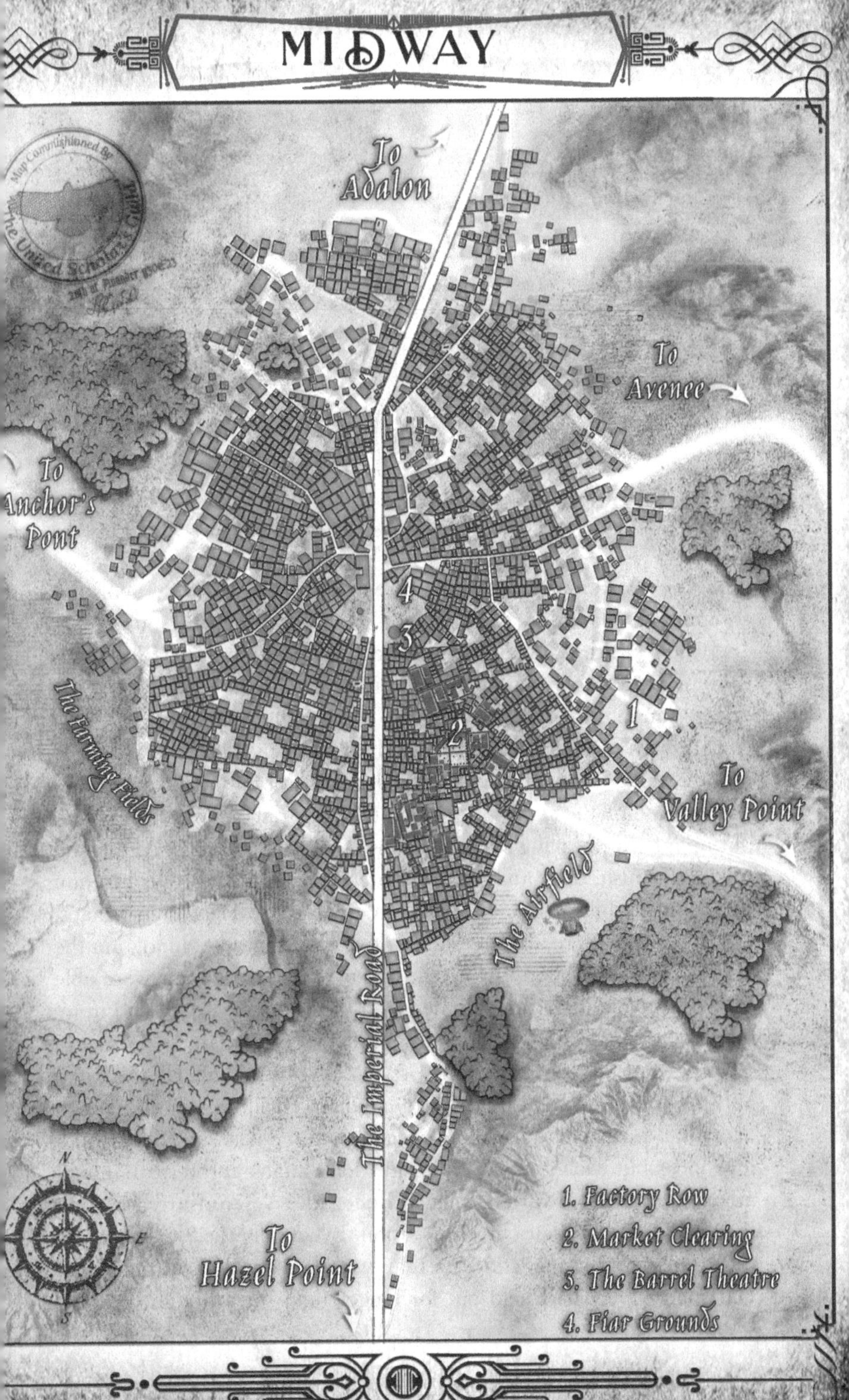

MIDWAY
Map Commissioned By
The United Scholars Guild
To Adalon
To Avenee
To Anchor's Point
The Farming Fields
To Valley Point
The Airfield
The Imperial Road
To Hazel Point
N
E
S
1. Factory Row
2. Market Clearing
3. The Barrel Theatre
4. Fiar Grounds

INTERLUDE IV
RENEGADES

RONICK WALKED AMONG THE HANDPICKED PLATOON, REVIEWING equipment, weapons, and orders with each of the three squad leaders, when Darringer galloped toward their position. The Renegades were preparing to execute a mission into the city of Midway, and the orange sun in the sky meant Darringer was right on time.

Midway was now controlled by the Bonemen. Over the last three months, the Sagean soldiers had established a dominate presence, but unlike some of the small cities along the Imperial Road, Midway had put up a fight—leaving some portions of the city in ruins. At the end of the skirmish, the remaining dissenters were put into concentration camps in the hills to the west of the city. In the wreckage and chaos, the Renegades were able to establish two teams of spies hidden in the city. Having been there before the takeover, the two teams were able to cause havoc, interrupt shipments on the Imperial Road, and more importantly, gather information about the Sagean's army.

The Sagean was desperately trying to control the Uhani River and the Imperial Road in order to conquer Tovillore. The Bonemen army had pushed to take the Renegades' home base of Fort Mare a few times, but each strike was a simple feint attack and retreat. Those attacks had been thwarted, but the Renegades were unsure how long they could stay in their current position. Eventually the Sagean would move west. It was a concern that weighed on both Ronick and Darringer. They had held out for longer than they thought possible already, and Ronick wanted to strike back—liberating Midway was a significant strike.

Darringer dismounted, tossed the reins for his horse to a soldier, and approached Ronick. "You sure about this, Ronick?" he asked.

"Yes, sir," Ronick answered, checking his blades. It was a nervous tic of his.

"Then why are you nervous?" Darringer asked, eyeing him. Darringer was observant and always an excellent judge of character.

"I would feel better if we had Vera with us, but she's still recovering. The plan is solid, sir," Ronick said.

"Go over it one more time with me."

"Yes, sir. The first team causes a distraction in the east quadrant of the city, near the factories where we already have escape routes in place. We'll be using our remaining explosives, but I think it's worth it. Team two frees the prisoners and protects their escape. The third squad ushers the freed people through the southern hills and toward the river. Everyone circles back to a secondary position on the river, where we have already scouted a secure launch point. We cross back over to our position here, and we're back in Fort Mare by morning."

"I see are a lot of ways this plan fails."

"But it's worth the risk," Ronick said.

"Yes, it's worth the risk. Seems to me the first team is in a precarious position. Those factories are heavily guarded."

"My plan is they will be using passages that the Bonemen haven't caught on to yet, on the upper high-rise connections and steel catwalks. We have been infiltrating this city without being caught since it was taken three months ago. If they hit the right buildings, I'm confident they can get out."

"Which team are you leading?" Darringer asked.

"I'm leading team two. Freeing the people is the mission. I can't let that fail."

"Sounds about right."

"Gerald is with team three, and Harlen is with the first squad."

"What about the locks?"

"That's where this new guy, Tavish, comes in," Ronick said, indicating the short and stocky fellow sipping something leisurely from a tin mug nearby.

"Is he up for it?"

"He has to be."

THE BONEMEN WERE HOLDING WHAT THE SAGEAN CALLED THE NEW World sympathizers in a large cage near the farming fields. The lights from the Midway airfield shined brightly in the distance, but the glow was not enough to cast any significant light to the area. Ronick moved his team into position in the trees south of the Governors Mansion. The concentration camp was built at the back of the mansion, which was now the south headquarters for the Bonemen in Midway. The cage holding the sympathizers was barely lit by torches near the perimeter and guarded by only three soldiers walking the grounds. Most of the Bonemen were either inside the mansion or housed in the apartment complex a block away.

On the eastern edge of the city, the horizon came alive as the first team initiated the distraction. Explosions could be heard booming and echoing off the condensed building facades and narrow alleyways.

Ronick waited for the triple blast that would signal their time to move. The blast came and went, and the Renegade soldier next to Ronick shot up to charge in, but Ronick quickly pulled him back down. There were still no movements at the camp.

"Something's wrong," Ronick said.

Another explosion shook the ground, and a giant ball of fire bloomed up into the night sky near the factories. An unplanned escalation, but it seemed to do the trick. Sagean soldiers filed out of the Governors Mansion and into the streets.

"Move," Ronick told his team.

Six of them ran to the gate, and three with bows remained back in the cover of the bushes. Ronick reached the metal cage, with an arrow zipping past his face. It took out a soldier at the gate, and the two remaining guards were struck by arrows before they could react.

They reached the gate, and Ronick grabbed the new guy and shoved him toward the lock. "Tavish, you're up."

"This isn't exactly as you described," Tavish complained, rummaging through his bag of tools.

"Can you do it?" Ronick asked.

"Yes."

"Then do it."

Cries and shouts began to take up inside the cage as more and more people started to see what was happening.

"Wayne, do you see Colton yet?" Ronick asked his second in command.

"Yes, he's coming over," Wayne said.

Ronick turned around to see Colton running toward them, Tavish still trying different configurations to pop the lock. Overhead, alarm horns blared out into the night from all over the city.

"We need to hurry. They're calling the machines in," Colton said. His face was still bruised from the night he was captured.

"We're trying," Ronick said.

"Got it," Tavish said. "It was a lot like an old mordsturn lock but…"

Ronick cut him off. "Don't care, move."

With the aid of three men on each gate, they flung the huge doors open and began waving people through.

"Ronick, there's more inside," Colton said.

"Inside where?"

"Inside the Governor's Mansion. They turned the entire sublevel into a prison. A lot of the folks from the showman's troupe are in there."

"Fine, Wayne, go grab Tavish and bring him to me."

The lockpick had scampered off with the group of people, and Wayne had to chase him down and drag the squatty man back.

Bonemen soldiers started to fire charged pulsator rounds into the escaping crowd from the upper levels of the house. Ronick's men launched volley after volley of arrows. Ronick found a dead Bonemen guard beyond the gate that had taken arrows in the shoulder and chest and grabbed the man's gun as he scrambled to the inner doors of the house.

At the door, two soldiers came barreling out as they reached the steps. Ronick threw the gun to Wayne and unsheathed his swords.

Wayne took the first one with three shots into the doorway, and Ronick dispatched the second.

The small inner room was in disarray, and the muffled sounds from outside gave way to the yelling of Bonemen inside unprepared for an attack.

"Wayne, make your way to the upper level. I'm going to take our locksmith to the basement," Ronick said.

"Yes, sir."

"Don't be a hero, just see if you can convince them to stop focusing on the prisoners. I'll be back up to help," Ronick said.

"Got it," Wayne said, moving back through the other rooms.

Colton held a door open, glanced beyond, and waved Ronick and Tavish forward.

"Down the stairs and to the right," Colton said.

"Thanks. Colton, get out of here," Ronick replied.

They rushed down the stairs into a guard station with two guards on duty. The Bonemen stood quickly at the intrusion, knocking their chairs to the ground. Tavish stayed back, while Ronick clashed swords with the first guard and kicked him to the ground. Then he spun away and attacked the second man. Their blades crashed, and the guard's sword deflected into the stone wall. This produced a small opening, and Ronick darted in and cut the man down. Ronick turned and charged in to kill the second guard before he could gather himself off the floor.

Ronick's heart pounded, and he gulped air. "Tavish, it's clear. Free the remaining prisoners."

Ronick leaned against the wall, catching his breath, and Tavish pulled the guard's keys off the dead man's waist, jingling them as if to say "you didn't need me for this." He ran along the corridor, opening every cell and telling the occupants to run.

"Ronick, I need your help," Tavish called to him from the back.

Ronick bounded down to the farthest cell, where three ladies were chained to the wall. They looked like sisters to Ronick, and Tavish was struggling with some of the cuffs. One woman was bound with rope and gagged.

"What's going on?" Ronick asked.

"These keys aren't working on the cuff," Tavish said.

Ronick looked at the three women. "Why is she gagged? Did she bite one of the guards?"

"No, Rhondi just wouldn't shut up, so they gagged her," one of the women answered.

Ronick watched Tavish fumble with his lockpicking kit and decided to try and break the chains instead. He slid his blade through the anchor pin and tried to lever it loose.

"Are you trying to cut me or yourself?" one of the women asked.

"Let the man work, Jeweli," the second woman said.

"Got a better idea?" Ronick asked.

"Yes, there's a pickaxe in the window well. It will make for a better lever."

Ronick retrieved the pickaxe from the other room and used it in his second attempt. With some effort, the pin finally came free. Tavish found the right mechanism to free the cuffs, and they moved to the last woman. Tavish freed her, and the five of them ran for the stairs.

At the stairs, gun blasts filled the hall. The bright bolts of charged rounds disintegrated into minor explosions in the walls. Colton was protecting a wounded Wayne, who sat leaning against the doorframe with his arm decimated by pulsator shots.

"Run," Colton said, and he started to fire both guns in his hands. The group scrambled through the small room, out the back door, and back into the holding cage.

The night air hit Ronick like a hammer. There was such a sulfuric smell that he immediately started coughing. A thick cloud of smoke had settled over the area, with orange and red blasts from charged guns flaring in the chaos. Outside the metal gates, Gerald was still helping people escape. He held up a man with a long, stylized beard.

"Gerald, what are you doing here?" Ronick said, reaching him.

"I came back for you. Darringer sent me back when you didn't show up at the river," Gerald explained.

"Archibald?" one of the women said, and they freed Gerald of his burden and helped the other man away, Tavish running away with them.

"Keep going, toward the river." Gerald pointed.

Ronick turned around, hoping to see Colton and Wayne appear from the smoke, knowing they wouldn't.

"Anyone else?" Gerald asked.

"No, let's go," Ronick said.

At the river's edge, a single boat remained to usher them across, with a lone man waiting inside, a lantern at his feet.

"Finally," the man said, the whites of his eyes clear in the darkness. "I was about to leave."

As the boat filled up, Gerald and Ronick waded into the water to push it into motion. The mud of the riverbed seized Ronick's boots, and he nearly fell on his face. The way the river cut through the land, most of the water was pitch-black from bank to bank. They only had to reach the darkness, and they would be unseen and safe.

A series of gunshots blasted from the tree line behind them. The shots failed to reach them. The sound of gunfire and Bonemen soldiers calling out orders overtook the noise of the river. Ronick glanced behind them. A squad of Bonemen soldiers in bronze armor had cleared the trees and stood at the riverbank, firing rounds aimlessly into their retreat. The soldiers couldn't see them.

A few shots slapped the water near them randomly, and Ronick winced but kept walking. With the current well past his waist and the boat moving now, Ronick tried to get in, but the suction of the mud made him stumble again. Next to him, Gerald fell below the surface entirely. Ronick picked his friend up, at first believing Gerald had also struggled with his footing. From the weight of him, Ronick's thoughts changed, and fear charged through him.

Another shot at them hit the water, a few feet from Ronick's back.

"Leave him and climb in," the boatman said. Ronick glared at him, ready to strangle the man for the suggestion. He was one of the newer soldiers from Prine, Ronick realized, he didn't know a torquing thing.

"I won't leave him. Either help me put him in the boat or we all die," Ronick sneered.

Whether from the fire in his eyes or his voice, the kid jumped up and helped pull Gerald aboard. Ronick moved with the boat, the water rising to his neck. He didn't want to risk giving away their position, so he remained in the water. Floating with the boat to the other side, he watched the far shore, frustrated that he was powerless to strike back and afraid to look at the lifeless form of his friend.

BACK AT FORT MARE, THERE WAS A MISSION DEBRIEFING FOLLOWED BY a funeral for those lost in the liberation. Four of the six men on team one were among the losses. During the debriefing, Ronick learned that Harlen had decided to place some of their bombs inside the ammunitions factory instead of the abandoned buildings that had been marked out as distraction points. In the end, the deviation had cost the men their lives, but it had also been the distraction that was needed.

Then, of course, there were Wayne and Colton, two men Ronick had come to rely on. Wayne had joined them after Pardona, and Colton had helped them from day one inside Midway and was brave enough to remain in the occupied city, supplying reports and managing spies along the Imperial Road. The loss most strongly felt among the men was Gerald.

All the original Renegades were in attendance because of Gerald. A man as nice and giving as Gerald was rare, and Ronick missed his friend. Gerald had a calming ability on the soldiers that bridged the gap between the men and the leadership. What started as a group of survivors fleeing the Scree from the small towns had become a major force resisting the Sagean and his Bonemen.

Ronick stood at the back of the gathering, listening to Darringer eulogize the fallen.

"When a man is dead, reverence for life is not only necessary but essential for the living," Darringer announced. "Every person carries with them thoughts and dreams, aspirations and achievements, joy and sorrow. When those things leave this world, they cannot be replaced. We gather here to say goodbye, and to say thank you. For the energy of a person's life is magic, and when that magic is gone, we mourn what was lost."

"Are you all right, Ronick?" Vera asked. She had quietly sidled up to him without his noticing.

He looked at her face and winced. The small cuts were healing from her abduction, but the bruises had yet to subside. Vera had stayed behind to heal, and her reaction to the losses was anger more than sadness.

"I'm fine," he lied.

"Are you though?"

"I will be," he said. In truth, he had never been more frustrated.

"Fighting the Scree was horrible, but there was little difference between them and the beasts. These Redeyes are the same, I guess. However, the Sagean and his army of Bonemen are somehow worse because they're not infected by a disease. They're still human. They just chose to be the way they are." She shook her head.

"They're all infected and mindless," Ronick said.

"Maybe they are, because I'll never understand how they can believe so strongly in the Sagean that they are willing to imprison their neighbors."

"It's getting worse too. The real Sagean fanatics—the Lionized that wear those detonating necklaces—they have a special place in the army now. I don't know. It's getting harder," Ronick admitted.

"It is, and unlike the Scree or Redeyes, it's only a matter of time before the Bonemen retaliate."

"What do you want me to do, Vera?"

"I don't know, Ronick, but we need to start seeing the bigger picture."

"And what is the bigger picture?" Ronick asked.

"I don't know, but that Redeye that tied me up—it wasn't working for the Bonemen."

"All right, we'll talk with Darringer tonight about the next move," Ronick said.

In the open field beyond, Ronick noticed a soldier struggling with the white Nyrogen horse. "I'll talk to you later," he told Vera and stepped away from her. "I got this one," Ronick said, taking the reins to Ghost and walking her back to the stables. When he got the spirited horse inside, he pulled the odd glove from his pocket to look at it again. The material, so light and incredibly strong, shimmered in the sunshine. He had found the glove under the horse's saddle not long after Learon had left the horse in his care. It was an odd cloth the likes of which he had never seen, and somehow, he knew it was important.

"Ronick, riders are at the west gate," a soldier said.

Ronick took the runner's horse and rode for the west gate. There were four riders, one of them flying the banner of Atava. Ronick told the guards to open the gate, and the men from Atava strolled into Fort Mare, looking weary-eyed and tired. An older man with a perfectly manicured beard dismounted and surveyed the city.

Ronick approached suspiciously but introduced himself. "I'm Ronick, of the Renegades. I help protect this city. Who are you and what brings you to Fort Mare?" From behind him, he saw Darringer arriving too.

"Ronick, it is good to put a face to the name. I'm Morgan Farris, I was sent by Lady Olean of Atava, we came to speak with you and Darringer."

"About what?" Ronick asked.

"About joining forces with us in Atava," Farris said.

"I'm afraid you made a long and dangerous ride for nothing, Mr. Farris. We're doing just fine here," Ronick said.

"Let's hear him out, Ronick," Darringer said.

"Are you Darringer?" Farris asked.

"I am."

"Can we go somewhere to talk?"

"Yes."

Darringer led the man named Farris to a room overlooking the Wells, where they often used to meet with the city managers. Farris's men waited outside.

Farris found a chair. Holding his riding gloves in his hand, he waited for Darringer to speak. Ronick stood at the windows, where he could keep an eye on the man's companions in the street, in case he had to signal to the sniper on the adjacent roof.

Farris eyed Ronick a moment. "Let me ask you. How long do you think you can hold out here in the Jaws?"

"We've survived this long," Darringer said.

"And it's amazing what you have done, but once the Sagean stops seeing you as a nuisance, he will send a full force to destroy you. After what your group did in Midway two nights ago, I suspect that day is coming. If we have heard about it in Atava, the Sagean has heard about it, and all our reports categorize his state of mind as unstable at best."

"Fort Mare survived the first war," Darringer said.

"Only because General Moonstone had so many other armies swirling around the Old World. The Sagean is coming for you, and Fort Mare is in the Jaws. With his men pushing from the east, he will hold his beasts in the forests, where they're positioned perfectly to strike you when you retreat to the west. It's a long ride to the Broken Hills, and with so many under your charge, I would estimate only a fraction would make it to Atava. That's why the road was named the Jaws in the first place. If your enemies are in the forests to either side, they will crush you. We will protect your people as you travel to Atava, and once you're in Atava, those ancient walls will hold back his beasts and his automatons."

Darringer locked eyes with Ronick. This stranger was making good points, voicing worries they had shared for some time.

"What about his bombers, the airships? We have reports that a fleet of airships could destroy us all," Darringer said.

"Those are all destined for the New World."

"So far," Darringer said.

"Isn't Atava just another trap?" Ronick said.

"I won't lie to you. If the Sagean brings his full force to bear on the city, we would be trapped. But an army like that takes time to move across the land, and we would have time to prepare, seek aid from Rodaire or Skyvier, or escape if needed," Farris said, and he shifted in his chair. "Let me ask you. What about the Dragons?"

"What about them? We've seen the same one as you, I suspect. A giant orange one that passes nearby every three days."

"Isn't it funny how it's exactly every three days? We know there are more. There's the grey one over Rodaire, the black one. I have walked the walls of Atava, and I can tell you, they were built to defend against Dragons and possibly other creatures we don't know of."

Darringer stood up and gazed out the window next to Ronick. They had been together since the start. Darringer found Ronick in the first village after his own was decimated. Months later they were here together—a lot of time, bathed in blood.

"I'm with you, whatever you decide," Ronick told him.

"We both decide. But regardless of what we do, we need allies," Darringer said.

"Maybe some should stay, Darrin. Can we trust the Atava ambassador, Lady Olean? She voted to elect the Prime when there was still a United Coalition," Ronick said.

"You can trust her." Farris spoke up. "As soon as the Prime was elected, she began making changes to the city. Her vote for the Prime was one of self-preservation, and when the Prime began making changes to the Coalition, she separated herself from the other ambassadors. They had no way of knowing there was a Sagean behind it. But when the Sagean revealed himself, she immediately acted to secure Atava's independence and survival."

"What about the return of the dead emperor? Did she know about that?" Darringer said.

"No. From what we have learned, the High Order families brought about his return," Farris answered.

"And the Dragons too, I guess?" Darringer said.

"The timing aligns, but we don't know," Farris replied.

"I'm tired of feeling alone in this, I'm tired of being outnumbered —I'm just tired," Darringer said to Ronick.

"I know we struck them hard two nights ago. If you think this is the wisest thing to do, then I'm with you," Ronick said.

"We need all the help we can get. We need to find Learon," Darringer said.

"When we need him most, he'll find us," Ronick replied.

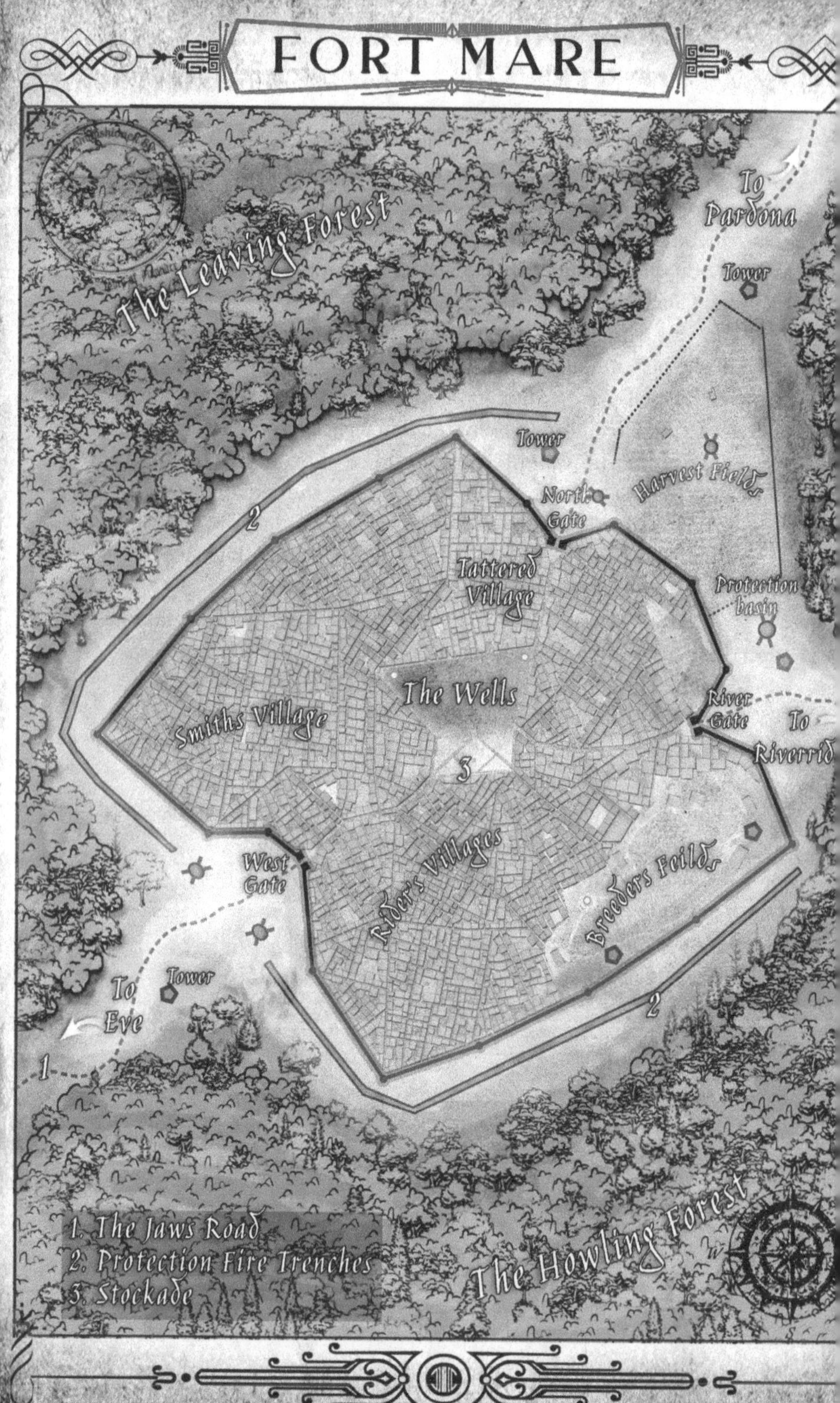

FORT MARE
The Leaving Forest
To Pardona
Tower
Tower
North Gate
Harvest Fields
Tattered Village
Protection basin
The Wells
River Gate
To Riverrid
Smiths Village
3
Rider's Villages
Breeders Feilds
West Gate
To Eye
Tower
2
2
1
The Howling Forest
1. The Jaws Road
2. Protection Fire Trenches
3. Stockade

Part Two

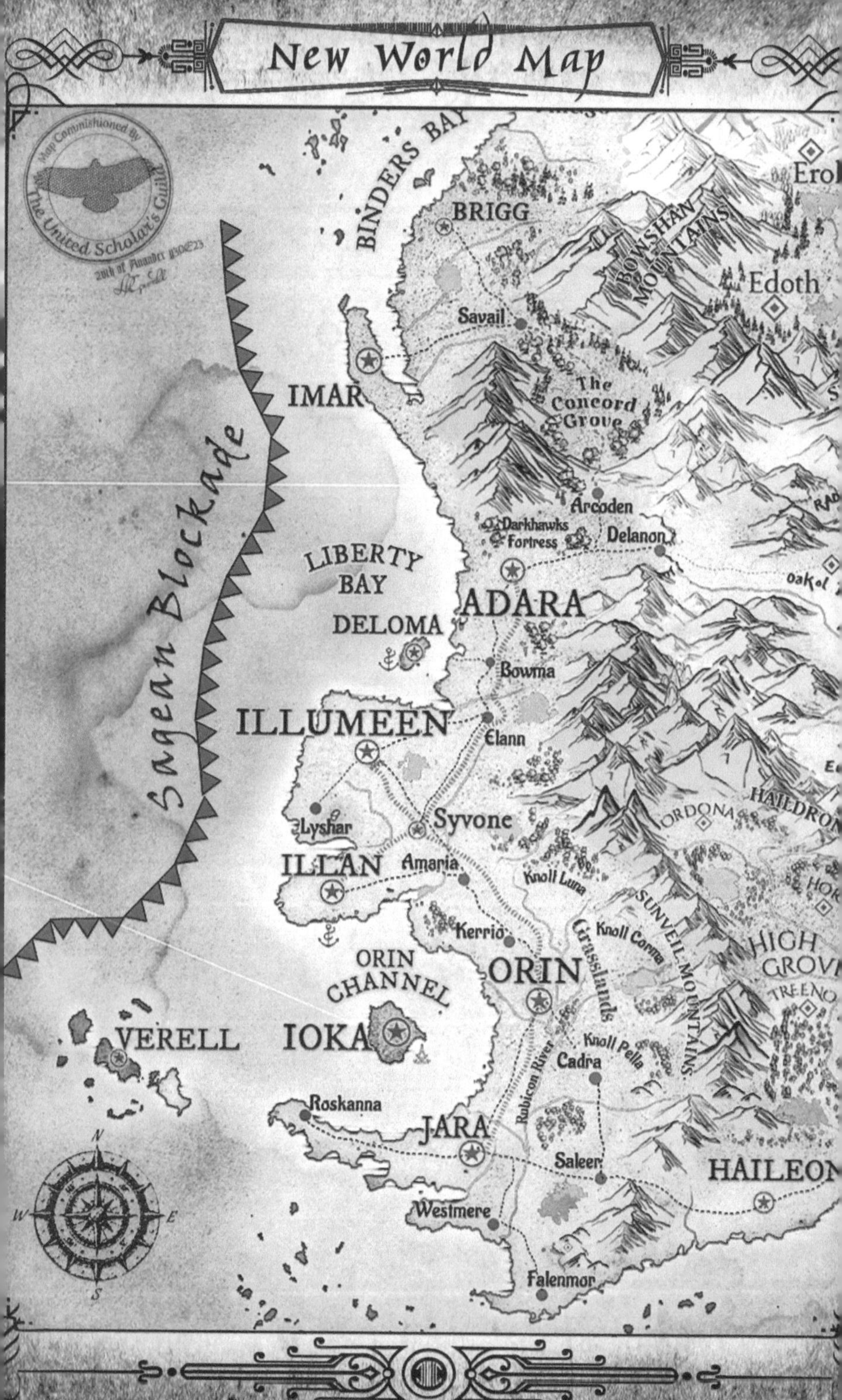

New World Map
Map Commissioned By
The United Scholar's Guild
20th of Anander 930E23
Sagean Blockade
BINDERS BAY
BRIGG
Savail
BOWSHAN MOUNTAINS
Erol
Edoth
The Concord Grove
IMAR
Arcoden
Darkhawks Fortress
Delanon
Oakol
LIBERTY BAY
DELOMA
ADARA
Bowma
ILLUMEEN
Elann
HAILDRON
Lyshar
Syvone
CORDONA
ILLAN
Amaria
Knoll Luna
SUNVEIL MOUNTAINS
HOR
Kerrio
Knoll Corina
HIGH GROVE
ORIN CHANNEL
ORIN
Grasslands
TREENO
VERELL
IOKA
Knoll Pella
Cadra
Roskanna
Rubicon River
JARA
Saleer
HAILEON
Westmere
Falenmor
N
E
S
W

ELEVEN

PATHFINDER - KOVAN

THE OLD OCEANSIDE COTTAGE WAS JUST AS HE REMEMBERED IT. THE white shutters were locked in place over the windows, boarding the house tight against the winter gales off the sea. Kovan tried to recall how long it had been—ten years? fifteen?—since he had been there.

It was the only place he had ever felt peace. Ellaria and Kovan had settled there seven years after the war. It was a seaside escape for war heroes. They were alone in the house for years before deciding to expand their family. It wasn't an easy decision. Having been on the front lines of the war, it took a long time for the pessimism surrounding the future to subside. As it sometimes can be with older couples trying to have children later in life, it took many years before Ellaria became pregnant. Even then it was only after they had stopped trying that it happened. Their little Zoe was born in the winter, on the shortest day of the year. She didn't come out screaming, but quiet and with eyes as bright and wondrous as Kovan had ever seen. At the age of four, she fell into the ocean. Kovan jumped in to save her, and for his entire life he believed that in the freezing dark waters off the north cliffs of Illumeen, he had lost her. He recalled clutching her hand and somehow never surfacing with her. And that's what he lived with. He endured that failure, and it tore him apart. The loss tore them both apart, and somehow, they couldn't find solace in each other. Grief can be so consuming and so lonely.

He was tortured with the memory of her small hand slipping out of his grasp, beneath the water.

That was the terrible reality he lived with, until the third memory cube peeled back the truth.

"Kovan, what are we doing here?" Learon asked.

The kid was understandably annoyed at Kovan's last-minute diversion. After they left Ellaria on the docks, they boarded the wind-drifter and took off toward Jara in the southeast. Even though all the attacking fleet of ships had passed, they were still warned not to take off. Bazlyn navigated the craft back north along the Rubicon River. The intention was to fly all the way to Elann, but Kovan made them divert to Athoria Lake outside of Illumeen. His only goal was to find his daughter and to find Tali. He had decided at the last moment that in order to properly search for Zoe, he had to start at the beginning.

After landing at the lake, he sent Bazlyn on to wait for Ellaria in Delanon, where he hoped to meet them at some point. Together with Learon, they headed for the cottage. They arrived with the sun over-head. The fields of tall grass were brown and mostly wind-beaten by the winter. The house too looked weathered. Still simple and beau-tiful on the hillside, but the paint was peeling, and the exposed wood had turned grey. It felt like a mirror image of himself in building form. If a house could live and pay homage to its former residents, this one was expressing the exact tiredness Kovan felt.

"I'm looking for something," Kovan said, tipping a statue over to retrieve the key. It was covered with soil and stained, but it still worked.

"What?"

"A…" He hesitated, not wanting to say it out loud. "Just wait out here. It won't take me long to find it."

The key slid in easily enough, but the door was stiff in the frame. He pushed to pry it into action and nudged it ajar with his shoulder. A small change of air expelled dust, like ghosts escaping into the sun.

Inside, the furniture was still draped with linens, but cobwebs spread in every corner and a fine layer of dust marked his footprints through the house, with very little light peeking in from the gaps in the fastened shutters. Kovan went across the hearth room to the bedroom door in an archway under the stairs. Inside the room was more dust and the smell of damp. The wood bedframe was empty, the feather mattress discarded long ago. It was a lonely-looking space now, as though the building itself had forgotten what it was. Two large highbacked chairs faced the glass doors overlooking the ocean, but they looked solemn and dying instead of welcoming. A warm fading sunlight filtered in across the floor, and a lose shutter swung outside with a slow creak in the wind.

He tried not to focus on the details of the place, but everything was so familiar and at the same time so foreign. It was an odd experience to visit a place he used to know so well. What spots in the floor creaked, where the drafts leaked, even particular patterns in the stained wood grain were all etched in his senses.

He crossed over to the closet. Stacked high on the shelf was the wood box he was looking for, with some of the last mementos he had of Zoe. Inside was a small blanket, but right on top was the necklace. It was the obsidian necklace that he came for. When he had risen from the waters the day she drowned, he awoke a day later still clutching the protection stone. He remembered cursing it and all alchemy and magic.

Kovan cradled the stone in his hand and caressed the delicate gold chain with his fingers. Then carefully, he placed the necklace inside a small leather pouch. Unable to stop himself, he lifted the old baby blanket free and placed it to his face. Unwillingly, he collapsed heart and soul into the softness. He buried his face into it and sobbed. After a long moment, he opened his eyes, and wiped them clear.

A flood of memories came over him. All his memories so easily accessible now. A song came to his mind that he had not heard nor sung in twenty years. A song he would hum softly or sing to his Zoe in the first months of her life. In the late-night feedings when he so desperately wanted her to sleep and he himself was half-awake. It was not a song for babies, but a song he heard when he was a kid and loved. It brought a smile to his face.

Something else in the box caught his attention. Three photographs remained at the bottom, sliding softly in the tilt of the box. The photographs were now dull and discolored, and there was nothing left of the people in them. Nothing he could recognize. Whatever there was, or once was, had been stolen, and he needed to get it back. He had to. He realized while staring at the relics of his past life that if all he ever did with the rest of his time was get back what was taken, then that would be the best thing he could do. Seeing the best version of yourself captured in time was cruel, even crueler to see it faded, but his goal now had a clear vision, to match the song of his heart.

He took what he came for and replaced the rest carefully back on the shelf. He locked the house back up and motioned for Learon to follow him to the shed. There he gathered more supplies. Behind a false panel in the wall, he found his old weapons and armor from the war, waiting for him. Scratched and dented, dull and dusty for its burial of twenty years. The sword, the swirl-patterned pommel and sheath, dry and in need of oil. He retracted the blade from the scabbard and pressed his palm to the edge. His hand came away with a thin cut. It was still as sharp as the day he'd last cleaned it and put it away. When he decided that he had lingered long enough, he returned to Learon, who sat holding Elias's cat. The mystcat had appeared on the deck of the *Savona* and hadn't left Kovan's side since. The sight of Elias's cat reminded Kovan to give Learon Elias's Elum blade.

"Here, you'll need a sword to go with your bow," Kovan said, handing over the old Shadowyn sword.

Learon hesitated, but took it. "Where to now, Kovan?" he asked.

"To the Rudedog Tavern in Telantry Square, to find the best pathfinder I know."

THEY ENTERED THE TAVERN JUST AFTER THE BLUE, WITH LEARON trailing behind him a few steps. Kovan had seen the change in Learon from an innocent and kind-eyed kid to a steel-eyed and tormented fighter. But even if Learon's posture had changed to always being on guard, his predisposition to take in the surrounding city remained. He would always be someone enthralled by the world around him, both by the architecture of God and man. He watched Learon gazing at the buildings and hoped that this trait of wonder inside him would never die, as so much else would be asked of him before the end.

Entering the tavern, the mystcat bounding in before them, Kovan ignored looks from the patrons and headed straight toward the back bar, where the bartender was animatedly arguing with her supplier. He knew Devon would remember him, but he could only hope she would be willing to let her husband go with him.

"Are you trying to kill my customers!" the bartender yelled. She was a big woman, and her voice boomed even in the loud space of the tavern.

"The man at the end of the bar said it was fine," the deliveryman argued, leaving his hands on the dolly full of crates, where some of the slats were stained from the contents they held.

"Valdimar. You can't listen to him. He drinks anything. This is my bar. I make the purchases, and I have to stand behind everything I serve, and this is tainted drip," she said.

"No, no. It's finely crafted, Madam Devon." The peddler started to make another sales pitch, but to his dismay, she poured out the spirits on her hand and shoved it into the man's face.

"See! Can you smell that?" she demanded. "I can. You're bottling the heads from your distiller, mixing it with the dregs of maric-powder and more cane."

"No, we would never," the seller protested.

"But you did, the maric produces that sour, putty smell. Sure, it only tastes like dirty spirits. I'm sure you've added so much cane on the bottling to make it passable, but this torqued poison will kill some-one," Devon said.

"How about twenty ambers a case instead of forty?"

"Get these barrels out of my tavern and leave my sight before I grab my short-barrel blaster and send you back to Lyshar, toe up with the wagoner," she yelled.

After the man left, Devon wiped the countertop clean and grabbed a bottle of clear spirits. Then she looked Kovan in the eye, with a "what the hell do you want" sort of look on her face.

"I'll have your house ale," Kovan said.

"No, you won't. You'll have what I pour you. You and this... Kovan?"

"He's old enough," Kovan said.

"Uh-huh, anyways, our house stuff is crap."

"It's your own house ale?" Learon said.

"That's right, and it's for tourists. How about a shot? That's what you're supposed to do when you see an old friend." She didn't wait for him to respond and grabbed four shot glasses.

"Fine. I'll have a shot of emberbroth," Kovan said.

"No. I'm out of my Logan Valley stock, and the stuff shipped from the crescent is piss-water. How about cane-vapor? Finest batch from the bay."

"Sure." Kovan smiled.

She aligned the glasses and poured four indistinguishably even pours without effort or obvious care. Kovan thought maybe she was listening to the sound of the liquid fill up in the cups to know how even each was. She pushed two cups toward them, kept one for herself, and slid the fourth down the bar. She slammed hers and poured another with a grin.

As though the sound of the pour was a loud clock chime, the drunk alertly ambled toward them. He caught the glass off the counter and slammed it back without losing a drop. Kovan shook his head, realizing who it was.

Learon sipped to taste his.

"Kovan, since when do you travel with daisies like this?" she asked, motioning to Learon.

"He's… still in training."

"Training for what, the Darkhawks?" Valdimar asked. He had arrived, grinning ear to ear. He had black hair and a face that seemed to be always winking. Kovan knew better than most that it was just an unconscious reflex for the sheer amount of bullshit that effortlessly spewed from the man's mouth.

"For life," Kovan said, and he hugged is old friend. "How you been, brother?"

"I'm great. Look around, I've found the end of the rainbow. I got everything I need. So, this one is still green, huh?" Valdimar said.

"Not so green, but he's learning how life kicks you around," Kovan replied.

"Hah, yeah, it fights dirty too. One day you wake up and you're the bar drunk, right, babe?"

"Sweetie? You're an idiot," Devon said.

"Then, honey, you're a moron," Valdimar said.

"I must be."

"Is that what happened to you?" Kovan asked.

"Oh no, not me. I found my calling."

"You're calling is to annoy me into the grave, Rooster."

"I entertain the patrons, sweetheart."

"By drinking all my emberbroth?"

"I'm just getting on their level," Valdimar said with his hands out. He always punctuated his stories with hand gestures. "If you're not on their level, they don't respect you," he said, drawing out the end of his words like he was saying something poetic.

Devon rolled her eyes and poured herself another drink.

"Wait, did you call him Rooster?" Learon asked.

"Yeah, I fed him once and he never leaves. And now he clucks around here all day long and night. And like a rooster, he coos a big game, but he runs when danger is near."

The old drunk smiled wider. "I can't help it if they can't catch me. I'm fast, babe. Plus, I'm a lover not a fighter. But I'll admit, I'm a bit of a fight starter, not a fight finisher," Valdimar said with a sort of dance, but then like he saw something shiny, his attention diverted to the far side of the bar, and he left the conversation.

"You're not going to leave that cat, are you?" Devon asked.

"I would if I could, but no," Kovan answered.

"So, what do you want, Van?" Devon asked.

"I need him. How bad is he?" Kovan asked.

"He's good, I mean he's always bad, but he's better. He's slowed down, Van."

"With his drinking?"

"No, not that. Just in general. Age does that."

"Well in that I can't argue. We've all slowed down, but is he still sharp enough to guide?"

"What, him? That's our pathfinder?" Learon said, dumbfounded.

They ignored the question and continued. "So can I have him?" Kovan asked.

"Please, you'd be doing me a favor." Then she called down the bar, where Valdimar was telling a joke to some men at their table. "Rooster, find your things. You're going."

"What, come on, someone always telling me what to do."

"Not someone, me. Van needs you."

Valdimar came back over. "Where to, Van? What are you looking for? You want a route to the High Grove, or maybe we go to the best ladies house in Syvonne?" He hit Learon in the shoulder, obviously believing he had said something funny that Learon didn't catch.

"We need a way to the Shadowyn."

"Of course you do, and I need to be twenty years old again. My man, Van, when you come back around, you come back around, my friend. I see you're wearing that old armor of yours, too. Did they get you to lead the war again?"

"I have my own battles to fight. Do you know the way? I thought I remembered you saying you did."

"That's the rumor I started. First, we need to go to Elann. I'll go get my bag," Valdimar said.

"You sure you're ready now? We could give you an hour or two," Kovan asked, unsure of his friend's state to ride.

"I'm always ready to roll. I have a travel bag packed with the essentials, but I have to go find it." He looked to his wife. "Honey?" he called out slowly.

"Don't 'Honey' me. Get off your drunk butt and get it yourself," Devon said.

"Fine. I'll go look for my own bag. I swear I do everything around here," Valdimar said with a wink toward Kovan.

Valdimar disappeared for a short time behind the bar and returned with a duffel bag that opened at the top like a doctor's bag. It rattled and clinked like it was full of bottles. From the heft of it, that appeared to be exactly what was inside.

"I know what you're thinking—yes, the party travels with me," Valdimar said.

"Are you only bringing alcohol?" Learon asked.

"No, I have clothes and oatmeal in here."

"Oatmeal?" Learon replied.

"The torquing truth. Oatmeal's the great tonic of our time, gentlemen."

Leaving with Valdimar was an arduous task full of multiple stops, as he was friends with everyone, and everyone had something to say to him. One gentleman as they were leaving handed him what looked to Kovan like a pouch of Moonlighters flower. A plant commonly smoked by the Harrinari in Karnika.

Valdimar took it and loudly proclaimed, "My man, you know how I do."

Kovan wasn't sure if it was a statement or a question, but the man who gave him the smoke hugged him and laughed and proceeded to the bar.

Traveling through the rest of the town went more or less the same. If Valdimar wasn't talking to an acquaintance, then he was talking to strangers. Though, in truth, he was a man that didn't know a stranger. When they reached their horses, Valdimar told them to hold on and walked over to a man they saw peddling on the street who had taken rest on a street corner. The stranger was surely homeless.

"What now?" Learon grumbled under his breath.

"It's just his way," Kovan told him.

"What could they possibly have to talk about? This guy is our pathfinder?" Learon voiced his concern again. "Our guide and hope of finding the Shadowyn rests on a guy they call Rooster? I think she may even have called him 'Roosty' back there. He's clearly popular, but honestly, I think I would rather have Devon in a fight."

"He's what we have to work with. Don't get it twisted, he's scrappy too. Valdimar has traveled all over the New World. He knows people wherever he goes," Kovan said.

Valdimar handed the homeless man a small bag and walked back to them.

"Can he even climb up on his horse?" Learon asked.

Valdimar returned still wearing his large smile, which faltered at seeing the horse. "You know, guys, it's a whole new world out there with machines and motorized carts. We can't, you know, travel in one of those?"

"I trust a good horse over a machine any day," Kovan said.

"Of course, you do," he replied without malice. "All right, but if I fall, assuming I can get up on this thing, you two are going to have to pick me up. And by the looks of it, I'm going to fall."

"Let's go, Roosty," Learon said.

"Hey, only my family can call me Roosty. Now just tell me which one to get up on, because I'm seeing like four of them, and they're all moving around."

"Try the middle one," Kovan suggested.

It took four attempts for Valdimar to climb on his horse, and that was after Learon had helped put his foot into the stirrup.

"I said there were four of them, how was I to know which one was the one in the middle?" Valdimar complained, grasping around to grasp ahold of the saddle. When he was finally up, he hugged the horse. "It's all right, big guy. Keep me safe and I'll keep you safe," he muttered to the horse and then sat up tall, his back straight, and winked at them both. As if they hadn't waited ten minutes watching him struggle.

"Are you ready?" Kovan asked.

"Ready? Sure. You two just keep me posted on when we're going to stop."

"We won't stop before nightfall, unless the horses tire."

"Not even if your ass starts hurting."

"Not until nightfall," Kovan repeated.

"All right, all right. I guess that makes sense, because my ass already hurts. But what if I have to get sick?"

"Let's go," Kovan said and turned his horse toward the road, heading east at a slow trot until Valdimar got his bearings. "You said Elann, right?"

"Yes, past Wolf Lake."

Learon turned to the pathfinder. "What did you give him?"

"Give who?"

"The homeless man back there?"

"I gave him whatever money I had. I think some of Devon's too."

"Isn't it all Devon's?" Kovan chimed in.

"Mostly, yes, but I earn my money. Believe me. You don't want to know the things I have to do for a little bit of money from my honey."

Kovan couldn't help but laugh and shake his head.

"Do you have enough to return home when we're done?" Learon asked.

"I'll figure it out. I'm not worried about it. If I have it to give, then I give. Plus, my woman owns the best tavern in Illumeen. She can afford whatever I give away."

"Does she know that?" Kovan asked.

"Oh, God no, and don't you tell her what I did. She'd kill me."

TWELVE

LONG WALK - ELLARIA

ACCORDING TO THE CAPTAIN, THEY HAD LANDED SOUTH OF THE Whelk Forest, northwest of the small city of Kerrio. The decision was made to head east for the small city, where a train could take them to the Grand Station at Syvonne. Atwood and Shaw hated the idea, and suggested it was going backward not forward. The captain produced his map and waved it in the air.

"I've done the calculations, and more so, I know this land. Kerrio is closer, and that's the way I'm going," Captain Fryk said.

"That doesn't mean I'm going that way. We should head for the tributary and go north along the river to Amaria," Shaw argued.

"It'll take two days just to reach the river," the captain fired back.

"My companions and I will go to Kerrio with you, Captain. I trust you," Ellaria said.

She did trust him. Any captain willing to sacrifice his ship to save everyone on board was not going to lead them astray now.

"We will follow too," Admiral Vaughn said. He was a balding man, with a wideset jaw, and an upper lip that almost never moved when he talked. He had a commanding presence, and Ellaria trusted him more than any of the governors.

Ellaria didn't argue the plan, but she dearly wanted to put Atwood and Shaw in their place. Those two would argue the direction of the wind, even if it was blowing at their face. She didn't doubt that they didn't like the idea of going backward, but mostly they didn't like Captain Fryk giving orders. The other governors were more mild-mannered. Zulhorn kept quiet, and Ramell seemed content to let the captain continue as the leader. Though in truth, Admiral Vaughn was the highest-ranking officer there.

Ellaria would always be an outsider among them. They knew they couldn't order her around, but they weren't humble enough to take orders from her.

In a half-days time the group came to a muddy makeshift road curving through a valley of dead grass. A few farms were visible in the distance, and one had a herd of sheep visible from their vantage point.

"Is that…?" Wade asked Ellaria.

"Sheep, what about them?"

"It's just, it's livestock, in the open?"

"There are no beasts here, Wade. No need for the lookout towers along the roads or gated fortifications. And no need for the blue fires at night."

"I guess. I knew that, but to see it is another thing," Wade said.

"You'll also find that most people here don't carry weapons. These are farmers and builders. Even wildlife that is hunted for food, like deer or boar, they don't call it Silva meat; they call it game."

"I never realized how much harder life is in Tovillore."

"Over here, Tovillore is called the Old World," Stasia corrected him.

"She's right. Most people here call Tovillore, Rodaire, and Skyvier, the Old World, or the West. Which is ironic because the Harrinari call the people of the New World, Westlanders," Ellaria said.

"My point is, how can the Westlanders be ready to fight a war against a foe that is so much harder-skinned?" Wade said.

"We're going to find out, but in my experience, people will fight for their survival when attacked," Ellaria replied.

The hike to Kerrio was long, made longer by the absence of news about the war. The first sign of the war came when they found a small trampled road with wheel tracks depressed in the dried-out mud. A few hours after setting their pace on the road, the entire party stopped to rest and were passed by a pair of riders, their horses draped with the king's colors and kicking up clumps of dirt.

The ship captain stood to flag them down, and Vaughn followed him as soon as he recognized them as soldiers.

"Where did your group come from?" the young soldier asked, scanning the countryside.

"We were shipwrecked last night," the captain said.

The soldier turned in his saddle to look out over the forest line and to the sea beyond. "Bad night to be on the water," he remarked.

"Sure, but those Bonemen got it good," Shaw commented.

"So did some of our own," the captain said, scowling at Shaw's bravado.

Vaughn cleared his throat and stepped in front of Captain Fryk.

At the sight of him and his coat, the soldiers made to dismount, but he waved them to hold.

"How much farther to Kerrio?" Vaughn asked.

"It's half a day's ride, sir. You all, being on foot, your group's a full day away. Is anyone in your group wounded?"

"Just some scrapes and bruises. Who are you with?" Vaughn asked.

"We're runners with the Sons of Knoll, sir. The rest of our squad is about a league behind, coming up the road. They'll supply you with what you need."

"You already have a new assignment?" Vaughn asked.

"We received word at dawn to pack up and head south, sir."

"On whose authority?" Shaw inquired.

"The daughter heir, sir. We are to be redeployed immediately to Falenmor. We are riding ahead to secure our train and supplies for travel."

"Then be off, and don't stop for anyone else," Admiral Vaughn said.

The soldiers crossed their right arms to their chests in respect to Vaughn, and without another word, the two riders galloped off up the road.

Stasia and Wade were standing at Ellaria's side during the exchange.

"I though Vaughn would ask them more questions?" Wade asked.

"He wanted news of the war, but as scouts, they wouldn't know anything, so he sent them on," Stasia answered.

Ellaria smiled at the girl's know-it-all nature and nodded that she was right.

When the Blue sun rose at midday, the band of soldiers had come upon them. The small legion was some forty in number, and all of them so young that Ellaria wondered if they had all their teeth. There commanding officer stopped to give their group water and talk with Vaughn and the governors. The squad's leader, Lieutenant Mills, was older than his charges. His blond hair was tousled in the same manner as Wade's, and he wore a mustache that looked silly on him. *A child pretending to be a man, leading other men,* she thought.

Mills gave them the information that he received. "A rider arrived at dawn. He had carried good and bad news."

"News of the blockade?" Atwood asked.

"The blockade is gone. The Bonemen landed troops and sent half their ships north. The front lines are being established as we speak. They say the bulk of the Sagean's forces landed at Illan and the Illumeen coast. Some at Lyshar and Roskanna. They also dropped troops behind our lines, but not in any significant numbers yet."

"Then the war rages as we speak. They would have met forces in all those locations," Vaughn relayed to the governors, before following up with another question. "Did any Sagean ships make it through the channel?"

"No, sir. That ocean contraption worked. But scouts report that many of the Sagean's ships have now turned north toward Liberty Bay," Mills said.

"I suspect they'll find that less inviting than the Orin Channel," Vaughn said.

"What's the bad news?" Ellaria spoke up.

"Word is their air attack was most effective in Orin. Their bombs destroyed a lot of the city."

"How are we responding?" Atwood demanded.

"I don't know, sir," Mills replied.

"What about Illumeen?" Shaw asked.

"I don't know, sir." Mills shrugged.

"Thank you, Lieutenant Mills. You go on ahead. Don't let us slow you," Vaughn said.

"You're not slowing us, sir. We are making camp tonight to arrive in the morning for the train."

They traveled another two leagues before they made camp for the night, and Ellaria sat as far from the fire as she could stand to keep her distance from the governors.

"You don't trust them, do you?" Wade asked.

"These weasels? No. They're less predictable than the Coalition ever was. At least those power-hungry egomaniacs were satiated by their own wealth. These governors are being put to the test. The Coalition folded"—she snapped her fingers—"like that. With just a little pressure from the Court of Dragons. These governors want to protect their small morsel of power more than they want to protect the people they're supposed to be in service to."

"At least this time tomorrow, we'll be on a train to Syvonne," Wade said.

"Thank the Blue, my feet are killing me," Stasia chimed in.

"And you, Echoryn Solhara?" Ellaria asked the young Tregorean woman. Ellaria was still unsure why Echoryn had chosen to travel with them and not Learon. Those two seemed as close as brother and sister. So far, through the whole ordeal, the young woman had not said a word. Even now her attention was transfixed, studying some flower on a nearby bush.

"I don't like it here," Echoryn said flatly. "There's too much air and water. I feel exposed out here."

"We are," Ellaria admitted.

"And I think you're right not to trust these governors. In just two days we will have arrived at a city, with transportation," Echoryn said.

"Meaning?" Stasia asked.

"Meaning, why would anyone wishing us to make good time suggest we walk another way?" Ellaria said. *Could there be more behind their reluctance. More than simple lust for power.* "If there is subterfuge about, we need to figure out who the spy is."

"How do we do that?" Wade asked.

"Keep your eyes and ears open. It's a long train ride to Syvonne. Spies often reveal themselves," Ellaria said.

Fires were going in multiple spots, and the sheer amount of people camping on the side of the road made for an obvious target. Ellaria couldn't help but scan the sky. It was a clear night except for a subtle orange haze in the south.

The soldiers were in a fine mood. They were gambling and laughing around the fire, and when they had food prepared, they called out for everyone to join them. The governors grabbed bowls, and Wade took some back to the others, but Ellaria lingered by the soldiers a moment.

They were telling stories and laughing. She overheard some of the men boasting about a woman they had seen in the city the month before. Ellaria didn't hear the whole story. What she did hear, she found trite and superficial, but nothing out of the ordinary for a group of young men. Something about the banality of it, their youthful preoccupation with such an insignificant event. Her shoulders dropped and a lump came to her throat. It only took forty years for the world to test the limits of humanity with war again, and she didn't think she still had the stomach to watch the young die.

"Miss, I'm sorry. Did the boys offend you?" the lieutenant asked.

"No. No need to apologize," Ellaria said, but she had lost her appetite. She stood and poured the contents of her bowl back into the pot. She wasn't about to steal a meal from one of the men. Then she returned to the grass near Wade, Stasia, and Echoryn.

When she settled into a comfortable spot near the fire, she pulled out Elias's letter.

Ellaria,

There is much I must tell you. A simple letter would never be enough, but I tried explaining everything I know in case I never see you again. Thank you for keeping me safe and dragging me out of Tovillore. I'm sorry if I scared you. It wasn't me and I couldn't control it. I couldn't control him. I have momentarily survived what was ailing me, but the damage has caused a misalignment of my body and spirit.

For the last forty years, I believed the Wrythen was the cause of my sickness. That the use of my powers was calling out the dark entity. I never considered that it was the Sagean. During my battle with the emperor, when the Wrythen appeared, I believed the Sagean was destroyed. Somehow, he had escaped and taken refuge inside my well of energy. There, his spirit remained dormant unless I used my powers. Emanating as much energy as I did in fighting our way out of the emperor's tomb, I inadvertently freed the Sagean.

The Kihan healer has done his best to stabilize my spirit and block the Sagean. A temporary fix, but none of that matters now. More importantly, in the final moments of my soul sickness, when I was able to regain control, I glimpsed a plane of existence the Ancients called the Unity Maze. Mia once told me about this world the prophets see, where the paths of fate exist, but I had no understanding of it until now. Seeing this flashing reality, and the many versions of life, I was suddenly aware of events and choices still to come. I've seen the Last Battle, and you, my friend, must be there, to guide and protect the Trinity Guard.

I also remembered things from the past, terrible things. I know you don't know what I'm talking about, but soon you will. What I came to remember was that we were all betrayed by Mia. Experiencing the Unity Maze,

I know now that her actions were spurred by her visions. For right or wrong, she did everything in the name of saving the world. When you find her, with revenge in your heart, just remember all the extremes you went to to save the world. I can't say any more than this; otherwise, I risk directing you onto another path, and your journey is dangerous enough as it is.

In the end, what matters is I believe we will all be reunited. Sometimes things must be broken before they can be put together. By binding the very imperfections, we become something stronger and more beautiful. When everything comes back together, I believe that's when we will be strong enough to defeat the Old One.

My time is up, and to have any chance of fighting by your side again, I must take drastic action tomorrow at the temple. Depending on how things play out inside the temple, I will be sending Tali to Mia through the portal spell connected through twin necklaces. Tali wears the sister necklace I made for Mia a long time ago. I believe Mia is somewhere in the New World. I have implored Kovan and Learon in my letters to them to seek out the Shadowyn. It's important that they do, and that they don't go running off to save Tali, and I don't believe she needs saving.

All of us are on our own journeys. For some of us, it's a trail of belief; for some it's one of redemption; and for others, their journey is about love or perseverance. For Tali, she must discover what matters most to her.

After tomorrow night the world will once again go to war. I'm entrusting you to save it once again. It's an unfair ask, and I'm sorry. I need to tell you a few more things to help you in case you never get the Tempest Stone to work.

In my research about the Ancients, there were many mentions of two groups of people that I believe are also at the heart of this matter with the Wrythen. Sometimes I heard them referred to as the Vygoths, or they were referred to as the Watchers. I believe both of those are the same beings and they evolved to become what we now commonly call the Fates—the supposedly immortal beings watching over our world. My mother believed in the Fates; the Kihan believe in them too. The Zenoch, as well as the Harrinari, have their own Gods, but their religions also include the Fates. What I have come to realize is that the Fates, or whatever you want to call them, these Watchers were real. If they were real, then some of them might exist today. The good news is that I don't believe they are another enemy to defeat, but they certainly will have their own agendas. I think I have met one or two in my travels, when I was going by the name Julian Sawyer and working as an archeologist. One goes by the name Maki, and he resides in Ravenvyre; another is named Poe. I don't know if they brought the Wrythen to our world or created it, but the Old One and the Fates are connected somehow.

If I don't come back, you are to go to my vault at my home in Polestis and use the obsidian pillar. I spoke with Meroha, and she told me that there was an attack on my home in the north, but I don't believe they would've ever been able to access my vault. There were too many protections. Tali can get through them, and everything inside is yours. Please use what's inside and find a way to defeat the Wrythen.

If the Old One survives, the world will not. Use the Wave Gates if you must. There are lot more scattered throughout the world. They are creations from the Fates. If you use them, be wary. I don't know what lies behind every one of them. I've written down the symbols that I recall, and what locations they may lead to, but they can be unreliable too.

Lastly, I've set Meroha on a quest of resurrection. It involves her homeland of Kotalla. The Kihan are going to help her to liberate her country, but it's a longshot. There is a second method that could bring me back, but don't pursue it. I fear for the ramifications if you do. I'm prepared for my last fight to be tomorrow. I have a living connection to this world from long ago, so I am hopeful Meroha and the Kihan will be able to bring me back. If not, just know, I love you.

Ellaria, you are and always will be my best friend. You were always the best of us. Remember, you don't have to win this war on your own.

Until we meet again.

Love,

Elias Qudin

Ellaria carefully folded the letter up and stored it away. Elias had studied more about the Ancients than anyone she ever knew. If he said the Fates were real, she had to believe him. *Even if it does sound crazy.* If he thought he could come back from the dead, maybe he could. Mayock had done it, but she suspected that it was only because Elias was a Luminary that the Sagean was able to do such a thing. The thought of being betrayed by someone so long ago, and only coming to realize it now, was terrifying. She needed a drink, and she walked over to Wade and Stasia and took the small bottle of ember-broth that Wade had conned someone out of.

"Hey," Wade said.

"Trust me, I need this more than you do. Your blood still moves fast. Mine is slow and tormented and it needs to be eased," Ellaria said, and she threw back the bottle. When she handed the empty bottle back to him, his wide-eyed look of confusion amused her.

She sat down back in her spot, thinking about the Fates. In addition to Elias's suspects, she could think of another candidate as a living Fate. The Mistress of Merinde had to be high on her list. Though the older woman seemed mad, maybe it was her madness that was the key piece of evidence. *If I was immortally bound to this realm, I would go mad too,* she thought.

With the ideas of madness in her head, she spotted Echoryn across the fire, looking intently at the foliage and flowers around the campsite. The girl worried her. She was more insular than she had been before in the Tregorean Province. If her powers of prophecy were beginning to take her over, Echoryn would surely be on the path to madness too. *Perhaps we all are.*

WHEN THEY REACHED KERRIO, THE PLATFORM WAS BUSTLING WITH people: troops heading north and south and a few bands of civilians.

The platoon of soldiers they came with took up a massive section, loitering around the loading area. As the soldiers waited for their train, some played card games, some stood smoking at the edge of the walk, and the lieutenants sat going over their orders. When Ellaria could compartmentalize their fate, she found their company made her smile, and their free spirit, an uncanny defiance to the turning of the world, invigorating. *Have I ever been that young, had that glow to my skin and free exuberance to my blood?* She couldn't recall.

Ellaria approached the squad of soldiers to say farewell. She found Lieutenant Mills sitting with the supplies, his feet up on a stack of duffel bags. He examined a clipboard, intently. Mills's small company, Sons of the Knoll, were spread out and waiting, swallowing the entire platform. A hundred and fifty men, with so little fat to their bodies and skin. The vibrant youth awaiting the death knell was like watching a bird's nest in a hurricane for Ellaria. She desperately wanted to protect them.

"I wanted to wish you luck, Lieutenant," Ellaria said to Mills.

The young man stood, "Thank you. And which region are you a governor for, miss?"

"Oh, I'm no governor," Ellaria replied, somewhat offended.

"Oh, my mistake."

"You said you were heading south."

"We're catching the train to Jara, and then it's on to either West-mere or Haileon. I'm not sure. We expected a message from our superiors, but the magnotype lines are down. We can't send a message out, either.

"Well, be smart wherever you're going," she said.

"It's not the front line, but someone has to defend the south."

"It might just be the front line when you arrive."

"You think so?" the lieutenant asked, his eyes wide.

"I do."

"Pardon my disbelief, ma'am," another soldier interrupted them. "But no way is a force going to make it through the Dead Wake."

"I hope you're right, youngster," she said, but the more she thought about the geography of the war, the more she saw the weak points. When she looked at it from her enemy's eyes, and the daunting task of an invading force, the more certain areas began to look like obvious targets. She surmised that the Dead Wake wasn't impenetrable. It only took one good captain, and once one ship found the route, a fleet could.

"Can I give you one piece of advice, Lieutenant?" Ellaria said.

"Sure."

"Assume the enemy never sleeps and is always closing in."

"I will."

"Good. Then may your aim be true and your steel sharp," she said, and she walked back to her side of the platform to wait for the northbound train. Her worry for the soldiers, the war, and all the ones she loved hung over her like a blanket of lead.

THIRTEEN
JUDGEMENT - TALI

THE WAGON RATTLED ALONG THROUGH THE ZENOCH LANDS. THE interior canvas was lined with fur to shield against the cold-blasted air. Tali's hands were bound behind her with rope. Two strangers accompanied her. One, a soldier with a face like a block of ice, and the other an official of some sort.

They had been traveling for a week now on a road they called the Temmerant, and in her brief moments outside the wagon, Tali had determined that they were traveling east. The tall snow peaks of the Territhrune Mountains had changed to peaks on the distant horizon, and the forest thickened. Beyond this, she knew very little of what was happening or where they were taking her. The wagon followed a large river at times, and as the road weaved around the land, they often rolled over stone bridges where smaller rivers intersected their path. Two days before, they had passed a city. Tali could hear it in the distance, but she was never allowed out to see it. Being trapped inside the wagon was as good as being blindfolded. As they progressed though the Zenoch country, she could smell the pine trees, the mud of the road, and something of flowers.

Anger and anxiety were both potent and churning in her blood at a constant rapture. Her powers were gone. Almost like the man in gold had known she was weak and stole the last bits she had away. Her sense of the elements was there, but even that sense seemed to be fading with each day. The thought of that evil gem touching her again made her skin crawl, and a shiver twitched at her arms. A revulsion she powered through with gritted teeth so she could avoid vomiting. *Where are they taking me? Why did I trust Mia?*

Tali fumed at the thought of Mia having betrayed her. If she had her powers, she would lay waste to the man in gold, and then use his staff to beat Mia. Being stuffed in the wagon against her will, a prisoner of these people, left her with little else but desires and schemes for vengeance.

Revenge was her best barrier against fear, and even then, the fear was slipping in through the cracks. Even if she could get ahold of the yellow viper-eye, *could she reclaim her powers?*

She fingered the loose strands of the knot at her wrist. The sunlight on the seat next to her felt strong, like it always did. It oscillated with long pulsing waves that rippled the air. A simple act of collecting the ripples was all she needed to do. It was as easy as breathing. She tried again, but nothing happened. *If I can feel them, why can't I draw them in?* Her hands grew colder, and her head burst with pain, like an ice pick had slammed through her temple. Suddenly she couldn't breathe, her pulse raced, she was drowning. She focused on the flowers and the smell of pine in the air to calm herself.

Every time she tried to draw on the energy, the outcome had been the same. A sharp pain behind her eyes, followed by trouble breathing. Panic flooded her, until it quickened to a state of hyperventilating.

She closed her eyes and listened to the wheels rattle. The surface had changed. There was crunch to it, and the car jostled in a slight flailing like she had felt in the winddrifters. They must be driving on a crushed gravel, she thought.

"Almost there and I can be home," a voice said softly.

Tali opened her eyes. "What?" she said, believing the guard had spoken to her.

"Quiet," the guard ordered. He scowled at her with his jaw clenched. The dirt-crusted stubble of his beard and tired eyes gave away just how exhausted the man was.

Looking at him, she knew he hadn't said anything aloud. She could still hear people's thoughts, she realized. Conceivably, it was like how she could still feel energy but not touch it. Either way, she wasn't skilled enough at *listening* to take advantage. It had always been a fleeting skill for her, one she had never learned to control. When she had picked up on other people's thoughts in the past, they always came to her unwarranted, unannounced. The voices intruded on her own mind, not the other way around. If there was a way to enhance this gift, the answer eluded her.

Tali glared at the other attendant. She suspected the woman was someone of high-standing based on the gold at her sleeves and her makeup. The woman took notice of the exchange and made a note of something in her journal but said nothing. Tali closed her eyes and tried to sift through the noises around her in the same manner that she concentrated on various energy vibrations. For Tali, finding energy was simply a matter of looking for it. Energy had subtle intonations, a flow she could feel. Tali extended the reach of her senses but tried to ignore the pulls of energy to search for the voices. She found only silence.

Tali exhaled in frustration. She'd stretched her senses to their limits and nothing. *Unless,* she thought, *it's not about enhancing anything but being more receptive to the person.*

She opened her eyes and stared at the woman writing in her journal, studying everything about her. She had high cheekbones and dark hair with flecks of blue that shimmered in the sun. Tali wondered if the blue in the woman's hair was natural, as she had seen other Zenoch with similar coloring. Tali shook her head; *she was getting off track.* Refocusing, she noted the woman had long eyelashes and almost colorless eyes. Her face was adorned with bright silver makeup around her eyes. It complemented her darker blue skin and was drawn to points down the side. Above her eyebrows the silver became an interlacing pattern that disappeared into her hair. She wore a scarf bundled tight and thick to her chin and cheeks. Her lips moved slightly with her breathing. Her cloak lifted out of sync with the scratches of her pen on the paper, and suddenly Tali could see the words the woman was writing.

... I came at the request of High Elder Jinree Sen'Lo. I have seen no sign of aggression from the captive. She seems sad and lonely, but she has not fought us. She has not even asked where we are taking her. I believe her bewildered state is an

effect of the viper-eye. She must still have her powers, as she has not asked for extra clothing or blankets, and the trip from Roal to Cadon has grown very cold. Colder at this time of year than I have ever experienced. Maybe the Fates have drawn a dark cloud around us in this task. I too feel solemn about my charge, and I have seen it on the faces of other men on this trip. I have wondered if the captive's disposition is affecting us all. A route of seven days has taken twelve and exacted a toll, I fear.

If it is the will of the Spirit Elders, I shall request that the Luminary is brought to the temple in Darkanna for your inspection. Though I suspect Twilight Elder Ashrata Nea'Ko has other ideas for her. I request that a decision be made with the utmost haste and be delivered to me with speed. There is no telling what length Nea'Ko will go to prove the might of our people in the face of one touched by the source. His caravan is ahead of our own by a day and a half, and he will no doubt have something prepared for this outsider when we arrive. It's possible he will want her bones for a new axe. When we reach the temple, I still hope to learn more of the Harrinari leader Nea'Ko took prisoner.

Please advise,

Your humble servant

SunCrystal, Lunoka Trava'Ko

The words were etched into the journal, and the woman carefully tore the sheet away. Tali's mind snapped back. Lunoka rolled the letter into a tight scroll and sealed it by tying a silver strand of braided thread around it. She tucked it up her sleeve and snapped her head up at look at Tali, as if sensing she was being closely watched.

Tali looked away and sighed. At least some of her gifts had not betrayed her. *The woman is right about one thing,* Tali thought. *I am lonely.* No one was coming to save her, and Tali was slowly losing her confidence that she could save herself. There was an emptiness inside, too. The bonds formed from trying times are more vibrant than blood, and the distance between her and her friends was so great now that despair was rotting her tired heart.

It was after the Blue of the next day before the wagon finally stopped. Tali assumed they had reached the Zenoch capital city of Cadon. Heavily armed soldiers, pulled the wagon's canvas open, and Lunoka stood to exit. The remaining guard inside grabbed Tali by her arm. In a flash, a blade was at the guard's throat. Lunoka's hand held it tight and steady, and her face came close.

"Though she is a prisoner, she is still a woman of grace. Show her respect or find your head in the gallows, Protector," Lunoka warned, her voice venomous and low. Her threatening tone had punctuated the man's title with a particular despisement of the term.

His grip loosened on Tali's arm, but a red blotching on her skin remained.

"Thank you, I'm coming," Tali said, but the woman scowled and exited.

The guard made Tali go in front of him, and she stepped out to a bright shining world. Her eyes adjusted to the sun; the power and warmth of it felt so close.

A squad of thirty men filed in around her, including three leaders distinguished by their gold robes. Each of the leaders wore a mask over their face. The mask was charcoal at the top, and the lower half was painted gold. Most of their blue skin was covered by cloth, paint, metal, or jewels.

The masked man at center stalked forward, with his long striped staff held proudly in front of him—the same man in gold who had captured her, the leader, Ashrata Nea'Ko.

"Luminary. You are to be judged by the elders," Nea'Ko said.

"Judged for what? I just want to go back to my friends," Tali said.

The gold man waved a soldier forward. "Take her inside."

With spears pointed at her in a circle, the soldier with a large axe at his hip pushed her forcefully in the back to start moving up the massive set of stairs. Tali took to the steps ploddingly. The stairway was flanked at the sides with giant boulders of granite. The granite was stark and chiseled.

The stairs led up to the promenade, with a darkened opening on the uppermost level. Tali searched for an escape, but all around was either more soldiers or some impossibly steep drop-off to the city below.

At the top, Tali paused to catch her breath and was shoved in the back again to continue. She turned to face her agitator but could only grind her teeth and keep going. Tali was marched into a grand hall of a Zenoch temple. It was a cold space with massive columns and tapestries draped at the sides. The windows at the outer halls were blocked by giant wood doors, and the hanging iron chandeliers somehow made the room darker. The glow of candles didn't reach the heights of the towering ceiling or the floor. From behind her the Zenoch entered, with Lunoka speaking at Nea'Ko's side.

"At the behest of the Spirit Elders, I sent the Harrinari leader back home weeks ago, Proxy Lunoka Trava'Ko. Now if you'll excuse me, I must attend to our guest," Nea'Ko said.

"You don't mean to make your judgment today, do you?" Lunoka asked.

"Of course. A Luminary has trespassed in my lands. This cannot wait," Nea'Ko said.

"You must wait. At least until the Spirit Elders have had a chance to determine her fate."

"I will determine her fate. As the Twilight Elder, I oversee the Zenon Valley. Now, I've agreed to this summit with the Harrinari, but I will not suffer the insurgence of spies or Source-touched witches crossing our borders."

"The Spirit Elders will not be happy," Lunoka said.

"The Spirit Elders know the order of power and the charge of my station."

Lunoka Trava'Ko stared at Tali a moment. There seemed to be a pain behind her eyes as she turned to leave the room.

"Are you leaving, Proxy Agent? You'll miss the sentencing. This will be a great day for our people. Her punishment will serve as a symbol for the might of our nation," Nea'Ko asked.

"Your own strength is all you care to showcase. As the hierarchy standing dictates, I concede to your wisdom, Twilight Elder, but I must bid you farewell."

Lunoka walked out, and Nea'Ko stared her down, his jaw set hard as steel. Tali wondered why the other leaders dressed in gold said nothing.

The fury on the leader's face was enough to frighten his subjects to obedience. Everyone in the room bowed their heads while he snaked through the hall to his throne. *There is no council of elders here,* Tali decided. *Only one tyrant and his disciples.*

Nea'Ko leaned over his knees, still holding the staff, and gazed at Tali through his mask. He lifted it free and placed it on the armrest of his throne. Then he spoke to her, though it sounded more like he was talking to himself.

"I long for the day when I am the lone High Elder left, and my wisdom is unchecked." He stood again and walked closer to her. "I wonder what the extents of your power might be. I have heard of you, you know? I have heard of the Luminary girl named Rue Dark-eyes from the Old World," Nea'Ko told her.

His admittance startled her, and she hesitated to answer him. "How do you know that name?" she asked.

"We are not as insulated from the outside as you might think."

From the dark corridors at the back, a small squad of Bonemen soldiers emerged, carrying their power-charged eruptor rifles and wearing white capes.

"Did you know that the Sagean has returned? He offered a proposal to my people for the capture and termination of any Luminaries. I confess I'm interested in your powers. Even though they are fragile and easily quieted. Still, I wonder, what were you capable of, girl, before the viper-eye silenced you?"

"Call me girl one more time and you'll find out," Tali said.

"Oh, you're harmless now." He rolled his fingers in rhythm on the metal of his staff and smiled. "I simply wish I could somehow claim what's inside this gem. Tell me this, Luminary, have you found the Aurora Altar? Is that why you were in the wilderness north of Erol? If not, why are you here?"

Tali stayed quiet, confused by the man in front of her. Nea'Ko was jealous of the very means of his subjugation. He despised all that had more power than him, including inanimate objects. Weighing how to answer such a man's questions, she simply said, "I don't know what you're talking about."

"Tell the truth—you are here to destroy my people!" Nea'Ko shouted.

"I just want to leave your lands and return to my people. They are fighting a war, that's where I need to be."

"Oh yes, the war. Like the Great War before it, only those who profit off the death and destruction shall see the other side a winner. I mean to profit."

A man like this can't be reasoned with, Tali thought, but maybe she could make him realize what he would lose. "If you allow the Sagean to win, you will see your power dwindle to nothing. I promise you, he will not stop with the Free Cities. Once he claims them, he will turn his sights on the Zenoch and conquer your land too."

"You are here to kill me and take my lands. I won't have it. I see it in your eyes. You are a killer. I must be the one to stop you, before you…"

"Would you please shut up," Tali blurted out. It was from either having spent so much time with Kovan or her own exhaustion, but she couldn't take the ranting of this lunatic anymore. "You obviously know what you are going to do to me. So, let's get on with it. Throw me in your prison, kill me, send me to the Sagean with a little bow wrapped around my neck, but I'm tired of your preaching, Goldie. You are utterly weak and powerless, and you know it, so you profess and boast about the qualities you truly lack and long for."

She hadn't meant to call him Goldie; the name had just popped in her mind, but it cut through the amusement on his face.

"Very well," he growled. "As an enemy to the Zenoch, you will serve your penance on the Rock and shine as a symbol of our strength against the demons of the Source." He motioned for his guards. "Take her to the Suffering Rock."

Three men hauled her out of the room, her sliding feet skipping on the joints in the stone floor, back out onto the upper pavilion, where the granite walls sloped hundreds of feet down the hill. The monolithic stone was stark and defiant. When they got closer, she could see a set of iron shackles anchored on the surface.

Nea'Ko tapped the granite with the yellow gemstone on his staff. "This Suffering Rock will give you time to contemplate how cooperative you want to be."

"You put too much faith in sticks and stones," she growled and tried to kick her captors, but received a blow to the head that knocked the light from her eyes.

UNSURE HOW MUCH TIME HAD PASSED, SHE AWOKE TO FIND HERSELF bound to the shackles and displayed for the city below. For the people's amusement and fascination. Tali rolled her aching head on the hard stone surface.

There was a radiant heat to the stone from baking all day in the sun, and the points where it touched her skin burned, but unsheltered on the face of the stone, the wind had no buffer and it wiped at her face endlessly. Her nose was running, and she tilted her head to wipe it on her shoulder. In doing so, she caught a glimpse of the steep drop to the ground below. She closed her eyes. Tali knew that soon the night would fall, and the cold would come on ten times over. She had no doubt that she would freeze to death.

Below her, Nea'Ko came strolling out. His gold cloth shimmering brightly, he removed his mask and looked up at her with a sorrowful expression.

"I really don't want to leave you up there until the morning. I don't believe you will live through the night. So, are you ready to speak truth yet, my dear?" he asked. A devilish smirk curled at the side of his mouth and betrayed his obvious excitement.

Tali had barely opened her eyes to look at him. The blow to her head throbbed like a knot of rope behind her neck, and drowsiness came in waves of nausea and blurred vision.

Overhead, the crack of thunder rattled the sky, and the gold man's smile widened. "If you survive the night, I will hand you over to the Sagean's men. If you confess now, I can show you mercy, and kill you swiftly. Your choice?"

Tali licked her lips and found she had very little saliva to do it. "With the wind out here, I can't really hear what you're saying, Goldie. I'm sure it was quite something," she said in her best impression of Kovan she could channel, and she smiled at the cruel man and said, "See you in the morning, Goldie."

Fourteen
Weary Travelers - Kovan

Sure enough, every morning Valdimar ate a bowl of oatmeal and washed it down with clear spirits. For most of the trip, the weather had been miserable, but Valdimar's constant jokes had made the grueling nature of riding across country easier for all of them. There was hail and sleet driving at their backs as they rode through the city of Elann. Kovan turned them up the skinny confines of Makers Street where it wound uphill, with small shops on either side stacking along the slope. He pulled them to a halt and dismounted outside the small confection shop. The steep incline of the street angled across the window storefront, ending sharply at the raspberry-colored door, with a thin sheet of ice was forming near the step. There was an assortment of sweets in the window, a tower of chocolates and candy, and the inviting smells like only Mimmie's shop had.

"'Mimmie's and Pippie's Confections,'" Valdimar read the sign aloud. "What are we stopping here for, Kovan? I didn't take you for a man with a sweet tooth," he asked.

"Well, you don't know everything, and everyone. This is Mimmie's shop. She makes the best candy in the world. Believe me this stuff is worth more than crystal, and more than gold."

Valdimar gave Learon a side glance, looking for help. "Lee-air-on, my friend. I'm only half sure, candy is what we're stopping for. What do you think?"

"It's pronounced Lear-in," Learon corrected him.

"Are you sure?" Valdimar said.

"Pretty sure."

"You both stay here. I won't be long," Kovan said.

"But it's cold, Kovan. My legs are numb, and I don't want to say out loud what else on me is frozen," Valdimar complained.

"Fine. Come inside, but don't touch anything and don't say anything."

Inside the shop, a young blonde woman stood behind the counter with a pleasant grin, filling out some sort of ledger.

"Is Mimmie in?" Kovan asked.

"I'm sorry no."

"Do you know when she'll be back? Or how about Pippie?" Kovan asked, looking to the back.

"I'm sorry, they retired two springs ago. I'm Mimmie's granddaughter, Diana," she said.

A small clatter from something hitting the floor interrupted them, and she tilted her head to look past Kovan to Valdimar and Learon. They were gawking at everything on the shelves. Valdimar was particularly interested in a violet teapot with flowers he was fiddling with.

"Can I help you guys?" Diana asked.

"I'm sorry I missed them. We've been on the road a few days. It's a pleasure to meet you. My name is Kovan. I used to come into the store and visit with your grandmother a long time ago," Kovan said, removing his hat. "Please tell me your grandmother handed down her recipe to you."

"Which one? Her candy recipe or Pippie's recipe for fudge?" she asked.

"For the hard candy," Kovan said.

"Absolutely." Diana beamed and pointed toward a glass cabinet of bowls full of multicolored shards of flavored candy. "Do you have a favorite flavor?"

"Yes—no—they're all my favorite," Kovan said.

Diana's face glowed with pride. She opened the cabinet from the back and began to fill a small bag. Valdimar, as if drawn to the smell, drifted over.

"So, what's your name?" Valdimar asked politely.

"Diana."

"Oh, a wonderful name for a wonderful person."

Absurdly, Diana smiled at him. She was apparently as nice as her grandmother, Kovan thought.

"Say," Valdimar continued, leaning over the counter, "such a wonderful person as you are, would you happen to have something hot to drink for three weary travelers?"

"Sure. I'll bring you three some hot chocolate. How's that sound?" Diana asked.

"That would be divine, you really are a wonderful spirit," Valdimar said.

Kovan gently pulled Valdimar back away from the counter before his friend could continue. "Honestly, thank you," Kovan said.

"You know my Mimmie, huh?" she asked.

"Yes, from long ago. It's good to hear they retired. I remember Pippie always telling Mimmie to stop giving away free samples," Kovan said.

After their hot chocolate, they returned to the cold. The rain had stopped, and the sun was finally breaking above.

"Worth the stop for the sunshine alone, huh?" Valdimar said.

"I promise you it will come in handy," Kovan replied, holding the multicolored bag of sweets up to the sparkling light, before securing it in his saddlebag.

"'Handy candy.' I like that. I mean who could resist?"

"Now where?" Learon asked.

"We enter the forest east of Wolf Lake," Valdimar said, rolling Moonlighters flower in a small paper to smoke.

"Elias said the hidden village was in the north reach of the Haildron Mountains. How did you find it?" Kovan asked.

"An old farmer, his hand, and two sons needed help tracking some missing horses beyond Wolf Lake. I had heard rumors of sightings of the Shadowyn in the area. It's always been a place where people disappear. I must have been feeling rather heroic at the time, so I agreed to help out. Anyway, we tracked them as far as the creek bed east of the lake, but we were forced to turn back," Valdimar said.

"Why?" Kovan asked.

"We were met with heavy rain, and the woods there are… I don't know how to explain it. They're eerie. A man can be easily turned around in them. Almost too easily. Once we crossed the stream, the hair on my arms stood on end like we were being watched. I don't mind admitting, I was happy to turn back. The group I was leading was anxious to leave, especially after one of them swore they saw a leopard."

"A leopard?" Learon asked.

"I guess. The rain was coming down in sheets, man, and we were having a hell of a time. The youngest of our group cried out that he spotted a leopard or a panther in the upper brush."

"I've heard the Harrinari keep lions. Could it have been one of those?" Kovan asked.

"Yeah, they do. I've seen those massive things. They have them in prides near their settlements. I suppose if the Harrinari have lions, maybe the Shadowyn have something similar, but I don't know. Before we turned back, I saw a curious hole in the woods where the trees were unnaturally arched. I investigated it and found some tracks. It looked to me like a path was beyond it that could lead deeper into the mountains. None of the men wanted to go in, and I've never went back."

"Take us there, Rooster," Kovan said.

"I will," Valdimar said, speaking through a sizable cloud of smoke puffing out of his mouth, "if I can remember the way."

Beyond the lake, they traveled for another two days. Valdimar guided them deeper into the mountains to the hidden trail head. Kovan was ready to try another way when the canvas of split trees came into view.

"Ta-da, the hidden road to the lands of the Shadowyn lies beyond," Valdimar said magnanimously, wiping the sweat from his brow.

"Thank you, Valdimar. We wouldn't have found this without you," Kovan said.

"I know."

They dismounted to investigate the area. With the forest creeping in, the overgrown path was barely distinguishable. The land around them had some of the first green grass Kovan had seen in months, but Kovan could understand what Valdimar meant about feeling like eyes were on them. There were so many tall trees, but yet a silence to the area like the wildlife was hiding.

"What do you think?" Kovan asked.

"I think I like the grass. Put your toes in the grass," Valdimar said.

Kovan turned to his old friend, confused, and saw he had taken his shoes off to walk in the grass. "You need to stop smoking that Moonlighters weed," Kovan commented.

"True," Valdimar admitted.

"Are you coming in with us or going back?" Kovan asked his old friend.

"In there? No, not me. You're both brave men. I'm not saying I'm scared to go in there, mind you. I do wrestle bears," Valdimar said.

"Excuse me?" Learon said.

"Oh yeah. A big honey bear, every night."

Kovan laughed and said, "You know one of these days, your wife is going to beat you silly, my friend."

"My woman has to keep me happy, 'cause I'm the only one who can put up with her."

"And?" Kovan prompted.

"And she's the only one that has ever put up with me," Valdimar admitted.

"That's right."

"What can I say? All the best relationships are forged through friction," Valdimar said.

"I'm going to stop you right there," Learon interrupted. "I don't want to hear anything about, the friction."

"A wise man, too," Valdimar said.

"You can go home now, Rooster." Kovan handed him some money and rations to make it back down the mountain, then helped him get back into the saddle.

"You know. I'm going to trade this horse back and use the money for an autocart back to Illumeen?"

"I know, Valdimar. Hey Roosty, you know you should probably—"

"Don't say it. I'm not going to stop drinking, not now. Not when I'm still in my prime."

"I know you are."

"I'm going to live this life to the fullest, my friend."

"I know. That's not what I was going to say. I wanted to tell you that if the war reaches Devon's tavern, you need to get out, head to the High Grove. Even if the Sagean takes the coast, his armies won't press into the highlands for a long time."

"You don't think we're going to win this time around, do you, old man?" Valdimar said.

"Not without Qudin. Not unless I can find who I'm looking for."

"Well then, I bid you good luck, brother. I love you."

They embraced in a hug and whispered a goodbye. Valdimar shook hands with Learon and turned back toward the way they had come, the sounds of a poorly hummed song drifting away as he went.

"I can't believe I'm going to say this, but I'm going to miss him," Learon said.

"Me too," Kovan said. At his advancing years, saying goodbye to old friends always made Kovan wonder if he would ever see them again.

"I was just getting used to him. He sure brings a lot of joy to life, doesn't he?"

"That he does, kid. It's easy to forget how import that part is. Now let's see where this path leads us."

FIFTEEN
YOUNG PROPHET - ELLARIA

THE TRAIN SPED THROUGH THE COUNTRYSIDE. THE FIELDS OF unprotected crops and free-roaming animals was a sight equally awe-inspiring for Ellaria as the great cityscapes full of statues and mono-lithic representations of human ingenuity.

There was a fear that the emperor's modified beasts would make their way to the New World one day, but it never materialized. There were no blue warding fires along the road, like in Tovillore, and trade flourished because of it.

Ellaria pulled her eyes from the passing view and left her room for the main cabin. The skinny corridor lurched with the landscape as she stepped out. In the walkway of the next train car, she discovered Echoryn shivering on the floor.

"Echoryn, what happened?" Ellaria asked, kneeling to comfort her. She looked frightened and weak.

"I…" she stuttered but went quiet.

"Here." Ellaria instinctively reached out to help her off the floor, but Echoryn convulsed at her touch and collapsed more tightly into herself, like a bear was attacking her.

"Don't touch me," she cried.

"It's all right, I'm not going to hurt you, no one is going to hurt you. But we should get you out of this hallway and into your room."

Echoryn looked up into Ellaria's eyes, then quickly scanned the hall and nodded her agreement. Ellaria backed away when it was obvious Echoryn was moving under her own power. She went a few paces ahead and opened her cabin door. Watching both directions for strangers, Ellaria waited in the hall until Echoryn entered, then followed.

Echoryn closed the drapes at the window before she sank into the bed. A soft red glow from the sun filtering through the cloth settled over the compartment. Ellaria sat on Stasia's adjacent bed.

"What happened?" Ellaria asked, but Echoryn didn't respond. Instead, she pressed her hands to her head and took slow and deep breaths. A subtle wince on Echoryn's face suggested there was actual pain underlying whatever had scared her.

Ellaria gave her a moment to calm herself. Looking over the cabin, she couldn't help but appraise the meticulous nature of Stasia's side. The neatly made bed, with sheets smooth and taut, and a small shelf of accompaniments, each object succinctly arranged and angled just so. A small smirk crested Ellaria's mouth. It was the opposite of Wade's compartment.

"If there was ever a simpler display of proof that love is blind, I don't know it. Look at Stasia's things—how she can fancy Wade is a mystery of the heart," she commented. It was a jest she hoped would change Echoryn's thoughts and allow her to drop her guard. Echoryn opened her eyes to glance at the space and gave a slight self-contained laugh.

Ellaria pressed again. "What's going on Echoryn? How can I help?"

"You can't, no one can," she answered softly.

"It's your abilities, right?"

"I can't stop the visions. Every time someone bumps into me or even if I'm just in the room with them for a long moment, images come. Flashes. Sometimes worse," Echoryn said.

"Worse, how?"

"Sometimes, when I see something strong enough, it's more like I am the person experiencing it."

"I'm not sure how to help you. I know very little about prophecy," Ellaria said. She stopped to think about the only prophet she had ever known, but for some reason she struggled to remember Mia. *No doubt a consequence of the betrayal Elias told me about.*

Ellaria shrugged off the fog and continued, "Maybe it was just so long ago that I've forgotten, but what I remember of the prophet Mia was that she had a sadness that Elias couldn't break through. I also remember she never talked about it. I think it made things worse for her. You should talk about it. Elias used to say it was an ability more closely connected to the Source than his own."

She looked confused. "The Source?"

"That was Elias's word for God."

"I don't know how to talk about it."

"Start with how it works," Ellaria suggested.

"It's complicated. The future is uncertain, but the pieces are in place. Like a game of stones. There are many ways the end plays out, but the pieces are in position from the start, and so there are some predictable outcomes. When I touch someone, or a piece on the board, I get a greater glimpse of the game. The stronger the piece, the greater the glimpse. What I see are the trajectories of energy. The choices and events are all connected like branches of a tree or a maze. Sometimes it feels like if I could just make out enough of it, I could solve the maze. Anyways, the reality is much more complicated, because unlike a game board, people don't stand alone. They're entwined with one another and with fate. Does that make sense?"

"No, not really, but I appreciate the attempt."

"Good. I don't want to explain it further, as it turns my stomach, like touching a wound and knowing pain awaits. It's unpleasant. There is a certain amount of, well, for lack of a better phrase, of spirit transference. I can see the person's memory as if it's my own, but it's not a memory of the past. It's of the future. It's like a memory in reverse."

"That sounds uncomfortable. What about someone like Learon?"

"What about Learon?" Echoryn said defensively.

"I know you two got close during his time in your province. Wasn't it difficult to be around him?"

"Well, yes. But there's more to it than just the dead calm of viewing someone's life. Like a memory, any vision elicited by a person comes edged with their personality. Cruelness, jealousy, admiration, it's all there. Because they're not my own feelings, I sense them with infringement. My visions with Learon are powerful, but he is uncommonly kind and passionate."

"Memories in reverse?" Ellaria commented.

"Correct."

It was a fascinating topic for Ellaria. There was little to no information about prophets. They had been known to exist, even before Elias discovered Mia. However, whatever books existed on the subject either were burned or remained in the possession of the Court of Dragons. Edward had revealed to her that a substantial collection existed on the island of Denmee. One of the few positives about her time as Edward's captive was how trusting he was of her. He was more and more forthcoming with her, until he found her messaging the others and grew irate and forced her to be part of the experiment. Echoryn's explanations did leave a few key questions unanswered.

"So, what awful thing did you see before I found you just now in the corridor?"

"I saw a thing of black mist and red eyes. It spoke to me in a room I couldn't make out, but it was almost like I wasn't there. Or, the person I was inhabiting, they weren't in the room. The mist was in their mind."

The Wrythen, Ellaria thought, and continued her questioning. "What did this black mist say?"

"It wasn't a mist, Ellaria. It was a being. It was terrible. It must have been the Old One. I don't recall what it said to me."

"Try," Ellaria urged.

"It's more than just a formless being, I remember that. At some point the presence became stronger than the person I was experiencing it through. Grotesque images of a man tortured inside a swirling mist flashed. Almost like the mist was a presence around a being at the center."

"Was this thing aware of your presence?"

"I don't know. I don't think so."

It sounded like Echoryn had a vision from both a person talking with the Wrythen and from the Wrythen itself. A scary thought she didn't want to share with the young woman. "Can you recall anything that was said?" Ellaria asked again.

"I, I don't…" Echoryn paused and grimaced as if in pain. "Yes. The Old One was thanking me for my service," Echoryn said with a shudder. "And I, I…"

The girl convulsed again, her skin drained of color, and she took heavy breaths. Prophecy was a visceral experience for the girl. Ellaria instinctually clutched the girl's hand with her own to calm her before remembering that she could unintentionally hurt her. When Echoryn did not react to the touch, Ellaria continued and spoke softly.

"It's all right, Echoryn. You can stop. Let it go. When you recall more, and with more ease, I would be very interested to learn of it. Until then, rest."

Ellaria didn't wish to stop, but she couldn't stomach watching the girl relive the experience.

"Thank you, Ellaria. I'm tired," Echoryn said weakly.

"That's fine. You're safe. I will leave you here to rest. Don't worry, I'm going to the dining car now. I'll let Stasia know you're in here. Rest and we'll talk again."

Ellaria got up and went for the door, then turned back, needing an answer to the most important question. "One last thing, dear. Who's the person? Whose future did you see?"

"I don't know, but I think it was Governor Atwood's," Echoryn said.

SIXTEEN

SHADOW LANDS - KOVAN

AN HOUR IN AND THE TRAIL WAS ALREADY SWALLOWED BY THE terrain. Bushes and rock shaped a thin path, just perceptible beneath the moss and leaves. It was nearly unfollowable, and at various points Kovan and Learon had to stop and debate the way. The often-disappearing path moved in an endless series of backtracks, turns, and diversions, but they progressed deeper into what was known as the Crescent Tip of the Sunveil Mountains and higher still.

Eventually, they found themselves beneath a sheer slope of granite. The mountain face cut in jagged steps from the peak to their feet, with harsh-shaped shadows at the base. Kovan gasped for breath, worn out from the trail.

"We can't possibly climb that." Learon exhaled. He held an arm at his side as though his lungs ached. Kovan could tell he was faking his level of exhaustion.

"Really, kid, none of this has tired you out?" Kovan asked with a nod to the pretense.

Learon stood tall and smirked. "Not really."

"Well don't pretend just for me. That's more infuriating."

"Sorry."

Kovan rolled his eyes. Sometimes Learon was too polite. He wished the kid would throw something back at him. He missed the verbal sparring he was used to with Elias. "Never mind, kid. No, we can't climb this. I can't climb it anyways, but there must be a way through."

"We could have missed a turnoff, or maybe…" Learon jumped to the ground and threw the reins to Kovan. He stepped closer to the rock face, where the cloak of shadows was cast down from the sun and disappeared. One moment Learon was walking slowly in the shadows, and the next he had passed beyond Kovan's sight. A slight panic of alarm made Kovan's hair stand on end.

"Learon?"

There was no answer. After a pause Kovan was about to call out louder when Learon appeared again. First as a shape in the darkness, then fully into the light.

"I found it. Why are you yelling?" Learon said.

"You disappeared, and I wasn't yelling."

"It sounded like you were."

"I said nothing louder than the level we're speaking now."

"Really. Well, the cavern back there somehow amplifies what's out here on the other side."

Kovan nodded his understanding. "So we go forward, but we go quietly."

They went over some simple hand gestures to use so they could communicate in silence. As they made their way in, they walked both of their horses through the shadow-concealed gap.

A steep switchback escalated up the mountain face of the slot canyon. The path was narrow and treacherous. Kovan signaled to slow down at points where the trail had washed away or crumbled to the width of the horse. The horses' sides scraped along the stone surface.

As soon as they reached the top, Kovan had an unsettled feeling in his gut that they were being watched. The terrain changed to a hilltop of thick trees, bushes, and rocks, plenty of places to watch from and never be seen. An hour later, the path ended at another ravine with a stone bridge leading to a bamboo grove. The bamboo trees created a dense forest, making it impossible to see what was within or beyond.

"I guess we cross the bridge," Learon said.

"I guess," Kovan said, looking all around for whoever protected the passageway. "Though, I'm unsure if we will even make it across."

"You think there's someone in there?"

"I have no doubts. The question is whether we'll have to talk our way in or fight our way in to be invited."

"Who invites a person into their land after fighting them?"

"People who value fighting, Learon. People like the Shadowyn."

They started to cross the bridge, wary of every step. The stone bridge had low walls on the sides and two sets of anchor columns on each end. The pedestal columns held sculptured stone leopards sitting atop like guardians. The suspended span of the bridge was achieved with a soft arch to the stone and connected to the hillsides almost as if organically grown over. On the far side, there was a small clearing with seven stone pillars of various heights. The path continued beyond in the form of a stone road overgrown with grass.

On the vacant road, an old woman materialized from the shadows. She carried a big basket full of berries slung over her shoulder. She used a tall wooden walking stick that went above her head, and walked slightly hunched over. She advanced toward them but turned and took another trail heading up the side hill.

"Hello," Kovan called out, but the woman didn't look back.

Kovan and Learon were three steps off the bridge when four warriors dressed in black appeared on top of the tallest pillars. The warriors' faces were covered, except their eyes, and their swords were drawn. On the road ahead, the old woman was gone.

"That's great. So, it's a fight," Kovan grumbled.

Learon stepped cautiously into the clearing. "We are friends of Q…"

His words were cut off when two of the warriors in black jumped to the ground and attacked. One of them crouched low and held their blade in an odd position behind their ear, while the other bounced on their feet and held their sword pointed backward and partially shielded by their body. The remaining two warriors sheathed their swords but remained crouched on the pillars above, watching.

Kovan loosened the gun at his hip but didn't draw it, choosing to rest his hand on the grip and observe. Learon, however, had drawn Elias's

Elum blade and took a defensive stance to counter the Shadowyn's attack. Kovan was ready to step in but found he was curious to see Learon fight, and realized that the two warriors not engaging were similarly as interested in Learon as they were their own fighters on the ground.

The sight of Learon's sword caused a moment of conflict and confusion between the Shadowyn attackers. Kovan noticed the spectating Shadowyn exchange a look of worry between them. Kovan took his hand off the handle of his pulsator. He recognized a test when one was before him, even if it was someone else being tried.

Learon and the two warriors clashed swords; Learon's speed was something to behold. He easily deflected every slash and kept both opponents in front of him. Kovan was sure after only a few movements that these two warriors were both still in training, but it was apparent early on that the skills of the two Shadowyn would not be enough to defeat Learon.

Learon countered every blow and had the patience to step back, breathe, and defend again. At one point, one of the warriors charged toward Learon. Learon swiftly grabbed the attacker by the wrist, blade and all, and pulled them past. In the exchange of momentum, Learon spun, disarmed the attacker, and threw the warrior off their feet through the air. The attacker landed on the ground with a cry. It was woman's voice. Learon stopped briefly, startled by the woman's voice, and the second attacker lunged.

"Learon, watch out!" Kovan yelled.

Learon moved just in time to avoid the attack. He rolled low and to the side, and when he stood, Learon held two swords. He had claimed the fallen Shadowyn's sword while he dodged. As Learon held both swords, Kovan could see the distinct difference in the blades now. While the Shadowyn attackers had similar swords in size and shape, the blades were not equal. They were not true Elum blades.

A third Shadowyn jumped down, and the fourth, and they surrounded Learon, leaving Kovan alone. On the road, Kovan saw a shadow change, and he reached into his satchel and flung a small bag overhead to the roadway.

Learon and the Shadowyn paused, and Kovan drew his gun. In quick succession, he blasted the tops of the four pillars where the

Shadowyn first appeared. The blasts echoed and boomed in the valley. The warriors slithered back and pointed their blades at Kovan, and the bag landed.

On the road the old woman appeared again. She reached for the bag of Mimmie's hard candy with a smile.

"We come in peace, if you let us," Kovan said loudly. "We carry the blade of Elias Qudin and request permission to enter your lands."

The old woman, whose face was brightened by the candy, now looked downcast. "For what purpose?" she asked.

"So that I might train with you," Learon said, his eyes bouncing between the four opponents before him.

"Why?" the old woman asked.

"I made a promise to Elias. I'm trying to keep that promise," Learon said.

The old woman approached, and the Shadowyn warriors sheathed their weapons and cleared a way for her. She had white hair pulled back and wrapped in a bun behind her head. She had a soft welcoming face full of wrinkles, but calculating blue eyes.

"Did he leave this world? Is he dead?" the old woman asked.

Learon started to respond, stopped, and finally said, "Yes."

"Why do you hesitate, you don't believe it?"

"No. I don't," Learon said.

"I see. I am Naomi. I'm the High Maven of the Shadowyn."

"I'm Kovan Rainer, and this is Learon," Kovan said.

"Come on then. I can't stand around here all day. The rain will be here soon, and I hate when my hair gets wet." Naomi turned to leave and held up the bag of candy. "I'm keeping this, by the way."

"I brought it for you. You're welcome," Kovan said.

The Shadowyn warriors waited for them to follow and then filed in behind them. Twenty paces onto the road, archers came out of the trees and joined their traveling party.

"Did you know the candy would work?" Learon asked.

"I remembered Elias once telling me a Shadowyn saying about strangers at your door. 'Thieves offer whispers. The devil offers opportunity, but friends bring you food,'" Kovan said.

"Were you going to watch them kill me?" Learon asked.

"You looked like you could handle it. Trust me, if they wanted us dead, they would have killed us in the slot canyon."

"You think so?"

"Yes."

As they talked Kovan noticed the woman Learon had disarmed walking behind them with her arms crossed and giving Learon a scolding look.

"I don't think she likes you, kid," Kovan said.

Learon turned to her and offered her, her own sword back. "Sorry, this is yours," he said, holding the sword hilt out to her.

Kovan viewed the exchange, and the woman's eyes narrowed and her scolding look became darker somehow.

"No," another warrior in black said definitively. "That is yours now. Ahjana will have to earn another."

The woman mumbled something under her breath that sounded like a curse.

"Way to go, slick. I think you made it worse," Kovan said.

"I think you're right. I'm terrible with women."

"All men are. Are you going to be all right here?" Kovan asked. Though Learon had seen much and been through a lot, he always projected such an ease about himself that Kovan worried about him.

They rounded a bend, and the sight of the most pristine and tranquil village Kovan had ever seen came into view. A sprawling settlement, like a small city, of scattered black wood houses in the meadow. The mountains to the north held multiple waterfalls, with the thinnest streams of water cascading slowly over rock and disappearing into the trees. Buildings shared the land with the trees, a winding stream, and a lake that unfolded in multiple parts. The road before them to the lake became a tunnel of branches, vines, and leaves, with small hanging lanterns on the sides. The entire area smelled like lavender and fresh leaves after a rainstorm.

"I think I'll survive," Learon said.

The old woman led them into the village to some small houses on stilts in the middle of the tranquil lake. She crisscrossed along the waterways to the highest perched hut and opened the door for them. Inside was a small space with a band of slotted windows. There were two alcoves, one with a bed surrounded by shelves with trinkets. The opposite side had a large desk with drawings and papers, all gathering dust.

Naomi shut the door after they had entered, leaving the guards behind.

"I have not entered this room for a long time. Even when Elias returned briefly about two years ago, he didn't stay in here. I thought one day my son would return for good. I was wrong," she said.

"Your son? I'm sorry we didn't know that. Elias never said," Kovan said.

"No, I don't suppose he would have. My son always liked his secrets. Even as a boy, he wasn't very forthcoming. Not that he was hiding something, just that he never wanted to burden others. From the day he found out he was a Luminary, he understood that his burden would be to stand against the empire. Your father had uncommon fortitude," she said.

Learon stared at the floor without looking up.

"You didn't know that Elias was your father?" Naomi asked.

Learon stood frozen and didn't respond. When he looked back at the old lady, his eyes were glossy.

"Or you didn't believe he was? He didn't tell you?" she asked again.

"He didn't. I think he tried. It's just…" Learon stammered.

"Unexpected?" Naomi said.

"Yes."

Kovan shuffled over to the young man and put his arm around him and changed the subject.

"Naomi? Elias, left me a letter telling me he left some object here that could help me find someone I'm looking for."

Naomi smiled and went and stepped up on the bed. "I know exactly what you're looking for. Something to give you direction," she said.

She reached above her head into the rafters with her walking stick and knocked down a small wood box. She walked back and handed it over to Kovan.

"It's a curious relic," Naomi said as she removed the lid.

Inside was a bronze compass that fit in Kovan's palm. There was no spinning needle like in a typical compass. Instead there was a top circular dial overlay on the crystal face and five gems inlaid on the outside ring. The crystal face was like colored glass with a geometric pattern. The outside dial was full of symbols and numbers that were indecipherable. To Kovan it more closely resembled an astronomical clock like the one that existed in Ravenvyre, which was rare.

"Protect that with your life. I trust that if Elias wanted you to have it, than he trusted you to protect it and keep it hidden."

Though the thing was light, the invaluable things in his possession were mounting up. Between this and the Tempest Stone, Kovan was now the caretaker to relics he didn't understand. "What do you know about it?" he asked her.

"It was the key to the empire's oppression," Naomi said.

Kovan didn't know what he did, but the compass lit up and soon symbols in the crystal glass bloomed and illuminated the dark room with a faint glow. Geometric patterns in the glass bounced around, and Kovan rotated the circle halo at the top. The gems on the outside filled with light. Kovan rotated the compass in his palm and watched the light roll to one side as if pulled in a direction.

"I guess it works," he said.

"You think it will help you find Tali?" Learon asked.

"I hope so," Kovan said.

Naomi observed the compass reading, her eyes narrowed. "You are to travel northeast and to the wastelands. When you're ready, I will take you through the master's garden, and you'll go through the valley of mist."

"I'm ready now," Kovan said, and a sudden disturbance landed at the windowsill. The mystcat scratched lightly on the glass.

"Well, there you are," Naomi said, opening the window. Merphi cried and softly rubbed on Naomi's leg before it climbed a bookshelf on the opposite side, where it sat staring out the high windows.

"I should have assumed Elias's cat would be following you, Learon," Naomi said.

"She's not. Merphi has been following me," Kovan said.

"Hmmm." Naomi sighed but offered nothing else.

"More than ready. My traveling companion is back," Kovan said and looked at Learon for assurance that he would be all right.

"It's all right, you should go. Go find her. Thank you for helping me get here," Learon said and handed the Elum blade back to Kovan. "Elias gave it to you, not me. Besides, I'm here to earn one of my own."

"Thank, you. We'll see each other again, and soon. In a month, you will find Ellaria and the others at the summit in Karnika. If you're done by then, find a way to join them," Kovan said.

"I will."

Naomi and Kovan left Learon in Elias's room, and she took him to another section of the village, through a simple garden with hedges and empty beds of weeds.

"The weather makes me fear that the flowers will never return," Naomi said.

"The bamboo grove was green and alive," Kovan observed.

"The grove of bamboo trees is always green. But the cold of winter has settled in."

"I must ask. When did you know Learon was your grandson? Before or after you stopped the fight?"

"After he drew Elias's Elum blade. I'd recognize Elias's sword in the dark. When I recognized the sword, my old eyes truly looked at the young man wielding it and saw my son's eyes and my father's chin. Old blood has the ability to show itself on the face of new generations like ghosts."

"He's special, you know, Learon."

"I could see it."

"He's half Tregorean. Though they call themselves Kihan, and he's something called a Nimbus Warrior."

"You seem to know him well, and you knew my son?"

"Yes. He was like a brother to me."

"Then tell me, why do you believe Elias asked him to come to us?"

"I think part of it was to make up for lost time. They had only just found each other. Maybe Elias wanted him to know something of his family."

"And why do you really think he wanted him to come here?"

"To prepare him for a great battle. A battle with a being much stronger than the Sagean."

"Is this the same entity that haunted Elias?"

"Yes."

"Then I will make sure he is prepared."

"Good. Learon is special, and he possess an uncommon amount of courage and kindness, but he lacks belief and confidence. I believe he has known for a while that Elias was his father, but back there he acted like that was the first time he had heard it."

"I will heed your advice," Naomi said.

"There is a summit between the Zenoch and the Harrinari people."

"We were told."

"But you're not going?"

"The Harrinari and the Zenoch know where we stand. There's no need to reappear. You should know that there will be bloodshed."

This caught his attention and he quit shifting his things to look the woman in her eyes. "How do you know?"

"The Harrinari never go to Radmana. It is a sacred place, but one cursed with blood. I was surprised the Zenoch agreed to the location. So surprised that I worry there is something else at play."

"I'll keep that in mind," he said. They reached a vast staircase of stone descending into the valley, and Kovan stopped. He reached into his pocket and pulled out the compass once again before leaving.

"At the bottom, my people will be waiting with your horse and some supplies for your journey. The wastelands of Karnika are very dangerous. Assume everything can kill you and you should be alright. There is a river ten days from here directly east. You must head there first. You are looking for someone special?"

"My daughter."

"Then take heed, you will find your daughter, Kovan. A parent's bond with their child is special. It's unlike anything. It's unique to nature."

"What if that bond hasn't been nurtured in many years?"

"Was it once before?"

"Yes."

"Then the bond still exists. Bonds of love leave a residue—a mark of energy only the spirit knows, and the spirit never forgets." Naomi leaned on her tall walking stick, overlooking the mist-filled valley below. "I can send some of my shadow with you, as far as the wastes edge. We are allowed to go to the border where the land starts to crumble and turn to rust, but no further," she offered.

"I appreciate it, but I don't need a caravan. One man is less a threat. A group of strangers makes people nervous."

"They'll follow anyway, so don't shoot them."

SEVENTEEN
TRAIN LINE - ELLARIA

ELLARIA CLOSED THE DOOR TO THE CABIN AND MADE HER WAY ALONG the tight confines of the train corridor. The swirling decorative walls and carpet were extravagant and almost made her forget the look on Echoryn's face as she recalled the Wrythen.

What little she was able to say was troubling, and Ellaria could only assume there was more. Her thoughts were swirling. *How was Atwood connected to the Wrythen?*

The door moved aside, and Ellaria entered the dining car. She spotted Wade and Stasia at the bar. They waved her over and she fell in beside them.

"Do you need a drink?" Wade asked.

She scanned the bar top for what their glasses held and admitted a drink would do her good. "Please, a wine."

Wade stood to flag down the bartender. "Red, white, pink, purple, what's your preference?" he asked Ellaria.

"A red if they have it," she answered and sank into her chair. A quick look around the room and she spotted Atwood straight away. He sat at a table with Vaughn, Shaw, and Ramell. The plan was for most of these governors to be leaving her company soon. Once they reached Syvonne, her half was going on to Adara, while the others would wait for trains to their own cities. Governor Zulhorn was there too, sitting at a table by himself.

Wade slid her a drink and sat back down before wiping his hands on his shirt afterward. "Sorry, I spilled a little when the bartender passed it to me." He lifted his glass for a toast. "To traveling fast."

While they drank and Stasia began to fiddle with Wade's collar, adjusting it at the back where it was folded oddly, Ellaria looked at the couple longingly. They were in love. She knew they had a deep friendship and one always on the edge of intimacy, but they had crossed over at some point in the last few months. Ellaria had seen it before, how the terrors and stress of wartime could drive people into each other's arms.

"I like this development," Ellaria commented and smiled.

Stasia blushed a little, but Wade looked at her oddly. "What development?" he said, confused.

"She means us, Wade." Stasia kissed his cheek.

"Not to break up a good evening, but—" Ellaria started to say, but was cut off by Wade.

"Oh, here it comes. What impossible feat are you going to ask of us? You want us to stop the war, assassinate the Sagean, improve the weather maybe."

"Wade," Stasia admonished him.

"Well, he's not wrong. We need to do those things. At least the first two. But I'm talking about something more immediate." She leaned closer. "We need to keep a close eye on Atwood."

It was Stasia's turn to look confused. "The spy?" she asked.

"I think so, yes."

"The Sagean and his devotees hold sway even here," Wade stated, a mixture of contempt and weariness to his words.

"From what Echoryn told me, he could be a spy for the Sagean or for something darker, or both. I don't know. I don't understand it all yet, but I mean to," Ellaria said.

The dining car was full of people, and Wade struck up a conversation with two brothers sitting at the other end of the bar. They were another group searching for the sword rumored to slay Dragons. Ellaria found them idiotic, but Wade was enthralled.

"Let me get this straight—you're going to the north to search the Concord Grove because there's a governmental conspiracy that a sword is hidden there?" Wade asked.

The older brother, who was shorter and led the conversation, scratched at his goatee and nodded emphatically. "Yes. It's a large valley, a basin really, shared between the New World and the Zenoch. The Zenoch would never forfeit land they controlled. Yet this spot was part of one of the first treaties established and is technically a No-Man's land. It's allegedly crawling with Darkhawks that patrol it. They're hiding something there."

"Who is they?" Wade asked.

"I think that King Danehin knows the land is sacred. Why else would the Darkhawks fortress be built so close?"

Ellaria had to chime in. "The treaty for the grove was bartered by the empire long before the Great War. The Zenoch didn't argue over the lands because to them their land ends at the Bowshan Mountain Range, and anything and anyone beyond it are their enemies. The treaty was a simple acknowledgement that the empire was going to build a road through there, and they didn't want to be attacked. The Darkhawk fortress came later during the war. The position was ideal to ship troops on a northern route that could cross the Anamic Ocean without the emperor knowing. The Darkhawks proving ground is further east, and there is no way the Desolation blade, the only sword that can kill Dragons, is buried in a meaningless valley."

"Really. It sounds like you should be leading your own expedition to find the Desolation blade," the older brother said.

"I'm sorry. I'm trying to help the king win a war. You kids have your fun though," Ellaria said.

"Won't you need the sword in case the Sagean turns the Dragons against the New World?" the younger brother asked. He was tall and handsome but with devious eyes, partially covered by a wide-brimmed hat.

"I hope it doesn't come to that," Ellaria said.

"Well, if you did have to look for the crystal blade, where would you look?" the younger of the two asked.

"I have no idea," Ellaria admitted.

"Sure, you do. We'll buy you a drink if you tell us your top three places to look. You're evidently a scholar of some sort."

"Two drinks," Ellaria bartered.

"Absolutely," the younger brother said.

"Deal," Ellaria said.

The younger brother clapped his hands together and grinned from ear to ear. "Buy her a drink, James," he said to his older brother.

"Happy to," the older brother named James said.

The bartender handed over another drink to Ellaria. She took a sip of the wine and placed it down. By this time, a small crowd had gathered to listen in, including Governors Shaw and Vaughn.

"I would start with what we know," Ellaria began. "Mostly what we know are myths and legends. Supposedly, the sword was forged by Caleb Reaver from the bones of Dragons. There's a chicken and the egg problem already, but let's move on. Nevertheless, most scholars believe Caleb was a real warrior who lived two-hundred years before the Luminary Wars. If that's so, he would have probably been a king in the land of Telatheor, an ancient land that most believe is present-day Tovillore. However, there are other known people to have wielded the sword. Both were woman—Quinn Starfire and Avari Nova. Starfire was supposedly a Tregorean warrior a hundred years before the Luminary Wars, and Avari Nova, who we know significantly more about, was the queen of Ravenvyre during the Luminary Wars. She was the last person to have had it, and the legend goes that she hid it away because it was too powerful for mortals. Some say she cast it into the Brovic and cursed the Brovic forever. Having lived in Ravenvyre as a kid, I know that there are many tunnels beneath that city too. The biggest question is, Was it hidden, or, like most valuable objects, was it simply buried with the person or was it handed down as an heirloom and lost?"

"What do you think? And what about the stories that the Harrinari have it?" James asked.

"There is some evidence that the lands of Karnika are much older than we realize and that some of the ancient cities could have existed there, but scholars have never been able to study the area. Also, it's said an Oakol king held the sword at some point. Who knows? I think if I had to pick three locations, I would look in Ravenvyre. The second place I would look would be Lowtalla and the south of Rodaire. There was a small skirmish about thirteen years ago there over the heir to the Ravenvyre throne. It's possible some thread of its whereabouts could be learned there. The third place I would look would be Azan Island in the Zulu Sea. The kings of old were said to meet on an island centrally located between each province. We don't know what island that was, but scholars think it was Azan Island. There are ruins of a castle there and more ruins in the sea that have never been explored."

"So, nowhere in the Free Cities, the High Grove, or Karnika?" the younger brother asked, his grin fading.

"Oh, who knows, maybe the Zenoch have it. My best guess is that it was probably lost in the Brovic. Point is, it's a fool's errand," she said.

"Maybe we should go east then, Bro?" the younger brother said.

"Oh, what does she know? Callen, she obviously works for the king. They probably already have the sword," James said.

Ellaria rolled her eyes and turned her attention back to her wine. The crowd dispersed, and Wade leaned over to her. "Maybe we should be looking for the sword."

"Oh Wade," Stasia said, hitting him on the shoulder.

"I'm just saying. It couldn't hurt to have it. I bet the emperor is looking for it. Who knows, maybe it's the thing we need to kill the Wrythen."

Ellaria swirled her wine and added another burden to her growing pile.

Wade and Stasia eventually called it a night and retired back to Ellaria's room. She had offered it up to them for the night so they wouldn't disturb Echoryn.

Soon after they departed the dining car, the two governors came over to sit with her. She was listening to the rhythms of the train and the punctuations of metal sliding by, almost too intently to notice their arrival.

"Miss Moonstone, can we sit with you?" Shaw asked.

She looked the man in the eyes, careful not to glare, but her face was not friendly. She made them wait for an answer before eventually relinquishing. "Sure," she said flatly.

Shaw and Vaughn brought their own drinks with them and took the two chairs opposite her.

Vaughn leaned into her ear before taking his seat. "At the station I received a letter from General Marr, asking if you can come with me to Bowma and meet with our head engineer, Pryor, before going on to meet Marr and Danehin in Adara?"

Ellaria nodded, and Vaughn, having relayed the request, sat down. It was an odd request that would add at least a day to their journey, maybe two.

"I suppose I can. Why?" she said.

"I'm not sure. Pryor will fill you in."

"Was there anything else?" she asked.

"I had a question for you, General," Shaw said.

Calling her general was a first, for him or any of the governors. "Go on," she said.

"I'm curious why you had Princess Dalliana move forces to Falenmor."

Ellaria was reluctant to admit if she had and decided to tread lightly, as she always did with these politicians. "You don't see a need for forces in the south?" she asked.

"Not unless we are at war with the unknown inhabitants of Manashera."

"Well, Mr. Shaw, I don't like the unknown. Those comfortable with the unknown might as well start pushing daisies through the dirt."

"I just hope we don't need those extra forces in Illumeen. It would be a shame to ruin such a glorious reputation with a blunder. But I'm sure you've thought of that."

"It wasn't on my orders, but it's wise to protect our flanks," she said.

Behind her at the end table, an argument broke out between Atwood and Ramell. The shouting stopped almost as soon as it started, and Ellaria never caught the reason. She looked to Vaughn and Shaw, who appeared equally stunned by the outburst. Shaw's eyes narrowed, and he spun back to the bar top.

Vaughn, who'd stood at the commotion, stared intently but didn't approach them. The two men finished their drinks in silence before parting.

"Have a good night, Miss Moonstone. I'll see you on the platform in the morning in Syvonne." Vaughn grabbed his black hat and tipped it to her. "Shaw," Vaughn said, and he left.

Shaw stared at Ellaria a moment, and she thought he was ready to start in on her again, but whatever was on his mind, he thought better of it. He grinned and stood.

"Miss Moonstone, I apologize. As you can understand, I'm concerned for my people."

"That's understandable, Mr. Shaw, but the war is here. There were men fighting and dying tonight on the coast as we sat here drinking. If we want to defeat the enemy, we need uncommon fortitude, but we also need to work together."

"Agreed," he said and bid her a goodnight.

After Shaw left, Ellaria stayed a minute to finish her last drink. She wanted to make sure that when her head hit the pillow, she would be out until the train arrived at the station. She tipped the bartender and left the dining car. As she reached for the sliding door, the train pitched, and a slight dizziness hit her. *Maybe, one drink too many,* she thought.

Ellaria stopped and placed her hands on the wall to steady her balance along the corridor. Outside the glass the scenery slipped by at a deceiving speed. The land from Kerrio to Syvonne was mostly rolling hills. In the distance a small town was lit up in the night, moonlight bathing a stone bell tower and a series of farms after that. The scenery began to blur in her vision.

The train's rhythm, once steady and unnoticeable, trembled at her feet. Ellaria grasped for the side panel to still her nerves. The landscape beyond the glass became too blurry to focus on. She felt her eyes rolling back as she tried to concentrate on it. A sudden sense of nausea hit her stomach, and she fell to one knee, her legs giving out. Her eyelids sagged uncontrollably, and panic wrenched at her insides. Something was very wrong. If someone was trying to kill her, they may have succeeded without a fight.

With the last bit of resolve she could muster, Ellaria pulled herself along the corridor, fumbling at every door she came to. The fear of being found helpless in the open spurred her on. Finally, a handle turned, and she stumbled through the opening into an empty room. She managed to shut the door and slump against it. In the empty cabin she was startled by the sound of her own heavy breathing.

With her ear to the floor, she heard footsteps coming down the hall, closing in. Ellaria tried to reach up and lock the door, but the handle moved, and she fell into a pair of feet.

"Ellaria. Oh my God. Ellaria, get up," the voice urged.

Ellaria blinked up at the person who was trying to get her to her feet. There was a long moment of bumping into things, and Ellaria found herself in a bed. Plopped onto it like a sack of flour, she found she couldn't speak or see. The rumble of the train was now a shifting wave, and she was rolling away with it.

"Drink this," the voice said.

The feel of a trickle of cold liquid running down her lip was the last thing she noted before succumbing to a deep rest that her body ached for.

EIGHTEEN
WILDERNESS - TALI

WITH THE NIGHT CAME THE BITTER COLD, AND IT SEEPED IN UNTIL her bones felt like hollow tubes full of ice. The first part of the night had been the worst. The temperature change felt almost instant once the sun set, and the frozen air pressed in. At first, Tali gazed at the lights of the sprawling city at her feet to pass the time, but there was no comfort in them. Chained on the rock and freezing, the loneliness of her misery was hers to cherish in perpetuity. As the night wore on, her exhaustion found new depths and the feeling of her extremities grew numb.

Tali tried to watch the guards and track their movements to keep herself occupied, but she could hardly see much of the temple. Eventually, the city lights blurred, and over time they dwindled away until most of the city only held a soft glow, like that of a single candle in a valley of blackness. Even the lanterns of the temple died out, and with each one, she wanted to sleep so badly.

Tali didn't notice when he arrived, or how long he'd been there. She couldn't even feel the rope around her that he had placed to make sure she didn't plummet to the ground when he released her from the chains. She couldn't say how long she had been asleep, but when the warmth of Tyzo's hands touched her wrist, she winced from the sharp pain. His touch felt like a scalpel. She tried to cry out, but nothing escaped her lips. As he freed the shackle, her hand fell.

Her arms were so numb that she wasn't sure it hadn't fallen off her body to the ground below, until she saw it draped over Tyzo's shoulder.

Her eyes opened to make sure what was happening was real.

"Shhhh," he said. "We got you."

She must have been moaning, because she didn't remember saying anything. Somehow, she found herself on the ground and Tyzo was wrapping her with a blanket.

He lifted her off her feet and over his shoulder.

"We?" she asked.

"Is she alive?" Lunoka whispered.

Tali blinked to see the Zenoch woman, a blade in her hands. It glimmered with the moonlight, and blood dripped at the edge.

"Yes," Tyzo replied.

"We need to hurry," Lunoka said.

Tyzo carried Tali down the steps, over a sidewall, and into the forest surrounding the temple. He carried her a long way over the uneven ground, avoiding the patches of snow. Tali was only semiconscious for most of it. They stopped beneath a particularly twisted pine tree, and Tyzo placed Tali on the ground. He stayed there, bent over, holding his knees and gasping for breath. Tali sat up as best she could and held tightly to the blanket, shivering uncontrollably. There was a loud tapping in the forest, but she eventually realized it was her own teeth chattering. Tali put her hand to her mouth to stop it.

Lunoka was busy working on something on the ground. A small warm mist wafted up around Lunoka and she brought something over to Tali. It was a scarf, but steam was rising from it, and Lunoka proceeded to wrap it around Tali.

It was heavy, but the warmth was everything to Tali at that moment. She felt herself sag from a new wave of exhaustion. When she opened her eyes, Lunoka was handing her a waterskin to drink from.

"There are hot stones inside the scarf. This should keep you warm most of the night," Lunoka told her, and she stood scanning the darkness. "Tyzo, once she can walk, take her north to the lake as planned."

"What are you going to do?"

"I'm going to watch your back and make sure you're not followed. I need to return to my room before they suspect my involvement. Maybe I can ruin their search somehow. And Nea'Ko will search. If for no other reason than his own pride."

"And when we get to the lake?"

"From there Mianora will take her to Darkanna."

"Thank you," Tali mumbled as Lunoka dashed away.

THEY MADE THEIR WAY TO THE LAKE, WITH TYZO SUPPORTING HER most of the way. The trees thickened, and the ground became harder with more boulders until they crested a small rise. The vast winding shore of the lake stretched out before them like black glass. The night had become overcast, and the moonlight shrouded as they progressed. They reached a small cove and waited. Tyzo lit an old metal lantern and placed it on a large rock at the water's edge. Shielding all the sides but one, he projected the light into the lake. Periodically, he would make the light disappear and reappear, signaling for someone on the lake. When the light illuminated the rocky point of the cove, the lake waters beyond seemed to stretch on like a small ocean.

Tali said nothing. *What is there to say?* she thought. She wasn't quite sure she was rescued, and now she was saving her energy to strangle Mia once she saw her.

Tyzo tinkered with his lantern for ten minutes before they saw a light moving on the lake. In a rush Tyzo extinguished his lantern and walked back to Tali's side. He pulled a bow from his back and crouched down to whisper. "I think that's Mia on the boat," he said, looking all around them and back through the woods from where they came.

"I don't trust her," Tali said.

Slowly Tyzo walked a few steps away from her. She wasn't sure he had heard her until he whispered back, "She said you'd say that."

"Well, she got us captured in Erol. It was obvious she was working with Ashrata Nea'Ko. She gave me up."

"True," he answered, but continued to stalk around, looking for anyone pursuing them. The attention he was paying to what Tali was saying was beginning to frustrate her. She stood up with a scolding look that was betrayed by the darkness.

Tyzo registered her expression and walked back toward the lake. "Here she comes," he said in passing.

The four-oar yawl arrived, with Mia at the helm. Mia removed her hood and tossed a thick rope out for Tyzo to catch. Rope in hand, he pulled the squatty wood boat to ground, listless waves splashing at the sides, and he waved to Tali to get in.

"I'm not getting in that boat with her," Tali protested.

"Yes, you are. Even if I must knock you out," Tyzo said with a slight growl to his voice.

"Tali, you can't go back. You can only go forward," Mia said.

"Wise words won't excuse the fact that you let them capture me."

"Correct."

"Why?"

"Come with me and I'll explain."

"Get in," Tyzo said, he had his bow drawn and an arrow nocked. His eyes were wide and gazing into the dark canopy of trees. All three of them froze at the sounds of movement in the distance. At the crack of a branch breaking, the three of them turned to the sound.

"Get in the boat, get in now," Tyzo urged her under his breath.

Tali clutched her blanket and scarf and scrambled aboard. Tyzo, pushed off the shore but angled them along the bluff bank.

He handed the oars back to Mia. "Keep us close until we're past that mound," he said, pointing.

Taking up his bow again, he studied the tree line. Tali watched for movement but saw nothing. When they passed the headland of partially submerged boulders, Mia took them from the mouth of the cove into the middle of the lake, and Tyzo took up the other set of oars and began rowing them out. Lanterns emerged at the spot they had taken off from, but they were far enough into the lake now not to be seen. On the open water of the lake, the wind whipped up again. Tali covered her head with the blanket. She was starting to think she would never be warm again. The cold felt like it had soaked into her, intensified by the dread that had consumed her since being captured. With only her eyes peeking out from the cover, she gazed at the shoreline as it slowly faded to a silhouette of trees and hills, and they escaped under the clouded night. Tali tried to keep her eyes open to watch Mia, but she couldn't. The last sight she recalled was a strange glow in the sky, and it was calling to her.

Shadowyn Lands
Archway to The Five Peaks
Valley of Mist
Bamboo Grove
Thousand Steps
West Trails Bridge
The Maven's Quarters
Tera of The Masters
Warriors Village
Thunder Canyon
Sparring Sands
Training Grounds
Shadowyn City

NINETEEN

LESSONS - LEARON

"EVERYONE HERE HAS DEVOTED THEMSELVES TO THE BLADE. IT HAS been this way for many lifetimes. Did you come here believing you could learn it so quickly? I don't know if I am impressed by your arrogance, which by the way matches your father's, or if I'm insulted," Naomi said, her wooden sword pointing at his eyes.

"I want to learn," Learon said earnestly.

"Then attack me. I will not suffer fools. If one suffers the presence of fools, the prudence of self collapses," Naomi said.

She held her wood sword at the ready and waved Learon toward her. Learon tried a combination of moves but couldn't hit her. It was his fifth day of sparring with her. So far, all his lessons had been with her alone. Even though he was aware that there was a larger school full of students training day and night, she had not allowed him to intermingle with the village yet. They got up before dawn every day and meditated in the chill of the morning. This was followed by a training session that focused on details like grip strength and proper footwork. After lunch there was another meditation during the Blue period, followed by a sparring session, dinner, and a night meditation.

At first, he tried to take it easy on her. She was his grandmother, and she had to be almost eighty, but he paid a heavy price for that mistake. She beat him over the head with her walking stick with blows across his face that cut into his cheeks. He realized quickly she was a dangerous old lady, and swift as the wind in short microbursts. A life

209

of training, athletics, and exercise had kept her young. There was no frailty to her; in fact her presence suggested a strength that matched the steel of her gaze.

"By the look in your eyes, I assume you have faced mortal combat more than once. Understand, our way is as much a style as it is a code by which our warriors live and fight. The blade is the heart of our culture. Have purpose, be exact, swift, and always be sharp," she said.

He attacked, and she blocked.

She ambled to the side and flicked a branch on the ground into his face and slapped him with the tip of her wood sword. He wiped the dirt from his eyes, and still she kept talking. She always talked while they sparred.

"It requires the deepest commitment, from the most serious mind, and a passion for perfection. Not all our people are warriors, but often men are the slowest to train. Women have a much deeper understanding of their own abilities and tend to master the sword much faster," she said, grabbing her walking stick.

He attacked and spun the sword and slashed again, but the old woman sidestepped and blocked with ease. She held the short sword in her right hand and her walking stick in her left. She blocked and attacked with both but would lean on the stick in between.

"Do not be confused by the spins or the twelve sword forms and teachings. Battle has many forms, but survival is always paramount."

He went to rush in again. She thrust her stick out to stop him. She sat down on the bench nearby, visibly tired. He sat next to her, and they both looked out over the village from the small courtyard.

"You can get someone else to train me, Naomi," he said.

"I think I will have to. My old bones are failing me."

"I can't land a blow. You're not so old."

"You could if you wanted to. The fact is, I am old, but that's the way of things, my son," she said and winced. "I'm sorry. Do you mind if I call you that?"

"I already told you I don't mind."

"I think it's time you joined the others. But you will still come here for meditation."

"Of course," Learon said.

"You must learn how to intercept an attack and respond in force.

You also must learn yourself. The key to knowing the sword is knowing your own body. There is value in knowing your own speed, strength, and flexibility, as I have demonstrated. Like all great artisans, the craft of the sword is learned through arduous training. Skills are handed down from a master to an apprentice, but the most important lessons are learned through experience. Now, run off to the central training field. Speak to Cawdean. He knows why you are here, and he will get you inside."

"Thank you, Naomi."

"If you want to thank me, don't hurt anyone."

Learon left Naomi and followed the winding path to a large structure at the center of the village. It took him a few tries to find Cawdean, and he received more than a few odd glances while he wandered around, looking lost.

"You're Maven Naomi's special project, right?" Cawdean asked.

"My name's Learon. Yes, Naomi sent me."

"Come with me."

Cawdean showed him through to the changing rooms, around the weapons room, and to the hand-to-hand fighting arena before taking him to the training yard.

"Go find a spot, and I'll let Gadren and Osiah know who you are."

Learon walked out to the field, and within moments, all eyes were on him. He stopped at an open patch of matted golden grass and picked up a training sword. Learon tried to block out the onlookers and began to practice his sword forms on a wood dummy.

"Get back to work," one of the blade masters yelled.

Learon assumed it must be Osiah because everyone resumed what they were doing, but they continued to eye Learon as if he might become a bird and fly away. Naomi had told Learon of Osiah. He was the best swordsman in the village.

"You're the new novice, right?" a young man asked, walking up to him. He was about Learon's height, but he was slender and had an impish grin.

"I guess so. My name is Learon."

"My name is Jaden. What's the deal, are you from the Ordona?

You don't look like your Harrinari, or are you a warrior from the steam-world?"

"The steam-world?"

"Yeah, the Westlanders. Your cities are full of steam and machines."

"I guess I'm one of those, yes."

"Wow. We don't get many Westlanders here. Matter of fact, we never get any."

A group of students passing by waved and smiled at Jaden, and Learon got the sense he was popular. The sight of Learon had them whispering and casting sidelong glances. When a group of young women walked past, Jaden called out to one of them.

"Ahjana, did you see we have new blood?"

The woman stopped in her tracks and eyed Learon. He recognized the name from their first meeting. The grip on her practice sword tightened, and Learon bowed slightly. She raised her sword as if she was going to hit him, but lowered it and gritted her teeth. He was trying to be polite, but again it appeared he had insulted her. It seemed everything he did with this woman was wrong.

"Oh, do you know each other?" Jaden asked with a slight laugh.

"No," Ahjana said in what amounted to a growl. She had thick brown hair tied off in twin tails and tied back together again at the back. Without her face covering, it was the first time Learon had seen her. She had angular features to her face, punctuated by small pursed lips and hawk-like eyes. Learon thought she would be pretty if she wasn't always scowling a death look at him. She stomped away before he could speak to her, and he wondered if she was given her sword back.

"She doesn't like you much, does she?" Jaden said.

"I sort of disarmed her in combat," Learon said.

"You did. Well, that would explain it. They really scold you around here if you drop your weapon. It's one of the essential teachings no matter which way of the sword you pursue. It's a fundamental to all of them. If you are born in the village you are trained to hold a sword by age four, and you learn quickly not to let it go."

"Is she any good?" Learon asked.

"Ahjana is one of the steel-bound, apprentices in their last year.

She's very good and very fast. If you defeated her…" Jaden whistled but got distracted. At one end of the training ground, a group of men were making a ruckus and boasting about something. Something about the guys had upset Jaden, and Learon observed Ahjana walking away from them.

Jaden turned back and continued, "Anyways, if you bested Ahjana, then you're no novice. You're probably ready to go for the sword, too."

"And who are they?" Learon asked.

Most of the guys looked like typical tough guys, with more bravado than brains, the kind that would run from a real battle. Among them was the biggest guy in the entire yard. The man looked like molded stone and clay. He stood firmly on his feet and appeared unshakable, like the territh could move beneath him and he would hold his ground. His strength was obvious, but Learon wondered if the man possessed the swiftness of the Shadowyn masters yet. As Learon observed him, the young man began to spin and brandish his wood sword with flourish and speed. It was overtly fast, like he knew Learon was spectating.

"Oh, that's Aleph. He'll be going for the sword any day now."

He was obviously a dangerous man, and Learon had no interest in fighting these people. He only wanted to learn what he could and leave.

When the training session was over, Learon and Jaden stood outside the yard, talking. As other students walked by Jaden, more and more they began to mutter "rusty" as they passed. A few even bumped into Jaden as they said it. Though they never said a word to Learon, he guessed it was a punishment for Jaden for having talked with Learon. Once all the trainees had cleared out, they started to walk together into the north section of the village.

"Rusty?" Learon asked.

"It means soft, or ruined," Jaden replied.

"I'm sorry," Learon said.

"Don't worry about it. They're just threatened by you. My guess is Ahjana told them about you, and they're worried you will take their shine. They don't want you to get any help from me."

"I'm just here to train and then I'll leave."

"But you'll want to earn the sword, right? Most of the students here have been training their whole lives to earn one. The idea of an outsider getting a sword before they do is enough to set the entire school into madness."

Learon wondered if Ahjana was mad that he had bested her with an Elum blade, but now he appeared to be training next to her for one. He could understand her confusion, and it probably added to her resentment of him. Learon would have offered her an explanation if she asked him about it, but she never did.

The next two days went the same. Learon would stick close to Jaden during training and was excused from sparring. All the while receiving dirty looks from the steel-bound group readying themselves for the sword. As the training session ended on his tenth day in the village, Learon realized he didn't know what going for the sword meant.

"Jaden, how do you earn the Elum blade?" Learon asked as they walked out of the training yard.

"By completing the Trials."

"The Trials? What Trials?"

"The Five…" A series of bells rang out that Learon had yet to hear in the village, and Jaden stopped what he was saying.

"What's that?" Learon asked.

"We have to go to the Square. Come on," Jaden said, tugging at Learon's sleeve.

Jaden jogged through the streets to a sector of the territory that Learon hadn't been before. Nearly everyone was making their way to the same spot. All the trainees were rushing there, and even civilians from the village in the lower valley.

"Are we being attacked?" Learon asked.

"No, it's a contest in the sandbox. Follow me and just hope you don't get chosen to participate."

THE ENTIRE VILLAGE SEEMED TO BE MIGRATING TO AN AREA IN THE forest east of the main buildings. The crowd of villagers and fighters alike entered a small clearing and climbed a gentle hill of grass. At the top, people crowded in at the edge of a rectangular space and sat along the ledge of a stone retaining wall around the perimeter.

Learon reached the edge of the space to see a large arena full of white sand below. The sandbox was sunken ten feet into the ground. There were about thirty four-foot-wide grey stones arrayed around the box, resting in the sand. At the east end, a tall stacked-stone wall rose twenty feet above the adjacent perimeter wall. The tall wall had random stone shelves and an array of lit lanterns fixed to the surface.

Learon thought that if he had stumbled upon the serene pool of shimmering white sand on his own, he would have thought it was a meditation space. The excitement of the crowd told him different.

The sand was pristine, with a sweeping pattern of combed lines swirling throughout. The large flat stones were spaced equally inside the space and most of them had a wooden sword lying on them.

The crowd came to a hush as the Shadowyn Guard entered the clearing with the High Maven following them. Learon tried to smile at his grandmother, but she didn't look up. The guards carried long wooden poles and fanned out around the outside of the arena.

One of the guards came near Learon, a big man with a scarred face. He glared right at Learon and reached the pole up and to his side, pointing it at Jaden's chest.

"Cursed-steel," Jaden murmured under his breath. The guard handed the pole to Jaden and moved away.

Jaden turned toward the sandbox. "Wish me luck, or that the Blue shines on me, depending on what sort of thing you believe in," he said and used the pole to lower himself down to one of the large stones. He placed the pole in a sleeve on the retaining wall and picked up a wooden sword off the stone by his feet.

In all, nine trainees were selected—Aleph being one of them— but the crowd showed the most excitement when Gadren, the blade master and one of the trainers, lowered himself into the sandbox. Unlike Osiah, Gadren had made a point to stay away from Learon, so he didn't know much about him except that Jaden disliked him.

Everyone inside the box stood on a stone. Jaden and two other kids were told to move to the center stones. They did so by jumping from stone to stone and readied themselves for the contest to begin. A low rumble of drums around the area began to pound, and everyone but the combatants sat down. Learon followed and sat down on the ledge with his feet over the edge. A loud mechanical crash shook the grounds, and Learon looked around for the source, but no one else seemed to care. Three musicians with wooden flutes appeared at the west end of the sandbox and blew a short session of notes. When the flute music concluded, drums beat to a flurry and stopped. The contest had begun.

TWENTY

SANDBOX - LEARON

As soon as the drumming ceased, Aleph leapt to the center stones and immediately attacked two trainees. Both looked unfamiliar with being inside the fighting square and hesitated, while Jaden immediately jumped to a new stone. With three swift strikes, Aleph had knocked the first student off their stone and into the white sand.

Instead of him landing on the sand and limping away, as Learon expected, the sand swallowed him. The kid screamed as his head disappeared, his arms flailing until they were out of sight. The sand funneled for a moment, then ceased, and all that remained was a rounded depression where the kid had fallen in.

Learon stood up on the ledge, the shock of what happened nearly spurring him to jump into the square. Looking around at the hollering crowd, he could see that they seemed unfazed.

"Is that kid dead?" Learon asked a young woman clapping her hand against the wall with the other onlookers. She ignored his question and continued to spectate; her eyes fixated on the contest. Learon turned his attention back to the fight, but he refused to sit.

On one of the stones, a younger-looking girl seemed afraid to move, but her stone began to sink, and she was forced to jump. She landed awkwardly on the same stone Jaden occupied. He pushed her aside with a brush of his hand, and she too drowned in the sand.

Jaden then used some of the ledge stones on the high east wall to escape an attacker. Scaling the wall took time, but it allowed Jaden a

217

retreat to the far side of the sandbox. From the wall, Jaden dove to a vacant stone in the corner farthest from Learon. Jaden's forehead was dripping with sweat, and he had yet to clash swords with anyone.

Learon sensed there was more than pride and bragging rights resting on the outcome. Whatever the stakes were for this contest, those inside fought with complete determination, equal to anyone Learon had seen in battle before.

Elsewhere in the box, Gadren, the trainer, leapt after Aleph. In three bounding jumps, he had met Aleph at the center. By then, Aleph had successfully dispatched the second student on the middle stones. The middle stones appeared to remain stationary, no matter how long someone stood on them.

To Learon's surprise Gadren did not attack Aleph. Instead, they simply pointed their weapons at each other and nodded an understanding. With ferocity they each turned separate directions and attacked the remaining students. Gadren faced a tall man on sinking stones, and he crouched low, with his sword oddly positioned behind his ear. The attacking stance was the same one used by one of the opponents Learon had fought upon his arrival. Gadren won his fight and moved on.

Every battle Aleph fought ended with his opponent sucked beneath the land. One ended when the blow from Aleph's sword caused blood to splatter on the white sand. The wounded stepped off the stone in forfeit and Aleph moved on. Learon decided it was some rule of the contest that he wasn't aware of.

While the swords were only wood, the blow from a properly placed strike caused a lot of damage. A blow to the head would easily kill a man, and Aleph slashed with a dangerous amount of strength.

As the combat wore on, Learon started to see the inevitability of the two fearsome warriors making their way to Jaden. While it looked like the cornerstones didn't sink either, he was still trapped.

Aleph pointed his sword at Jaden and hollered, "Rusty." He then stalked back across the middle stones and jumped two stones in rapid succession, and attacked Jaden with a war cry as he landed.

Learon's own heart pounded in his chest as he saw Jaden fail to defend himself. It took only four moves for Aleph to disarm Jaden, then Aleph took his sword in both hands and crushed the pommel into Jaden's nose. The impact knocked Jaden back, and he looked ready to fall, but Aleph stood him up. Aleph's eyes were full of fury and malevolence as he began to punish Jaden. Shouting erupted from the bloodthirsty crowd when they realized Aleph was refusing to let Jaden fall. Blood covered Jaden's face, but none of it had hit the sand yet, and the crowd cheered every time a drop missed the sand.

Jaden's legs seemed to buckle, but Aleph again leaned Jaden against the wall to keep him up. Aleph slammed the back of Jaden's head against the stone wall, and Learon leapt into the sandbox.

A hush came over the crowd at first. Learon dropped onto a stone before the center stones. It sank slightly with his abrupt landing, but before it dipped below the surface of the sand, Learon had stepped free of it.

Gadren turned to see Learon, and a wicked grin came over his face. Learon had entered the arena without a weapon. Quickly, Learon grabbed a pole off the wall. The spectators around the edge erupted and everyone stood. Gadren got in Learon's path and made a move to strike. Learon blocked the attack and drove the staff into Gadren's chest like a spear. Learon lifted Gadren off his feet and slammed him into the sand.

Running at full speed, Learon claimed Gadren's fallen sword and made his way to Aleph. As Learon zeroed in, Aleph paused his attack, his chest heaving from the exertion of battle.

Learon didn't waste time contemplating how to attack. With his pulse racing, his abilities took over, and everything slowed. Learon lowered his sword into the sand and flicked a spray of it into Aleph's eyes. Learon ran along the vertical surface of the east wall, spun, and drove his sword into Aleph. The attack took Aleph off his feet and into the white sand. Learon landed on the corner stone, staring at the spot of sand Aleph had disappeared into. Learon reached for Jaden before Jaden could slip into the pool of sand and steadied him to lean on the wall.

The crowd had become silent, but the blood in Learon's ears pounded. The sound of gears in the ground was followed by a loud mechanical bang. Naomi and twenty guards were entering the square from the west end where a portion of the wall had receded into a set of stairs. They walked across the sand freely toward Learon. Above, the audience was being told to leave and reluctantly departed back to the village. Naomi and Osiah both looked quizzically at Learon. Neither appeared angry.

"Didn't I ask you not to hurt anyone?" Naomi said. Learon nodded and she turned to Osiah. "I thought we would have more time with him."

"You said he was struggling, Master," Osiah said.

"Possessing the skill for the Five Peaks and surviving them are two different things, Osiah."

"True."

"Will you train him until it's time?"

"Yes."

Naomi led Learon out of the sandbox and back toward the village. Halfway there, she guided him on another route through the northern hills, and through the bamboo forest on a subtle trail of beaten territh, with a hypnotic sound whistling through the grove. As the bamboo shifted and swayed with the wind, it produced a constant sound like light rain falling all around.

"Why did they do that to Jaden?" Learon asked.

"To lure you into the sands, of course. I'm sure they hoped you would get expelled for the infraction."

"That makes me even more angry, and Gadren's supposed to be a master?"

"Gadren is no master, just an instructor. He was very embarrassed for losing to you at the bridge. More so than Ahjana. He was demoted and has carried a grudge since. Don't be too harsh on them. The idea of an outsider angers them. Not to mention you are a significant threat to any man who thinks they're the best. I doubt they'll be the last men to challenge you."

"What are you talking about? I don't see how I'm intimidating to anyone. I don't care about any of that. I just want to learn what I can and get back to help my friends."

"Your path is much different from theirs. Mostly because young men are idiots, but they think you're a threat to their goals. Don't dwell on it any longer," Naomi said.

"Are we going back to the village?" Learon asked.

"In time. I wanted to let the village settle down before you were seen again. What you did this evening will be talked about for a long time. I want to show you something, and then you can go to dinner."

Among the bamboo trees, they entered an area that felt sacred, with jagged stones arranged on the ground. Naomi showed him to a shrine with a tall sculpture of a hooded man. The clay-colored stone form was simplistic and depicted a man sitting on his knees, a sword crossed over his lap. He held a feather in one hand. The age of the statue was obvious in its discoloration and the deterioration at various points. The tip of the sword had broken off long ago, but an inscription in the base was still legible and read *Galladeer Kerion.*

Learon knew the name as one of the myths of the ancient world, talked about with the likes of Caleb Reaver or Avari Nova.

"What do you know about Kerion?"

"Not much," Learon admitted.

"He was the leader of the Shadowyn and the reason we take refuge in this place. He was also a Nimbus Warrior. The tales of his abilities have been long known to our people. That is why I asked you not to hurt anyone. You are a being of war, Learon. A warrior of the Trinity Guard is rare. You are what the Fates call Source-born, bonded and bound to the fate of the world."

"You forgot harbinger of death," Learon said, quoting from one of the texts he remembered.

"You're also called the Warriors of the Last Battle, Riders of the Last Dawn, and those that stand against the night."

"And this world can't find peace without death and destruction?" Learon asked.

"I'm not sure who can find peace at all. Sometimes war doesn't end after the last battle is fought. They can last much longer than the people fighting them. New people, with new laws and new ideas, fight new wars and don't even realize it's the same war. There's an eternal conflict of ghosts and shadows, and you're a part of that. What I'm saying, Learon, is maybe this feeling you have, the thing holding you back, is not because you don't believe you're meant to fight this war but because you already have and you're simply reluctant to fight it once again. With your path obscured, only you know how to find your way through the storm."

"But what if I don't know the way?"

"You know they way, because the way knows you."

"What if no one follows?"

"The Trinity Guard is the flame in the darkness. In the darkest times, where there is light, people will follow. And as the Nimbus Warrior, you are the protector of the light."

Learon rested his hand on the stone figure and glanced back at his grandmother, but she placed a finger to her lips for him to be quiet and said, "No more questions for tonight. Go to dinner, and when you are ready, I will tell you the story of Kerion, the blue feather, and the Five Peaks."

Inside the dining hall, Learon lingered near the cook's station, unable to find a place to sit until he noticed Jaden waving him over. He had stitches under his left eye, and his face was a deep purple from his nose through both eye sockets.

"Are you all right?" Learon said, sitting down on the bench.

"Thanks to you," Jaden said.

"I owe you an apology, Jaden. It may have been a trap to get me into the sandbox. You were the bait."

"Well, I've never been anyone's bait before." He touched his jaw as he ate, and winced. "Not as great an experience as I would have thought."

The dining room was loud and packed with students. Learon watched the disorder with apprehension that his presence had gone unnoticed.

Jaden caught Learon scanning the room. "This place is a chaotic mess, pun intended. Especially after a sparring session like that. It's easier to find a spot if you sparred in the sand. The fighters usually have to go to the medic first like I did to get stitched up," he commented. "Somehow you don't have a scratch."

Learon looked at his own food and wasn't hungry. He struggled to shrug off feeling like he didn't belong here; or worse, he was wasting his time.

"Well done." A random guy slapped Learon on the back. He

wasn't the only one. More and more people were congratulating him as they identified him among them.

"I can't believe you jumped in. What's your punishment?" Jaden asked.

"Nothing," Learon said.

"Maybe they forgave you because you don't know the rules, but no one on the upper wall is permitted to jump in like that."

"I'm sorry, but…"

"Don't apologize to me. I'm grateful. I was about to get killed. Aleph is an animal. Seriously, I think he's part bear. Or… what are those giant wolves in your country? Wolveracks?"

"Yeah."

"I think he's one of those."

"You're crazy, Wynvaloren," another person said, passing by.

"Wynvaloren?" Learon asked Jaden.

"Hey, if you don't like it, you better nip it in the bud right now. Nicknames have a funny way of sticking."

"What's it mean?"

"Oh. Right. It means fearless wind-walker. Which is pretty wicked if you ask me. But I don't know. It's also a lot of pressure to live up to."

"I'm not interested in nicknames," Learon said. He didn't want to explain that he had enough already. "I'm not planning on staying here long. What I need is to know how I earn the Elum blade."

Jaden shook his head, and a man who never stopped talking was rendered silent by a simple question.

"What did I say?" Learon asked.

"Look, you're new, so I suppose you don't know, but that's not something we talk about at dinner."

"You were talking about it before the contest."

"Right, but I never outright said I needed the blade. We never look at the blades as a reward or an achievement."

"Oh."

"Of course, I'm messing with you. We all do, but you shouldn't talk about it in the dining room. Plus, only the best of the best makes it through and are even allowed to test themselves on the peaks to get one. Which includes you, but not me, obviously."

"The peaks," another kid said, sitting down next to them with his friend. They were both bigger than Jaden but not as tall. The second one was scarred on his left cheek. "What are you talking about the Five Peaks for, Jaden? You'll never survive them."

"Oh, I know that," Jaden answered with his mouth full. "Learon, this is Terrin and Brand, they're both High Grove–born."

Learon lifted his fork to acknowledge their introductions.

"That was crazy by the way, Wynvalon," Terrin said.

"Thanks, I think," Learon said.

"Anyway, Terrin, I'm no dummy. I know my skills lie elsewhere. My goal is to just be given a chance and make it through the first peak. I have no aspirations for the sword."

"What are the Five Peaks?" Learon asked.

"The Five Peaks, the Trials. Man, you don't know anything. How did you even find this place?" Jaden asked.

"I would ask why they even let you in, but we saw what you could do," Terrin said.

"A blade master brought me," Learon said, trying to provide an explanation that was satisfactory, without having to divulge any more detail about himself then he had to.

"Well, they did you no favors. The Five Peaks are five sacred peaks east of our lands. They're more like spires of territh, like the ground around them disappeared. The tallest ones rise above the clouds, but all of them live in this mist," Jaden explained.

"You've seen them, Jaden?" Terrin asked.

"Sure. You guys have only been here a year, but eventually the older students will dare you to go out there and come back. There's like fifty of them, the peaks."

"Like pillars?" Learon asked.

"Yeah," Jaden said.

"What's so special about them?" Learon asked.

"I don't know for certain; the masters don't talk about them. Everyone's Trial is their own, they say. But I think they must be magical," Jaden said.

"Of course they're full of magic. Mist like that doesn't just happen," Terrin said. "And from what I've heard, no one makes it past the third peak."

"Well, that can't be true. Don't you have to get to the fourth peak to get your Elum blade?" Jaden said.

"Yes, but there are fewer and fewer sword masters," Terrin said.

"Wait, if you get the sword on the fourth peak, what's on the fifth one?" Learon asked.

"Nobody knows the answer to that. Each peak is supposed to be a test. A test of strength, of will, of your soul—they say," Jaden said.

"There's a myth that only four students have ever made it to the top of the fifth peak. That Kerion the Great made them that way. And the fifth person to reach the fifth summit will be gifted with treasure and magical abilities," Terrin said.

"You can't believe every rumor, Terrin. There's been way more than four to make it, but there hasn't been one in a long time," Jaden said.

"What about High Maven Naomi? What rumors do you know about her?" Learon asked.

"Rumors are she was the last one to reach the fifth peak, and that she is a descendant of the Fates themselves. They also say her best student was Qudin Lightweaver."

"Qudin Lightweaver was never here," Terrin said.

"He was. Osiah told me himself that Qudin was the best swordsman he ever faced," Jaden said.

"If that's true, then Qudin definitely made it to the fifth peak," Terrin said.

The Hyperion Compass

TWENTY-ONE
INTO THE WASTES - KOVAN

IN THE EIGHT DAYS SINCE LEAVING LEARON WITH THE SHADOWYN, Kovan had crossed out of the north reaches of the High Grove and east into the wastes, emerging from the valley of mist into a desert of heat and wind. The Harrinari Territory was brutal land—hard arid desert soil and endless hills of cactus and bristle bushes. There were tabletop plains and tiered buttes as far as Kovan could see. At night he was forced to sleep against one of the wind-carved shelves of land to shield himself from the elements. He checked the compass multiple times during the day and closed his eyes to the glowing signal at night, with the vast blanket of stars overhead.

Most nights ended the same. He would settle in as comfortably as a man could get on hard dirt and weeds, examine the compass, come to terms with his regrets, and think about what he was going to say when he found his daughter. Eventually, his eyes grew too heavy to keep open.

Kovan hated to put his trust in a device, but he had faith in Elias and hope that the compass would take him to his daughter. Whether he was going the right way or the wrong way, it didn't matter now. Alone in the desolate land, he felt like he was teetering on the termination line, where the light turns to darkness. One way or the other, he was determined to find his way.

Kovan had every reason to believe that something was waiting to be discovered by him. The compass was leading him somewhere, and

Kovan was willing to bet his life that it was taking him to someone special. *Why else would Elias have left me such a curious thing?* he thought. He rubbed his thumb over the engraved ruins on the dial, worried he had made a mistake in keeping his quest from Ellaria. *But how could she ever understand if her memory of truth was lost?*

The darkness of the wasteland was alive with noises, calls from animals that went unseen in the day, and the feeling of many sets of eyes watching him. Kovan was too tired to care.

At first, he thought he would travel at night; but by the second night, he had twisted his ankle walking alongside the horse under the diminished light of a crescent moon. The ground was full of small fissures the size of a person's foot and deep enough to cripple his horse if unseen. Instead, he slept once the light was gone and was up once the brightening began. It wasn't good sleep, not with the noises, not with the wind, and a few times he thought he heard someone or something moving positions around him, but cursory investigations turned up nothing.

In the morning on the ninth day, he packed his things and checked his water supply. The Shadowyn High Maven seemed to know more about his path than she was willing to say, and more about the compass. *At least they gave me enough water for twelve days.* Kovan had hoped to stretch it to twenty, but he was going to be lucky to get another three out of what he had left.

Even in a saddle, he just couldn't keep up the pace he expected of himself. The combination of the wind, the terrain, and his old back made traveling slow. A pain had taken claim of his lower back just above his waist, and each step felt like a needle sliding in and out. His old and failing nerves sent pain down his legs if he rode for too long, and his knees felt brittle if he was on his feet for too long.

"Torquing devil," Kovan cursed as he measured out the rations of water: one for the horse, one for himself, and one for the mystcat. The mystcat Merphi walked by his side when he was walking. When he rode, the cat liked to run alongside the horse, often disappearing and returning to him at night to rest on his chest.

With the light of the dawn breaking, he started out again toward it. Naomi had assured him that a small river lay ten days to the east but warned of the dangers of the area. He assumed she had meant the Harrinari, but he now believed she meant the harshness of the land.

He could remember a trip out to this land once when he was younger as part of the Darkhawks squad, and he knew some of these plants were edible and some were poisonous, but he couldn't recall which was which. There was no wildlife to hunt or to clue him in on what was safe to eat. He had to focus on making it to the river. A desperation in him was like embers of fire awaiting air—soon it would ignite and consume him.

When the morning wind died away, the sun haze baked into the land and blurred the horizon in every direction. When he was alone and when time stretched, his thoughts fell more in-line with the version of himself who had awoken without his memory and lived a month as a new man. Reconciling the two versions was a constant clash within. In the solitude of traveling, Kovan's mind wandered, and he found himself thinking about time and decay. *Time is a thief, stealing all you cherish until there's nothing, nothing but dust and wind*, he recited. With each passing day, Kovan was starting to think he was doing time a favor. Soon he would be among the dust he was kicking up at his heels.

By midday on his eleventh day, the land began to show signs of human intrusion. The edges of a road, though worn and rambling, began to take shape, but the light of the Blue sun threw colors across the territh that looked supernatural. When Kovan reached the road, he pulled out the compass, unsure if he should follow the road or cross over it and continue traveling east. His dry and cracked hands twisted the outside dial, and the glowing symbols illuminated in the center. The top circles spun, and the lights moved until they settled on a single symbol. The arrow now pointed northeast. He peered up to the road again and was startled by the sounds of another person approaching.

Kovan quickly concealed the compass and drew his gun but kept the muzzle pointed down. *Where did the stranger come from?*

It was a man dressed in a garment that flowed in the wind at some points and was buckled tight at others. He wore goggles and an old hat. Kovan couldn't see any weapon, but what looked like a musical instrument was tied to the man's horse.

"Greetings, wayward traveler," the man said, his gravelly voice in sync with the arid landscape.

"Hello," Kovan said cautiously, his own voice equally ragged from disuse and dust.

A faint smile came on the man's face. "It's great to see you, my friend."

"Do I know you?" Kovan said.

The man removed his goggles and blinked, but even if he did seem familiar, Kovan didn't recognize him.

"Any soul out here wandering the wastes is a friend of mine," the man said.

"I'm looking for a small river, maybe a day's ride from here. Do you know it?" Kovan asked.

"The Magesto River," the stranger said.

"I'm sorry, no. I'm looking for the Reshanu River."

"Yes. Well, many things change over time, names more often than anything else."

"Can you point the way?" Kovan asked. Not that he trusted the man, but upon a quick scan of the baggage on the stranger's horse, there didn't appear to be any more than a single skin of water.

"I can. We will travel the road. It's not far."

"Lead the way," Kovan said.

The stranger repositioned his goggles and continued north. Kovan eyed him a moment before holstering his gun. The man was old, but Kovan couldn't say how old. Sometimes the man's face held a thousand age lines, and then they were gone just as quickly. The stranger stood upright with his chin up, and Kovan surmised that the man must be in good shape to be out there alone, but he also looked brittle in the baggy clothes. A small part of Kovan's mind wondered if this stranger had been following him. *Was he responsible for the noises I heard in the darkness?*

By the evening, the road had veered deeper into the wastes, and the mountains Kovan came from were no longer visible. But the river was there, running in a splintering of small streams, some no wider than a step.

The old man took a long piece of fabric from his neck and

submerged it in the stream. Kovan bent down to the nearest one, ran his hands in the water, and tasted it.

Expecting a rancidness, he was elated to find it was fresh and cold. Tasting slightly of minerals, it was sweet and refreshing. This land was harsh, sour, and inhospitable, and he was happy to find the water wasn't the same. He refilled his canteens and tried to wash away the dirt caked on his face.

"Thank you," Kovan said to the stranger, the cold cleansing of the water over his face sending a wave of relief from his cheeks down his spine. Kovan began to unpack, but the stranger waved him off.

"What?"

"We cannot rest here long, and we can't sleep here," the stranger said.

"Why?"

"The zinobats come out to the rivers at night, and Harrinari hunt the water's edge. Better to meet a Harrinari in the day than night while on their land, my friend," the man explained.

Kovan nodded his understanding. A meeting would come eventually, he thought nervously, cracking his old knuckles on his right hand.

They camped near some large boulders after inspecting them for snakes. Each man wrapped cloth around his face and his jacket tight over himself as the wind came into the valley, hurtling overtop the boulders at their back and whistling through the underbrush. Kovan placed his pack against the rock and settled down onto the ground.

"What's your name, old-timer?" Kovan asked.

"You can call me Oz," the man said.

"All right, Oz. Where exactly were you traveling from, and where are you going?" Kovan asked.

"I came from the south, and I'm heading north. And you?" Oz asked.

"You can call me Kovan."

"So, what are you doing out in the wastes, Kovan?"

"I'm looking for someone."

"This someone, are they with the Harrinari?"

"That's what I'm here to find out."

There was a long silence that Kovan broke with a question. "Do you play that instrument?"

"I can play it, but no, I'm not a musician."

"Seems like an awfully bulky thing to lug through this land if it's not part of your livelihood."

"I didn't say it wasn't, but it is not mine. It belongs to an old acquaintance of mine. One day when our paths cross again, I'll return it to him."

Kovan thought of Elias's Elum blade on the horse's saddle and understood the sentiment.

With night upon them, for the first time, Kovan could see a soft glow in the distance. One that suggested a civilization—or the Harri-nari's version—a town or possibly larger. The wind continued, and in its passing, Kovan could almost swear he could hear whispers.

He blinked and concentrated, but while he was sure he could hear many voices, he couldn't listen to any single tone nor understand them. "Do you hear that?" Kovan asked the stranger.

"Of course. It's the whisperers of the wastes."

"What is it?"

"Some say it's the sounds of another world breaking through to ours."

"Another world?"

"We'll there's the world we can see, and there are many we can't."

Oh great, he had inadvertently found himself another Elias. "Let me guess, our eyes are limited?" Kovan said, recalling something Elias was fond of saying.

"Everything about us is limited. Our greatest strength is our creativity, the ability to invent tools to help us compensate for our own limitations. There are many worlds beyond our perception we simply haven't built the tools to see yet. Sometimes nature provides the tools to see. This valley and the wind that swirls around are one such tool."

"Do you know what they are saying?" Kovan asked.

"That is a better question, but my only answer is it's best not to worry."

This time Kovan heard it, uttered perfectly and low as though in his ear,

Follow the path of stars, unite the Trinity.

Kovan pulled his coat tighter with his left hand and gripped his gun to rest the metal on his chest to sleep, with the mystcat curled up near his head.

KOVAN COULDN'T REMEMBER FALLING ASLEEP, BUT HE DREAMED ALL night of phantoms moving around him in the wind. They conversed with him or about him, but he couldn't see them. In the morning, he awoke from a nightmare that washed away from his mind with the light of the day. He opened his eyes to find the old man staring at him. Startled, Kovan scrambled to sit up and fixed the barrel of his gun on Oz. The man smirked and reset his goggles to shade against the morning light.

"The ghosts of yesterday haunt you, my friend."

Kovan picked himself up and dusted himself off before answering, "In my experience, burdens are carried and not found. Everything I bring with me comes from yesterday. Are you free of such things?"

"No. They haunt me too, but yesterday was so long ago that I've had the pleasure to forget most of it."

After Kovan checked his supplies and fed the horse and Elias's mystcat, they set out again, but this time to the north. The valley was ominous from the start, but they continued anyway. The land always looked deserted in all directions, but tracks on the ground suggested things moving around just out of eyesight. At one point Kovan spotted horse tracks that looked fresh but no horses, or he found animal tracks but no animals. Kovan couldn't help constantly checking over his shoulder.

In the afternoon when the wind kicked up, their pace slowed.

Neither man was very talkative. It was the stranger who heard the threat first. His hand flashed out flat and to the side, telling Kovan to pause.

Kovan stopped and knew enough not to ask why. He scanned the hillside and quickly looked for the nearest cover.

"How many?" Kovan whispered.

"Not sure. Three riders I think, based on the tracks we've already seen."

"Doubled back?"

The man nodded and whispered, "Wait until you see their colors. Yellow and blue and we may not have to fight. If they wear green, they're Eenod tribe and have followed us here. If they wear purple, they're Meer tribe, and if that's the case, be prepared to die."

"I'm always prepared to die," Kovan said, priming his gun to power.

"Well, then pull out that electric-charged gun of yours and start blasting. Maybe you'll surprise me."

Without any cover, they moved back-to-back, and the man produced a weapon Kovan didn't know he had. With a flick of his wrist, a double-bladed knife somehow unfolded from a metal handle. *At least he won't be a liability if a fight starts*, Kovan thought.

Three riders crested the hill, wearing black. They passed by without incident and galloped west with speed.

"Who were they?" Kovan said, watching them go.

"Lor tribe. They rarely leave the eastern valley. I think that was a tidings ternary. They are carrying messages back to their homeland, in triplicate. Hopefully it means Alasne is succeeding in uniting the tribes."

They rested a few hours before traveling again at dusk. The stranger was not altogether peculiar, apart from his presence in general. What he was doing on the road was an oddity Kovan himself couldn't account for yet. Both men were traveling north, but it had gone unspoken where either man was heading. Since the stranger seemed to accept Kovan's mysterious presence here in Karnika, Kovan thought it only fair to allow the man a modicum of mystery, too.

When the night came, they made camp again. In the north, the hazy glow of the city they hoped to reach the next day loomed like a magnet, drawing both men closer.

A flash on the furthest hills to the west pierced the landscape, like a torch being lit and burning away. Whatever it was, the light was extinguished as quickly as it had appeared and wasn't seen again.

"A friend of yours?" Oz asked.

"No, I'm traveling alone," Kovan answered, perplexed. It was in the direction of where they had come from. He wondered if Learon had followed him, but he didn't believe the kid had any quit in him. There was no way he had left the training. If it was any other friend, they would have caught up to him by now. Someone else was following Kovan and keeping their distance.

Watching the land for another sign of life, Kovan finally gave it up and settled onto the ground. "We seem to be traveling to the same place?" he asked the strange old man.

"To the Oakol. Have you traveled to the Oakol before?" Oz asked.

"No. You?"

"Yes. I travel up and down the valley often."

"Where's home then?"

"My home is on Triden."

"Triden?" Kovan said, surprised. The man was a very long way from home. "There's nearly nothing there but mountains and rock and jungle."

"I like watching the ocean and the solitude."

"The Jade Sea is something," Kovan agreed, "and I guess I see the appeal of staring out over the Brovic, spending your days wondering what lies beyond."

"I know what lies within the Brovic."

Kovan tilted his head at Oz's reply. "What?"

"The end of the world, my friend."

Kovan stayed awake, staring at a blanket of stars unlike he had ever seen. The wind through the valley pushed any semblance of clouds away, and the stars were as clear as ever. Even if he wanted to look away, he couldn't, the mystcat had returned as she always did and slept on Kovan's chest. When Kovan was sure that Oz was asleep, he checked the compass. The light still held a strong signal in the direction they were going. He had found that he could get multiple signals to appear by touching the different gems around the dial. Each time, a new configuration of light appeared in the glass, and the direction arrow would rotate to a new alignment. In a panic he had shuffled through until he found the same configuration he'd first used, and he hadn't touched the dials again.

Somewhere in the distance, a rustling on the land interrupted the night. Kovan quickly closed and pocketed the compass and stood up to look around. He waited on his feet for his eyes to adjust to the darker depths of the landscape and spot the disturbance or a light, but nothing stirred. Eventually, he lay back down. The mystcat cried in annoyance as it rested on top of him again, and together they listened to the voices in the wind until they fell asleep.

A friend is hunting you.

In the morning they set out on the road. The rising sun filled the valley with a sparkling light. It reflected off the land and specks of metals and crystals in the dirt. The heat of the sun slowly vanquished the bitter cold that had settled into the ground overnight. Kovan had spent almost two weeks in the wastes and become accustomed to the ever-changing land, even growing to like it. The sights and sounds of the Karnika wastes seemed dishonest, but there was an order to it, a secret way that made Kovan comfortable.

They traveled for most of the day on horseback, until both men felt the need to walk. Surprised they had not yet reached the city he' seen in the night, Kovan was staring off into nothing, when he stumbled over a stone emblem in the ground. Partially obscured by the blowing dirt and identical in color, it was easy to overlook. In fact, staring at it, he thought it might vanish if he looked away. He would never have seen it if he hadn't tripped on it. The hardened clay had a series of lines etched on it in a picture that reminded Kovan of a constellation.

"Not much further now," Oz said.

They walked another five paces when the dust started to gather in front of them and lift from the ground like smoke. As though the sky was sucking up the surrounding land, dirt from their feet pulled toward a wall forming in front of them.

Kovan stepped back, his mouth gaping. "What's this now?"

A stricken look crossed the stranger's face. "A warding. That shouldn't be here."

The wall of red-and-brown clay began to solidify into a shape. Soon the edges folded over, cutting the silhouette of shoulders and a head. A face lifted higher, like a sleeping giant awakening from the land, a guardian of the wastes.

Kovan cursed and drew his weapon, almost laughing to himself that he had no idea how to fight such a monster.

The giant of dirt rushed toward them. They were blown off their feet and blinded by dust pelting their faces. The larger chunks whipped fast enough to cut tiny gouges into his skin.

Together, they crawled back beyond the clay plaque embedded in the ground that had obviously triggered the sand giant. When they reached the open ground, the charge of the giant halted and stared at them, its empty eyes hungry.

Kovan felt along the ground blindly, wiping the dust from his ears and his face. He hid his face in the crook of his arm to shield his eyes a moment. A soft cry from the mystcat startled him as Merphi purred up to him.

"Where have you been?" he asked the cat.

Her once white fur held a gentle coating of brown and red. She purred against his head with a wet nose, and then she pranced over to the seal. The eyes of the giant shifted to the new threat. When the cat crossed the unseen barrier, the giant reared up and opened its ghostly mouth. A patch of darkened clay looked ready to gulp the land. Merphi continued forward without a care in the world. The mystcat disappeared into the haze of blowing sand, and suddenly the giant stopped and the dirt that made it faded back into the ground.

Their horses had not been afraid of the sand monster, but they were agitated by the wind and blowing sand and had started to drift off. It took Kovan a while to catch both of them and walk them back. The old man was finding his feet and muttering under his breath. This was the first time Oz had appeared agitated.

"You have any idea what that was?" Kovan asked.

"I know what it was, just not why it was here. It's a mage's creation, a sand giant for trespassers."

Kovan coughed and spit dirt out of his mouth and wiped his eyes. In a matter of ten steps, they were surrounded by warriors, some on horseback, others riding giant brown bulls with massive horns. All of them had weapons, all of them ready to kill.

"Put you gun away, Kovan. These are the Oakol," Oz said.

TWENTY-TWO
RED EYES - ELLARIA

Ellaria awoke to the sound of multiple voices arguing around her.

"Would you two stop? She's waking up." Echoryn's voice was firm but quiet.

Ellaria slowly opened and closed her eyes, but the light in the room made her wince. It was morning. Whether it was the next morning, she couldn't say.

"Can someone shut the blinds?" Ellaria sighed and rubbed her eyes. There was a dull pain just behind them and a deep muscle strain at the back of her neck.

"How do you feel?" Stasia asked. The girl was sitting nearby. Wade was nervously pacing, and Echoryn was huddled on the next bed, holding her knees, her face stoic.

Ellaria adjusted to her surroundings and could see the strain of the night worn into each of their eyes. She remembered having been poisoned. The real question was why she was not dead. Images of Echoryn dragging her through the corridor flashed in her mind, and the taste of a bitter tonic sat dryly in her mouth.

"Thank you, Echoryn. I believe you saved my life," Ellaria said.

"You're welcome."

"Did you have a vision, or was I just lucky?" Ellaria asked.

"I had the vision of you poisoned back at the docks in Ioka, but I didn't know when exactly it would happen," Echoryn said, but what

238

she didn't explain to the others, and Ellaria understood from their last conversation, was that her visions were often in first person. Echoryn had experienced the poisoning.

"So, how did you determine it was going to be last night, and how did you find an antidote?" Ellaria asked.

"There was a stone bell tower in a small village in my vision," Echoryn answered.

Ellaria smiled, recalling the blurring landscape, and said, "I think I remember that."

"As for the antidote. When you were dying, you thought about the plant that could have saved you and knew it was growing near where you had camped a few nights before with a group of soldiers."

Ellaria smiled again, recalling Echoryn looking over the foliage as they ate dinner with the soldiers two nights prior.

"The real question is, Do either of you know who did it?" Wade asked.

Ellaria looked at Echoryn and shook her head. "I'm not sure. But I think it was Shaw or Vaughn."

"Not Atwood?" Wade asked.

"Shaw and Vaughn came over after you two left and shared a drink."

"Well, I can't say any of the governors would completely surprise me. None of them like you," Stasia said.

"Killing me so I don't have a seat at the table is a little much," Ellaria said.

"It's not just that. Whichever one did it, they're not who they say they are," Echoryn said.

"What do you mean?" Stasia asked.

"They're not themselves. In the vision, I saw a pair of red eyes standing over Ellaria," Echoryn explained.

"Red eyes, are you sure?" Ellaria said.

"Absolutely," Echoryn said firmly.

"It's got to be Atwood," Wade said. "Echoryn said she already had a vision of him."

"It could've been Shaw. Hasn't he been against you this whole time?" Stasia asked.

"It's Atwood," Wade said, self-assured.

"To be fair, they're both mudfoots." Ellaria stepped in. "What I would like to do is see their reaction to me walking around. You three should go to the dining car for breakfast, and I'll come in a little bit afterwards, and—"

"No," Wade cut her off.

"What do you mean no?" Ellaria said.

"It's no good. I'm not leaving your side while someone is trying to kill you," Wade said adamantly.

Ellaria smiled at him. "Your chivalry is misplaced, Wade."

"It's not chivalry. It's good sense. Someone wants you dead for the same reason I know we can't lose you. I've seen some of these governors, and the New World is in trouble if we lose you… Honestly, all of them being spies makes me feel a little better. That's good news for our side. They're all idiots," he said.

Ellaria laughed and said, "Most people in power are, Wade. That's why you can't trust any of them."

A knock came to their door, interrupting their scheming. They looked from one to the other. With everyone they trusted accounted for, *who was knocking?*

A second, more urgent knock pounded.

"Ellaria, are you in there?" the voice behind the door was Vaughn's.

Ellaria answered the door, but only marginally opening it, just enough to see their new arrival's face.

"Vaughn, what do you need?" Ellaria said.

"You're all right?" Vaughn said, surprised.

The hair on the back of her neck stood on end. "I'm fine," she said.

"Let me in, we have a problem," Vaughn said.

"I don't think so," Ellaria said, and she snapped her fingers behind her for someone to hand her a gun. Wade handed her a pencil. She looked at it and threw it back at him quickly and pointed to the gun in a bag on the bed. Wade handed it to her, and she kept it hidden behind the door.

"I think Shaw is a spy. Now let me in," Vaughn said.

By the colonel's appearance, she knew he was genuine. A man

with rarely a hair out of place or a crease to his shirt looked like he had slept on the road.

Ellaria stepped back. Vaughn swept the door aside and bounded in. He scanned the corridor in both directions and shut and locked the door.

When he turned to face her again, Ellaria had the pulsator gun pointing at him. The cramped compartment was full with both people and a lot of anxiety.

"What's going on?" Ellaria said coldly.

Vaughn put his hands up and backed into the door. "It's Shaw, something's wrong with him. I overheard him talking to someone in the darkness of the luggage car. He spoke gleefully of poisoning you. I almost turned to find you then or barge in to confront him, but..."

"But what? Who was he talking to?" Ellaria said.

"That's just it—there wasn't anyone else there, but I heard another voice. The voice I heard was dark and commanding and it made my skin crawl," Vaughn said.

She didn't react.

Vaughn eyed her a moment and continued, "I'm no easy blood either, Ellaria, but that voice turned my insides cold. As soon as I could, I went looking for you..." He paused again and set his jaw. "You don't seem surprised by any of this. What's going on?"

"I think it's the Scree. There's something wrong with them," said Ellaria.

"The ones that suffered that terrible affliction?" Vaughn asked.

Ellaria exhaled with exhaustion. She knew most of the governors had dismissed her report about the Scree, the soul gem, and the Genesis Chamber at the temple in Nahadon. "There's a lot more to it than that, but yes," she told him. She was reluctant to explain the Scree again. Explaining that people's souls were stolen and returned or not returned was an insane conversation.

"Make it simple for me, what are we dealing with?" Vaughn asked.

"Spies, people now beholden to someone or something that is controlling them. They are not themselves anymore."

"I'll assume you're right. I never did understand anything of magic, and I'm not going to try now. There's more to worry about here," Vaughn said.

"Right. Like who else is compromised?" Ellaria said.

"Do you think it's happening to all of those who were once the Scree?" Wade asked, concern for his own sister prompting his question, no doubt.

"That's a good question, Wade. I don't know."

"What about King Danehin?" Vaughn asked.

A void formed in Ellaria's stomach until she remembered: "No. The Court of Dragons restored him before the Temple of Ama, because Verro Mancovi was set on using him in the transference."

"So, what do we do about it?" Wade said.

At that moment, the train whistle blew loud and long. They were arriving at the station in Syvonne.

"We go about our business like nothing happened. Whoever attempted to kill me will attempt it again, but they may wait until after I've met with Chief Engineer Pryor. I suspect whatever he means to give me, the spies will want to intercept."

"Dangerous bargain, Moonstone," Vaughn said.

"What else can we do? Plus, I'd like to study them a bit," Ellaria said.

"But won't they know you're watching for them now?" Stasia asked.

"Right, but they don't know that I know about both of them," Ellaria said.

"Both of them?" Vaughn asked.

"Oh yeah, Atwood is also compromised," Ellaria told him.

"We stay on the train and head to Bowma like nothing has changed, but aren't both men supposed to leave us today?" Stasia asked.

"Yes, and my guess is, once they see me walking around, they'll both find a reason to stay aboard. The Pryor meeting is probably worrying them for some reason."

"I suspect you're right; they have each peppered me with questions about our side trip to Bowma. At first, I thought it was just that they were infuriated that the king was entrusting you with something.

But they were adamant about finding out what Pryor was supposed to be giving you."

"I'm sure it's nothing," Ellaria said.

"This is going to sound crazy, but is it possible that Pryor has the Desolation blade?" Wade asked.

"No way, you think?" Stasia said.

"I don't know, but Atwood and Shaw think it's something important enough to kill someone over."

AT THE GRAND STATION IN SYVONNE, ELLARIA STEPPED OFF THE TRAIN for a moment to make sure she was seen. Neither Atwood nor Shaw seemed to skip a beat at the sight of Ellaria, but she didn't suspect them to be rattled so easily. She loudly complained about the train food upsetting her stomach, anticipating that Shaw would assume he had misjudged his dosage. Ellaria scanned the crowded platform, which was full of soldiers, either deploying to the coast, to the north, or taking refuge in the crossroads city. Ellaria took a deep breath and returned aboard the train to watch the governors from a window.

The rest happened as Ellaria imagined. While Ramell bid farewell, both Shaw and Atwood made excuses to remain with the envoy, demanding that they too needed to have an audience with the king in Adara before he left for Karnika.

The others kept an eagle's eye on the men all the way to Bowma, but oddly Ellaria felt more relaxed. She appreciated having her enemies in clear sight.

Once in Bowma, only Ellaria and Vaughn disembarked. It was a half-day excursion to the coast and the military complex stationed in the ocean between Bowma and the island of Deloma.

Inside the complex, Ellaria strode past the enormous submerged fuselage, with its giant turbines churning in the water, on her way to meet the head engineer. The scientists told her the turbines produced most of the electricity in the nearby cities. The constant hum reverberated on the walls inside the facilities, and when Ellaria stood close enough, her teeth rattled.

The size of the machine was awe-inspiring, but it was the size of the underground complex that was truly unbelievable. Where the fortified tunnels wove underwater, the feeling was unsettling. She stopped along the ramparts before it split into the five access arms, each leading to the five prototype submerger-shuttles, all in various stages of completion, underwater ships for the war. Each machine had a navigating capsule, where a large glass view port provided clear sightlines all the way around. The spherical compartment was offset at the top and bottom by massive fins.

The head engineer finished his conversation with the tinkerman and came over to greet Ellaria. "You must be Ellaria Moonstone," the engineer said, lifting the goggles free of his head, his face full of soot marks and smelling of oil. His black hair was greasy and matted down.

"I must be, so I am. And you're Pryor, no doubt?" Ellaria asked.

"That's me."

"So, Mr. Pryor. I was told you wanted to see me."

"Yes. I was told by the king to trust no one but you," Pryor explained and lifted a strap off his shoulder that connected a long metal tube.

"And this is what exactly?" Ellaria asked.

"They are the final specifications for the air defense system in Illumeen."

"I'm not going to Illumeen," Ellaria said.

"No, the one in Illumeen is complete. These are for a second launch station under construction in Adara, with some modifications. You're to deliver them to Danehin at the Darkhawks fortress."

"I see," Ellaria said, and she opened the canister just to make sure she wasn't missing something.

"Sorry for the long trek down here. You seem disappointed."

"I'm just confused. I thought… well, I thought maybe someone had found the Desolation blade. You know, something top secret."

"Well, that would be something. I've heard of a few teams that are searching for it, but everyone has come up empty as far as I know. Honestly, I could have delivered the plans or had a runner do it, but the king was insistent."

Ellaria wondered if the king had discovered treachery of the

Redeyes, and she responded to Pryor with an observation: "Maybe Danehin thought it would be enlightening for me to see your creations, Mr. Pryor."

"These?" Pryor pointed to the ships behind him. "These are just toys. They're just a fraction of what we have built."

"They are fascinating. You built them for underwater travel."

"They're odd-looking ships, but they were designed for maneuverability and can reach fast speeds. That's why they have the dual propellers."

"All of this is the High Tide Program, then I assume you were the mastermind behind whatever machine drained the ocean at the Orin Channel?"

"The sea depletion trench, yes, I designed it. I heard it was very successful."

"Terrifying, but yes, successful. How about this air defense machine, did it work in Illumeen?"

"You haven't heard?"

"No, we've been traveling for days. Heard what?"

"Illumeen is under siege, but the Sagean forces have started pulling out. They didn't attack like we anticipated. It was almost like they knew we had a way to take down their cloudparters. We haven't activated it yet, didn't want to tip our hand to support ground forces. So, we don't know how well the launcher would have worked."

"Interesting. Was the launcher kept as big of a secret as the depletion trench?"

"About the same, I guess. Only the top military leaders know about any of the projects."

"What about the governors?"

"Well, yes. Some of them are informed because of the resource expenditure."

"Thank you, Mr. Pryor. I'll see that Danehin receives these," she said, tapping the canister. "In the meantime, you should double security down here. And if you know of anyone on your team who was inflicted with the Scree disease, you should have them reassigned immediately."

At sunset, the train traveled the final stretch toward Adara under a pink sky. The vibrant colors were bright but fading, and the scattered clouds turned black in contrast. The four of them, Ellaria, Wade, Stasia, and Echoryn, sat in the dining car. All the governors were there as well, except Governor Zulhorn.

Ellaria had the canister of schematics on the table, and she sat admiring the view when the sky started to move, and the darkness of the clouds came alive. A giant Dragon as dark as the night enveloped the clouds and moved in sync with the train, charging toward them.

A collective gasp from all the travelers ensued followed by a scream when the newly charged gas lamps were suddenly extinguished. The glow of them remained as an afterburn on Ellaria's retinas.

In the confusion, someone charged toward her. Wade grabbed Ellaria at the shoulders and pulled her to the floor. A knife plunged through her empty chair, the blade sticking out the back, and a blast from a pulsator gun flashed in the cabin.

Atwood fell dead next to her on the floor.

More cries and commotion in the small car erupted. Wade and Ellaria got to their feet and found Vaughn wrestling with Shaw near the door. Wade rushed in to help.

Between the two of them, Shaw was quickly on his knees. Vaughn pulled the curtain ties off and secured Shaw's hands behind his back. When Shaw lifted his head, his face was bleeding from a gash above his eyebrow, the blood dripping down his face from which two red eyes stared at Ellaria.

"He comes for you, Moonstone," Shaw said in a voice that sounded hollow and disembodied. Shadows in the landscape changed again and Shaw laughed.

The dimly lit land had become black under the wings of the Dragon overhead. A cloaked figure rode atop like black living mist. The size of the creature this close was unfathomable as it kept pace with the train. Panic set in among the passengers, and screams from other cars could be heard over the charge of the train.

"What's happening?" Wade said.

"Did you see someone riding on top?" Stasia asked, with a tremble to her voice.

Ellaria nodded.

Shaw grinned and spoke again. "You're all dead now. The Wrythen has come."

Ellaria ran to her bag and immediately dumped everything out to find what she wanted. The Dragon's flight glided over the land just beyond the glass. Every beat of its huge wings shook the train car.

Ellaria found the transcendence sand and bloodstone powder and looked up as the Dragon's head settled alongside them, its teeth and jaw as big as the train car. She removed the stopper and poured the powder on the carpet.

"What are you doing?" Wade asked, alarmed.

"Shut up and let me concentrate," Ellaria fired back, but the moment was descending into chaos quickly. Gunfire from charged rounds of pulsator guns pierced through the cries, but the energy-charged rounds did nothing to the creature. The screams from passengers were throwing off her concentration.

Ellaria flattened the powder into a circle and drew out the sigils for a shield. She pulled the small knife from her wrist and cut her palm. Muttering an incantation, she dribbled blood over the sigil.

"If this is helping, do it faster," Wade urged.

Ellaria ignored him and put her hand over the sigil. The reddish powder lifted from the floor and started to spin in a slow building storm within the train car, expanding further until the entire room was covered in the speckles of glimmering dust.

Looking up to assess the Dragon's position, she saw the black-mist rider with eyes of fire. The being flung its arm out, and Ellaria was thrown off her feet.

The entire train was ripped from the tracks. A thousand feet of train cars, passenger cars, storage containers, pallets of supplies, and machinery collided with the ground. As the train tumbled, the shielding spell isolated the dining car from destruction, but not the people inside from injury.

Ellaria slammed back into what was just the ceiling and then to the seats. She gripped desperately, and her feet flung back as it rolled again. The derailment came with a deafening crash.

The sound of metal breaking and pulverizing and the crunch of steel sounded like the fury of the sun. Everything inside was tossed around, bodies and small debris slamming into the revolving floor.

Their train car came to a screeching stop, scraping over a rocky plateau of land.

The shielding spell had saved their lives, but the shield wasn't meant to last forever. Moments after they had come to a stop, the windows blew apart.

Outside, the wreckage was scattered as far as she could see. Ellaria stood on a stone shelf of land that plunged away to a low prairie.

The black Dragon and its rider soared away toward the ocean where the sun had just dipped beyond the horizon.

TWENTY-THREE
SPIRIT ELDERS - TALI

TALI WAS ROUSED FROM HER SLEEP BY THE BOAT SLIDING ASHORE ATOP a bed of rock and weeds. Startled, she shot up quickly, the blanket falling away. The sun had risen during their crossing of the lake, but the sky was still clouded over, and there was very little warmth to the morning. Tyzo was already ashore. He helped Mia out and held out his hand for Tali, his blue fingers sticking out of his archer's glove. She took it and climbed out.

"How are you feeling?" he asked.

"Better," she said. "How long until they catch up to us?"

"We're safe," Tyzo said.

"No, we're not," Mia said, fixing her boots. "We have to go."

"The Spirit Elders know we're coming, right?" Tyzo asked.

"They do and they'll receive us at their temple, but the soldiers may or may not let us pass. The Spirit Elders don't know who is loyal to them and which soldiers are loyal to Ashrata Nea'Ko."

"How are we getting there?" Tyzo asked.

"Tyzo, you will stay here. We will go alone along the main road."

"No, I don't like this idea," Tyzo said, shaking his head.

"If they see an armed man, they may attack us. If they see just me and her, they'll let us through," Mia explained. "Trust me, Tyzo Eraw'Sa, I remember."

Tali wasn't sure she understood the exchange, but Tyzo's shoul-

"

ders sagged slightly. He grunted his displeasure, but he gave up his argument and began to collect firewood.

"It's a long walk, let's go," Mia said, and she started off into the woods.

Tali groaned to herself and approached Tyzo before leaving. She put her hand on his muscular arm.

"Thank you, Tyzo. I would be dead without you," she said.

"You are welcome."

"Any words of wisdom?"

"Show the Spirit Elders respect and expect to be presented with a request."

"I will. Thank you again," Tali said, and she rushed to catch up to Mia.

They began hiking over a set of hills and a small mountain pass, and snow covered most of the way. They walked for hours without stopping or speaking until they reached a road. The infrequent rays of sunlight sprawled on the surface at tiny points scattered around. The dirt was compacted, and small crushed charcoal stones were spread across the breadth of the road. A crunch sounded with Tali's every step.

"You said you would explain why you betrayed me. Explain," Tali said. Her tone left no question about her agitation.

"I'm sorry, Tali. There were some things I hadn't foreseen."

"Some?"

"Yes."

"Like being captured?"

"No."

"Being left for dead on that rock?"

"Correct. I didn't remember that."

"Remember it? You said something else about remembering to Tyzo. Are you making life-and-death decisions based on memories of visions?"

"Something like that. It's complicated."

Tali couldn't believe what she was hearing. She became more angry with Mia as the conversation continued. "Then explain it so I can understand, because it didn't feel complicated when I was freezing to death."

"First, you must understand that I have seen many of these events before and most of them from uniquely personal perspectives. When a seer gets a vision, it is often through the eyes of the one experiencing the moment. That experience stays with you, and once I write it down, I never forget. The recording of a vision is prophecy, and it is part of the magic."

"So how is it that you don't recollect something, if you never forget?"

Mia winced at her question. "Because the maze has shifted. A choice was made I didn't foresee, or a doorway opened that was previously closed," she replied, but then continued to speak to herself. "Maybe there are dead ends missed? Could there be more players? More branches I've missed or paths I've lost? No. Of course, the ninth derivative realm... and the ninth of the ninth of the ninth is clouded..."

"Are you all right?"

"Shhhh. The Morning-star... the capture... and she didn't fight... the gem... Ashrata Nea'Ko... the Harrinari witch... the—"

"The Harrinari witch?" Tali interrupted.

"Shhhh. The Spirit Elders... the yellow gem... and she didn't fight, but she didn't try," Mia repeated. Suddenly she stopped on the road and grabbed Tali by the arms, and looked at her with a scrutinizing glare. Tali felt like her gaze was boring into her brain like a tick, looking for something.

"Do you believe you have any of your powers?" Mia asked.

"No, the gold man took them, remember."

"Yes, yes, but you didn't fight, you didn't run. And later you didn't try to escape the caravan to Cadon, or fight Ashrata in the temple. What's wrong? Lunoka's report said you were sad. What's changed?" Mia said, but it wasn't a question. With their eyes still locked, Mia's pupils grew wide, and she let Tali go.

"Are you all right?" Tali said.

"Fine," Mia replied, turning away.

Mia resumed walking, but Tali stood dumbfounded. She was starting to realize that Mia might be crazy. She now had more questions than answers.

"Did I hear you say the ninth realm?"

"What?" Mai asked, startled. "Oh, I'm not sure actually. It's just how I think of them."

"Them? Them what?"

"It's how I keep track of the maze we're in. It's always a multiple of three. Bonds, paths, choices. It's always a trinity, thoughts, emotions, actions. Like the Trinity Guard, a Luminary, a Fusion Mage a Nimbus Warrior. It's the paths of life: the soul, the mind, the heart; one to be, one to think, and one to feel. It's choices: go left, go right, go straight."

"Because you can't go back?" Tali asked.

"No. You can't go back, and you can't stay still. That's death."

Tali was reluctant to ask any more questions, she feared the answers would cause more confusion for the both of them. Mia was complicated, and in her way, she had answered. Mia's misguided allegiance to visions dominated her actions. Mia called it a maze, but it felt like chaos when she spoke about it. Her mind was apparently enraptured by it, caught inside her own visions like a web. The conversation felt like a twisted abyss of wild vines that Tali didn't want to get sucked into.

They walked a long time before structures came into view on the rise beyond. When they got close enough to see people, Mia pulled her hood off but stopped Tali from doing the same.

"Keep it on, and try to look cold and miserable," Mia said.

Tali almost laughed out loud. They passed through the village streets unthwarted. Every building was remarkably pristine, and most were covered with dark-grey wood and topped with black tile roofs. There were thin obelisk towers among the buildings, each appointed with ornate stone reliefs at the top where small vertical openings broke up the detailing.

Further inside the village, Tali noticed drawn bows protruding out of those openings, tracking their movements. As they reached the stone steps leading up to the temples, a light snowfall began. Tali, already tired from their trek, glared up at the daunting number of steps and took a deep breath as they began their ascent.

When they reached the top, the sun was turning blue overhead. Even concealed behind clouds, the blue hue of the flaming ball of life was obvious. The ground at her feet swayed, and Tali tripped to her knees. Her wrist took most of the impact, and she cringed.

"Get up, we have to hurry," Mia said.

"I'm sorry, I'm just so dizzy," Tali replied.

Mia gathered Tali to her feet and urged her to keep up as she rushed the nearest building—an open portico with a giant roof and no walls. Inside, a hundred soldiers in grey armor were kneeling in finely spaced rows.

Mia put a finger to her lips and motioned for Tali to kneel in the back row. Unexpectedly the glow from the sun began to illuminate the outer walkways in a sheen of blue, and the soldiers began to hum and chant. The chant was a low, repeating mantra like a song, and she wasn't sure what the sounds they were making meant. If they were words, they weren't words she knew.

"Gelelow-ega-Gelelow-ega-oh-Segon-ega-Ada-nedee-Nahey-go-lano-Din-hithall."

They paused after the seventh time for a short period and then repeated. Tali's skin felt like bugs were crawling on it, or that ants were at her neck. She was intruding upon something she had no understanding of, and her instinct was to run. Trapped there as an unwilling participant, her mind started to drift. Her first thought was how incredibly hungry she was. She had not eaten since the caravan, and even then, they fed her sparingly. Her thoughts turned to the sensations of the crisp, clean, snow-filled air, the smell of pine, and the fragrances of wild bergamot and geranium that surrounded her. The chant went on for a long time, drawing Tali in to the ritual of it, and soon she heard Mia speaking to her.

Without talking, Mia said, *"You know he's still alive, right?"*

Tali didn't have to ask who she meant. Mia was talking about Learon, and she sent back, *"How do you know?"*

"Trust me."

"I don't think I can."

"He's alive or you wouldn't be here."

"But I can't feel him."

"You will, in time."

Tali wiped the tears from her cheeks and blinked her eyes open, realizing that the chanting had stopped. Surrounding her were the soldiers, all with highly polished axes in their hands, some with blades of striated metal that looked like white lightning. Mia stood at her shoulder, offering a helping hand.

"No sudden movements," Mia said.

"Mianora," a soldier said with a bowed head.

"Rogo, I'm here to see the Spirit Elders," Mia said.

"They're expecting you," he said, "and her."

The two of them were led by the soldiers out of the portico and to the three largest buildings on the topmost plateau. They were ushered into the center square, and the soldiers dispersed to the edges of the pavilion, where the stone at the ground changed colors in forming a ring around the area. Once in position the entirety of the squad kneeled on the circle with their axes on the ground before them and their open palms out. Three very old people wandered out from the temple structure, draped in gowns of silk and fur with gold stitching. One man walked with a cane and had a bright white beard extending down from his light blue face almost to his waist. The second, an old woman, wore her grey hair pulled back and gold earrings. The third was also a woman, but she wore no gold, only heavy robes and thick fur around her neck, and her hair, while grey, still held some peppering of black.

Tali quickly kneeled with her hands open for the elders, in hopes that's what Tyzo meant by showing respect. The old man smiled but never looked at her. The two women looked on, unimpressed.

"We thank you for the respect, young Luminary. Please stand," the old man said.

"Prophet, we all know why you are here. We have a problem with our Twilight Elder. What are you proposing?" one of the women asked.

"Spirit Elder Annika Lor'Si, I know that Tali can free the Harrinari leader, and together they will defeat Ashrata Nea'Ko," Mia said.

"And the alternative paths?" the other woman asked.

"The alternative paths, Spirit Elder Jinree Sen'Lo, all result in a significant amount of death," Mia said.

"Death and darkness have sway over our lands no matter the path," the old man said.

"The wrong path could see your entire nation eradicated, Spirit Elder Hurazo Kena'Ko," Mia said.

"That is impossible," Jinree Sen'Lo said.

"There are Bonemen at the temple in Cadon. Which can only mean Ashrata Nea'Ko is working with the Sagean lord," Tali said.

"Is this true?" Hurazo Kena'Ko asked.

"Yes," Mia said.

"So the Sagean has returned, and the morning star has arrived, the end of ends has truly come," Jinree Sen'Lo said.

"Yes, Spirit Elder, and the Unity Maze is nearly completed, and this young woman is one of the tethers," Mia said.

"We see that," Hurazo Kena'Ko said.

"Do we? I see a young woman too weak to stand properly," Annika Lor'Si said.

"She was tortured on the Suffering Rock by Ashrata," Mia explained.

"Was she now," Annika Lor'Si said.

"And she hasn't eaten in a long time. I can hear her stomach from here." The old man stomped the stone floor with his cane. In a matter of moments, a tray of food was brought out by a young girl dressed in black. She placed the tray at Tali's feet and hurried away.

"Please eat, young lady, before you fall over," Hurazo Kena'Ko said.

"We have long feared this day from the moment you came to us fifteen years ago, Mianora. Since that day, everything that you have said would come to pass," Jinree Sen'Lo said.

"Then you know Ashrata has fallen and cannot be redeemed," Mia said.

"We know. It is with great reluctance that we must break with the Twilight Elder Nea'Ko. However, the other Twilight Elders have sworn fealty to him, and he controls the Zenoch army. We only have the loyalty of our Duskmen here in Darkanna," Jinree Sen'Lo said.

"You have the loyalty of people, Spirit Elder," Mia said.

"The people should never be called upon to overthrow their own rulers. No, I don't believe we can go against him," Annika Lor'Si said.

"Spirit-Tree Hurazo Kena'Ko, you are the oldest and wisest, and it is your clansman that we seek to topple. Annika and I defer to your judgment as the old ways would have us do," Jinree Sen'Lo said.

The old man hobbled his way to Tali and reached aimlessly for her hand. Only then did she realize that he was blind. He took her left hand in both of his.

"Hmmm," he grumbled. "My grandson has been tainted with evil for a long time, but I am very reluctant to cause more horrors for my people. At my age, I don't have the right to make this decision. I've lived a long life and may not live through what is to come. It is the reason the Spirit Elder's voice is in service of wisdom and not law," Hurazo Kena'Ko said.

Tali was sure he was going to finish by rejecting them, whatever that could mean. His hands were pulling away when he felt Saphree's gifted bracelet at Tali's wrist. He stopped, felt it, smiled, and addressed her directly.

"There's an old Zenoch saying, dear. The difference between daughters and sons is simple. 'Daughters, you protect from the world; but sons, you protect the world from them.' If Mia's visions come true, I believe the world will kneel before you, my dear. So, I wonder, should I protect you—or protect the world from you? You can either leave now with our protection and return to the Westlanders to help them with their war, or you can stay and help us?" Hurazo propositioned her.

Tali finally had her way home. Her breathing almost stopped. She could find her friends, she could find Learon, and she could start fighting again. But what would that mean for the Zenoch, she thought, and what could it mean to have the Zenoch on her side in a war against the Sagean or the Wrythen?

"How can I help?" she asked.

"You must free the Harrinari leader. Ashrata has imprisoned them in the temple in Cadon. Once you have freed them, return to us. We will get the Harrinari leader back to their people, and they will defeat Ashrata," Hurazo Kena'Ko said.

"How do I free them and not get caught myself?"

"You can't."

THEY RETRACED THEIR STEPS BACK TO THE LAKE TO TAKE THE BOAT back to the temple in Cadon. Tyzo, couldn't believe Tali had agreed to rescue someone she had never met from the temple prison without her powers.

On the lake, Tali stared at the sky, wondering about the lights she had seen the night before.

"Mia, what did Ashrata mean when he asked me if I knew the way to the Aurora Altar?"

"I told you the Zenoch believe in signs and symbols. They see the aurora light as a magical thing and believe there is a place where the light comes alive."

"Not exactly," Tyzo interrupted. "Legend says there is a sacred altar beneath the most powerful aurora that can harness the powers of the Fates. People have searched for it, and valiant warriors have sought it, but it's never been found. Some say it's guarded."

"By what?" Tali asked.

"I don't know. Sometimes men have gone on long journeys in the north to find it and were found torn apart."

Tali shivered. "I had another question, Tyzo. In Lunoka's letter to the Spirit Elders, she said she feared that Ashrata wanted my bones for an axe. Why would he want an axe of bone?"

"Did you see Duskmen in the temple of Darkanna? More importantly, did you see steel of their axes?"

"Yes."

"Their axes are formed with crystal binding and the bones of their elders. The Zenoch believe that the magic of a person, their strength, is in their bones," Mia said.

"It is not simply a thing of magic and strength. It is also the tradition of honoring our elders who protect us from the afterlife," Tyzo interrupted again.

"Ashrata craves power enough that I doubt he understands the difference," Tali said. "So how do I free this Harrinari leader?"

"I honestly don't know," Mia said, shaking her head. "My vision was that Ashrata imprisoned you after you fought and killed a bunch of his soldiers. Somehow the two of you got free, and I took you both to the Spirit Elders."

I guess it's plan B, Tali thought with a smile, recalling Kovan's propensity to improvise. Then the realization came to her as the boat returned to the south. The Spirit Elder had already told her the answer; she just didn't want to hear it.

"How do you free a prisoner without being captured?" Tali asked them as they stepped to the shore.

Tyzo and Mia looked at each other but didn't answer.

"You don't. You let yourself be captured," Tali said and appraised Tyzo as his face fell. The key to her plan was for Ashrata to depart for the summit in Karnika. Tali suspected Ashrata would take his entire army to show off his power and force the Harrinari into subjugation.

She just hoped Ashrata wouldn't take his prisoners as trophies.

TWENTY-FOUR
TRAINING - LEARON

"I DON'T KNOW WHY I'M EVEN HERE," LEARON MUMBLED UNDER HIS breath.

"Why are you here?" Osiah snapped, attacking and easily landing a blow on Learon's shoulder. The sting traveled to his fingers, and he dropped his sword.

Apparently not as *under* as he thought, retrieving his wooden sword. Learon sighed. "I'm here because of a promise I made, but after three weeks, I still don't know how to keep that promise."

"At least you're smart enough to realize that just being here is not the same as showing up. Learon, your mind drifts to battles that are beyond your control," Osiah said.

"Battles I could be fighting right now," Learon said, slashing back at Osiah in frustration. Osiah blocked the onslaught and stepped back.

"Your time here is at its end, Learon," Osiah said. "Naomi will take you to the shrine after this, and tonight will be the ceremony to prepare you for the Five Peaks."

"Oh," Learon said, yet he didn't know what else to say. He wasn't surprised by the news; he knew from talking with Jaden and the others that a warrior was never given more than a day's notice for the Trials. The end was coming with apprehension. No one could resist the sense of peace this place provided. Part of his trepidation was that the tranquility felt so much like home. Learon had made friends here, but he also knew something was missing. He had to move on. Being torn about wanting to stay and wanting to go was the most unsettling of all.

"So, as this is our last session, I thought I would truly attack you," Osiah said, pulling the sword back in his stance, his eyes growing narrow and earnest.

"I appreciate a final lesson, and whatever you have to teach," Learon said, bouncing on his feet.

"It's not for you. I have to know what you're capable of," Osiah said, and he charged in.

For a grueling ten minutes, they sparred, neither man giving ground or landing a glancing blow.

"You're still holding back," Osiah growled and swept past, but missed when Learon ducked and rolled away. "Move faster. Where is that magical speed of yours?"

"It only comes when I need it most," Learon complained.

"Do we have to switch to steel?" Osiah said, catching his breath.

"No."

"Then stop holding back and finish me," Osiah said, and he came sweeping in with one of his favorite moves. It was a low, spinning dash that Learon knew well, both how to execute and defend against. Learon's swift feet found the ground to meet the strike, but instead of spinning, Osiah burst from the ground and vaulted over Learon to strike behind him. Learon reacted on instinct and spun the short sword to block and immediately strike as Osiah landed. With a real blade, the steel would have cut deeply into Osiah's thigh. As it was, the blunt force of Learon's strike crumpled the tall man.

Osiah cried out, but bit it back with a look of astonishment at Learon.

"I'm sorry," Learon said, reaching out to help his instructor up.

"Don't be sorry," Osiah grunted, getting to his feet and gingerly putting pressure on his leg. "I have taught you all the forms I know, the counters, the dashes, and the feints."

"Will it be enough?" Learon asked.

"It's up to you to pair what you have learned with the gifts you were given. As you just did. When you do that, you will find very few opponents that can defeat you."

"But there will be some who still can?"

"The biggest threat any warrior faces is themself. For some this is a simple lack of ability. For some it is arrogance that blinds them. Your weakness, Learon, is belief."

Out of the shadow of the building, Naomi stepped forward, a colorful shawl over her shoulder and her walking stick holding her weight. "I hope you two are finished. I'm here to take the boy for meditation."

"We're done," Osiah said.

"Take me where?" Learon asked.

"Back to the shrine."

It was a short distance to the shrine inside the bamboo grove. The walking path was one of Learon's favorites now. Along the path were spots where he could see the whole village, and it was also one of the few places where the full extent of the stone stairway to the Five Peaks was visible.

Learon and Naomi took their time in reaching the shrine. Naomi, with the aid of her walking stick, was never in a hurry, and Learon was happy to keep whatever pace she set.

"I wanted to come up here for our last meditation because I wanted to tell you a story about Kerion, the feather, and the Five Peaks," she said. "As a great warrior, Kerion won many battles in the lands we now call Karnika. In his time, those lands were lush and green. They were not the wasteland of dirt and wind they are today. There are places where you can still see some of the remnants of the giant buildings that populated the great cities and, in the night, you can hear the ghosts of the ancients. Near the end of the War Without Sleep, Kerion faced the Invading King from Bravasha."

"Where is Bravasha? I've never heard of it." Learon asked.

"It was destroyed thousands of years ago and lost in the Brovic mists. Now be quiet and don't interrupt. Kerion's Trinity was incomplete, and he faced a mighty mage king with an army four times that of Karnika's. The many cities of the valley refused to align themselves, and the king, with his endless force, conquered one city at a time with ease. Kerion came to the High Grove to seek the help of the mountain tribes. No man had ever ventured over the Storm Mountains, as they were called then, and the tribes thought no army ever could. But the leaders of the Ordona tribes, being wise and humble, heard Kerion's pleas for their help.

"The leader asked only three things from Kerion: for him to prove his skill, to prove his spirit true, and prove his heart was pure. To prove his skill, Kerion displayed an accuracy with a bow and arrow that the Ordona tribes had never seen, but it wasn't enough. The leaders were unimpressed and told him only a warrior so skilled that they could shoot a blue feather off a blue-tailed grackle would be worthy. However, Kerion knew that the bird was sacred to the High Grove tribes. Fearing he couldn't perform such a shot without killing the bird, Kerion decided to move on and asked how he could satisfy the other requests. They brought him to a place not far from here called the Pillars of Morro."

"Morro?"

"Their word for the territh. They brought him to a special grouping of five peaks that rose up and out of the mist and into the clouds, and they challenged him to reach the tallest peak. After a secret ceremony, Kerion set out on his own. He returned from the pillars a week later, handing the leaders an old stone placed atop three peaks, a branch from the tree that stands alone on the fourth peak, and a crystal specimen from the fifth peak. They all agreed that his spirit and heart were true and pure, but his skill was not enough for them to send their warriors to fight by his side. But after his trial, he knew how to pass the test of skill. He climbed to the top of the north ridge, by the thin falls, where all could see him, and he cried out into the sky. From the treetops, a blue-tailed grackle came to perch on Kerion's arm and gifted Kerion a feather.

"The Ordona agreed to follow him into battle, and after he had defeated the mage king, Kerion returned to the High Grove and made a home here in the north. As a way to repay the Ordona, he promised to train the best soldiers the world would ever know and protect their lands against those that would seek its ruin. The Ordona then guarded this village from outsiders, and Kerion watched over the Five Peaks."

Her story ended, and they had reached Kerion's shine. Learon walked toward the old stone statue sitting alone in the forest of never-ending rain and asked, "How was Kerion able to defeat this mage king without his Trinity?"

"I can't say, because I don't know," Naomi answered.

"Did Elias know this story?"

"Of course. This was one of his favorite places in our village. I suspect it was the main reason he wanted you to come here. Though maybe he had other motives."

"When was the last time you saw Elias?"

"He came here about two or three years ago. He asked me if our people knew anything about the Old One. He stayed about a month, going over every ancient text."

"Did you know anything about the Old One?"

"We had only one text that spoke of it, and it said but two things —that the world has fought it more than once, and the ancient cities of Karnika were destroyed by it. I also told Elias that I believed whenever it got here, it has never left."

THAT EVENING AT DINNER, LEARON TOLD JADEN THAT HIS TRIAL WAS the next day.

"Tomorrow," Jaden said, his mouth full of food.

"Like you said, they don't give you much notice," Learon said.

"So, your ceremony, when is it?"

"It's tonight. What is it, by the way?"

"I don't know, but I would eat up if I were you. I mean, I've heard rumors, but you don't want to hear those," Jaden said.

"If I didn't, how could I stop you from telling me?" Learon said.

Jaden smiled and leaned closer. "There's a rumor that it's a blood ritual. I've also heard that you receive a thousand cuts, one for every step to the mountain eye. Another rumor says that you drink the black blood of a demon from a sacred horn."

"Where's Terrin?" Learon asked, looking around the dining hall.

"He's with the medic, getting stitches," Jaden said.

"There was another sandbox battle?" Learon asked. He hadn't

even heard the bells. Between training and meditation, he had been separated from the village almost entirely.

"Yeah. I looked for you, but I guess you were in meditation."

"I guess I was. Who won?" Learon didn't want to choose the obvious name, and said, "Ahjana.?"

"Yes. Did someone tell you?"

"No. Really. Well, maybe she'll earn a sword now. So did Aleph fight?" Learon asked.

"No," Jaden said, but he immediately stared down at his plate of food.

"What?" Learon asked.

"Aleph went for the peaks six days ago."

"Really? Why didn't you tell me that?"

"I just didn't want you thinking about it. I figured you would get called soon."

"Did he get a sword?"

"I don't think so. He just came back. I heard he only reached the third peak. I guess he was really dehydrated and talking crazy about a leopard that attacked him."

"Wow. Six days, is that normal?"

"Sometimes people are up there six days, sometimes three, sometimes seven. I guess it depends how far you get. I do know that there's no food out there, so the longer you're out there the harder it is to return."

Learon got a second helping on Jaden's recommendation. When he returned, they chose to talk about training. Osiah still ran the main sparring grounds when he wasn't giving Learon one-on-one lessons. They laughed about Osiah's scowl, and Learon smiled and felt relaxed with his friend until dinner ended, and his nerves returned to their frayed state.

Back at his room, a robe and slippers were waiting for him. Learon packed his things and knew he wouldn't be returning no matter what transpired on the pillars. When the moon was the only light in the sky, a knock came at his door.

Naomi smiled when he opened it. "I'm glad to see you're ready."

"I guess I am," Learon said.

"Then follow me," she said.

They headed for the water, where their footsteps on the wood bridge walkway added sound to the night. A symphony of noise that included frogs, chirps from the bush crickets, and other insects.

Inside the blade master's house located on the lake, Naomi led him through sliding panels and out to the back garden, where only masters were allowed. The back deck stepped down to the water and was lit with orange box lanterns. Osiah waited at the water's edge behind a stone table with a wood box on top.

Osiah lifted the box lid, and smoke rolled over the table and spilled to the floor. A single small turquoise cup with writing etched in the glass was waiting underneath. Naomi handed him the glass, which was too heavy for its size. The liquid inside was cloudy, and steam collected at the top like smoke without lifting away.

Learon wasn't sure he was allowed to talk, but he had to know: "What is it?"

"It's a tonic made from the leaves of sacred trees only found on the peaks. It won't harm you," Naomi said.

Learon looked at it again and took a second to soak in the moment. The drink smelled powerfully floral. The sight of the moon shining on the still surface of the lake sparked a memory of the lake near his father's cabin, and the way the moon enveloped that hidden meadow. The *pool of the moon*, his father would call it. It was a sight that made Learon feel like he was glimpsing the hands of fate as it touched the world. Whether it was a sign or not, Learon tipped his glass to the moon in recognition and drank. It was smoother than he expected, and tasted like flowers, the territh, smoke, and a hint of citrus. When it was gone, he wanted more.

He placed the glass back on the stone and asked, "Is that it?"

"No. Walk into the lake until your head is fully submerged and return," she said.

Learon nodded and walked down to the lake, his eyes fixed on the collection of white lotus flowers floating on the surface amid the reflected moon. Each step forward felt faster than he meant to go. At the edge of the water, he realized Osiah was behind him, waiting for the robe. Learon untied the rope at his waist and handed it over. He turned back and stepped into the lake. The water was ice cold, and he nearly flinched as a shiver ran through his body and his blood turned cold. Learon continued into the lake until his head was well beneath the surface.

Under the freezing water, he wished he could take a deep breath of the clear water—an odd sensation that passed. He counted to ten and came back to the deck. Osiah and Naomi were gone, and his robe was laid out and waiting. The lanterns were blurred trails of light, and he felt exhausted. He got dressed and returned to his room to await the next steps.

***

Naomi arrived before dawn to escort him to the Five Peaks. Learon's few hours of sleep were beguiled by vivid dreams that dissipated from his mind the moment Naomi knocked at his door.

She was dressed in the fanciest robes he had ever seen. Learon was in bed but had slept very little when the knock came. She stared at him when he opened the door and she saw his hair.

Following the ceremony, he felt like he needed a change on the outside to reflect something changing on the inside. Learon was twenty-two years old and had achieved nothing he had set out to. Caught up in the whirlwind of this struggle he had never intended to be a part of, he was so far removed from the kid trying to find out about his father's death. That kid was angry and guarded, and if given the choice, he would have preferred to avoid confrontation. His old appearance suited an older way of thinking that he was way past now. His long hair felt like a relic of his old self that he had shed, and it was time to move on. So, he cut his long hair until it was so short it spiked up on his head.

Learon waited for Naomi to comment, but she didn't. He grabbed his pack and coat and silently followed the maven of the Shadowyn as she led the way through the sacred garden. In the back corner, the shrubs and dead flower beds dwindled, and the white stone perimeter wall opened at a small moon-door made of arching charred wood, weathered to a dark grey. A small shadowed path interwoven among the tall trees snaked away from the village and to the east. About fifty feet beyond the garden, his grandmother stopped.

"This is your last chance."

"For what? To turn back?" Learon asked, confused.

"No. That was settled earlier when you drank the shadow-smoke. It's your last chance to see the village. I have seen how you appreciate your surroundings. Is it architecture you like, or nature?"

"I suppose I find inspiration in beautiful things, but I don't need to look back. Elias used to say, 'If you know where you've been—'"

The old women cut in, "'Then there's no need to ever look back. You might forget where you're going.'"

"That's right."

"Elias was an excellent student, and a good son," she said. Naomi tapped him with her walking stick. "Come on then."

Learon continued to follow her, though he did sneak a glimpse of the peaceful hideaway and hoped to return one day to find the serenity of the village the same as he left it.

They came to a place where the path split into two routes: one leading down to the valley and another leading to the stone steps. From the fork in the trail, he could see some of the valley of mist beyond.

"You are a part of this," Naomi said.

Learon looked around at the slopes of struggling wildflowers, evergreen trees, and distant mountain peaks with snow and tried to soak it in. For reasons he didn't know, he felt a connection to this land like never before.

Naomi glared at him. "You're missing it. I'm not talking about the landscape; I'm speaking of nature. You are part of it. The you who searches for truth, the you who loves, the you who fights and kills—humans, Harrinari, Zenoch, Kihan are all a part of nature. Friends and enemies alike. No matter what lengths we go to defy it or circumvent it.

"Because you are nature, you must develop a respect for nature. Different from the respect you give the Elum blade, as though it is something dangerous that you respect in order to conquer. You must relate to nature and respect it like you would your mother, with love and gratitude. Don't get me wrong, nature will kill you, but it's harmony you should seek. Reshaping nature to our advantage is human, but disruption of place is not mastery, nor is it dominion. To hold dominion over anything is an illusion of immortality."

Learon could only smile at his grandmother and wondered how

long it would be until he too was talking in riddles.

At the foot of the gigantic set of stone steps, Naomi stopped. The stairway climbed to an impossible height, and if it wasn't a thousand steps, it looked like it. The stairs were thirty feet wide and lined with trees the entire length up to where a natural hole punched through the mountain ridge. Learon estimated it would be light out when he reached the top.

"I can't go further. At the top you will find the Five Peaks. There is only one way to cross from peak to peak, and you must reach the top of every one in order to cross over to the next. At the top of each, you will find something for your journey. That's all I can tell you. Every Trial is different; your experience during your Trial is yours alone."

"Are they magical?"

"They are more than that. There are few places in this world that exist as vertices of energy. This is one of those places and from the vertex, you will be able to sense other points of energy. Trust your senses, but"—she tapped his chest—"trust that more."

Learon faced the stairs and turned back to his grandmother, the magnificent woman he had met only a month ago. At that moment words failed him, and all he could think to say was: "Thank you."

"One more thing," she said, and she reached in her pocket and pulled out a pendant on a thin strip of black leather. After she gave it to him, her face faltered, and he could see it meant more to her than the value of the metal and gem.

"I couldn't."

"Please. It is the best answer I can give you, to a question you have yet to ask."

Learon opened his hand to see a black triangle pendant with three lines revolving to meet at the center. A red stone was fastened in the middle. It was a symbol for something, but he didn't know what. "What is it? What does it mean?"

"It's a symbol of the Fates, of the Unity Maze. It represents the Trinity that must come together to defeat the darkness. It has been in my family for generations. It should stay in my family."

Learon stared at the pendant without looking up.

"Now go, my son, and discover what life has in store for you."

Oakol
To Delenon
Windmire Road
Canyon Trail to Radmana
Dry Creek Prairie
OAKOL
High City
Peddler's Field
OAKOL GATE
Diviner's Mound
RASHANU RIVER
Scorpion Hills
THE KARNIKA WASTES
Map Commissioned by The United Scholars

TWENTY-FIVE
OAKOL - KOVAN

THE PERIMETER OF THE HARRINARI CITY CONSISTED OF SMALL OPEN huts and mud-built structures, arrayed along a red stone wall. The convoy traveled to a central gate constructed of giant tusks, the likes of which Kovan had never seen, and he couldn't say what animal they once belonged to. Beyond the gate, dominating the hillside, was the city of the Oakol. As they passed through the gate, Kovan could swear he felt a shimmer of heat, but coupled with the heat already in the air, it was faint and possibly his imagination. Still, there was something to the sensation that was reminiscent of the feeling he got when they crossed the curiously marked symbol before the giant sand monster came to life out in the wastes.

He looked to his traveling partner Oz to see if he too perceived the wash of heat. Oz appeared to grimace but said nothing. Unlike Kovan, Oz wasn't restrained in any way.

"Oz, you seem to have earned their trust. Where are they taking us?" Kovan asked, growing agitated at the lack of communication. They had tied up Kovan and placed the mystcat into a cage.

"Stay quiet, Kovan, and don't trust everything you see," Oz said.

Pavak was the name of the man leading the escort that brought them from the wastes to the city. His tattoo looked like a winged beast with a wing visible at his neck. The tattoo expanded to the side of his face. He had piercings with silver at his nose, eyebrow, and ear and looked like he had barely an ounce of fat on him.

A short way into the city, their escort stopped abruptly, and the leader Pavak stopped and kneeled at the foot of a woman. She wore a hood the color of the sand. It was a light linen that wrapped at her shoulders like a shawl, and she also had a collection of gem-filled bracelets on each wrist. Of more interest to Kovan was the woman's skin. Like most of the Harrinari, she was covered with an assortment of tattoos, but her tattoos were different. There was a pattern to them but nothing recognizable, and from what Kovan could make out, the marks covered the woman, probably her entire back. Every bit of her exposed skin suggested a tattoo either starting or finishing.

He had to assume this was the Witch Woman he'd heard of, uniting the tribes. He was expecting an old woman, but this woman looked like she was only forty, if that. The Harrinari, as he understood, functioned much like the Zenoch. They gave superiority to their elders, though they did not adhere to the Zenoch's numbering system. The woman's eyes shined bright and green and from a distance. They held a captive glare of both serenity and sadness.

The woman and Pavak were too far from Kovan to hear their words, but the exchange was clearly intense. The woman was angry, but Pavak was arguing in her face. She looked to Kovan and Oz to study them, and her eyes settled on Kovan. Her gaze held him intently. She motioned to another warrior and gave them instructions. The second warrior walked straight away to the cage they had put Merphi in and freed the cat. She dismissed Pavak with a glare of fire, and he returned to the traveling party and proceeded to escort Kovan and Oz deeper into the city.

Shuffling along, Kovan wished his hands weren't restrained so he could check his compass. It would probably be taken from him the moment the metal appeared in the sun.

As they walked through the city, it became clear there was a second inner sanctum behind another sandblasted wall, with another mage-spelled gate. At this second gate, the archway was shaped like a moon-gate but larger. It reminded Kovan of the tavern on the island of Nima where Poe had given him his memories. Though he doubted a recluse of culture and arts like Poe had ever lived within.

The moment they passed through, another shiver trickled throughout his body, this one cold and unmistakable.

Oz coughed, and Kovan rubbed his neck. "Some sort of warding, or is another sand giant going to appear and smack us around again?" Kovan asked.

"A warding. Alasne is gifted," Oz commented.

"Is Alasne the Witch Woman I've heard about?"

"Shhh. Don't say that. Whatever you do, don't call her that," Oz warned.

Kovan had more questions, but they were interrupted by Pavak.

"Missionary, Alasne will receive your report in the Rover's Hall," he told Oz before speaking to Kovan and saying, "Follow me, drifter."

Oz put two fingers to his temple and nodded a farewell.

Pavak took Kovan to another building that looked like a bowl turned over. The size of the building was disguised by the outside shape, but inside there were multiple levels. Pavak led him to a lower-level room with a dirt floor covered with an intricate rug woven with a thick coarse thread, and left without a word.

An hour later, the woman he saw before entered the room, with armed guards waiting in the hall. Kovan was lying back on a group of pillows and lifted his hat to see her enter. Her head wrap was down, and the tattoos at her back came up to her neck. She had markings on her face too, but now Kovan could tell they were makeup lines. Her long dark brown hair had many small braids in it, a style almost too young for her, and a lock of white hair. Standing before him, he could see the age lines at her eyes.

"I don't suppose you brought food?" Kovan asked.

"I didn't, but I'll have some brought to you."

"And my horse?"

"It's being taken care of."

Kovan nodded and placed his hands out for the woman to cut his bindings.

"In a minute. First I want to talk with you."

"You don't trust me?"

"We don't know you."

"But Oz, you trust that old man?"

"He's the Peregrine Man, a missionary for Oakol and all the Harrinari, since long before I was born."

Her response made Kovan more curious. "Is his service reparations for some digression?" he inquired. It was obvious the man named Oz was not one of the Harrinari, so why would he be in service to a people unless he owed them something?

"To my knowledge, his servitude is to a sacred pact, a promise to our people, the details of which are older than me. If you are wondering if you are bound for a similar fate, I can reassure you, we are more likely to keep you imprisoned than have you as an emissary."

"So, I'm your captive."

"For now, let's call you a guest. Believe me I know what it's like to be imprisoned. You're not a prisoner here. However, please don't try to leave the city. I'll know if you do."

Kovan didn't argue but was unsure what the difference was. "What do you want to know about me?" he asked.

"First, I'm curious to know who you are and how you came to our lands."

"Kovan Rainer. Nice to meet you." He tipped his hat rather awkwardly with his bound hands. If the woman recognized the name, she showed no signs of it. Kovan leaned against the wall and said, "I came from the west, over the Haildron Mountains."

"From the High Grove?"

"Yes."

"Are you here to assassinate me?" she asked plainly.

The question caught Kovan off guard. "What? No," he said.

"Then why are you here? If you are an emissary for the West-landers, you're early. The summit isn't for another two weeks."

"There is an envoy on its way here, with the king of the West-landers as you call them, but I'm not part of their group."

"Then what are you doing here?"

"I'm looking for a friend," Kovan said.

She narrowed her eyes as though his answer drew more suspicion. "The wastes are no place to search for someone. How did you come to have a mystcat companion? You're not a Luminary. Is it your friend's then?"

"No. The cat belonged to another friend of mine. Why it follows me, I can't say. I did appreciate you releasing her."

"You're welcome. Is that how you passed the guardian?"

"What? Oh, the sand monster. Yes. Your monster is terrifying, but it's afraid of cats."

Alasne feigned a smile. "The sand guardian was extra protection; we have a tribe still holding strong to the old ways. Stubbornness and bravery flow equally within Harrinari blood. I will cut your binding free. I hope you understand our reluctance. We are preparing for a lot of Harrinari to be here in two weeks. There have already been multiple attempts on my life."

She stepped forward and pulled a long knife from a sheath hidden behind her back. Kovan held his hands out, and a moment flashed where a different version of himself may have taken the knife and fought his way out. This new version of himself was a little too trustworthy, an effect from the memory cubes, but also, he thought, from Tali's influence.

Alasne cut the ties and stepped away. A guard came in then with Kovan's pack and dropped it on the ground. "For obvious reasons, I couldn't give your guns back yet. I have some things to take care of, but we will speak again soon."

"Maybe next time we can discuss when I'm leaving," Kovan said.

"Maybe," she said with her back to him.

Nothing is more irritating than wasting time, Kovan thought, and as soon as he was alone, he rushed to take the compass out from an inside pocket in his vest. He activated the thing and opened the shell. It lit up a few different colors this time, depending on the direction he pointed it. He was slowly figuring out how the device worked, and he selected the small blue crystal as he always did, by rubbing his thumb over a colored gem until the cosmic symbols changed in the glass. The inner circles responded and revolved around, and the needle realigned. He wasn't at all sure what the symbols meant, or the inner circles, but a needle pointing a direction to follow, he understood that. The light was brighter than before, and he hoped it was some measure of distance.

Kovan waited an hour and decided he was free enough to walk

around the city. He cleaned himself up as best he could and decided to see how far he could track the blue light. He walked leisurely through the building, expecting someone to see him and force him back to the room, but no one did. His presence had earned little to no notice.

Outside the building, guards eyed him but said nothing.

Kovan strolled around the dusty city, weaving around the small paths between buildings. Most of the roads were barely big enough for a cart, and the evening sun was dwindling and casting long shadows along the corridors.

As night came, Kovan felt like he was lost trying to follow the needle while navigating the maze-like roadways. Following the light of the compass as it waned and grew became obvious in the dark. An old man lifting the lantern outside his door eyed Kovan with suspicion, like Kovan was about to steal his food.

At last, he rounded a corner onto a large square with shabby tents, small peddlers, and street urchins, and the compass glass sparkled as though the needle had found its mark.

Sitting on a blanket at the mouth of an alley were a young woman and a boy huddled under another coarse blanket. They were looking at something in their hands, and a taller boy was standing in front of them. Kovan followed the compass directly to the small group of kids, his own pulse quickening. From a distance he could tell the girl wasn't Tali, but she was almost the same age, just about the right age for his daughter.

Kovan weaved through the traffic of people and stepped to the kids. They looked up at him as though they had been caught stealing.

"Can we help you, stranger?" asked the young man who was standing.

"I'm…" Kovan stammered, he didn't know what to say. "I'm looking for someone."

"Who are you looking for?" the younger boy said, and he shot to his feet.

Kovan was still staring at the girl, trying to find recognition in a stranger's face. A small commotion behind them startled them all, and two soldiers were coming through the square. Kovan looked down at his hands, and for the first time, he noticed the compass was clearly pointing to the tall boy, not the young woman.

"Desdar?" said the deep voice of one of the soldiers, speaking to the taller boy. "There's a hunting party leaving. Are you still coming?"

"Of course. Can Elmore come too?"

"Sure, but we're leaving now," the soldier said.

Kovan, realizing his mistake, pocketed his compass and started to slip away.

"Who are you, and what are you doing here?" the soldier said, reaching out to touch Kovan's shoulder.

"He's with me," Alasne said from across the square. She was leaning against a wall with her hood up, watching the entire exchange.

Kovan hadn't noticed her at all. *How long has she been following me?* he wondered. The soldier quickly pulled his hand back, and Kovan continued out of the area, Alasne following.

When they reached an empty street, she spoke to him. "Just let me know when you admit you're lost, and I'll point you in the right direction."

"I will," Kovan said, stopping at an intersection. He began to take a right, and Alasne shook her head slightly, so he turned left.

"Well, I hope you had a good look around," she said.

"I did."

"And what were you doing in the garment district?"

"I don't really know," Kovan admitted.

"And I suppose you don't know why you were talking with those kids, either?"

"That's simple. It's like you said, I got lost and was looking for a way back to my room."

"Well, that's easy. Let me help you," Alasne said. She whistled and a soldier came running from down the street. "Please see this man back to his room at the Shell House."

"Yes, Exalted One," the soldier said.

"Rest easy, Kovan. In the morning, I will have a group of soldiers lead you out of the valley in whatever direction you want," Alasne said, walking away.

"Thank you," Kovan said, but he didn't know what direction he wanted to go now.

Kovan couldn't sleep. He was the most comfortable he had been in months, and yet his mind raced with thoughts about the compass and what he was going to do. *Why would Elias send me to get the stupid device if it doesn't work?* His thoughts continued in this vein. When Oakol warriors came to his room in the dead of the night, Kovan was already awake and heard their feet shuffling outside his door.

"Come in already," Kovan hollered out, and sat up in his bed.

The door opened, and Alasne followed two soldiers into the room, with others waiting in the hall.

"Kicking me out already?" Kovan asked.

"No. Actually, I need your help," she said.

"My help? With what?"

"That boy you spoke to last night, he and the entire hunting party are missing."

Kovan got to his feet and began to gather his things to go. Alasne's eyebrows curled while she watched him.

"You're eager to go looking for him? Why?" she asked.

Kovan paused a moment and then continued to pack. "You came to get me. It must be important," he said, trying to brush off her question.

"Fine, but I'll figure out if you're hiding something. Bring everything. You won't be coming back. When our search is over, you can head west and meet up with the Westlanders' convoy, if you like. We're riding out in five minutes."

"We? Are you going?"

"Yes," she said, walking out of the room.

Kovan finished getting his things and joined the search party along with his horse. Between the dirty looks and murmurs, it was clear his presence wasn't welcome; but if there was opposition, no one said anything.

Alasne was mounted on a horse already and stood next to an

officer with a similar insignia on her shoulder as Pavak, the man who'd brought Kovan and Oz into the city. Pavak was a lieutenant, so Kovan assumed this woman was too. She had shadowed eyebrows and one of those faces that always looked like it was scowling, eyes always rolling in annoyance.

"Nikki," Alasne addressed the officer, "I'll take Kovan with my group to the west in case they got off course. You lead your group to the south where they were last seen, and we'll return in two days' time," she ordered.

The tall, muscular officer sat scowling at Kovan, on the verge of protest, but she bit her tongue at the last moment and angled her horse away.

"Mount up," Alasne said, throwing Kovan a bundle of cloth, "and put that on."

Kovan unfurled the cloth and put the headscarf around his face. The mystcat emerged from an alleyway, and Kovan opened the saddlebag for it. Merphi jumped to the lid and slowly climbed inside. They rode through the city and regrouped at the main gate. Nikki's squad had picked up more men. Two soldiers were escorting a pair of red-haired lions back into cages near the entrance.

"There's a storm coming, Alasne. We need to leave the red lions," Nikki said.

"So be it," Alasne said, and with a wave of her hand, the gatemen began retracting the doors. Through the widening gate, the beginnings of a sandstorm could be seen stirring across the valley below. The wind swirled and lifted three-foot-tall waves of dirt-filled gusts.

"This storm is a bad omen, Alasne. The Great Diviner above shows his fury this night," Nikki grumbled.

Alasne took the comment without reply and pointed to the gate master. "Close the doors and allow no one into the city until we return," she ordered.

She started into the wind, Kovan following at the back.

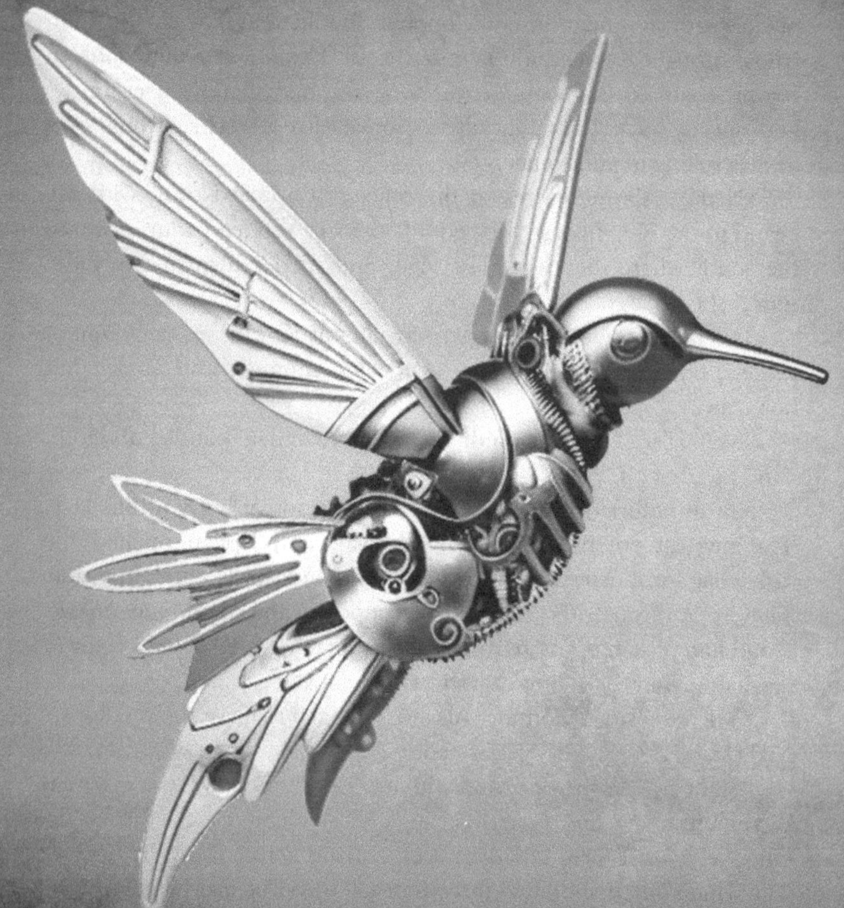

WARBIRD MESSENGER

TWENTY-SIX
CAPTURED - ELLARIA

THINGS HAD GONE FROM BAD TO WORSE QUICKLY. AMONG THE wreckage of the train, they found only three survivors. All three were soldiers on their way to Adara, reinforcements for the ground troops stationed along the coast of Liberty Bay, where, according to them, fighting had begun. Governor Zulhorn was among the casualties. They found the old faithful man's train car completed demolished.

The worst injuries from Ellaria's car had been the few people who had suffered concussions in the crash. Minus some minor wounds and bruises, everyone in their train car had lived. Everyone except Shaw and Atwood. Shaw had at some point hit his head in the tumbling and never woke up.

In total, there where sixteen people stranded in the plains between Bowma and Adara. They were arguing whether they should keep moving or wait for help when the shooting began.

At first, they believed the soldiers coming up the hill from the east were a New World platoon on recon to investigate the crashsite. Wadc and the two treasure-seeking brothers had waved them on.

It wasn't until they were roughly four hundred feet out that Ellaria and Vaughn recognized that the colors and troop formation up the hill was out of place. At three hundred feet, they began to open fire on Ellaria and the rest of the survivors' camp.

The group scrambled for cover and toward the west.

"We need to make it to the forest," Vaughn said, pointing to the tree line in the distance.

After fifty feet, Ellaria realized they couldn't move fast enough. When two of their numbers had been shot and killed, she knew they wouldn't make it. Vaughn had come to the same realization, and they threw their hands up and kneeled on the cold dead grass.

"We're surrendering?" Wade said incredulously as he kneeled with them.

"We have no choice, young man," Vaughn said.

Ellaria could see the worry in Wade's eyes, and Stasia trembled next him. Wade moved his head, searching everywhere for an escape, but the land was nearly barren. Their only chance now was to persuade the squad of Bonemen to take them as hostages and hope New World troops arrived to save them. The smoke from the crash had been substantial, with very little wind to push it out. It was likely troops were coming, but the odds weren't promising.

Ellaria thought on their chances and began to rummage through her bag with one hand while keeping her left arm raised in the air, all the while tracking the enemy as they slowed their approach. A small band had broken off toward the train wreckage to investigate.

"Ellaria, what are you doing?" Vaughn said. "You'll be shot."

She ignored him. She and Echoryn were too far away, but Wade wasn't. When her hand found the vials of shadow-dust and wind-maker powder, she pulled them free of the bag and threw the pouch over to Wade.

"Use these. Shadow-dust first and then wind-maker powder. You see that cropping of trees five hundred feet to the west and the hills beyond? The forest is just over the hill. You and Stasia run as fast as you can. The king's men will be here soon. Tell them we've been captured," Ellaria ordered.

Wade looked stunned, and Stasia tugged at his sleeve.

"Go now," Ellaria urged.

Wade crouched up to his heels, took a deep breath, and picked Stasia off her feet to run. He threw some shadow-dust on the ground as they turned their backs. The area surrounding all of them plunged into darkness, the lack of wind leaving the darkness to linger longer than normal. Shouts from the Bonemen could be heard as they closed on a sprint.

Ellaria flinched as a few pulsator rounds blasted into the cloud of smoke. Wade and Stasia emerged out of the cloud on the far side, and Ellaria's heart sank. A civilian in a uniform that Ellaria recognized as the bartender and the two brothers had taken the opportunity to run.

Another black cloud formed in front of them, and the small group of five ran into it at full speed. Six Bonemen ran past Ellaria and the rest of them kneeling in the grass and charged toward the second black cloud.

A third cloud bloomed and a fourth, then a smaller fifth. *Smart girl*, Ellaria thought, assuming Stasia had suggested multiple clouds. Soon they would run out of dust, if they hadn't already, but they had reached the small cropping of trees and were heading west to the forest.

More shots rang out, and one of them fell to the ground. Ellaria gulped and hoped it wasn't Wade or Stasia. The man lifted his arm in the air; it was the bartender. A sense of shame settled in her stomach that she had hoped the wounded man wasn't Wade.

As her eyes followed her friends escaping, a set of muddy boots stopped in front of her, and an eruptor rifle was aimed at her.

She glanced up to the officer standing in front of her. Based on his short cloak of white and the golden metal mask, he was obviously the leader. His eyes narrowed at her, and she could tell by the venom in his look that he was contemplating shooting her right there, but her age had stopped him. His phifer cloth armor showed signs of scorch marks.

A sixth cloud bloomed at the hillside, and then the cloud moved rapidly, spreading out back toward them. The black shadow-dust was propelled into the valley by the wind-maker powder.

The cloud grew grey and brown, until it swallowed the area. The wind reached Ellaria, and she shut her eyes as the gust blew through, lifting her hair back.

The leader of the Bonemen cursed and signaled his men to round up the remaining hostages.

When the leader had a good sense of how many he had captured and who everyone was, he swiftly walked toward the soldiers in their number. Ellaria bit down on her tongue hard enough to make it bleed so she wouldn't shout out, and she closed her eyes. The leader executed the men in uniform unceremoniously and motioned for the rest of them to be huddled up together and their hands tied.

The troopers chasing after Wade had come back empty-handed. The leader fumed and cast Ellaria a nasty look.

"You can't kill us," Vaughn shouted. "We're New World officials of some standing and warrant the status befitting prisoners of war."

Ellaria narrowed her eyes but kept quiet.

"We'll see about that. What are your names?" the leader asked.

"I'm Nevrin Zulhorn from Imar and this is Lady Irabel Thenan from Logan, and her aid," Vaughn said without hesitation, giving false names for himself and Ellaria.

The leader wrote them down on a small piece of paper and waved a soldier over. The Boneman soldier handed over a small mechanical artificer's bird. The leader placed the note inside the warbird's chest and closed the tiny compartment. He muttered a few words, and the mechanical humming bird flushed back to life. Its gold wings fluttered and it flew out of his hands and toward the north.

"We'll see how much you're worth, Nevrin Zulhorn," the leader said.

* * *

It was nightfall when the tiny warbird was seen again in the sky, with their fate sealed within. The night had come with a cold wind, and no sign of help.

"Line them up," the Boneman leader ordered.

The small bird landed in his palm, and the chest folded open. The leader read the note and cast a look at Vaughn. He whispered something to the soldier next to him, who was armed with a charged eruptor rifle. The soldier nodded his head. Ellaria couldn't keep her hands still. For one of the few times in her life, she was truly terrified. She looked over toward Echoryn, who appeared calm, and Ellaria exhaled.

The next few moments were chaos.

Blaster fire exploded out along the valley, followed by the sound of horses charging in. The Bonemen scrambled and tried to return fire, but the attack had vaulted in from three sides. Unlike the guns of the Great War, the electricity-charged rifles didn't create miniature clouds of smoke that twisted and turned in the wind. The power-charged tungsten bolts fired through the air with burning colors of orange and red. The spread of gunfire was a collage of color and speed, terror, and ferocity.

When a Boneman standing nearby was fatally wounded and fell to the ground, Ellaria pulled the body over to her, Vaughn, and Echoryn to crowd next to it as a shield. It was poor cover, but the Bonemen soldiers where all outfitted with excellent armor, and it was all they had. The dead soldier's pulsator gun had fallen a few feet beyond her reach in the dirt, and she stretched for it.

The Bonemen's leader, sensing defeat, turned back to Ellaria and ran to take her hostage.

Before he could reach her, a hulking form dismounted a horse and fired rapid blasts of gunfire from a bronze double-barreled surge-blaster. The gun was unique and gleamed in the moonlight. King Danehin wheeled around on his heels and continued to fire into the remaining ranks of the Bonemen soldiers. On their journey to the New World from the Tregorean Province, he couldn't walk. The king looked completely healed now. Danehin had always been a warrior. His exploits in the Great War at the age of fourteen were the stuff of legend. Ellaria was not surprised to see him charge in, but she was shocked to see him wielding a gun instead of his typical great sword.

When the skirmish was over, Wade came riding straight to Ellaria and Echoryn. Danehin finally drew his sword from his back, and he slammed the giant broadsword in the ground and hollered out.

"Huzzah!"

The surrounding New World soldiers answered the call and hollered back, "Huzzah, huzzah!"

The king ambled over to Ellaria, a big grin on his face. He was a big man and built like a house. When he smiled, it enveloped his full face and was one of Ellaria's favorite sights.

"Ella," the king roared, "sorry to keep you waiting."

"King Danehin," Ellaria said with a bowed head.

Danehin grabbed her in a bear hug and whispered in her ear, "You can call me Arno, old friend."

Ellaria shook her head. "It wouldn't be right, King Danehin."

"What if your king ordered you to?"

"You're not my king, King Danehin."

"Ha." The king laughed and rocked in his stance. "How I've missed you, Ella. Come, we have much to talk about."

"Am I missing something? Have the Bonemen taken Liberty Bay?" Ellaria asked.

"God no. But they landed troops all along the plains, and now they're spread all along the countryside. We're having a hell of a time weeding them out. We'll talk about it all, I promise. It's past time you directed our forces."

TWENTY-SEVEN
THE PEAKS - LEARON

LEARON STOOD AT THE TOP OF AN ENDLESS STAIRWAY WHERE THE mountain broke free into a giant archway. The sea of mist and the pillars of territh stretched out before him. In the light of the dawning sun, the Five Peaks glowed a subtle golden hue, beckoning him forth.

Learon walked down a small winding dirt trail and crossed a small bridge of rock and tall grasses toward the first peak.

The column of twisted ground rose high above him, and for the first time, he understood the daunting task ahead of him. Each peak was sheer, jagged, and massive. His first obstacle was getting to the first peak, which required a leap off the boulders at the edge of the ravine.

Learon backed away from the edge. He didn't want to look at the gap or assess the distance. It was the first peak. He had little to gain from worrying about whether he could make this first jump.

With his pack strapped tight around his chest, Learon ran as fast as he could and sprang off the edge. He soared through the air longer than he thought he would, landing on the first pillar at the crest of the mist from the valley below. The surface appeared a split second before impact. He landed with a crash and scraped his palm. Standing, he winced at his hand and the tiny cuts. In a small puddle of standing water, he quickly washed his hand and dried it on his shirt, then he began his climb.

First, he made his way up a minor slope and into a shaded perch of flat stone. While he had spent many years in the mountains, he had very little experience rock climbing, and he would have to rely on gut instinct in choosing his route. To start he had decided to stay in the shaded areas while the sun beat down over the cliff side. Learon continued to boulder his way along a makeshift route to the top until he found himself facing a wall of stone. His eyes picked out a route of handholds, and he began scaling the cliff wall up the incline. The climb relied on pure strength and conditioning. A few times the wind picked up and Learon would pause, but he was afraid to break for too long. In half a day he had reached the top of the first peak.

At the top was a wood chest beaten by the rain and dilapidated to the point that Learon hesitated to open it. Rolling the latches over, he lifted the lid to find a length of rope strung to a grappling hook with three claws and single cup of water. At least he hoped it was water.

Learon downed the water and tied the rope at his waist. He swung the hook lightly to get a feel for the weight. He found a spot where a few large boulders projected roughly off the face of the second peak and launched the grapple as best he could to catch on the jagged surface. His first throw failed, but on the fourth attempt, the claws lodged tightly to a collection of rocks above his original aiming point. With the rope in hand, he stepped to the edge of the first peak.

The clouds at the mountain's peak promised wind and rain, but neither had yet materialized. Learon figured he needed to get to the third peak before the weather slowed him down. Unless one of the peaks offered food and more water. There was only so long he could survive on these peaks.

With a gasp, he swung out over the gap. The treetops in the canyon passed below in a blur. Learon slammed into the stone wall of the second peak with a painful crunch, nearly losing his grip on the rope on impact.

His feet flailed below him against the stone surface until his left foot found a hold. He dug into it twice before using it to steady his dead weight. Leveraging himself, Learon began another ascent up the cliff face and navigated to a small plateau halfway to the top. He found a small flat spot just wide enough to support him and laid on his back, catching his breath. "I hope there's an easy way down once I get to the last peak," he said aloud to sky.

With his new vantage point, he could clearly see the third peak and glimpses of the fourth and fifth beyond. It looked impossible to cross over to each. Lower down on the peak, at the edge of the mist, he spotted a bridge of rope and wood planks.

Learon sighed. There was an easy way to cross over to the third peak. But his relief was fleeting when he realized he still needed to reach the top before he could go back down to the bridge. There would be something at the top. Most likely something he needed.

Trying to remain focused, he continued his climb up the second peak. His arms had begun to feel heavy each time he neared another resting point. It was as if the ledge was purposely cut into the spire to rest.

About halfway up, the weather started to change. The night was going to be cold he realized. He eyed a high plateau on the mountain face on the third peak. With some effort he might be able to reach it before nightfall, he thought, but in the moment of distraction his foot slipped.

He dropped and slid down the rock face. Frantically he found a new foothold to halt his fall. His heart raced. He had been lucky to have had it happen on a gentle slope instead of one of the steep inclines. His forearms had taking the brunt of the mistake, and blood oozed out of a long gash in his right forearm until it dripped off his elbow. Learon caught his breath and charged ahead.

The day passed in quiet solitude, his own rhythmic breathing accompanying the sporadic crunch of dirt and rock at his feet.

His muscles ached, and during the Blue sun, he rested at a particularly precarious spot with his back against the bulk of the rock and his feet off the edge. There was just enough room to bandage his arm, and he winced while wrapping it up. He gazed out over the valley was mesmerized by the sea of land stretched out below. A feeling was growing inside him as he got closer to the top. It existed only as a whisper now. He couldn't explain it, but it was a feeling he longed for, and he continued to climb.

As he reached the top of the second peak, he breathed deeply. He was weaker than he expected. He bent over and wiped the sweat from his brow, his chest heaving from the exhaustion of hours of physical exertion. The air was the most clear and fresh his lungs had ever felt. A wave of energy soaked into his blood, and as his blood spread through him, rejuvenation coming over his entire body. Learon stood and gazed out across the sea of mist and pillars of land. His senses stretched and a peace calmed his mind, but it faded just as quickly. The sense of peace and connection he had been feeling was stronger now, but still not mature enough to hold on to. So far, the peaks had not been the trial he expected.

The wind was whipping around him stronger than before and seemed to constantly change directions. At the top, there was another chest. This one contained a brown sack, but no water. Unsure if he was supposed to or not, Learon untied the string at the top of the bag and looked inside. It was full of shards of multicolored metal used for the Elum blades. He tied it closed and lifted it free of the box. It was heavy and cumbersome as he swung it over his shoulder.

Scanning around, Learon realized there was no way to reach the third peak without climbing back down to the bridge, carrying twenty extra pounds of metal.

Learon exhaled and began his descent. Climbing became a meditation as he shut out the wind and focused on his own breathing, and on the rewarding micro sounds of his climb. He focused on his fingers on the stone texture and his feet on the chipped grooves. Every detail became important companions providing confidence of grip, purchase, and progress.

He reached the bridge faster than he thought possible. Learon crossed the bridge to the third peak with the evening sky falling over the mountains. The elongated light illuminated the specks of crystals and metals in the cliff face, and the peaks sparkled with vibrant hues.

The moment Learon stepped over to the third peak, the sensation of place and connection escalated. He looked up to the top and studied the mountain to discern the best route. The best perch and first resting point was a long way up, and something else caught his eye. There appeared to be some black specks floating in the air all around the pillar as it pierced the sky. Learon couldn't be sure, but he thought whatever they were, they were alive.

Again, Learon started to climb, but the instant he mounted the rock wall, he heard a growl from behind him. Turning his head to find the source, he spotted a large shadow moving around the second peak. The shadow of the giant wildcat slipped around the edge and out of sight. Learon stared at the spot and waited to see the animal reappear. When he thought it was safe to continue, he began his ascent. The act of climbing again brought a calmness and focus that spurred him further than his strength should have allowed.

His focus on moving up the mountainside had brought him among the mass of black specks. What he had thought were specks of floating debris, he could now see were giant bats, thousands of them flying around and encircling him. The beat of their wings made the skin at his neck crawl.

Learon continued to climb, but his pace had slowed significantly. He shifted his weight in the footholds and looked for his checkpoint.

The perch was roughly twenty feet above him now. The bats had begun to take more notice of him the higher he climbed, like they were protecting the peak. Their numbers seemed to come in waves, and when they dissipated slightly, Learon moved up another series of holds. He wasn't sure if he could make it to his perch in the night. Another wave of them came at him. This time the bats started to hit the wall near him, some of them crashing into his side and head. Learon pressed his face against the stone and closed his eyes, waiting for them to pass.

When he opened his eyes, a flash of blue passed through his sight. It was there, and then it was gone. It was caught up in the blackness of the bats all around, flying at a different speed than the bats as it passed around the side of the peak.

Learon waited to see it again and realized the bats were circling the entire peak repeatedly. While he peered at them, the blue shape returned. It was a big beautiful bird with bright blue tail feathers. The blue-tailed grackle flew in and out of the bats as though they weren't there. The bird made eye contact with Learon and soared closer to him. Then the bird dove a few feet lower and disappeared around the mountain.

In that instant, Learon decided to follow the bird. He lowered himself down the mountain, and the onslaught of bats decreased as he did so. Feeling along the rock surface, his hands found a deep groove. He pulled himself further and found a crack in the cliff face the size of a man—a cave. The darkness within the passage was pitch-black, but there was a wild blue light beyond the entrance.

The cave was narrow and damp. Inching along, his presence was hard to disguise, as everything he did seemed to echo into the cavernous space. When Learon reached a wider space, he realized the cave was a crystal-filled fissure. The blue light inside was the result of the moon above filtering down through the giant fissure that extended all the way to the upper crest. The light gleamed off the quartz crystal stalactites and stalagmites. Nesting in the stalactites above were more bats, fluttering and moving slightly.

Before he had entered the cave, Learon was tired and unsure how much further he could go without sleep, but now he felt rejuvenated by the crystal. He began to climb up the vertical cave passage. Learon started at a rock column and progressed rapidly to the main rift, passing by the hanging bats, who paid no interest to him.

He reached the top of the rift and emerged at a large plateau and found it wasn't the top of the peak. The summit was still a few hours' climb, but the bats were gone, and the wind was buffered by boulders located at the edge.

Learon placed his things down and decided to rest for the night. He made a small fire and rested against the boulders. His muscles ached, but the many scrapes and scratches on his hands and arms were healed, and his fingers were nicely callused over. Unwrapping the bandage he found the large gash was gone, only a scar remained.

IN THE EARLY MORNING, BEFORE THE SUN HAD ARRIVED, LEARON WAS back to climbing. To his relief the remaining route was a series of boulders and shorter ledges he could lift himself atop.

The night's sleep had brought a new determination to his efforts. With the realization that he was halfway through, he was more confident now than any time in the village. Every step brought him closer to the fifth peak, closer to completing his Trial, and closer to reuniting with Tali.

At the top of the third peak, the new day's sun shined with a blinding glow. The light was magnified by an array of a hundred swords stuck into the ground. All of them were sharp, and the steel shined like mirrors, but none of them were Elum blades. Three massive rocks were tilted together at the middle of the summit. Beneath the leaning boulders, Learon found another wooden chest. Try as he might, he couldn't open the chest. Learon examined the boulders a moment. They were smooth, and the grey color was equally as out of place as their positioning.

There was a flat stone in front of the chest with an etched image of an Elum blade. He looked back at the blades and wondered if he needed to draw one out, but they weren't Elum blades. Learon set his things on the ground to think. Then the thought occurred to him, and he placed the sack of metal he'd found on the second peak on the flat stone. The chest latch clicked free.

Learon opened the box and found a blue feather and one cup of smoking liquid. This was unmistakably the shadow-smoke. He didn't hesitate; he downed the drink and took the feather.

He stood to inspect the rest of the summit. The sea of mist all around had thickened, and the peak itself seemed to be among the clouds. Behind the boulders another bridge of rope and wood had magically materialized.

Learon shivered with uneasiness and crossed over, gripping the side rope lines tightly as he went, the bridge swaying in the wind.

TWENTY-EIGHT
RETURN - TALI

"I WAS TOLD, YOU ALLOWED YOURSELF TO BE CAPTURED. WHY?" Ashrata Nea'Ko asked.

Tali's eyes flickered to the gold staff in Ashrata's hand and the yellow gem. Then she turned her head down to her chains. The getting caught part of her plan had been easy, but seeing the man in gold grinning at her from his throne was the difficult part.

He laid the staff over his lap. "You came back for this, I see. I admire the courage to return here. There may be use of you. I could kill you. It would have to be public and gruesome—you shamed me by escaping."

"But you don't want to do that, do you?" Tali said.

"I don't?" Ashrata replied.

"No. You won't damage a gift for the Sagean."

"You would be a generous gift to give," Nea'Ko agreed.

"But you're not going to hand me over to Sagean."

"Why is that?"

"Because I can help you."

"How? How can you help me?"

"What if I helped you kill the Spirit Elders? They undermine your power, and I can get close to them."

"Interesting."

"They are trying to stop your plans to destroy the Harrinari."

This surprised him—either their plans to stop him or her knowledge of it.

"And what do you propose?"

"Let me help you. When you go to meet the Harrinari, assassins will follow. Be wary of the borderlands."

"I own the borderlands. The Ri clan have strong ties to the Ko clan."

"That's where the most likely assassin is waiting. But I'm sure you understand the ways of spies and assassins?" Tali said.

"I do, I do. Interesting. I'm leaving for the lands of wind and sand today. While your offer intrigues me, I don't trust you. I would take you with me, but I can't very well have you near me and this." He spun his staff. "I think I will keep you alive."

With a flick of his wrist, the guards holding Tali let her go. Ashrata turned his back to her.

"Come on," he said, and the guards shoved her with end of their lances to start walking.

Two more guards joined in at the front and lit the hallway as they descended into the darkness. They wound down a wide stairway that switched back again and again with offshoot passageways connected to the various landings. At the final level, the blackness and gloom stretched out before them, with the hint of a small light in the distance. Their steps echoed in the expansive space, and from the darkness a woman's voice called out.

"Hey Goldie, is that you? Where did you go? It's lonely down here, you fancy metal-cladded buffoon."

Tali held back a grin. Ashrata grumbled under his breath, and Tali noticed his hand tightening on his staff until his knuckles went white. The prisoner locked in the depths of the Zenoch temple still had spirit, a spirit that Ashrata obviously detested.

Twenty feet from the steps, they came to an iron gate with intricate patterns in the welding. The symbols and script were constructed into a latticework wall with a circular door. Ashrata produced a key and inspected Tali for her reaction. With his eyes on her, she tried to hide the fact that the cage made her skin crawl. The prisoner within still ranted, and a growing pit inside Tali's stomach was churning violently.

"Watch your step, Luminary," Ashrata said, holding the gate open for her.

She stepped hesitantly over the lower iron and into the prison cells, and instantly felt two sensations. One, a terrible oppressing sensation like being pulverized underneath the weight of a mountain, but the other was a feeling of comfort.

The woman inside went quiet as they entered. Ashrata told his guards to stay and took a lantern from them to lead Tali deeper into the room. Tali's eyes darted all around, trying to take measure of everything and trying to find the source of the feeling she sensed.

"This is the warded Zenoch prison. I have had it specially fortified against energy wielders such as yourself. Though we both know your energy belongs to me. Tell me how it makes you feel," Ashrata said, unable to hide his crooked grin.

Tali was only barely paying attention to Ashrata, and hoped a simple scowl would satisfy his ego.

The room eventually opened into a wide circular space with small cages lining the outside perimeter. In the furthest one, with barely a speck of light to illuminate it, stood a woman. Her age was hard to tell. Tali guessed she was in her forties. The prisoner was slender, with long brown hair that looked wet, and she was almost naked save for a set of thin garments like a bathing suit.

The woman slowly approached the front bars to her cell as though she had no care in the world, but she didn't touch them. In fact, Tali could see her hands were covered with gloves. The woman's face was hollow, and among her many bruises were an endless number of tattoos on her legs and arms. She glanced at Tali in a quick study. The prisoner possessed a penetrating gaze from a set of sparkling green eyes that made Tali feel like the woman had learned everything about Tali in that one look. She blinked and then she stared daggers at Ashrata.

"Goldie, it is you," the woman said sweetly.

"I've brought you some company, Alasne."

"Are you going to put her next to me so we can play?" Alasne asked.

"I don't think so. I wouldn't want any blood to be spilled. Besides, I don't think Tali here wants to get wet."

Ashrata looked to the sidewall, where a bell was hung in a niche high up in the stone wall. Behind the bell in the niche, interlaced gears softly clacked with each notch turn. After a few notches rotated around, the bell rang out with a single dong.

Ashrata stepped back three steps behind a grate in the floor, and without warning a loud crash broke the silence. The woman backed up into her cell as a large tidal wave of water pummeled her, completely washing out the cell and flowing rapidly to drain at Tali's feet.

The woman walked back to the bars and tried to conceal a shiver, but her skin showed goose bumps all over, and she was soaked from head to foot. She shook her hair like a caged animal.

Ashrata ushered Tali into a cell across from the woman.

"Make yourself comfortable, Tali, and don't let Alasne bother you. She has been down here all alone for some time now. When I return, I will personally deliver you to the Sagean and claim my reward." He locked the cell and appraised his prisoners. "It appears I have got quite a collection now. The envy of any emperor," he said and walked away.

"Going so soon, Goldie? Come on, we never get to talk anymore. Tell me again how powerful you are."

"You laugh, Alasane, but with Tali's powers captured in my viper-eye, there is no one left who can stop me. I will soon have all that I deserve. At Radmana, there is said to be an ancient relic of great power, and with it, I will lay waste to your people. When the summit gathers, I will take control of your little alliance of tribes and kill the leaders who resist," Ashrata said, and he strode out of the prison, tall and proud, the light from his lantern casting a bouncing shadow back toward them.

"Don't go. Take me with you," the woman called after him. "So I can shove that staff of yours down your throat. My people will kill you, Goldie. They'll crush you with your own gold…"

Ashrata had left the room and slammed the iron gate, which echoed stoically in their confines. Yet a soft light lingered down the hall where he must have left a lantern, and presumably guards, waiting. They listened to his footfalls stomping up the steps until the sound of them faded away.

Across from Tali, she could barely see the woman in her cell, but in the darkness, she knew that her eyes had softened and her entire demeanor along with them.

The woman clutched her own arms and spoke. "So, sister. How the hell are we getting out of here?"

* * *

The room was draped in darkness, and the air was dust filled. With every inhale Tali took, she coughed.

"It tastes like moldy leaves, right?" Alasne said.

"What?" Tali said.

"The air. Someone once said 'freedom is cool clean air.' A day in here and you'll never hear wiser words. Ashrata said you had powers that he stole. What's he talking about?" Alasne asked.

"I'm a Luminary, but he trapped my powers in that evil gem of his."

Alasne laughed.

"What's so funny?" Tali asked, upset by the woman's reaction.

"It's a lie."

"What's a lie?"

"Goldie can't take your powers. Didn't you have a master to train you at all? No one has power over you other than the power you allow them."

"But I don't have my powers anymore," Tali argued.

"Yes, you do. He's only tricked you. The viper-eye can't steel your powers. At most it can weaken you because you're giving your energy to it."

"I don't understand."

"Tell me, do you sense the flame of the lantern? Even from far away, I bet you do."

Tali thought about it, and while something itched at her from beyond the cell door, she couldn't focus on it. She shook her head. "Well, that gate complicates matters," she said, loosening the tie at her hair and catching the two varium crystals she had Tyzo help her hide within."

"So, what's the plan? You have one, right?" Alasne asked.

"I have a plan," Tali said.

"Good. You don't seem like someone who lets themselves be captured without a plan to get out."

"First, I must know. Are we alone down here?" Tali asked.

"What you see is what's here. No guards to monitor us, no light to help us, and that cursed gate to trap us."

"I meant, are there any other prisoners?"

"No, just us. Why?"

Tali nodded her understanding, but she was confused. She had felt him—Learon was here, he had to be. Tali put her hand to the stone walls and closed her eyes.

"So, are you going to tell me the plan or surprise me? I like surprises, so that works for me, but I'm cold and time is precious to me and my people," Alasne said to no response. "Hello?"

"Shhhhh," Tali said, trying to concentrate.

In the silence, a click and clack rattled above, and water came splashing out of Alasne's cell.

"Why is he torturing you?" Tali asked.

"…Goldie has a funny way of showing affection, is all," she replied. "Why do you think? He's a psychopath."

"I mean why like that?"

"Oh, it's the same reason for the gloves. He doesn't want me to write anything or draw."

"Why?"

"You have a lot of questions, sweety. I'm not saying I don't like the meet-and-greet going on here"—she shivered—"but I would love to tell you all about myself, once we're out of here."

"You're right. I'm sorry, I'll hurry," Tali said. She approached the bars to her cell and audibly exhaled, looking for the weakest spot.

"You're in worse shape than you look," Alasne said, and she paced around her cell. *Some rescue. At least my hero is something to look at.*

"I'm not a hero."

Alasne stopped in her tracks. "I didn't say that out loud. How do you do that?"

"I don't know. It's something I can do."

"I wish I had that power, then I wouldn't be in this cell. I came here to meet with the Zenoch Elders. Goldie poisoned me and killed my men. If I would have known what he was thinking, I would have killed him on the spot."

"Well, it doesn't always work, and I don't know how to control it."

"Wow, you're a real mess, you know?" Alasne said.

"Oh, I know, I'm a gem." Tali placed the crystals at the lock as Kovan said he had done to escape his cell in Ravenvyre. "Now let's see if I can get this to work."

With the crystal in position, Tali kicked the iron gate and fire erupted at the latch. She kicked again, and the cell door swung free and rattled against the bars and back.

Tali jumped to her feet and rushed over to Alasne's cell to do the same. In short order, her cell door was open too. Alasne ran out and launched herself onto Tali with a giant hug. The young woman was freezing, and Tali wrapped her in her cloak.

"Thank you," Alasne said, with glossy eyes.

"Don't thank me yet. We still must get past that mage's gate."

"I could get us out in a flash if I had some blood and a way to draw," Alasne said, showing Tali her gloved hands.

Tali untied the gloves and threw the leather to the ground. Alasne reached down and grabbed a thin sheet of stone that flaked off in the blast of their doors. She grabbed Tali and cut her arm.

"Ow! What the hell?" Tali said, recoiling from the woman.

"I'm sorry, I need your blood. I'm too weak as it is. Otherwise, I would use my own."

Tali stared at her, confused, as the woman walked swiftly over to the elaborate gate. She stood facing the gate and waved Tali over.

"Watch," she said and began to draw a series of connected symbols on the gate in Tali's blood. When she was done, the blood glowed bright and white. Until it faded. Alasne grabbed Tali's hand, and they walked right through the gate like it was smoke. The gate reformed when they were through.

"If Goldie had stolen your powers, the blood wouldn't have glowed like that," she told Tali. "Now, if we hurry, we can catch Goldie and kill him before he gets his army to the south."

"We can't."

"What do you mean 'we can't'?"

"Like it or not, Ashrata has the backing of his people. If we kill him, it will solidify his position and the Zenoch will undoubtably start a war with the Harrinari. No, we must get back to the Spirit Elders and let them gather their forces. They asked for time, and I must give it to them."

"I can't go north. I must go back to my people and warn them."

"The Spirit Elders showed me; they have a way back to your lands that will put us ahead of Ashrata. Trust me."

"Do I have a choice?"

"Of course you do, but I trust you'll make the right one."

"Why?"

"Because I was told you were a great leader. But mostly because I think you love the idea of being there united with your people when Goldie arrives."

Alasne smiled. "I knew I liked you as soon as I set eyes on you."

TWENTY-NINE
HUNTING - KOVAN

THE WIND ON THE KARNIKA WASTES WAS RELENTLESS. THE SHAPE OF the land escalated the ferocity, funneling it through the valley and trapping it. The sandstorm they rode out into in the night was punishing and had shown no signs of letting up. What started as three foot tall gusts of dirt, had doubled in height and frequency.

Their search party had split in two directions. Nikki's squad headed to the southwest and a place they called the Scorpion Hills. Kovan's group, with Alasne leading, headed west toward the river. It wasn't a big group, only six soldiers, Alasne, and Kovan. By the morning they had reached the river and spread out to search for any signs that the hunting party had come through. The wind and blowing dirt made their investigation difficult, but soon after arriving, they found something.

"Over here!" a soldier called out.

Kovan rushed over to find the soldier and a medic caring for a wounded man. The man lay dying on the ground, his clothes blood-stained. Kovan looked over the wounds as the medic dressed them.

"Some of these are bite wounds, like he was attacked by an animal," the medic said as Alasne arrived.

Kneeling by the man's side, Alasne addressed the dying man with a stern but empathic tone. "What happened, where's the rest of the men?"

"A ghost attacked us," he said, and he gulped for breath. "A demon of steel."

"And Desdar, the boy. The young boy, where is he?" Alasne asked.

Kovan found her question curious. If she was out here for the boy, then the compass hadn't made a mistake, and she knew the boy was gifted.

"Taken…" the man said, and he coughed out blood.

The field medic quickly tore the man's shirt off and tilted him partly up onto his side. It must have been agony for the man. Blood pooled freely below the body, soaking into the dirt, and his screams ended abruptly. The medic sat back. With a clear view, Kovan could see the burn marks on some of the wounds now, and he turned to Alasne and grabbed her, hauling her back from the body to the largest nearby rock. She tried to jerk free, and her men turned their weapons on Kovan.

"Take cover, we're being targeted!" Kovan yelled.

There was a moment of uncertainty among the soldiers, and in that void, a bolt of bright orange metal blasted through the medic's shoulder. A bad shot if they were aiming for the medic, but a deadly shot if the gunman had been aiming at Alasne.

"Those are eruptor rifle wounds," Kovan said to Alasne, who was huddled behind the rock.

"What?" Alasne asked in the erupting chaos. More shots rang out.

Her remaining five soldiers scrambled for cover. Only one carried a pulsator, and he fired a few rounds back into the hills, directing the other men to move to various points. Three others, with bows, found protected positions and set a volley of arrows toward three points on the hill. Their precision in the wind was miraculous, but they struck nothing.

"The dying man was bait," Kovan explained again.

"Yeah, I get that," Alasne replied.

"So, can I have my weapons now?"

Alasne nodded. "Sure, they're in my saddlebags, on my horse."

Kovan growled in annoyance and started to crawl out along the ground. A charged round blasted a spot a foot from his head, and he scrambled back. "I'll wait, then," he said.

"Are you stupid, or crazy?" Alasne asked.

The gusts were charging through the low land of the riverbed, and the sheets of sand were starting to blind their view in all directions. The storm had been gathering in strength at each passing moment, and it now howled through the land. Alasne's men were steadily progressing over the river and up the slope to their attackers, but Kovan lost sight of them in the storm. The noise was unbearably loud.

"Stay here," Kovan yelled.

"Where would I go?" Alasne replied.

Kovan rolled his eyes and sprinted out to where they left their horses. Staying low, he was beaten by the dirt on all sides. The sand was caking into his eyes, and he was soon lost. The mystcat found him, and then Kovan found Alasne's horse, by luck, when he ran into it while trying to make his way back to the large rock for shelter. With its colored metal chaffron and tail guard, it was the only one slightly visible.

Carrying the cat under his coat, Kovan led the horse back in the direction he thought he should go but found nothing. His heart hammered in his chest as he spun to look in every direction, and the cat squirmed, clutching to him, her claws digging into his chest.

"Kovan," Alasne's voice called out to him, and he moved toward the muted sound with his hand outstretched.

"Alasne, I can't see anything," Kovan replied.

"Over here," she called again, and he veered his direction slightly until his hand found the boulder, and he brought the horse in as far as he could.

Kovan dropped to the ground and wiped furiously at his eyes. The crust of dirt scratching his eyeballs seemed like it was piled under his eyelids. He could hardly open or close them.

"Use this," Alasne said, placing a wet rag into his hands.

He pressed the rag into his eyes and dug out everything he could until he could blink again. "Thank you," he said, and he noticed the air underneath the boulder was calm and the noise in his ears had dissipated. With his eyes working again, he could see the outside sand hitting against an invisible shield and rolling across it. He stood and looked around. Alasne was busy drawing something on the underside of the rock. She had produced a dome-like barrier with an alchemy spell. The magic of her drawing shimmered off the rock surface and reflected in her eyes as she worked. The age lines at her eyes faded, and her skin brightened. She completed her drawing and looked at Kovan watching her.

"I guess we wait this thing out," Kovan said, ignoring what he had just seen.

"As fast as it came on, I think it will pass through by nightfall. Or at least settle enough for us to find my men and this assassin."

Kovan rested back against the rock, a wave of exhaustion hitting him, and he rested his eyes. He couldn't get comfortable enough to sleep, but he was too tired at the moment to do anything else but sit there. He put his hands to his aching ears. They were wind blasted and frozen, and it was all he could do to try and warm them.

"Are you all right?" Alasne said, watching him.

"Just uncomfortable. Don't worry about me."

"You seem like someone who is used to sleeping anywhere."

"I am, but alas comfort is a luxury for young bones, Exalted One. The older you get the more you find that you spend a great deal of time in search of being comfortable. You don't know what I wouldn't give for the perfect chair."

Alasne smiled. "I'll have my people make you one if you help bring Desdar home."

It was the opening he wanted, but he had to tread carefully with his question. "Is he special?" Kovan asked.

"Why do you ask?" Alasne replied.

"Otherwise, you wouldn't have left the city yourself to find him."

"He is. He is a ward entrusted to us by the Varu tribe."

"Oh," Kovan replied. It was not the response he was looking for, but even with her explanation, she seemed to be holding back. "We'll get him back," he said, closing his eyes.

WHEN THE WINDSTORM DIED DOWN, IT WAS REPLACED WITH HAIL THAT pummeled the ground in inconsistent splatters. With the sheets of dust gone, they could now see the river and the hills beyond, but no sign of Alasne's men.

"Would they have survived the storm?"

"Yes, but they may have scattered, and I'm afraid the assassin could have picked them off one by one."

"We need to go search the hill we were attacked from."

"You think we'll find my men there?"

"Or something that points us in the right direction."

They left the shelter of the boulder and searched the hills where they were attacked from. Kovan inspected the area, and Alasne's men were gone, but there was more to learn.

"What are you hoping to find? My men are not here," Alasne asked over Kovan's shoulder as he crouched around a small rock formation.

Kovan aligned the view from one rock back to the riverbed and nestled onto it. "Here. The shooter sat here. He stabilized his rifle on this flat spot."

"How do you know it was a he?" Alasne asked with her hands on her hips.

"I don't, but..." Kovan stopped midsentence as something shiny caught his attention. In the ground, covered by loose dirt, was a small bronze gear the size of his thumbnail. There was also a flaked shard of steel plate, with a chipped edge. He looked more carefully at the dirt and began to see some pawprints, or what was left of them after the storm.

"What's that?" Alasne asked.

Kovan rolled both pieces in his hand a moment, thinking about the whispering wind. *"A friend is hunting you."* "I'm not sure, but I think I found a piece of our demon hound," he said.

"A dog shot at us?"

"Something like that," Kovan said. He was sure now what the pieces had come from and who had shot at them, but his hypothesis made him more confused than ever. "Is their anywhere nearby where the land would create a natural barrier from the storm? A ravine or trench? Somewhere your men would go?"

"Yes, further west, there is a series of trenches where the land is shelved, and it splits to create a series of low creek beds. Why?"

"We will find what we're looking for, I'm guessing. Both the assassin and your men."

ALASNE GUIDED KOVAN FURTHER WEST WHERE THE LAND BEGAN TO break like she had described. It appeared like the hard clay had been broken and pulled apart. The small trenches were ten feet deep and ten feet wide.

Alasne dismounted. "These fissures are scattered all around, but the largest is four hundred feet into the hills, there," she said, pointing.

Kovan jumped to the ground and studied the area, trying to think like the assassin. He left his horse on the flat land and crawled into the channeled space, sliding on the slope to the bottom.

Once inside, he found tracks of soldiers. It wasn't hard, because there were a lot of them, and most were fresh. Kovan kneeled to inspect what looked like blood on the dirt, and he whistled for Alasne.

She came to the edge above him, her hands on her hips and scowling. "I'm not a horse, Kovan."

"I know. But I didn't want to yell out. I don't know how our voices travel in these channels," he explained and showed her the tracks he found. "They came in here."

"Who, my men or my enemies?"

"Both. I think your men are being led into another trap."

"Why do you think that?"

"I found blood too, but no signs of struggle in the tracks. Almost like someone was leading your men into the channels with a blood trail. From the looks of it, all your men."

"All of them?"

"I think the second group has doubled back this way."

He showed her where the bloodstain was, and she circled it with her finger and traced an arrangement of symbols around the circle. When she was finished, she placed her hand over it and whispered something beneath her breath. The tattoos on her skin began to change. Kovan stepped back. She finished and looked to the west.

Without saying a word, she began to draw something else and waved him forward.

Kovan took another step away and said, "I'm good."

She stared him down. "Oh, would you get over here, you big baby?"

Kovan shuffled closer and leaned in to see her drawing. It was a quick map drawn in the dirt.

"This is the central artery of the channels," she said, pointing to the center. "Whoever the blood belongs to is moving around outside the area. I bet my men are in the trenches and moving toward the gathering point."

"Hmmm," Kovan said, his mind working.

"Hmmm what? You suspect one of my men is behind this, don't you? Someone has betrayed me?"

"No. I think someone I know has betrayed me. A bounty hunter, a friend, and they're working with the Lor tribe to get us both. I felt I was being followed for a long time, but by someone equally unfamiliar with your land. We passed a group of Lor tribe riders coming out of Oakol. We thought they would attack, but they never stopped."

"The Lor wanted me to uninvite the Varu tribe from the summit and I refused. I told them everyone gets a say at the summit in two weeks. Hostility between the Lor and Varu is not new. It's a very old rivalry, but you think the Lor are working with an outsider?"

"Yes. I'm sure of it."

"So, do you have a plan or only theories?"

"I have a plan. You're not going to like it but I have one. Let me ask you, how do you hunt a hunter?"

"I don't know. I..." Alasne began to argue, but a flash of understanding crossed her eyes. Through pursed lips, she grumbled, "You're right. I don't like it."

Kovan checked his weapons and primed his pulsator, spun it in his hands, and holstered it back before looking at her to answer, "Trust me, it will work."

THE MANY CHANNELS SNAKED THROUGH THE WIND-BLASTED LAND, AND Kovan watched Alasne pick her way through the trench, following a path of trampled ground. She moved swiftly, agitated by Kovan's plan.

Kovan found the ground uneven above and picked a crooked path through dry bushes, with a watchful eye on the Oakol leader. It wasn't easy keeping up with her pace. As the trenches converged, the land grew dense, and the size of the boulders increased. The first scattering of trees offered more concealment, and Kovan's progress slowed accordingly.

Alasne caught up to her men in the large canyon at the center of the network of channels, and Kovan came around the far side of the depressed land to get a better view. He studied the surrounding foliage, searching the perimeter for the assassins' movements, hoping his own approach wasn't being anticipated by someone who knew him well. He caught his breath and wiped the sweat off his palms.

Looking back, he had lost sight of the Oakol moving around in the trenches. *Come on, Alasne, lead them in,* he said to himself, waiting to see her and her men take the clearing. In the cratered area, a small shape sat tied to a dead tree trunk. From a distance, the kid appeared to be alive.

Kovan scanned again and found the three Lor men, their bows nocked. Their aiming point moved back and forth between the kid and the two openings into the space from the serpentine paths.

Alasne and her men entered the clearing, but instead of finding cover, they walked in with their guard down.

"Damn it, lady, what are you doing?" Kovan said to himself.

When the arrows flew from the Lor men in the blind at the Oakol, Kovan quickened his pace. A loud blast echoed in the bowl of rocks, and Kovan froze in his steps. The arrows and a bolt of tungsten shot from the opposite end, but hit nothing. The Oakol vanished in a shimmer, and the attack struck the ground. Kovan smiled and his head whipped around to find the sniper.

He scrambled around the hillside as a volley of arrows emerged from the trench, aimed back toward the Lor in hiding.

Alasne appeared in the area again, and the sniper took aim once more.

Three shots from Kovan's gun blasted into Blackthorn's mechanical dog, and a fourth took Blackthorn through the side.

Kovan put his foot on the rifle, forcing it out of Blackthorn's grasp. "It's over, Blackthorn," he said, his pulsator gun pointing at his friend's face.

Blackthorn slumped to the rock he was using to steady his shot, blood spilling down the rock face. He looked up a Kovan and smirked. "You always were clever," he said.

"You were never a desperate man. It was you who followed me. You started a fire that night on the wastes. I suspected someone was there, but it went out suddenly. You've been tracking me this whole time?"

"I was going to take you that night."

"Why didn't you kill me in the night while I slept? Why wait to grab the kid?" Kovan asked.

"Call it good sport, old friend. I anticipated you would be with the rescue party."

"Who sent you? Why come for me at all?" Kovan growled, his jaw clinched as he stared at the face of his friend. Blackthorn coughed and spit blood. Kovan cringed, and part of his insides recoiled in horror.

"Targo and the syndicates, but that's the job, Van."

Kovan bristled with contempt, and disappointment shadowed his face.

"Oh, don't look at me like that. Not while I'm dying. We all live this life with the same motive, Van; to get by, to pass the time," Blackthorn said.

"I never passed the time hunting my friends. You could have come to me. You didn't have to die for a mark."

"I've never had anything else but the hunt, have you?" Blackthorn winced.

Kovan took his friend's hand to keep him from slipping to the dirt completely and waited until his spirit left for good.

Alasne's men found Kovan still standing over his old friend and escorted him back down the hill to Alasne, picking through Blackthorn's things and taking the mechanical dog with them when they left. Kovan wanted to stop them but said nothing. *Their lands, their custom*, he thought and looked on, quietly disapproving.

When they met back up with Alasne, she was setting the boy on a horse as she commanded her general, Nikki, to ride back to Oakol at once.

Alasne waved at him and accompanied Kovan back to where they had tied their horses off beside the trenches.

"That was some trick," Kovan said.

"A complicated spell, but useful. I've ordered my men to follow you west, if that's where you're heading."

"It is. I'd like to meet up with my friends, but I'll return with them for the summit," Kovan promised and mounted his horse. Looking to the two soldiers waiting in the distance, he smiled. Alasne was not offering an escort, she had ordered him to be followed until he was off Harrinari lands.

"Tell me, Kovan, why didn't you travel with your friends? What were you looking for?" Alasne asked.

"Not a what. I was looking for a person."

"The boy?"

"Not the boy. Someone else, a young woman. But like the boy, she has powers."

"This young woman you're looking for, is her name Tali?"

"Yes. You know her, you've seen her?" Kovan asked excitedly.

"I've met her. She helped me escape a prison a week ago, but she left here not long before you arrived."

"Where was she going?"

"She returned to the north, but with a promise to be back for the summit, a promise I need her to keep. My plans for a united Karnika depend on her."

"Then I will certainly see you again. A lot depends on that young woman."

THIRTY

IT HAD BEEN A WEEK LIVING AT THE DARKHAWK FORTRESS. THE LOCAL guide to Karnika was expecting them in Delanon in two days. So far, they had accomplished nothing. The king wanted Ellaria to weigh in on the war stratagem and devise a sound plan before they all left, but after days of strategizing, they were nowhere.

The fortress was a huge building in the hills of the Shonari Mountains. The structure was thirty stories in height from the lowest floor to the top ramparts. Some of Ellaria's group, like Wade and Stasia, were loving their time there. Echoryn was miserable and had locked herself in her room. Given her visions of so many soldiers' fates, wandering the halls was too much for her to handle.

As for Ellaria, she was going crazy trying to find the best way to defend the New World from the Sagean's invading forces. Standing at a thin vertical window cut into the stone wall, Ellaria stared down at the training grounds, watching her old guard. Semo was leading a new regiment through hand-to-hand fight training. As Semo walked among the ranks with his mechanical leg. Ellaria smiled at seeing the warrior rejuvenated, and cursed herself for having not spent more time with him.

"Vaughn returned this morning," the king said.

"To the front?" Ellaria asked. She turned back to the long table and the map of the New World spread on top.

"To Deloma to lead the sea battles. He took your notes with him, but he couldn't wait any longer to find out the rest of our stratagem," King Danehin said.

"It's for the best. Without the train, it will take him a few days to arrive," General Marr said.

"The Sagean forces had been after the train line for the past month. I didn't think they would actually get it," the king commented.

The king had been lamenting the impact on supplies for days. One of many challenges that faced Ellaria.

"Technically, the Sagean didn't sabotage the train," Ellaria informed him.

"I know, the black Dragon did. Are we sure the Sagean doesn't control the Dragons?" the king asked.

"If he did, do you think we would still be alive?" Ellaria replied.

"I suppose not," the king said.

"A black one—that's the first time we've seen a black one up here. How big was it?" General Marr asked.

"It was giant. Maybe even larger than the others I've seen," Ellaria said.

"Hell, they're all giant," the king said.

"What color is the one up here, again?" Stasia asked. When she wasn't studying reports from the field, she would sit in on their meetings. General Marr was annoyed by her presence, but Ellaria found her youth refreshing, with the added bonus that Stasia possessed a uniquely clever intellect.

"It's the same red one from the south we think, and menacing as all hell," the king answered.

"Any attacks?" Stasia followed up.

"We had one small battle with it, when it attacked some fishing vessels last month. One of our battleships engaged. It was a short fight; I can tell you. The Dragon burned them to nothing. Their fire just lingers on the surface of the ocean. It's unnatural," General Marr said.

"I hate to interrupt, but back to the matter at hand. Are we losing the war, Arno?" Ellaria asked, looking the king in his eyes.

"Not yet. That's why your here," the king answered and began to pace behind the table. Now inside the confines of the Darkhawks' fortress, the king had ditched his weapons for a large ornate staff.

"I keep looking at these maps and, I don't know..." Ellaria mumbled.

"It's war, and if I recall correctly, you're pretty good at it," the king said.

"I know it's war, and our necks are always in the noose. The trick is repeatedly slipping the rope. But the Sagean's tactics so far have been curious..." Ellaria stopped, the king was nodding, but she noted a wince as he walked back and forth.

"Is it your legs, still?" she asked, concerned.

"It's my torquing back," the king answered.

Conrad Marr jumped in. "We're clearly not losing the war. Look at the map, General." As the general in charge of the king's army, he didn't really want to hear what Ellaria had to say, but he respected his king too much to say so.

"I've been looking at the map. I've read all the reports. Conrad, what can you tell me that I'm not seeing at first glance?" she asked the general.

"We're holding the Bonemen back at Illumeen and in Liberty Bay. We were sure they would attack to split our forces, which they really haven't tried. Obviously, we had a major victory in the Orin Channel, and it set the Sagean's plans back a lot," General Marr said.

"That victory is months gone by," Ellaria said dismissively and decided to ask the same question she asked every day. It was the first question she asked when she had arrived, and still, she was unsatisfied with the answer. "What about our spies?"

Marr threw his head back, exacerbated, and didn't answer.

"I keep telling you both. Spies are the lifeblood of a war. They're worth more than any ground gained. Without more knowledge, we're spitting in the wind here, fellas."

"It's still dark on that front," Marr answered.

"That's more than a week now without word. What about the Sagean's spies? How many have you weeded out?"

"Besides the Redeyes?" the king asked.

"Yes. For the moment let's leave those ones out."

"We've found our fair share. Most had to be killed. We do have one converted spy. We found the man wandering our supply stores. He has a good memory too, because he had no papers on him. He was transcribing everything after the fact, but we found his reports in sealed cases. He's how we knew about the assassins after the king in Adara," General Marr said.

"And now where is he? Is he reliable?" Ellaria asked.

"We sent him back to the enemy to spy for us and feed them false intelligence but haven't heard back. We think he's reliable. We did exactly as your notes from the Great War suggested. No torture. We made him feel safe, provided comfortable housing, fed him, and basically treated him like family—"

"You mean treated him with decency, like a human being?" Ellaria interjected.

"It worked. He came around and started talking to us. When we thought he was ready, we sent him on his way a week ago."

"And our organization of 'Doomed' spies?" she asked.

"They've been effective in starting skirmishes on the mainland, in Tovillore and near Andal, but the Sagean is so singularly focused on the New World invasion that he has let the anarchy grow in his own land."

"That goes against what we were told in Ioka," Ellaria commented.

"Don't believe the false narrative. Civil unrest is everywhere over there. The emperor isn't concerned with Rodaire breaking from his control," Marr replied.

"Because he thinks he can easily crush them after he's done with us. Gentlemen, Adara is a battleground of intersecting highways, and yet we have no lines of communication flowing to us. If that doesn't change, things are going to go very badly," Ellaria said.

"Thankfully, the Sagean seems content to strike and fall back like a snake. So far, it's been effective, but only in the chaos it sows. Otherwise, were routing them," the king said.

"Sadly, I don't share your optimism. Maybe we are routing them on the coasts, but they've also split our forces and our attention. The most concerning reports are of the many airborne forces dropped behind our lines using gliders before we figured out how to spot them."

"We're eradicating those, right, General Marr?" the king said.

"Yes, my king," General Marr said.

"If we were, then we wouldn't need a spy to tell us about the team of assassins that made its way inside the Adara capitol building, looking for the king," Ellaria said.

"You're right, the air-dropped troops have been unexpected. We planned a multitude of air defense crafts, but outside of the attack on Orin, they haven't tried anything like that again," General Marr said.

"That's because they were tipped off to your airstream catapult in Illumeen. Is the one in Adara compromised as well?" Ellaria asked.

"We've made the changes to the propulsion system as indicated in the final schematics you delivered from Pryor. I am assured that both are operational at this time," the king said.

"I can only assume that the Sagean was using the airborne troops to sabotage the train lines, to avoid the air defense catapult," Ellaria said. She walked to the window again, unable to stare at the map with the small figurines representing armies and real people any longer.

"Something is coming, I can feel it," she said, and she gazed back out at the barracks and training grounds, now quiet below. Inward philosophic self-reflection was part and parcel to her mechanism for perseverance, even if it was usually born from paranoia. Sometimes her thoughts strayed to the level of consuming her. She had never been this worrisome in her youth. Never so full of doubt and fear.

Danehin came over to stand next to her.

"I have to be honest, Arno. I'm not sure I can still lead men to their death so callously like I could forty years ago," Ellaria said.

"You were never callous, Ellaria. You were always clear minded if your orders held the burden of cold truth, that's because that's all there is in war. It's natural to feel things in a deeper way with age. Don't lose sight of the goal," Danehin said.

"They're all so young," she said.

"Don't let those pimple-faced morons dissuade you. They're all brave and honorable; they're full of fire and they need their energy directed at a goal or they'll burn up. Don't let your age cloud your vision for the young. They're not so stupid as to not know why they're fighting. They need someone to lead them, to aim them at the right target for the right reason. Think of them as arrows in your quiver, Ellaria, and you're the only archer I trust," the king said.

She turned away from the window and smiled at her old friend, a resolve settling in. "Thank you, Arno."

She could also feel the stain of a day catching up to her. It was late, and with the meeting winding down, a yawn escaped her lips before she could stop herself.

The clock chimed the late hour, and the king cracked his knuckles. "I'm turning in."

"I have to go check on my sergeants before the morning. Good night," General Marr said and excused himself.

"I'm going to stay and look this over a bit longer, if you don't mind," Ellaria said.

"Mind? I'm grateful. We all are. But don't forget our engine carriage leaves in the morning for Delanon," the king said.

"I won't forget, but I promised a battle plan, and I mean to leave one behind while we are at the summit."

Danehin left the room, and Stasia woke in the armchair when the door closed. Ellaria hadn't noticed that she had dozed off.

"Still at it?" Stasia said with a stretch.

"Yes. Something doesn't feel right. Can you bring me an extra lamp?"

Stasia handed her the brass base, and Ellaria slid the lamp into position. Something about how the battle was playing out wasn't adding up. "The emperor had been mixing attacks of desperation with patience. Most of our coastal battlements are tempory ground. Ground gained is easily lost. The Sagean knows this and has focused on small, scattered attacks while disguising his ship movements. General Marr thinks that the victory at the Orin Channel and the reclaiming of the water off the coast of Illan has thwarted the Sagean's best shot," Ellaria explained.

"What do you think?" Stasia asked.

"I don't know, child." Ellaria sat back down and rubbed the

bridge of her nose and eyes. Her eyes were dry and tired. "According to our spies, the Sagean is mad for revenge. He's desperate, not only to take over the New World but to crush me and Danehin in the process. Some of his army's moves have shown that. The bombing of Ioka and Orin, attacks on the train line, and the assassin's attempt on Danehin. The rest of his movements have been sporadic, and honestly, restrained."

"Well, here." Stasia handed Ellaria a small hand-drawn map. "Maybe this will distract you for a moment and clear your head."

"What's this?"

"I've finished mapping the Dragons' flight patterns, based on all the information I've had access to here. Notice anything interesting?"

Ellaria looked back down at the map, which Stasia had color coded, marking the general descriptions of each Dragon sighting. Ellaria smiled at the details first, then lowered the paper to look at Stasia after seeing what she was referring to. "None of the Dragons overlap."

"That's right."

"None of them? Do you think they're territorial?"

"Maybe, but a single species, born of the same small location, doesn't typically become territorial over different climates and habitats."

"Unless the climates don't matter to them?" Ellaria suggested.

"What's more interesting, I crossmatched it to some wind maps and ocean currents, and the Dragons' flight patterns aligned."

"I assume there's more?"

"There is," Stasia said, her eyes wide.

"With you there always is, my dear."

Stasia smiled at the compliment. "Well, this got me thinking, and so I wondered what effect they might be having. The Dragons that is."

"And?"

"Well, there are fish that eat nothing but algae and essentially regulate the oceans. Bats, well, they regulate the insect population, and we know how important bees are."

"Yes. So, you think the Dragons are up to something, something inherent to their species. But what?"

"I don't know, but do you remember that scientific journal you showed me that noted how they measured that the Brovic effect was diminishing for the first time in the sixty years that they've been tracking it?"

"Yes."

"Also, it's been so cold this winter. Globally our winters are usually short. The freezing season and the thawing seasons on either side of winter are long, but the heart of winter is never more than thirty days. Today marked fifty-six days. And there's one more thing. I've been tracking the sun."

"What about it?"

"The Blue is going away. The hours the sun turns blue are always when the sun is approaching its zenith until it exits its zenith, roughly two hours. The time of the Blue is well documented for every day of the year, and I can tell you the duration is shortening."

"Because of the longer winter?"

"Yes, and it's diminishing by the day. Indicating winter will never end."

"Let's not jump to conclusions," Ellaria said.

"Understood, but the Dragons are affecting our atmosphere, and that change is resulting in a colder Territhmina and the blue effect of the sun to fade."

Ellaria let out a long breath. *As if I don't have enough to worry about.* "So are you saying we need to find the Desolation blade and kill the Dragons?"

"I don't know."

"Wait. How much data do you have about the sun?"

"A week's worth, why?"

"I want you to run calculations that compare the rates that the Blue is fading to the data in the scientific report about the Brovic curse receding."

"That's brilliant," Stasia said, her eyes lighting up with a new task.

"If we need to find the Desolation blade, we're in trouble," Ellaria said.

"Who knows, maybe those brothers from the train will find it in the Concord Grove after all," Stasia said in jest.

Ellaria bounced out of her chair and huddled over the map, a new and terrifying thought coming to her mind.

"I was only joking. What is it?" Stasia asked.

Ellaria had studied the map and army positioning, and knew she was missing something. She had finally realized what was bothering her, what she wasn't seeing. The pieces of small bits of information charged through her head like magnets coming together: the failing magnotype lines, the image of the Boneman leader's warbird flying north, spy reports, restrained attack patterns, covert missions to interrupt the train lines to Adara, and it was the conversation with the brothers seeking the sword...

"Stasia, go through that stack of field communications and look for anything from the north, anything. I want to know when the last time was that supplies or troops traveled through the Concord Grove. Prioritize reports from Savail, Imarr, and Brigg." Ellaria pointed and scrambled around the table to the second stack of reports.

"I've read nearly all of these. What are you thinking?" Stasia asked.

"I think we're in trouble, dear. I think the Sagean is at our doorstep. They've taken the Concord Grove without our knowing."

"How? We're still receiving reports of no movement in the ocean out of Imarr."

"They're not moving through Imarr. It's a much bigger city than Brigg, but Brigg is the better capture point."

"They would have had to go through Binder's Bay," Stasia said.

"Exactly. During the Great War, we sent ships from Binder's Bay north to Domal. The Sagean is using the same play but in reverse, wrapping his fleet through the Grey Sea and around the Ice Peaks to land in the north."

"I have an old report from Savail that the Zenoch were seen on the western slopes of the Bowshan. Another report here from Savail that a runner reported seeing groups of Ice People migrating south. The scout says the bitter cold is driving them south, and their wagons are caked in ice and snow."

"I don't care how cold it is, the Ice People don't leave the north, and they don't have wagons or carts," Ellaria said, the pit in her stomach crumbling in on itself. *Are the Zenoch part of the Sagean's allies?* she asked herself.

"Go round up Echoryn and Wade. We're leaving," Ellaria ordered. She rushed over to Stasia and snatched the field journal out of Stasia's hands. Without reading it, Ellaria scrambled through the doors and into the corridors.

STASIA'S MAP
Skyvier "White" -same as Zenoch?
"Black" ???
North "Zenoch Lands" "Teal & Silver"
Rodaire "Grey"
Tovillore "Orange"
Mainsolis Sea
"Red" Long-spiked Tail
Karnika
New World
"Yellow"
Anamic Ocean
Brovic Ocean
Nahadon "Green"
Manashera "Black" "Blue"
Merinde
"Purple"

THIRTY-ONE
INVASION - ELLARIA

ELLARIA RAN THROUGH THE HALLS OF THE FORTRESS, TRYING TO FIND the king's room. "King, I need the king!" she started to yell down the empty corridors.

General Marr found her running in the halls and jogged up to her. "What's going on? What's happened?"

Ellaria slowed slightly but continued to walk with speed. "We're being ambushed. Where the hell is the king's room?"

"This way," he said, leading her around two corners and toward a guarded room. Marr signaled the standing guards up ahead, and they knocked softly on the door. When Marr arrived, he pounded on the double doors.

The king answered in his pajamas, his eyes squinting. "Generals, what's happened?"

"The Sagean has taken the Concord Grove," Ellaria said.

The king's eyes flew wide, and he grabbed one of his guards by the collar. "Grab my clothes and follow us to the armory." Then, turning to Ellaria: "Let's go. Explain on the way."

They marched through the halls to the cable railcar that could take them to the lower levels. They needed to act quickly to fortify their defenses before the Sagean's army swept in. The moonlight illuminated the outside ramparts, which were lined with lanterns. They entered the railcar, and the king slammed the door.

He took his clothes from the guard who had sprinted along after them and began changing in the car. "Explain," the king demanded.

"I thought the Sagean would align with the Mistress of Merinde and bring forces up through Manashera. I didn't think of the possibility of him aligning with the Zenoch," Ellaria said.

"Slow down. How do you know the Sagean forces are in the Concord Grove?" the king asked.

"The New World is like a long snake. How do you catch a snake? If you're skilled enough, you distract it and then grab it by its neck. We've severely underestimated the start date of this war. Marr, it is my understanding that crime syndicates have grown stronger since the blockade. They were being funneled money and resources by the Court of Dragons. The Court of Dragons instituted the blockade almost a year ago, cutting the New World off from resources and communications. They have had that year in which to covertly insert spies among our own ranks. Probably stationing troops to the north to wait. All in order to attack us from an impenetrable position. Treaties with the Zenoch made it impossible to fortify the Grove. It is an entangling ground in the hands of the Sagean," Ellaria said.

"How have they acquired serious ground on us in a fortnight, and under our noses?" the king fumed.

"With the aid of the Zenoch, and by sailing their ships from the north and advancing through the Ice People's land. We can't keep a patrol in the Grove, because we're not allowed to. The Sagean knows this and took advantage."

"If the Zenoch are helping the Sagean, what does that mean for the summit with the Harrinari?" the king asked.

"I don't know. My guess is it's a scheme to attack the Harrinari leaders and assassinate the Witch Woman of Oakol. We've received word that the Zenoch asked for the meeting to be in Radmana, the Harrinari's most sacred site. But what's sacred to the Harrinari means nothing to the Zenoch. I wonder if the Sagean secretly chose Radmana in order to search the site for the Desolation blade."

"Let's eradicate them. We'll send a huge force north into the valley and wipe them out," General Marr said.

"By the Blue. The Concord Grove is vast, difficult terrain. It would be a hard place for us to scout properly. If they occupy it, I am certain they are entrenched and impossible to attack by now. The city of Arcoden is hemmed in now. The Sagean can maintain that narrow pass with a small garrison and funnel soldiers directly at our backs. We need to worry about Adara, now."

The railcar reached the lower level, and the group filed out toward the barracks. The fortress was quiet in the passing late night, except for a band of four men cleaning the halls.

They stopped, dumbfounded, and stared at the king.

"Don't just stand there, one of you run and get your commanding officers. The rest of you raise the alarm," the king ordered.

Within minutes, bells were ringing throughout the complex. Semo, along with six other lieutenants, greeted them in the hallway. The king explained the situation to them.

"Why haven't they attacked yet?" General Marr asked, and all eyes fell on Ellaria.

"My guess is that they were waiting for the train line to be knocked out and our main source of supplies cut off, a covert attack in one location that provides the opportunity for a surprise attack in another. My fear is they will know the king and I are together."

"Great, so they could attack any minute now?" a lieutenant Ellaria didn't know said.

"Here, yes. From the Grove, no. They won't attack until after dawn. They would be stupid to march forces into the rising sun."

"Semo, take Ellaria to see about our convoy to Delanon. She's leaving immediately," the king said, and he pushed open a set of double doors leading to the lower terraces and the base of the fortress.

Warning bells rang out at the towers on the hillside, and they turned their attention to the skies. On the far west horizon, three huge Sagean airships were heading toward the city.

"You were saying?" General Marr said.

"This isn't the attack from the Grove. This is a diversion trying to push us to the north," Ellaria said.

The king grabbed Marr's sleeve, "Arm the alchemy-canons and by-the-blue launch the wind-dancers," he ordered.

Marr ran back into the complex barking orders. Ellaria, Semo, and the king rushed down the steps out away from the fortress to the field where their caravan awaited.

The Sagean airships came closer, and smaller ships sprang free on a course toward the fortress. A siren sounded, and the pine trees on the adjacent hill swayed. The ground rumbled, and a series of trees fell to the ground as four small fighter planes were launched into the sky. A huge cloud of vapor rose up the hillside and was pushed away by the wind.

A massive metal tower was now plain to see among the trees, and the king's soldiers were trying to roll more small planes into launch positions. The entire launch area filled with steam as the contraption recharged and reset.

The ejected planes launched with immense speed up to the giant Sagean airships. The New World ships were almost graceful as they opened fire. The Sagean's gliders were equally nimble but bulky, multiwinged, and menacing.

When the first rounds hit the fortress, Ellaria and the king were sprinting toward their awaiting steam-powered carriage, and a large squad with Semo leading the way. The king was yelling for his guns so he could fight.

As the third and last airship came overhead, it slowed unnaturally in the wind. Charged bolts of gunfire attacked the floating ship, but to no avail. The rounds were cast away around the ship. Suddenly, the night sky was full of a thousand parachuting soldiers.

The Bonemen were air-dropping an entire battalion. Soon after they had jumped, the air around the soldiers changed, and the entire regiment was swiftly divided and scattered over the countryside like falling rain. Ellaria racked her brain for the mage's spell that could manipulate the wind in such a way, and her only conclusion was a Luminary on board the Sagean ship—an acolyte who had survived the Sintering Fountain, was responsible.

Small platoons of the king's men organized and went out hunting the parachuting Bonemen. The larger platoons were organizing into companies and awaited marching orders.

Before they could reach the caravan, they were cut off by Bonemen troops. They dodged the first attack and found cover in a small stone field house.

In the distance, Wade, Stasia, and Echoryn were finally running toward Ellaria. Echoryn was dressed in her tight camouflaged hunting outfit from Nahadon, and was hard to see in the darkness. Ellaria waved them on, but ground forces had begun fighting, and gunfire had stalled their movements. A platoon of twelve Bonemen advanced on their position, and Semo led the king's guard to meet them. Wade, Stasia, and Echoryn started sprinting the final distance to the field house. A stray shot of an orange electrical bolt hit Wade in the arm, and he fell to the ground. Stasia screamed and huddled over him. Echoryn produced a bow from her back and fired arrows with pinpoint accuracy into the platoon of Bonemen. She took out three men before they recognized the threat.

As soon as Wade was on his feet, the king ran out to get them, and this time a blast hit the king in his shoulder.

He screamed out in anger more than pain and fired his surge-blaster. Ellaria noticed he had held the gun with two hands before, and now his left arm dangled loosely at his side.

More of the king's men arrived and began to push toward the steam carriages to escape.

"Where's the wound?" Ellaria asked as Stasia and Wade caught up.

"My left bicep. I'm all right," Wade said.

Ellaria tore a thin piece of fabric off a sack inside the field house to wrap around it.

When the king came closer, she wanted to help him too, but his men were surrounding him like frenzied ants. Their group moved across the field, running the rest of the way, with Wade at her side and Echoryn firing arrows all over the place.

They raced through the night as explosions shook the ground. Two of the three Sagean ships had crashed down. The airstream catapult was working. The king's men were able to flood the sky with ships. Ellaria was tracking some of the small short-range ships as they screamed above her when a shot of a glowing red bolt took Wade in the leg. The velocity of the blast flipped Wade to the ground, where he cried out. The shock of a second wound instantly drained the color from his face.

A voice from behind urged Ellaria to keep moving. Ellaria turned back to see King Danehin rushing toward her. "I have him. Go."

Ellaria and Echoryn pulled Stasia off Wade, who was writhing on the grass, and they ran. Danehin lifted Wade over his good shoulder and ran.

The blood at the king's shoulder had soaked through, and the impact of the king's wound had splattered blood to his neck and underneath his chin, but he ran with Wade as if he was little more than a sack of dirty laundry.

They reached the carriages, and the king's men filed all around. The steam from the carriages puffed out a thick mist into the night sky.

"Medic. We need a medic!" Ellaria screamed.

Two men came running up toward the squad and were nearly shot, but one was shouting that they were a doctor. One was a short man with a black goatee; the other was tall. It was the brothers from the train.

"Let them through, they're with me," Ellaria said.

The taller one, named Callen, went toward the king first, but he pointed him to treat Wade. Ellaria gave the brothers a pouch of imbued stones and effirial salt for healing and felt a tap on her shoulder. The king stood over her, swaying in his stance.

"Give this to my daughter. She's the queen now," King Danehin said, handing his crown to Ellaria. The crown was a band of two jeweled feathers meeting at a center jewel.

Semo arrived back from speaking with the driver in time to see the king hand it to her.

"We have to go now; the platoon will keep anyone from following you," Semo said.

"Arno. Come with us, you can sail to the south and be with Dalliana," Ellaria pleaded.

"I must stand with my men against this assault," the king said.

"Please Danehin," she asked one last time.

Danehin shook his head and smiled his wide all-encompassing grin. "Goodbye, my old friend."

Ellaria hugged him and looked at Semo.

"Catch him," she warned, and she placed a coin of dreamer's smoke in the king's palm. King Danehin's legs buckled and he passed out. Semo caught him, but the weight of the king almost toppled both men. Semo's mechanical leg compressed and puffed out steam. A look of fury bloomed on his face.

"What did you do?" Semo cried.

"If the king dies here tonight, so do our chances to win this war," Ellaria said. She yanked one of the brothers up to his feet. "Help him get the king into the carriage," she ordered. She was convinced that King Danehin was growing reckless and that he wanted to die in battle like his father. Having him fall dead here and now would mean a certain loss of the north.

Semo helped the five soldiers get the king into the carriage and returned to Ellaria, a smoldering look on his face. "I'm going with you."

Unity Maze Pendant

THIRTY-TWO
PHANTOMS - LEARON

THE INSTANT LEARON STEPPED FOOT ON THE FOURTH PILLAR, HE could feel the vibrations emanating from the other points around the world exactly as Naomi had described. The shift in his senses to something beyond himself made him stumble and his head swam. When the motion sickness had passed, a crash of thunder broke in the sky.

Learon winced, and rain began to fall in a steady sheet all around him. The loud patter of drops drumming the rock was hypnotic.

Great, he thought, the rain was going to make everything harder. If he needed to scale a similar granite facade again, the rain would make it impossible.

The rain dripped over his forehead like sweat. He ran his hand through his hair and threw off the water, then pulled his hood up. He checked the straps to his pack and started out again. This peak was the largest of the five, with enough room to hike safely from boulder to boulder. There was a path that simply coiled around the mountain and up to the top of the spire, where a lone, giant tree stood tall, its elongated boughs projected into the drizzling air.

There were more trees on this peak than the other five combined. The black pine, red pine, and the moss-covered maples were all leafless and twisted in the winter, but the unique Cyprus trees were green and massive, with branches that swept over the side of the mountain like the tree had shaped itself in the wind. They were majestic, and Learon could close his eyes and feel their leaves moving.

Learon walked among the trees in the pouring rain, admiring their strength and purity. The path was thin and open on one side, and the steep rock face of the peak rose on the other. It struck him that the simplicity of this peak was troubling. As Learon progressed up the mountain, he noticed that the distance between this peak and the fifth peak was substantial. This was his first and best view of the fifth peak, and he could see it was a jagged column of rock that split into two at the top.

Learon continued gaining elevation. Sometimes he needed to stop and vault himself up to the next level of the trail, but nothing about this ascent was strenuous, even in the downpour.

What's the test here? What's the virtue in this? he thought when the sight of something living made him stop dead in his tracks, his heart skipping. He looked again, wiping the rain out of his eyes, but whatever had been there was gone. *An apparition, or was something really there?* he wondered. The peaks had continually played tricks on his mind, and he often wondered later if something he was sure existed had been real at all.

Learon stared ahead into the rain until he was sure what he had seen was gone, but he couldn't shake the feeling something or someone was watching him.

He rounded a corner where a large tree root emerged out of the rock wall, over the path, and back into the ground. Learon stepped over the root and continued the hike. At the next bend in the trail, he saw someone waiting. His mother was up ahead, standing in the rain.

He froze. She appeared beyond the edge of the mountain, like a ghost reflected in the raindrops. She was saying something, but he couldn't hear anything other than the sound of the pounding rain and his own heartbeat in his ears. When he could breathe again, he moved closer. She was calling to him. Her voice was hard to understand in the downpour.

At the very edge of the cliff, he came face to face with her. The specter called to him like she couldn't find him in the rain. Whatever she was saying, Learon couldn't hear her. He stepped as close as he could, and suddenly their eyes met and she stopped talking.

"Mother," Learon whispered.

She didn't answer. The shadowed reflection of his mother appeared so lifelike that Learon had the urge to go to her. "What is this magic?" he said aloud to himself. "Mom are you really here?"

She looked right at him as if in pain. Her stare cut right through him, and then she was gone, her form evaporating in the falling rain. Learon stepped back and continued up the winding path, shaking his head in disbelief. He climbed over a stack of boulders and realized he wasn't alone.

Others were there with him on the path. People he had left behind, people like Rose, the innkeeper from his hometown; his old friend Mr. Garner; Ronick and Darringer. Even Wade, and Stasia, and Echoryn. Some would appear and disappear just as quick, their ghostly forms slipping away in the rain as he neared them. All of them lost and looking for him.

Learon turned, looking in all directions, and the specters surrounded him.

Again, he wiped the rain away from his face and looked up to judge how far he had left to go to reach the top. He was distressed to see he had made very little progress.

Learon put his head down and tried to ignore the phantoms as he hiked up the mountain. He hesitated to look, but eventually he glanced behind himself and found that all the ghosts were following him. All of them with the same aimless look and calling out to him, all the people who needed him. The presence of them began to weigh on Learon. Their presence startled him every time one appeared on the path; and every time one of them left, Learon felt hollow. So many people he had left behind. So many looking at him to be great, to be special. *How am I ever going to protect all these people?* he wondered. The loneliness and pressure were piling up, and his breath came rapidly and short. When the path turned and he stepped over another large root projecting out of the ground, he stopped.

Is this a different root, or the same one from before? he asked himself.

On the rain-soaked ground, there were no footprints, but he could have sworn the root was identical to the first one he'd seen. *How many have I stepped over?* he thought. He peered up to the top of the peak and could see he hadn't made progress at all. In fact, the top looked further away.

Learon quickened his pace. After another bend in the path, he found his mother again, waiting up ahead, standing in the rain.

What is happening to me? Learon's heart began to beat faster, and he decided to run. He navigated the path and small boulders as quickly as he could, but he refused to look at any of the ghosts hounding him. It seemed the more he ignored them, the longer they stayed with him, and their voices grew louder but still intelligible.

He refused to look at them and continued until, again, he was stepping over a large twisted root. Learon cursed and sprinted but stumbled forward. Staring at the ground ahead, he gasped. He could see tracks in the mud now. His heart sank when he realized they were his own footprints, and they were vanishing as fast as he could spot them.

Learon stood and looked up into the sky. The rain poured over him and he screamed, "What do you want from me!"

His muffled cry echoed off the peak. Overwhelmed by the insurmountable weight of everything, he suddenly couldn't breathe at all. Learon fell to his knees. He was stranded on a path that was taking him in circles. Hiking up and up and getting nowhere, and no matter what he did, he was isolated from everyone.

Learon wiped the pouring rain from his face and closed his eyes, attempting to calm himself and lean on the hours of meditation with Naomi to regain a sense of control.

When his breathing eased back to normal, he stood and looked back toward the path and up to the top, even though he knew what he would find. The majestic tree stood swaying in the breeze, at the summit, still so far away. He had made no headway at all.

Learon reluctantly decided to turn back and head down the mountain, returning to the bridge where he had started.

Hiking back down felt wrong too. Learon stopped at the large tree root and sat down. He buried his head in his hands and laughed nervously. He had become as lost as the phantoms around him. He was stuck, unable to go forward and unable to go back. He held the necklace Naomi gave him and tried to think of what to do.

The torrent of rain continued, and Learon felt the presence of another apparition standing nearby. It spoke to him.

"Why are you stopped?" the voice said.

Learon looked up, and Elias stood on the path, his form shimmering in the rain.

"Elias?" Learon said, startled, but Elias didn't answer. He wasn't there, Learon concluded. He took a deep breath and closed his eyes again.

"Why are you stopped?" Elias asked again.

"I'm afraid," Learon answered.

"Afraid of what?"

"That I will fail everyone I care about. That I can't be what everyone wants me to be."

"Ask yourself, who are you really afraid to fail?"

"... Myself," Learon said.

"So, is it what everyone wants from you or what you want for yourself?"

"I don't know."

"Why are you stopped?"

"Because I must move forward. But I can't."

"Why are you following the path someone put before you?"

Learon opened his eyes to look at the apparition of Elias, but it was gone. He stood and looked up to the top of the peak again—but not to judge the distance, rather to find a place to begin his climb.

He found a secure handhold and began to scale the steep mountain face. All the climbing over the last two days had built a tactile memory in his fingers, strengthening them. The skin had grown raw in the process, but callused over to be tougher, and his grip was twice as reliable as when he started. His muscles ached, but he blocked that out and focused on the next position, the next foothold, the route of his choosing up the mountain.

The rain made the climb arduous and slow, but Learon didn't care. Compared to wandering the path to nowhere, he felt weightless.

When he reached the top, he pulled himself to the summit plateau using some roots in the ground until his weight was firmly past the cliff's edge.

Learon got to his feet, and the first thing he saw was the magnificent tree stretching out above him. The second thing he saw was that the ghosts had returned and encircled the peak. Beyond them, at the center of the plateau, a chest lay on the ground. Learon shook and clutched the necklace again for comfort.

He backed away and under a large branch of the giant Cyprus to shield from the rain. He was freezing and exhausted. As soon as he was under the tree, the ghosts' voices ceased and the sound of rain returned, but they still stood watching him.

"You're still afraid?" Elias's voice said.

"Yes."

"What are you afraid of?" Elias asked. He was standing in front of him, his hood off. He was more translucent than the others, Learon thought.

"Being alone," Learon admitted.

"Why are they here?" Elias asked, and when he spoke his image became clearer before it faded again.

Learon didn't know the answer. He put his hand to the pendant again for comfort. "Because I want them here with me," he said.

"Do you believe?" Elias asked and pointed at Learon.

Learon looked down at his chest and looked at the necklace Naomi had given him. The red stone was bright and hot to the touch. He held tight to the necklace and the red gem and tried to remember what Elias had told him once about them. How mothers of the Ordona tribe would give their children a gem of rose quartz to protect them on a long journey. A heart-stone, empowered with love.

Elias had said that belief was the first act of alignment, that if Learon could believe in the energy of a stone, he could use it. He looked at his hands where the wounds had been healed from the crystals in the cave.

Closing his eyes, Learon held the stone tight to his forehead. He stepped back into the rain and felt the same vibrations he'd felt with his first steps onto the fourth peak. Then Learon sensed the points of energy around the world: a great beacon in the west; a powerful beacon to the east; and two more in the north; and a surge of power in the southeast that threatened to swallow him and everything with it. Learon couldn't breathe, and he squeezed the stone and opened himself up to it. There was a great warmth inside it that enveloped him. He had a sudden feeling of being home, and he felt her presence in the north.

Tali was surrounded by tall trees and snow. A great lake spread out behind her, and she was walking with a young woman and a blue-skinned Zenoch man. She was far away, but she was alive. Learon opened his eyes, and the ghosts were gone. He stepped to the wooden chest.

The lid creaked open, and inside, wrapped in a wool cloth, was an axe.

THE RAIN STOPPED. LEARON REMOVED THE OLD AXE FROM THE CHEST and stood up. He stood alone at the summit of the fourth peak with the giant tree and an axe.

Learon looked closer at the branches of the tree and could see that the black wood was exactly what the handles of the Elum blades were made of.

He knew right away that if he cut a branch off, together with the metal and the blue feather, he could bring his materials from the peaks back to the village, and an Elum blade would be made for him. A sword unlike any other, one empowered by his trials, but something made him hesitate. He could hear his conversation with Naomi about taking one last look at the village. They both understood he wouldn't be returning. Certainly not to wait for a sword to be forged.

He wanted to reach the fifth peak, and be gone, *but how?* Learon saw no other way to cross over to the next mountain. There was no bridge waiting for him and no way to leap the chasm between the fourth and fifth peaks.

He walked to the edge of the summit and closer to the trunk of the giant tree. There, he braced himself while holding a large branch as he looked down. He wasn't sure what he hoped to find, but all he could see was mist. He started to contemplate if he could somehow attach the grappling hook to the tree and swing over. When the mist parted below, he could see that down the cliffside, there was a point when the skinny mountain peaks came close to each other. He estimated the gap he could see to be roughly twenty feet. Which meant that it was probably closer to thirty feet, and still too far to jump.

Learon felt like he was missing something as he went back to the chest, holding the axe in his hand. He looked back at the massive tree stretched out over the gap, and it dawned on him.

"No," he said to himself. He appraised the beautiful tree, in the fresh sunlight from the passing rain, and couldn't believe what he was about to do.

He took the simple axe's rough, splintered wood handle in hand and hoped the thing would hold up to the work. He swung with all his might at the trunk of the giant Cyprus. The edged blade dug into the trunk, and Learon shrieked.

A pain deep inside himself seared, and a profound sadness settled in his gut. Learon swung again.

"Ahhh!" he cried out and dropped the axe to the gravel. This time the sting shot from his toes to his hands, and tears came to his eyes. He caught his breath and wiped his face. The two swings had dug into the tree and chipped pieces to the ground. Learon unaccountably mourned the missing pieces he had violently removed. Judging by the damage after two blows, it was going to take him a long time to cut the tree down.

He swung again. This time trying to do two strikes back-to-back, hoping that he could anticipate the pain, but he doubled over and screamed. A profound, tangible empathy was taking over his entire being. Learon wanted there to be another way but knew there wasn't. He kept at it for an hour until the axe was more than halfway through. He pulled the blade out and let it drop to the ground and then curled up into a ball and trembled. He held tightly to the red crystal until the physical pain subsided, but the sadness remained. Learon continued to chop down the magnificent tree, each blow exacting a toll on him.

When the evening came, and the sunlight was dimming, he brandished the final blow and the tree fell into the ravine. It somersaulted and crashed into the sides of both peaks until it eventually wedged itself between the two.

Learon stared in disbelief; he now had a way to cross over. Then he lay down on the dirt, among the many shards of wood and chips of bark, and he wept.

THIRTY-THREE
BEACON - TALI

THE WIND OFF THE LAKE CHILLED TALI TO THE BONE. TYZO HAD BEEN waiting with the boat and took her and Alasne across in the early morning to the northern shore. As soon as they reached land, the three of them headed for the Spirit Elders temple, where Mia waited for them.

Tali pulled her cloak tighter around herself as they made their way through the snow-covered ground. Suddenly a warm feeling came over her, and the forest of trees and the snow at her feet vanished. They were replaced by a sea of mist and pillars of jagged mountains all around. Learon was there, and he was smiling at her, and then Tali's world came snapping back to her.

Her vision blurred, and she stumbled into the snowpack.

"What happened? Did you trip on something?" Tyzo asked, at her side in a flash, helping her up. Tali stared at his blue-skinned hand, recalling an old dream, and took it.

"What was that?" Alasne said.

Alasne was leaning against a nearby tree as though she didn't have a care in the world, but she was blinking and wiping her eyes.

"You saw that too?" Tali said.

"Not by choice. What did you do to me?"

"It wasn't me," Tali said. On her feet, she dusted the snow off herself and smiled. She had finally sensed him again.

"Are you all right?" Tyzo asked.

"I'm fine. Let's keep moving."

It took until they were almost at the road for the truth of Alasne to finally hit her. Tali stopped. "Wait, it's you," she said.

"It's me?" Alasne said, her eyebrows coming together.

"Yes. I don't know why I didn't see it before."

"And what are we talking about?" Alasne asked.

"You saw Learon."

"Who now?" Alasne asked, a single eyebrow raised.

"I thought I sensed him in the prison, but it was different, because it was you," Tali replied to herself.

"There you go saying that again. We've established the 'you,' but what the torquing hell are you talking about?"

"You're a mage."

"Oh, are we starting over? Hi, I'm Alasne, I have powers and control of alchemy and sigils and magic stuff, and you are?"

"I'm a Luminary and Learon is…"

"Your boyfriend," Alasne finished her sentence. "I get it. I'm sorry I spied in on your weird psychic connection."

Tali went quiet and squinted her eyes with annoyance.

"Oh, I struck a nerve," Alasne said.

"No. Learon is a Nimbus Warrior. Together, us three, we're a Trinity. I don't know much about it, only that a Fusion Mage completes our connection. We're guardians, chosen to protect the world."

"I don't know what to say to all this, but I'm not chosen," Alasne said.

"You're gifted."

"There are many people who are gifted."

"Not like you. I'm not going to argue. I know it's you," Tali said, smiling.

"Stop that. What are you smiling about?"

"Hope. I'm smiling because of hope. I haven't had hope in a while and it feels good."

"Well, don't get too cocky. The Spirit Elders might be luring us into a trap, you know."

Tyzo made a small nod as if agreeing.

"They're not," Tali said flatly.

"Fine, but if I'm one of these guardians, does that mean…" Alasne winked at Tali.

Tali closed her eyes and exhaled a breath of annoyance. "You're very frustrating," she said.

"Well, I don't want to add to the frustration, but we need to camp for the night. We're not going to make it to the Spirit Elders before dark, and the gates to the temple are closed at night, even to guests and expected visitors," Tyzo explained. Without waiting for their agreement, he left them and began gathering wood for a fire.

"Does he never smile?" Alasne asked.

"I don't know," Tali said.

THEIR CAMP WAS SET UP A SHORT DISTANCE OFF THE ROAD, TYZO having positioned it behind a bulk of trees. In her short time with the man, Tali had come to understand that worrying was Tyzo's natural state. After they were settled, he stayed awake to keep watch.

At first, Alasne couldn't fall asleep. She laid on her bed and whistled while staring at the sky. When Tali finally rolled over toward her, Alasne proceeded to pepper Tali again with questions about the Trinity and Learon and the Fusion Mage. To which Tali had very few answers. Sill suffering from her imprisonment, Alasne eventually grew tired and fell asleep.

Tali looked over toward Tyzo, who sat a few feet outside the camp, his eyes scanning the trees.

"Tyzo, you can't possibly stay awake all night after doing most of the rowing across the lake today."

"I'll be fine. Get some rest," Tyzo said.

"Wake me and I'll take a watch to give you a break," Tali said before laying her head down.

Tali's own exhaustion surprised her, and in a matter of moments she was sleeping. Her dreams were filled with obscured faces and giant creatures rising out of the ocean and destroying everything in their path.

They were giant bipedal creatures with four long arms, each

equipped with claws. They were like sea scorpions, but the size of wagons, and they closed on their prey in flashes of movements. All Tali could do was stare as people she loved were killed. At one point she was looking at Learon and Kovan hiding inside a small wooden shelter hiding from the creatures. When the building came crashing down on them, Tali was helpless and turned to run, but the beasts closed in on her from all around. She was crouched down and holding her knees, while the scorpions' grotesque clacking noises grew louder. Every muscle in her body trembled. Tali closed her eyes, waiting to die, fear seeping from her pours like sweat, when a blinding light lit up her closed eyes.

She awoke with a gasp and rolled over. The night sky was full of color, a glowing swirl of greens and blues. She got out of her blanket and tried to find a better view.

She found Tyzo still sitting away from the fire, his eyes drooping and barely open. Tali went over to him and helped him stand. He was very cold and dead on his feet.

Still, he argued to be left alone. "I'm fine, go back to sleep," he said.

"You're not fine. You're no good to us if you're too tired to fight an intruder. Come by the fire and get warm. I can't sleep anyways. I'll take watch until morning," Tali said, leading him back to the fire.

Tyzo scowled at her, but went to lie down without contesting.

Tali started to stroll around their camp, her eyes fixed on the glowing sky. The bright colors to the north were drawing her in.

Without realizing it, Tali had hiked toward the lights far enough that she had lost sight of camp when she finally looked back. Most of her footsteps were captured in the snow and traced the way back, but she pressed on toward the light.

She wasn't sure how long she had walked, but the wilderness started to change. The mountains grew taller, and patches of darkness claimed much of the surrounding areas. She passed a pair of tall stones, her eyes on the sky above, and almost missed the glowing symbols on the rock. They were symbols of the Ancients' language. Tali was too rusty to translate them, but she had a clear understanding that she was entering a sacred area.

She crested a hill, the snow ankle-deep and looked down upon a clearing with more giant stones. Something sat on top of a pedestal in the middle of the space. Tali hiked down and into the valley. The mountains around her were steeply sloped with multiple ledges covered in ice and drifts of snow at the base. Light from the sky reflected in the ice and stone, but the jagged rock formation and tall boulders concealed a thousand crooks of shadow.

Four steps into the stone filled valley and she could feel eyes on her and shapes moving in the darkness.

Tali whipped around, and the rocks and tall cliff points surrounding her were filled with ice-panthers. Some were like Mia's ice-panther, Koda, in appearance and size, but some were much larger and had darker stripes down their backs. Most had bared teeth.

Tali turned in a slow circle. When she was facing the short pedestal again, five massive ice-panthers blocked her way. They had closed in on her without making a sound.

"The Luminary is here," Tali heard a voice say in her head. It came from behind her and startled her.

Koda stalked up behind her slowly. He glared at her and stopped in front, between her and the other ice-panthers. On four legs, his back came to Tali's shoulders.

"The one who can speak to us?" a panther asked, the voice also blooming inside Tali's head.

"I was only following the lights in the sky. I didn't mean to intrude," Tali said, bowing her head.

"Of course you did," another panther growled.

"Zanshar, she is a descendant of the Gelelo-ayeli. She will not attack us," Koda said.

"Gelelow-ega Seego-nega devente uhnelana," the oldest-looking panther said in the lost language.

A few of the panthers growled around her.

"I'm a descendant of who?" Tali asked Koda.

"The Sky Elders."

Tali didn't know what that meant or why Koda would say such a thing. "And what did he say?" she asked Koda.

"Dwalla says that doesn't mean we can trust you. That the Sky Elders of the Blue sun were abandoned by the creator. Now be quiet."

"Will she save the Dinhithal from themselves?" the female panther asked.

"Yes, Naheya, she will. She is doing it," Koda replied.

"And the prophet, Mianora? She believes this child is the one?" Dwalla asked.

"Mianora has seen the end of the maze, great leader. She has read the tide of time, and her actions will ensure our future is safe. This child of the Mystics is the key. If we don't give her the Entangling Sphere, we will have brought the very shadow down upon us that we mean to defeat. She can speak to us, she has united the Trinity, and she will unite the world toward the Last Dawn. She is the great warrior, the TaoKoa."

"Then let her place her hand on the sphere at the altar and we will know if she is true," Dwalla said, and the panthers backed away from the pedestal.

Tali looked around at all of them and took a single hesitant step. When none of the giant panthers moved, she slowly walked toward the altar, passing over a metal band that encircled the pedestal. Koda escorted her partway but stopped short of crossing into the circle.

On top of the altar were four necklaces with cracked and broken jewels placed around a black metal sphere emanating wisps of illuminated smoke. Tali reached out for it. The sphere was warm to the touch and solid. The smoke tendrils crawled up her arm, and the glowing symbols on the surrounding stones grew brighter.

Tali's heart pounded, and the ground below her rumbled. The metal circle lifted out of the grass and snow, along with two others buried beneath it. The metal bands encircled the air around her, and a column of light enveloped her. The entirety of the glowing sky pooled above, and then the aurora funneled into Tali. The colored light struck her body like a jolt of lightning, and her nerves tingled from head to toe. Tali felt a warmth surround her, her feet hovered off the ground, and then it ended, and Tali fell back against the altar.

Koda began to drag her away from the pedestal. The entire area and surrounding mountainsides were now dark, and only the moonlight lit the landscape.

Sluggishly, the frayed nerves in her arms and legs calmed and she looked around for the ice-panthers, but only three remained: Koda, the one he called Naheya, and the leader Dwalla.

Koda stopped and nuzzled Tali with his nose. "Get on my back, and I will take you back to your friends," he said.

"Naheya will go with you," Dwalla said. The great ice-panther leader came closer to Tali. She could see his age in the clouding of his eyes and the grey around his face. "You were right, Koda. She has survived the Entangling Sphere. The guardian stones have been mended. She is the TaoKoa," Dwalla said, then he pressed his nose to her ear and whispered to her, "Be strong child, for you are one of the tethers of war that bind the world, our champion at the Last Dawn."

Tali could only bow her head again. "Thank you, Koda," she said.

"How do you feel?" he asked.

"Like roadkill," she said, looking over his fur. "How exactly do I ride with you?"

"Get on my back and wrap your arms around my neck, but not too tight."

Tali did her best to smile, she collected the mended stones off the alter and then awkwardly climbed onto Koda's back. She placed her arms around the panther's neck. Koda took off through the woods with Naheya close behind. Tali closed her eyes and held on, her blood still quaked from whatever the alter had done to her.

HALFWAY BACK TO CAMP, THEY RAN INTO TYZO AND ALASNE searching the woods for her. Tyzo nocked an arrow as the ice-panthers slowed to a stop.

"Tali?" Tyzo said, still holding the bow at the ready but aimed to the ground.

Alasne showed no fear of the giant panthers and walked straight up to Koda to help Tali down. Tali slowly sat back and dismounted off of the ice-panther. The cold of the woods hit her, but she was happy to have her feet on the ground.

Alasne instantly embraced her in a tight and desperate hug. "Don't do that again," she said.

"I'm sorry," Tali said and looked to Tyzo. "I'm sorry, Ty."

"I'm glad we found you. Alasne was in a panic."

"I was not."

"She was. She awoke with a scream and started to point the way to go to find you," Tyzo explained.

"Something happened out there. Are you all right?" Alasne said.

"I think so," Tali said. *"Koda, what was that?"*

"The Entangling Sphere was used to mend the amulets of the Fates."

"The ones needed to fight the Wrythen?" Tali asked.

"Yes. Only the rarest kind of Luminary can make it work."

"What kind?"

"A Luminary descended from the Fates."

"Is someone going to say something?" Alasne asked.

Tali laughed and realized Alasne and Tyzo couldn't hear her conversation with Koda. "Sorry. I was talking with Koda."

"We got that," Alasne said.

"Now we must be going back, but when the Last Dawn comes, the ice panther's will be ready," Koda said.

"Thank you, Koda, and you, Naheya."

The two ice-panthers bounded around the trees, kicking up snow, and sped off to the north.

THIRTY-FOUR
THE FIFTH PEAK - LEARON

LEARON LAY THERE IN THE BED OF WOOD CHIPS, A COMPLETE WRECK, holding his knees. His insides felt torn, and his soul bruised and aching at what he had done to move on.

Elias's presence returned. "A new tree will grow back, but you will never be the same. This is why the fifth peak has not been reached by many people." Elias was sitting on the stump, looking down at him with a soft grin.

"I'll never forgive myself," Learon said.

"All things have roots, but the roots are not the tree. The roots help a tree stand, but the tree chooses how to grow and live. It creates itself in the face of changing seasons, and it learns to bend with the wind. A tree unites two worlds and balances the energy of light and darkness. Nothing is more empathetic with the world than a tree.

"We too are of nature, and it's through our compassion toward all living things that we foster harmony in the face of evil, war, and hate. Compassion allows the forest of humanity to flourish. The interconnectedness of our existence extends beyond roots and fallen trees. Empathy is what holds our world together, and without it the tree would never grow at all. The empathy toward all living things will burn brightly inside you as long as you live."

"Is it really you? Are you really here?" Learon said.

Elias smiled. "Remember, nothing is gone forever which has taken root in memory. The soul has memory, and so we shall meet again," he said.

A strong gust of wind blew through, and Elias was gone. Learon picked himself up and headed down for the tree.

Crossing the chasm by navigating over a giant tree was a nightmare. The branches moved in the wind, and the entire thing shifted with each step.

When Learon stepped onto the fifth peak with the sun setting far beyond the mountain range, only a wisp of light in the sky remained.

Learon stepped to the mountain wall to climb the last peak and heard a growl behind him. A leopard was there, with black fur and spots of blue and green. It launched off a tree and swiped at Learon's legs. The sharp claws gouged marks in the rock, and it fell to the ground.

Learon hurriedly climbed the rock, but the moon was concealed behind clouds that made picking his route suspect and slow.

When the darkness fully enveloped the fifth peak, it came with an onslaught of hail. What started out has pebbles of ice blasting the cliff became large-rock-sized ice bombs that could kill a bird. The huge balls of ice hit him like clubs.

Halfway to the lower summit of the two-tiered peak he stopped. The wind at the top was blowing in all directions, and the hail was punishing. He found a skinny ledge with an overhang of rock that acted like a canopy and provided a small amount of shelter from the hail and wind. The ledge was wide enough for him to sit and stretch his legs but nothing more. Still, he decided it was as good a place to stop for the night as he was going to get.

Learon retrieved the grappling hook and lodged it in a fissure along the surface. When he was sure the flukes of the grapnel were fastened and wouldn't move, he tied the rope around his waist. Satisfied that he had safeguarded himself from falling, Learon leaned up against the mountain and tried to rest for the night. The hail departed as swiftly as it had arrived, almost like it was never there.

Every part of his body ached and screamed for sleep, but his mind raced. He thought of his friends scattered around the world; he thought of the soldiers fighting along the coasts, and of the Renegades in Tovillore, all trying to fight the new Sagean Empire rising around them. He thought about Tali. He was certain she was alive, and through his vision of her, he knew he could find her. He was determined to find her.

***

The growling woke him before the sun had come up. The leopard, *if that's what it was*, prowled the mountain, with a low growl emanating in a frustrating rumble. The colored spots and stripes at its face glowed in the mist that had settled in the crevasses between the twin spires of the fifth peak. Learon tilted his head to track the thing's movements and quickly shifted back. The simple adjustment made his precarious position on the small rock point unstable. The strap and spike he had used to hold him in place held, but his exhaustion was prevalent. Sleep had been almost nonexistent on the mutable ledge.

The time he wasted trying to sleep had been terrifying. His thoughts had been consumed with falling. Slowly, he disentangled the protective straps and lifted himself to his feet, gripping his hand to the folds of the rock. Small granules of dust trickled out below his feet, and the wildcat growled again.

He ignored the animal and started to scale the rock. His muscles suffered from some lethargy. His attempt to sleep had not helped his muscles, and it had done less for his mind. The culminating effects of the his trials were present in the aches of his arms and legs.

The climb, however, was solitude. The work of scaling the peak, the process of findings creases and solid edges, hand position, foot placement, and route picking had again cleared his mind. By the time the sun was warming the surface, he had reached the plateau where the peak split in half.

The final summit was within reach, but beyond a simple jump. The growling continued as the leopard was proving to be a better climber than Learon. If nothing else, it knew this mountain and had picked a route where it could continue to stalk its prey. Learon could see no way over to the top spire. The rock face was completely sheer, and even climbing it looked impossible, but to jump over to it was suicide.

When the growling had ceased, Learon decided he could attempt to climb down and find another way to the highest point. He spent the morning clinging to the mountain and eventually was forced to refuge again at the same small ledge he had spent the night on. No matter where he climbed, he couldn't find a way to the top.

As the afternoon sun come out of the Blue, Learon rested and mused that the Blue period had seemed faster than normal. For the next few hours, he tried to use the grapnel to cross the gap, but it never found a fastening point. So he returned to the lower ledge of the split peak.

With the evening coming on, Learon felt his own hunger crushing at his insides. His heart hammered in his chest at the realization that he had wasted a day. Learon's frustration, hunger, and exhaustion were compounding as the time lingered on. Somewhere below the ledge, he could hear the leopard moving around. Learon's own hunger and the leopard's were in sync. It seemed like something was always chasing him, always hunting him.

Is the mountain mad at me for chopping the tree down? I wouldn't blame the mountain if that was the case. If this is the guardian of the peaks, it might have just cornered its intruder.

When the evening came and the stars began to pile up in the sky, the mists in the valley started to rise too, until it cloaked the entire area in a fog too thick to see more than five feet.

The glowing leopard was still there, and the shining light from its fur would come and go in Learon's vision. He was coming to realize that the mist and the leopard were signaling that his time was up. The longer he stayed on the plateau, the more he had convinced himself he could make the jump. With the mist all around, Learon chucked his bundle of supplies as far as he could to the top peak. The pack landed with a loud thud that angered the wildcat, and Learon could hear it clawing at the stone below his feet. Learon wasn't sure if the leopard was real or if he was imagining it, but the sound of its claws as they gouged though the rock made Learon's skin crawl. The wildcat was coming for him, it would not allow him to reach the top. There was something up there, something powerful. Learon knew it now. The wildcat was not a real animal protecting its territory; it was a creation of the peaks to guard the final summit.

The mist breached the ledge surface and flooded in around his feet, and the leopard would soon follow.

It was now or never, Learon decided. He backed up as far as he could, his heel off the ledge, and ran. He leapt off the edge. It was a blind jump, and the landing zone came at him fast, appearing out of the mist. Learon landed on the top ledge of the fifth peak and nearly rolled off the other side.

He picked himself up and dusted off his clothes. Scanning from the top, he could see the four peaks like floating ghosts, the tops proudly lit by the moon. The silhouette of a cypress tree swaying gently at the top of the fourth peak.

He searched for a fifth wooden chest but found something else that took his breath away. A wall rising above his head made of crystal, shining in the moonlight with names etched on the surface. The last four names read Naomi Sawyer, Elias Qudin, Elias Qudin, and Learon Wynvaloren.

The mountain had given Learon a new name. More surprising was that Elias had apparently made his way to the fifth peak a second time. As Learon tried to puzzle out why Elias would do such a thing, he ran his fingers over the lettering, and in doing so, he dusted clear something fused onto the wall. When the moonlight shined upon the object, Learon couldn't believe his eyes. He had his answer to why Elias had returned, and he had what he came for. A grin came over Learon's face and he laughed. His laugh echoed in the valley of mist.

INTERLUDES V

- Aylanna -

INTERLUDE V
AYLANNA

AYLANNA ARRANGED A TENTATIVE ALLIANCE WITH BARAGON, THE captain of the Band of the Black Sails. The Rodairean had a small navy of galley ships, but she required the cloak of the Black Sails' flags to penetrate the heart of the Sagean waters.

They boarded the *Carmine* in Orvana, and it took them the better part of three weeks before they had crossed the Mainsolis and sailed around the Cape of Andal.

The trip served two purposes for Aylanna and Batak: the chance to lay low and the opportunity to meet with a new spy.

With the expectation that the Old One would be calling on her for progress on the Desolation blade, Aylanna felt the need to escape the city and the coming wrath of the Wrythen when it found out she had no leads to the sword's location.

The reignition of the Whisper Chain had afforded them precious intel from all over Tovillore, and they were using it to search for the sword that could kill Dragons, but every lead had turned up empty. No matter how confident the Old One was that she could find it, Aylanna was beginning to think that the sword was either buried inside the Sagean's tomb or lost to time. An active Whisper Chain also afforded them a new spy network operating as a separate branch from the main chain. One of the new spies on the network was operating from inside the citadel. Aylanna was eager to hear about Verro, and Batak was equally eager to hear about his son, Delvar. With a new and highly valued spy in their service, they had organized a secret meeting at the port city of Anvil.

The Black Sails' ships were longboat raiders made for speed and maneuverability. They were timber ships that would always be elegant in comparison to the massive iron tombs the Sagean had been building at the citadel. She had her first glimpse of the new ones crossing the Mainsolis Sea. A fleet of Sagean ships were moving around the Cape of Andal with them.

The large stone lighthouse of Anvil was located on the hillside and overlooked Anvil Bay, a small inlet on the long northern coastline. They arrived in the harbor in the afternoon, a cloud-filled sky in a perpetual state of threatening rain overhead. But for the winter's cold and snow, Aylanna welcomed the lack of sun, as she was still routinely suffering headaches since the Sintering Fountain had transformed her blood.

The harbor was full of chipper ships that traded goods all the way from Domal in the Grey Sea to Eloveen in the Zulu.

The *Carmine* docked at the longest wharf, and Aylanna and Batak disembarked. Her daughter stayed aboard. The small port city of Anvil was full of warehouses. The quaint city blocks were full of saltbox-style houses and buildings.

While they were navigating around the docks, a light, freezing rain began to drizzle. They found the site of their meeting place, a small tavern overlooking the smaller jetties.

The tavern was a aged wood building, and a large Hazon man worked behind the bar. Their spy was already there in the corner of the tavern. He wore a fine black suit and top hat, and he sat studiously and stiff in the booth.

Aylanna went to sit down while Batak got drinks at the far side of the bar to keep watch.

"Mr. Napar," she said as she sat down. She knew it wasn't his real name, but the pin on his lapel told her she had the right man.

The man nodded. He looked like an old and bruised piece of fruit. The look behind his face was withered, and his eyes, always moving around the room, had bags under them. She knew the man had been a respected mathematician at the Arcana before it was closed, before the Sagean had him taken to the citadel to work along-side the Sagean scientists.

"Before we start, you never saw me, I was never here," the spy said.

"Of course."

"The names you asked about—the young man and the gentlemen—they've been deployed overseas to aid in the war efforts."

Aylanna rolled her eyes at the spy's reluctance to use the names Delvar and Verro. "Do you know where exactly?" she asked. She looked around and leaned in. "Just use their names so my headache will go away."

The spy swallowed and bit back a complaint. "The young man was sent to the holding position in the north. I don't know where, but there's a rumor of a tentative alliance with the Zenoch. From there Delvar was scheduled to be sent on a mission of some importance with Shirova. Verro has a talent for wind and was sent to Adara, but I heard he was redeployed to go south and help troops in Manashera."

"Manashera?" Aylanna replied.

"There's been a development in the unexplored continent. The Mistress of Merinde was asked to position her army there, and they discovered the lands were not abandoned. Upon landing their army, they discovered the civilization of the Menodarins."

"Alive and well?" she asked. It had been long believed that the Menodarins, if they still existed, had migrated their people to the unexplored continent. Still, not much was known about the curious beings or their culture.

"Yes. What began as a stepping-stone turned into an assault and full-on invasion on Manashera."

"And what about the captain?" she asked, curious about any news on the Sagean himself.

"Edward, or the entity inside him, is a madman. It's difficult to still consider him a man at all, anymore. His scientist manufactured a way to keep him alive, but he has become another one of his experiments."

"We heard something of this already. His focus is still on the king?"

"He has taken a greater interest in the mainland of late. Massive armies have been sent to crush the Renegades housed at Fort Mare."

"We heard they made some waves," Aylanna said, assuming the Sagean was furious with the developments at Midway and the small group of rebels there.

"More than waves. The Renegades destroyed the largest ammunitions manufacturer plant and storage facilities. It has rendered much of his army limp and cut his gun supply in half."

"How about my land? What are the captain's intentions for Rodaire?"

"I can tell you; your reactivation of the Whisper Chain did not go unnoticed. A wise move, I assume it's helping you track the captain's movements around Tovillore. There's been no word yet, but the sense is that for the time being the Renegades are the priority."

"I'm surprised the captain didn't destroy our machine, then."

"Oh, he wanted to, but his scientists insisted on leaving it alone and immediately began working on a devise that could tap into the Melodicure machine, instead."

"Did it work?" Aylanna said, scanning the room herself. Suddenly, her own nervousness about being in the open was turning her stomach.

"It did, but they had to build their own sensor towers. As far as I know, they can't tap into the older ones yet, or we wouldn't be meeting. However, that's why the captain believes he has the king and his general cornered. The team was able to build a sensor tower on the New World."

Aylanna knew the sensor towers the spy was talking about were simply sigil-etched pillars with gems inside for the Melodicure machine to connect with. What he really had told her was that the Sagean had a spy inside the Whisper Chain headquarters feeding him information whenever he asked. The ability to track people had always been at the heart of the Sagean Empire. Aylanna had already ordered all the sensor towers in Rodaire destroyed.

"But you don't think the Chain is compromised again?"

"No. Or I wouldn't be here. If they make a move to take over the machine, you'll know?"

"Well, I didn't know that there are spies inside the headquarters, until now. I'll deal with that. What about this other development? This secret project you warned us about, what is it?" she said.

"Do you know about the Old One?" the spy whispered.

"I do, why?"

"I don't know what or who that is, but I know the captain is afraid of it, and the most important project he has his team working on is a giant magnetic field that is supposed to work as a conductor and amplify the captain's powers so he can fight this Old One and trap it."

"Then the light of the Blue help us all, the Sagean is crazier than I thought."

PART THREE

THIRTY-FIVE
ON THE BORDER - ELLARIA

AT THE BORDER CITY OF DELANON, DOCTORS MET THEM AT THE King's Post, a compound and estate overlooking the gateway to the Karnika wastelands. Soldiers had raced ahead of their caravan to prepare for their arrival, and a uniformed officer greeted them. He waited at the door to their carriage for the medics to enter first. After the injured men were taken inside on stretchers, the officer introduced himself.

"Greetings, Miss Moonstone, I'm Lieutenant Bristol. I run the offices at the Post here. We have everything ready for your trip to Oakol," the officer said with his hand out and pointing the way toward the estate entrance.

"It's General Moonstone, Lieutenant," Semo corrected him.

"I'm sorry, General Moonstone. Your guide is waiting in the sitting room."

Stasia tapped Ellaria on the shoulder and held out Wade's watch. There was a message from Kovan. *About time he contacted us*, she thought. *The man is infuriating.*

HERE, IN DELANON. AT THE AIRFIELD WITH BAZLYN.

Relief flooded over her, and she handed the watch back to Stasia. "Take it with you."

"What about you, yours still doesn't work?"

"Kovan has one, and that will have to be enough."

Stasia feigned a smile and followed the medical team.

Ellaria found the guide to Karnika sitting silently in a small room off the entrance. He wore glasses and weathered brown clothes that looked like the dirt of the wastelands had been stitched into the cloth. His skin was tanned, and his face gaunt.

He twitched slightly at the door closing.

"Mr. Miller, this is General Moonstone," the officer introduced them.

The guide stood and looked around. The guide wasn't nervous, quite the opposite. His eyes were calculating, and he looked directly at Ellaria when he spoke. "Hello, General, I'm Gavin Miller. Your guide to Karnika."

"Let me ask you, Mr. Miller, how far have you been inside Karnika? Have you made contact with all the tribes?" Ellaria asked.

"Not all of them, but I've traveled to the Uden Sea and have lived with the Varu tribe," he said.

"You come highly recommended; I was only curious. Can I expect that our supplies are sufficient for the trip?" Ellaria asked.

"Yes, General. I reviewed all the supplies. I provided a list of the items needed to the soldiers here, and they have diligently acquired all that I asked for. We are ready to leave once you are."

"Good. Have them divide the supplies in half. We leave first thing tomorrow morning. Now if you'll excuse me, I have a lot of things to do before we leave and not a lot of time."

"Of course."

Ellaria excused herself and headed for the medical bay. Wade was first because his bed was closer, and Stasia looked up at Ellaria with the same concerned look she had worn on her face the entire ride there.

Ellaria came to his side and held the young man's hand. Wade was still passed out, the result of the many sedatives given to him for the pain. The doctor, seeing her arrive with guards, came over to Ellaria.

"How is he, Doctor?" Ellaria asked. The field medic did their best with both the king and Wade. Their actions saved both lives, but both men were in serious condition.

"I have only just finished looking over him. Your friend will limp for the rest of his life, but he was very lucky with both wounds. They missed major arteries, but the leg wound has destroyed the man's femur bone," the doctor said.

"No need to amputate?" Ellaria asked and Stasia's eyes grew big.

"No. But he will be bedridden for some time, and the process to walk again will be a difficult one. I would like to look after him for the next month, and then one of the nurses can begin his rehabilitation."

Ellaria stepped closer to the doctor to talk quietly. "Well, you're not going to like me, Doctor, but I need this man and the king ready to board an airship, tomorrow."

The doctor flinched back. "Impossible."

"Make it possible. I don't care if you have to accompany them. I'm getting them out of here tomorrow. Now show me to the king."

They moved to the back of the bay where the king was resting. Nurses were leaving the room with blood on their hands, and Ellaria's heart sank.

The king had awoken on the ride, furious with Ellaria, but by the time they had reached Delanon, his wound had zapped all his strength. At fifty-five years old, his body wasn't recovering as fast as Wade's.

"What's the king's prognosis?" she asked.

"He took a significant number of pulsator rounds to the left side of his shoulder and chest that resulted in massive blood loss. I don't believe he would be alive without the field medics. The tungsten bolts usually cauterize as they penetrate, but his wounds indicate that the tungsten ball broke up on impact. It barely avoided hitting something vital, though it shattered his left clavicle, and we've just finished pulling fragments out of him. Some were lodged in his neck. All in all he's very lucky. Still, it has been a great shock to his system, and I'm worried about infection."

The doctor started to pull the curtain back, and Ellaria stopped him.

"Do you think the charged round was designed for that purpose?"

"It's possible. You would know more about such things than I do. I will say that the pieces of tungsten were quite brittle."

Ellaria nodded and wondered if the Sagean had been rushing the production of ammunition. The doctor opened the curtains, and they found the king was awake. He pointed at Ellaria and scowled.

"You. You're who I wanted to see. Hold on," King Danehin said and put up a finger. "Doc, by the light of the Blue, can I get some food?"

"At once, my king," the doctor said, and he scampered away.

"You look good," she lied.

"I look like death. I've spoken with death, and he can't have me. Now, before I pass out from the pain, what is going on, Ellaria? I assume you have some sort of plan." He paused and closed his eyes against a wave of pain. "And a good reason to have pulled me off the battlefield?"

At least his spirit wasn't broken, she thought. "Well, considering we already went over this in the caravan when you woke up before, I would say I made a wise decision," Ellaria replied.

"You drugged me. I was delirious in the carriage. Tell me again."

"Fine. Tomorrow night you're flying to the south to the fortress in Falenmor. Your daughter is already there."

"That's a great place to hide me if you want me to go crazy."

"I want you to live."

"Well, it's either the safest place in the realm or the next spot the Sagean will be invading."

"Oh, I'm certain the Sagean will eventually invade from the south. The small army I saw in Merinde will come up through the Dead Wake, and our forces there will send them back to the sea, with your daughter and Stasia commanding our defenses."

"And you?"

"What do you think? I'm going to save your kingdom, of course. It's what I do."

"How are you going to manage that?"

"I'm going to enter into an alliance with the Harrinari, even if it means we make an enemy of the Zenoch. With their help and resources, I can send their warriors toward retaking the north and a special force to the south too."

"Wars are slow and taxing. What if that's not enough? How long can the New World hold out?"

"A long time I think, but just in case, I have a secret mission still coming together in my head, one that takes the fight to them."

The king smiled and laughed, then winced in pain. "I like the sound of that. I don't think I'll ever forgive you though."

"You will. You'll have many more years to think on it, and when you hold your grandchildren one day, I'll await your gratitude."

"If that day comes, you'll have it."

Ellaria left the king and Wade to see to her remaining tasks. She found Semo waiting in the corridor and motioned him to follow her.

"Yes, sir?" Semo said, the steam pump at his mechanical leg repeating like a metronome as they walked.

"Semo, I need your three best riders and the three best horses they have stabled here."

"Right away."

She loved that he didn't ask why, but she knew the wheels were turning. "They'll be couriering a journal with battle plans back to General Marr. I've marked it with a protection sigil, but the riders should still be under order to burn the journal if they are captured," she explained and handed the journal over to Semo.

"I'll see that it's done, sir," Semo said.

"Will you be traveling with the king?" she asked.

"Or with you, General. If you need me."

"I need you to protect the king and Wade. Once you land, I'd like you to take over at the fortress. The army there needs to be ready for battle. Can you do that?"

"I can."

"Good. Get going. I need to go out to the airfield, but I'll be back. We will be leaving in the morning—all of us. One more thing. Tell the doctor to sedate the king, he needs rest."

Semo nodded and rushed off.

With things properly set in motion, she went to find the airfield. In case there were spies in the city—and she was sure there were—she needed two airships and two caravans to adequately disguise their movements as they left the city.

Ellaria strode onto the airfield with evening sun dying behind her. A variety of winddrifters were in the station, and she found the *Savona* at the back of the lot.

Leather boots hung over the side of the ship, the legs wearing them crossed. Ellaria guessed who they belonged to.

"Van, stop napping and come down here."

Kovan sat up holding the mystcat in his left hand and adjusted his hat out of his eyes with his right. He glanced at Ellaria and the small squad of soldiers with her and grabbed a nearby rope. He swung down from the deck, a heavy bundle of sandbags lifting on the other side of the ship, slowing his fall.

She embraced him before his feet hit the dirt. "It's so good to see you, Van," she said into his chest, as uncalled-upon tears welled in her eyes.

She began to pull back and apologize, and Kovan held her tighter and whispered in her ear, "I can tell when you need a good hug. It's all right, we can handle whatever happens next, together."

"Promise."

She used his shirt to wipe her eyes as covertly as she could and backed away. She mouthed, *Thank you*, knowing that he had purposely given her time to return to herself and not let the soldiers see her crying.

The small squad of men fanned out around her. The extent of her own guard brought a raised eyebrow to Kovan's face.

"What's happened? That's a lot of protection. Don't tell me you're queen now?" Kovan said.

"No. But the king was injured. I'm…"

"Taking control?"

"Yes. Is Bazlyn here?"

"He's in the city getting supplies."

"I need him to take a crew tomorrow morning to Falenmor. I sent Dalliana to the fortress there already."

"Smart, but dangerous," Kovan said.

"I thought you'd say that."

"Well, it's an ideal place to maintain control of the war, if the north has been lost. Has the north been lost?"

"Maybe. Yes. Probably," she admitted.

"The Concord Grove?"

"Yes, how did you know?"

"I came through the wastes. I met Alasne, the leader of the Oakol."

"Wait, what? You met with the Witch Woman?"

"Yes, and she's not fond of that name. Alasne told me she was imprisoned recently by the Zenoch leader. I figured if the Zenoch are already betraying the Harrinari before the summit, then maybe they were in league with the Sagean."

"Dying-light, Kovan. Why didn't you send word?" Ellaria said, her face getting hot.

"I only arrived here two days ago, and the king's men were already preparing for his arrival. By then it was too late. Then I heard your caravan was seen arriving and waited here for you. But there's more."

"More?"

"Tali is still over there with the Zenoch."

"You saw Tali?"

"No. She rescued the Oakol leader Alasne and returned to the Zenoch Spirit Elders to help them win a civil war I guess."

"That sounds like her. I'm glad she's all right, but we could really use her. The Sagean brought an invading force overhead of the Dark-hawk fortress two nights back, and I'm sure there was a Luminary aboard one of the airships."

"Another Luminary?"

"I would venture to guess it was one of the newborn Luminaries, one of the Court of Dragons."

"Well then, you are lucky to have made it here."

"That's just it, we were lucky, but not because of what the Luminary did. There was no lightning, no ground moving."

"Maybe they're not as powerful as a real Luminary?" Kovan said.

"I think you must be right," she said, scanning the field. She still had much to do before they left. "I have to get back, but I'll see you at dawn."

Kovan looked at her, downcast, but tipped his hat to her and bowed. "I'll see you at dawn, Your Highness."

THEY LOADED THE KING UP ONTO THE *SAVONA* BEFORE LIGHT BROKE on the next day. Ellaria asked only for two of Semo's most trusted soldiers to help.

Then Kovan and Semo helped lift Wade aboard. Stasia gave Kovan a hug and then Ellaria.

"Wade will come through, he's a good man," Kovan said.

"I know he is," Stasia said.

"When you reach the fortress, Stasia, I need you to help Dalliana. Do exactly as you did at the Darkhawk fortress. Go over every report. I trust you ladies to keep things going until I arrive." She handed Stasia a copy of the journal she sent with the riders back to General Marr. "These are the same battle plans I sent to General Marr. I also sent him a note to contact you in the south. We won't be long."

"All right," she said.

"Also, ask for the regiment we met in Kerrio to fortify your area. They were being deployed nearby," Ellaria added.

Stasia looked at her with gaze of concern.

"You'll be fine," Ellaria assured her.

Echoryn hugged Stasia and whispered in her ear. Then Echoryn climbed the ladder into the winddrifter. Ellaria made a mental note to ask about it later, before checking a pocket watch. They needed to get to their caravan into the wastes.

Kovan then handed her a bundle, something heavy for its size and wrapped in a blanket. She started to unwrap it and he stopped her. "Probably not a good idea to expose the thing we fought so hard to steal in the open like this," Kovan said.

"You mean, this is the stone?"

"Yes. I've had it hidden in a secret compartment on the *Savona*."

She shoved it back to him.

"I can put it back," he said.

"No, keep it. But keep it safe."

They finished their goodbyes, and Ellaria gave Bazlyn strict instructions on when to lift off. Semo and Stasia waved goodbye, Bazlyn's dog in Stasia's arms.

Ellaria had devised it so that the ban on air travel had been lifted, and the *Savona* would be the third ship leaving the field, shortly after the army aircraft had taken off toward the west and another decoy ship toward Orin.

At the staging area for the caravan to Oakol, Ellaria checked her watch again and told the guide the agreed-upon place on the map. The guide was taking the bulk of the forces and the steam carriages to wait at the river near Oakol. Along with two adventurous passengers. Ellaria had asked the brothers to go with the guide and help in any way they could. They agreed, and a wink between them made her roll her eyes. They apparently believed that treasure awaited them in the wasteland.

Afterward, she rode back to Kovan accompanied by Echoryn and their small pile of supplies. A small squad of soldiers rode with her. Kovan waved her over and lifted Ellaria's bag to strap it to her horse, but the top tilted, spilling some clothes and a few books out. Echoryn reached down for the small tattered blue book. The instant she held it, she dropped it and jerked back like lightning had shot up her arm.

"I didn't know objects could do it?" Ellaria said, staring.

"I didn't either, but it feels like everything has been triggering me lately," Echoryn replied.

Kovan picked up the book and handed it to Ellaria before repacking her things and safely strapping them down. Ellaria turned the book over in her hands. It was the small blue book she had taken from the library in Ioka. "What is it, what did you see, Echoryn?"

"I don't know, let me see it again," Echoryn said, mounting her own horse.

Ellaria held it out, and Echoryn took it hesitantly. She held it with both hands and closed her eyes. Ellaria and Kovan watched her closely, waiting for a reaction.

When her eyes shot open, Kovan nearly jumped out of his shoes. He backed away and mounted his own horse.

"I think it's a book of prophecy," Echoryn said, handing it back.

"It can't be, I've read it. A few times. None of it makes sense, it's more like poetry," Ellaria said. "It reads like…"

"Like dreams?" Echoryn asked.

"Yes," Ellaria said.

"That's because it is. You know how sometimes you can remember your dreams and other times you can't? Prophecy is like that—you remember moments, images, flashes, but the narrative is broken, the logic falls apart when you retell it. The truth of it can't be explained. You can't express it or think of it clearly enough. That's what prophets feel, those fading images of the future. You don't know at first until the things you see become real and you recall the clarity. Visions like the one I had of you, where I'm sure of a cause and an effect, those are rare. Those are when the Unity Maze spreads out like a giant living tree."

"Elias said something about the maze in his letter. What is it?" Ellaria asked.

"It's what prophets call the entanglement of souls."

"How do you know that what you're seeing is going to happen? How is it that endless choices can create inevitability?" Ellaria asked skeptically.

"I can't explain it, but I don't have to believe in it, because for me the dreams are real. They are as true as anything else. I have them. I didn't ask for them, and I can only trust that there's a reason for them, or a value to them," Echoryn explained.

"Can you alter events, then? I mean if you had to, could you?" Kovan asked.

Ellaria was surprised that he had been listening at all to the conversation. It was the sort he usually would have ignored.

"To alter one, yes, if I focused on that one event and all the intricacies of it. But to alter more than one, I think would cause me to go mad. Where would you stop? With each alteration, the visions would come back to me again and again. Also, I think to affect change would require either massive shifts or for me to do nothing but live and breathe the visions, day, and night. Small influences are the best I can do. Try to be there when someone needs me, or if I'm really worried about something, I might warn them."

"Like you did with Stasia today?" Ellaria noted.

"Yes, but I worry my warning may be the very catalyst for the event I foresaw," Echoryn said, her eyes downcast.

"Can you read it, the book?"

"I don't know. Maybe."

"Then put it with your things. It's of no use to me," Ellaria said. "I have enough on my plate already. I don't have time for prophecy."

"Not yet you don't," Kovan mumbled under his breath.

"What's that mean?" she asked.

"Nothing. Just that I can guarantee you, you won't eliminate prophecy from our lives so easily," Kovan said, and he kicked off into the wastes to lead the small squad of eight to Oakol.

THIRTY-SIX
RADMANA - KOVAN

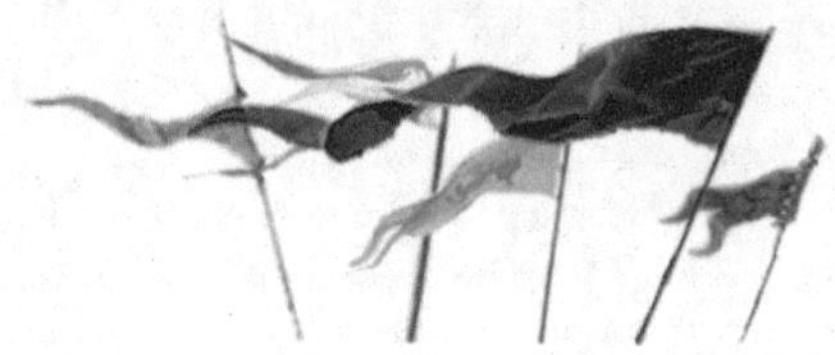

KOVAN LED THEM THROUGH THE WASTES OVER THE COURSE OF A WEEK and to the gates of Oakol. The area surrounding the city was packed with people. Tribes people, in various colored robes and headscarves, camped under different banners. Each banner displayed an animal representing the tribe. The symbol on Oakol's flag was a lion.

There were six tribes camped along the gate. Kovan estimated close to two thousand people, and the camps were pristinely kept. The assemblage of tribes were made up of mostly warriors, and each tribe kept a respectful distance from the neighboring group.

Kovan paused a moment but continued to the gate. "This is new," he said.

"This wasn't here before?" Ellaria asked.

"No."

At the gate several warriors appeared, with their spears pointing toward the horses. Alasne's general, Nikki, approached Kovan. She lowered the scarf covering her mouth.

"You have returned, Kovan. A man of his word is man of honor. Where is your so-called king?" Nikki asked.

"We are the king's emissaries. The king awaits word from us," Ellaria said.

Nikki looked Ellaria in the eyes and nodded stiffly. "You three may enter, but your men must wait outside the city. We leave for the sacred amphitheater tomorrow," she said.

"Then we will all wait outside the gates and watch for your lead," Kovan said.

"Uh…" Ellaria started to argue but tightened her lips.

Nikki glared at her and then snapped her fingers. Two warriors appeared with food and water for them. "We will see you at dawn, Westlanders," Nikki said, and retreated into the city.

In the morning, the gates opened at dawn, as promised. The giant metal circle, caked in sandblasted dust, rolled aside with a loud groan. Alasne rode out in front of a small army.

Kovan had awoken early to be ready and had already saddled the horses. He roused their accompanying squad of soldiers, but he let Ellaria and Echoryn sleep. He woke Echoryn first, who flinched, and her awareness seemed to be lost in the dream he had awoken her from. She rubbed her eyes and got to her feet without saying anything, an unspoken understanding of the situation. Ellaria, on the other hand, was typically not a pleasant person to wake, so Kovan nudged her as gently as he could, expecting the worst.

She opened her eyes, slowly to start, then alertly. "Are they leaving?"

"Just now, but we're all ready to go," Kovan said.

"Torquing ash, Kovan, I wanted to be ready," she cursed.

"We are ready."

"I-I wanted to be ready. I need to present the New World in the best light. Look at me. My hair is a mess, and my old face is like a wet rag in the morning."

"You look beautiful," he said, and she looked at him like he was crazy.

"Oh, shut up. You've now undermined the use of that word. See to the others and let's go. I want to ride at the front," Ellaria insisted.

From their horses they still had to wait for a small procession of tribe leaders to exit the city and join their camps. Once those leaders were prepared to lead their people on the way to Radmana, Kovan moved his group in behind Alasne and her force.

The trek to Radmana would take most of the day. What started as a road in the morning turned to an uneven trail over low hills and desolate ground by midday. The entire caravan of a thousand people stopped only once, at the start of the Blue. Up until that point, Kovan had been unable to ride any closer to Alasne. When the caravan stopped to rest, Alasne wandered back to them.

Kovan stood and slightly bowed his head.

"So formal now I see. What happened to the man who came here two weeks ago, angry, and thoroughly unimpressed by my city?" She took a quick measure of his company. "Or, are you simply on your best behavior for these beautiful women?"

"When I was brought here before, I was in chains, if you remember. I never said I was unimpressed, only focused," Kovan said.

"Right, on finding your friend," Alasne said.

"Have you seen her?" Kovan asked.

Alasne's shoulders sagged. "Not yet. And who's this?"

"This is Ellaria Moonstone, the general and emissary of Arno Danehin."

Ellaria bowed her head in respect. "Thank you for inviting us."

"I invited your king. Is he here?"

"No. But if you would allow me to ride with you, I can explain."

Alasne thought about the request, looking Ellaria over, and eventually nodded. "Yes, you both can ride with me, but not all the way into Radmana. I must enter the sacred site with the other tribe leaders by my side."

"As you want. Thank you," Ellaria said.

They rested, and when they were ready to move again, Nikki came back to gather Kovan and Ellaria and escort them to the front.

The caravan went through a valley, where the land spread out in an endless scattering of cracks. It appeared as if the territh below the dirt was sucking all the moisture away. The wind howled through the dying area, and there was no conversation to be had until their route took them in between cliff walls that rose high on either side: a canyon of raised plateaus all around. The tall sides were hard rock, angled out in jagged boulders.

"So where is your king, Ellaria?" Alasne asked.

"Our king was injured in a surprise attack before we were to set out to your city. He lives, but I had him sent to a fortress to heal."

"The state of your war has escalated, then?"

"Yes. The Zenoch have allied with the Sagean, and I'm afraid it's at your doorstep now."

"I'm aware of their treachery. This was our fear, this was the reason for the summit between the Harrinari and the Zenoch. Our two peoples have long been at a stalemate along the Shavin Mountains. I was afraid of what your war would mean to that peace, and here we are."

"War is a storm. It builds fear even in lands far from the fighting. I've seen it before. I've lived it, and those who hide from it are inevitably swept away like flies on a river, right into the boils of the rapids. You and your people are already drawn into the war. The question is, what are you going to do about it?" Ellaria said.

"So, you are *the* Ellaria Moonstone. The great general of the last war against the Sagean?"

"That is true." Ellaria seemed reluctant to admit who she was. Kovan wanted to say something but waited to pick his moment.

"And you lead the Westerners against the Sagean again?"

"It seems to be my life's curse," Ellaria said.

"She leads because of how dire the situation is," Kovan said.

"I know what you say is true. Your friend Tali filled me in on the greater evil that threatens all of us."

"If you have met and spoken to Tali, then you know how desperate we are for allies in the world war. Not against the Sagean, but against the darkness. The Sagean is but a champion of the Old One."

"A formidable champion to be sure, and one who is trying to draw my people into a war with the Zenoch... My hope is to persuade all my people to stand by your side," Alasne said.

Kovan saw Ellaria visibly exhale. Their path through the land had narrowed significantly.

"The entrance to Radmana is not far now. You'll see this gully eventually widens," Alasne said.

"What can you tell me of this sacred space?" Ellaria asked.

"Ellaria is a scholar, when she is not tasked to fight wars," Kovan explained.

"Radmana has been the sacred site for my people for over a thousand years. Generations of Harrinari have used it, going back to the Ancients. It's a space for magic, for rituals, and for duels to settle wars. Since the great destruction of Karnika and the scattering of the

Harrinari people, no one tribe is allowed to enter on their own. Our laws state three or more tribes must enter together. One must be an impartial tribe to witness and record the events. Since its existence, the Oakol have been the stewards of Radmana," Alasne said.

Nikki rode in next to Alasne. "The Zenoch have been spotted at the mouth of Eraja Pass, the man in gold at the head. They will be at Radmana by morning," the general said. Her tone was dark and angered.

"I take it this leader in gold, he is the one who imprisoned you?" Kovan asked.

"Yes," Alasne said bitterly. Her jaw flexed.

"And yet we allow him to come here still breathing. I don't know how you contain your anger, Exalted One," Nikki said.

"Anger is a poison that weakens the soul and clouds the pathways in your mind. The pathways that lead to your heart. Without those, empathy and understanding are impossible," Alasne replied.

"You forget, I know you better than that," Nikki said.

"Well, let's say I'm trying my best to control my anger," Alasne said.

Nikki huffed and waved for Ellaria and Kovan to fall back with her. They did as she requested and waited for the other tribe leaders to pass before continuing.

The rift had grown very deep, and the land above them had risen to a hundred feet or more. The shadows in the narrow space were stark and almost black. Kovan couldn't feel the wind on his arms, but it made an eerie sound as it stirred through the upper cracks.

The narrow passage opened as Alasne said it would. The last rays of the day's sunlight painted the clearing in oranges and reds. A tall entrance carved into the mountainside was before them. It towered far above their heads with a repeating facade of columns and large colored sails that fluttered with the wind high above. In the front courtyard a series of decayed ruins and remnants of ancient statues littered the ground. Though one remained, bright white in color. It was a man holding a sword, his resolute face to the sky. Kovan thought it had a likeness that resembled the man he met in the wastelands, named Oz.

Alasne's soldiers waited inside the entrance to take their horses.

Kovan dismounted and the mystcat jumped from his saddlebag and sauntered in before them.

Inside the great space was a massive rampart in near darkness except for the light shining brightly on the far side. The enclosed space was full of massive columns, and the Oakol warriors began lighting torches all around. Kovan and Ellaria crossed the concourse to the edge overlooking the center of the arena below and were both awestruck.

The center was a giant elliptical amphitheater like the great arena in Adalon. Most of the stadium was open seating, but there were three stories around the upper portion that contained pocketed windows, hinting at smaller viewing rooms within. From the ramparts down, the elliptical bowl cascaded to the ground in a series of benches, individual enclosures, and platforms. At the center was a circular silver platform engrained with copper sigils and spells: the main stage.

Kovan and Ellaria watched as the Harrinari people from their caravan dispersed throughout the structure. Each tribe had a designated area. They had not been instructed where to go.

Nikki eventually came and showed them to their rooms for the night. They climbed a series of stone steps to the upper levels, where they were given an expansive room with two smaller rooms connected inside. Everything inside was already lit with lanterns, and a table full of food waited for them.

"This is your room. The opening ceremonies start tomorrow."

"Are we allowed to walk around?" Ellaria asked.

Nikki's eyes narrowed, almost like she hoped they wouldn't have asked. "Yes, but do not pass through any doorway that you are not invited into. The magic that governs this place will prevent you from passing through openings where you are not welcome."

Nikki turned to go, and Kovan said, "Thank you," as she disappeared down the hall. "Well, what do you want to do?" he asked Ellaria.

"I would love to study every inch of this palace, but maybe we should eat first," Ellaria replied, and Kovan agreed.

After dinner the stadium was still alive with the sounds of the various tribes. From the small windows overlooking the interior, they could see that nearly all the windows around the upper levels were lit up.

Kovan, Ellaria, and Echoryn walked the corridors around the entire structure. Most of the rooms were behind wooden doors they had no business knocking on. Ellaria wanted to soak everything in, and Kovan wanted a good understanding of the structure. Based on the makeup of each tribe's congregation and the mix of dignitaries and warriors in attendance, the other tribe leaders were expecting a civil discourse, but Kovan was expecting a battle.

"We should have brought more soldiers with us," Kovan said, appraising the size of the structure.

"I know, but any real show of force would have elicited hostility," Ellaria said.

"You said as much before, but now that we're here, waiting on a confrontation, I sure would feel better if we had more guns on our side," Kovan said.

"At least Alasne brought a lot," Ellaria said.

The lower area of the stadium was full of the Oakol warriors stationed at the exit to the canyon road and at each of the stair entrances to the inner amphitheater.

Kovan sighed. "I hope it's enough." He was looking toward Echoryn with his statement.

"I'm sorry, Kovan, I don't know what's going to happen tomorrow," Echoryn said.

"Well, do we at least live through it?"

"I don't want you to answer that," Ellaria said.

"Good, because I don't know. All I know is that it's a significant turning point," Echoryn said, holding her shoulders.

They stopped at a balcony that overlooked the arena. Kovan tried to appraise how warfare would play out in such a unique space, if the Zenoch leader was intent on a fight.

As the night wore on, he convinced Ellaria that she could study all the carvings and reliefs in the morning light, and that they should go to bed. Back in their room, Kovan watched from the small square windows a patrol of the Oakol warriors at the top of the structure, where banners and large colored canopies rippled in the wind.

At some point, he dozed off with his head against the stone and was awoken by a loud noise overhead. He opened his eyes in time to see an airship pass through the sky. Kovan checked the time. The Zenoch leader would be arriving soon, and it appeared he had just received Sagean reinforcements.

Kovan began to clean and prepare his guns, double-checking the condition of the capacitor gems. After polishing Elias's Elum blade, he took the compass out. He rolled the dial and tried each of the gems in turn. The inner dials spun at his touch, and the glass glowed with symbols coming alive. He positioned the needle to gage the distances of what the compass was telling him.

"What is that?" Ellaria said. The light of the compass had awoken her.

"A compass Elias wanted me to have from the Shadowyn village."

"What does it do?"

"I think it locates people with gifts."

"You're kidding me, right."

"No. I'm sure that's what it does."

"That's an incredibly dangerous object in the wrong hands. What was Elias doing with it?"

"I don't know. His letter didn't explain where he got it. I see why he left it in the Shadowyn's possession."

"What did he want you to do with it?"

"Find someone gifted," he said, and he looked up at Ellaria. Her eyes where entranced by the object. He desperately wanted to tell her about their daughter, but he didn't know how. After thinking about the conversation for months now, he still had no idea how to tell her that her daughter was alive.

When the needle stopped again and the center sigil lit up, Ellaria's interest grew. "Look, those symbols in the glass, they're star formations, and based on the dial, I think this person is here in the building or outside."

Kovan felt his moment pass. "Yeah. It took me a week to figure out the symbol was a star formation, and it only took you ten seconds. What I don't understand is that if I touch one of the gems, the dials spin and new symbols come up."

"For different people and different abilities. I don't know of a fourth ability or a fifth ability," Ellaria said.

"And if I go back to the same gem, sometimes the stars have aligned differently."

"Different people with the same ability?"

"I guess so."

"Let's go through it one at a time," Ellaria suggested.

Ellaria retrieved a notebook and pen, and they went once around the dial. For each gem position, they noted the color, the symbol, the direction, and the distance from them. The second time around the dial, they recorded conflicting answers from the first. But on the third go around, some information began to repeat. They kept going and transcribed every new person the device located, until every pass repeated something they already had.

In total, the device found twelve people: four of them within a league of Radmana, and another eight as far away as a hundred leagues or more. They had no way to know the full extent of the device's reach.

The sun was coming up now, and Ellaria was studying her notes. Kovan stared at her. He loved to watch her mind work. A few strands of her hair continued to fall in front of her face as her head was bent over her notes. Kovan pulled it aside and tucked it behind her ear for her. She looked up at him and smiled. The lines at the sides of her eyes were as delicate and fine as her carefully manicured eyebrows.

"What?" she said.

"Nothing."

"You're staring."

"Am I?"

"Yes. Please stop."

"Fine," he said, sitting back.

She crawled over to him and kissed his cheek. "I need you to stop staring, because we're not alone. Once where alone…" She winked at him.

Kovan laughed, and Ellaria sat back down and said, "Look at this."

"Did you find something?" he asked.

"Yes. Two of these people are the same person."

"Are you sure?"

"Yes. Same sign, same location, but different gems activated to locate them."

"What do you think it means?"

"I don't…" Ellaria paused when a knock at their door interrupted them.

Kovan got up to open it.

Nikki stood in the doorway, disheveled and anxious. She had sweat on her forehead.

"What's happened?"

"The Zenoch arrived with an army of Sagean soldiers and giant beings made of metal. They've surrounded Radmana."

"Has fighting started?" Kovan asked, strapping his guns on.

"No. That's not all. The Zenoch leader, Nea'Ko, arrived with two Luminaries by his side. He wants to start the summit at the light of the Blue Sun. At that time he will speak with all the Harrinari leaders."

"What do you want us to do?" Kovan asked.

"Alasne believes this friend you share will show up. She wants you to remain out of sight until then."

"Then we will. You might want to gather your best archers and station them around the upper areas."

"Already done," Nikki said.

"Then I guess, one way or another, we'll see you out there. Good luck," Kovan said.

Nikki left and Kovan shut the door. The Shadowyn Maven had been right; there would be bloodshed in Radmana.

THIRTY-SEVEN
THE SUMMIT - ELLARIA

ELLARIA GAPED IN HORROR FROM THEIR WINDOWS AS THE ZENOCH filed into the space, their weapons shining. The man in gold directed his warriors to guard the exits. The Luminaries walked to the center of the arena, their cloaks whipping in the wind.

They were forced from their room by Zenoch warriors going door to door. Though the Zenoch couldn't enter the rooms uninvited, the Harrinari acquiesced to their requests, instructed by Alasne not to fight and to proceed to the amphitheater. The leaders of the tribes were escorted to the middle stage.

Ellaria, Kovan, Echoryn, and their squad of five snuck silently around the corridors, staying hidden. They moved to the lower levels and prepared for when the fighting started.

They came to the lower corridor of giant columns, and the space was full of Bonemen soldiers. Kovan stopped their progress and had them move back.

From the ramparts, Ellaria could see to the center stage where the Zenoch leader in shining gold stood. The arena was slowly bathed in a blue glimmer from the sun entering the zenith, and the leader in gold began to speak. His voice projected unnaturally loudly throughout the arena.

"I am Ashrata Nea'Ko, the ruler of the Zenoch. I have come to offer you the choice of either swearing loyalty to me or being crushed by my army."

Ellaria rolled her eyes. He looked and sounded like every other power-hungry man she had spent a lifetime fighting. She looked back to Echoryn and found herself staring at the barrel of a surge-blaster. Kovan put his hands up, and Bonemen soldiers motioned for them to walk.

The soldiers escorted them out to the center of the amphitheater. Nea'Ko, in his obnoxiously bright adornments, looked at them, furious at the intrusion. His hand gripped tightly to a long striped staff with a yellow gem at its head.

Ellaria recognized the Sagean acolytes Delvar and Shirova standing next to Ashrata. She assumed both acolytes were now Luminaries if they had survived the Sintering Fountain. Ellaria scanned around, but those were the only two she could find. Shirova whispered something to Ashrata, and his attention moved to Ellaria.

"The great Ellaria Moonstone," Nea'Ko said. "The emperor will reward me like no other when I deliver you to him."

He signaled to a far gate, and two automatons stalked into the arena. They were holding two wolveracks on chains. More Bonemen soldiers followed with torches. The appearance of the walking machines brought murmurs from the terrified crowd.

Suddenly, below her feet the ground trembled. A low muffled machine sound emanated from deep beneath the amphitheater, like thunder underground. Ellaria thought at first it was Nea'Ko's doing, but his face was panic stricken, and he eyed the Luminaries suspiciously. They in turn suspected the Zenoch leader of treachery as the air crackled around Shirova.

"Have you betrayed us?" Shirova said.

"It is not my doing," Nea'Ko proclaimed, scanning all around for the source of the noise.

A figure wrapped in a dark cloak walked alone into the arena, a hood concealing their face. The gold of Nea'Ko's lavish headdress shimmered with the blue sunlight as he shifted uneasily in his stance. His nostrils flared and his lip curled at a second intrusion.

"It was my doing," the cloaked figure said.

A large company of Zenoch warriors with black capes filed in behind them from a passageway at the ground level. The warriors spread out and climbed the stairs toward the Zenoch in opposition at the exits. Ellaria recognized the voice, and a wave of relief washed over her.

The Zenoch leader slammed his staff to the ground in front of the stranger in black. The figure removed their hood, and Nea'Ko's eyes widened and his nostrils flared.

Tali's dark eyes stared like daggers at Nea'Ko, framed by her black hair. Without emotion, she spoke. "I deny you."

Nea'Ko gritted his teeth and angled the staff and the gem at the tip closer to Tali's face.

Tali tilted her head as though examining the gem at the end of the staff, but there was no fear in her eyes. If Nea'Ko thought it would scare her, he missed his mark. In fact the color of Tali's eyes began to swirl, like Ellaria had seen before with Elias.

Tali reached up and grasped the glowing crystal and broke it off the end of the gold staff. A small ripple in the air reverberated, and Tali crushed the gem in her palm. The glow spilled out of it like smoke and coiled around her before evaporating.

She opened her hand to show the dust of the crystal.

"Impossible," Nea'Ko cried.

Tali smiled. "I told you to not put your faith in stones."

The flame-shaped scars at her temples began to glow, and overhead the clouds erupted with lightning. A bolt of brilliant white lightning—too bright to look at—struck her hand. Ellaria winced back, but the image was burned in her vision.

When she opened her eyes, Tali was glowing and Nea'Ko trembled before her.

Tiny bolts of lightning bounced between Tali's eyes, and her scars pulsed.

"You crave power so much, I thought I would give you what you want," Tali said, and she touched Nea'Ko's chest.

His body became light. Ellaria and everyone else in Radmana shut their eyes to the brightness. When it vanished, a heap of empty clothing plopped to the dirt. The gold headdress and mask clanged to the ground.

The moment of all in witness being wonder-struck passed, and in a heartbeat, the Sagean Luminaries flung their hands out—the battle had begun.

At an unspoken cue, the Boneman carrying torches came forward, and Shirova waved her hands. The flames of the torches sprung free and wild, like arms of an octopus. Shirova flung the ropes of fire at the leaders of the Harrinari.

Arrows loosed from the pocketed windows at the top of the structure. The ground rumbled. Delvar reshaped a voluminous mass of the ground and rock, the volume of which proceeded to grow and slam into a section of seats.

Ellaria had yet to move, but Kovan had disarmed the Boneman, reclaimed his own weapons, and began firing his gun. He yanked on Ellaria's shirt to pull her back.

She broke from his grasp and sprinted off to save Alasne from a flood of flames charging at the woman. Ellaria was too slow. The flames flew faster than she could run, and a shift in the dirt brought her tumbling to the ground.

The flame ropes hit an invisible shield in front of Alasne and evaporated. Her face was furious. She helped Ellaria stand and continued to weave magic. Lights flashed in front of Alasne, and symbols bloomed in the air as she brought forth and manipulated the elements with her fingertips. The tattoos on the skin of her arms and back swirled into new designs.

Ellaria knew she was staring at the Fusion Mage. She had read about the mages of old who could bind the Furies to their will, but seeing it was beautiful. The moment of shock faded with the blur of a wolverack racing by her and leaping into the crowd to attack the Harrinari hiding there.

The automatons swatted at warriors. Ambling through the arena, they delt devastation all around them, with their massive and powerful arms and their supercharged rifles. Arrows from above bounced off their bronze limbs.

Kovan continued to fire at Bonemen soldiers and ran for Ellaria.

The Zenoch fighting grew brutal and gruesome. Men attacking with axes and hatchets created a blood-fest. The Harrinari and black-caped Zenoch quickly laid waste to the revolting Zenoch aligned with Nea'Ko. As their numbers dwindled, the remaining threw down their weapons. But the Bonemen soldiers had no intention of surrendering.

Kovan blasted his gun into two running toward him and Ellaria and though he hit each multiple times, but they still advanced. Many of the Bonemen soldiers around the arena were fighting past the point of mortal wounds. It wasn't their phifer cloth armor; this was different. Ellaria had seen it once before—this legion had been indoctrinated by the Sagean's will to fight beyond death.

As the pair of Bonemen reached Ellaria, Kovan holstered his gun, drew the Elum blade, and dispatched them. With the short sword held in his right, Kovan attacked one of the automatons. Arrows vaulted at it from the high windows, and Kovan cut the main vein that powered the creature.

Echoryn pushed Ellaria down on the stairs as a wolverack leapt at her. Echoryn pulled knifes from her sleeves and faced the beast. The wolverack's long tail lashed around. Ellaria threw a vial of petrified blood-sand at the beast. It hit and exploded in a brown fog, and the wolverack's movements slowed. Echoryn attacked and cut the beast down.

"We'll never last out here with the Luminaries," Kovan said, pointing to the middle ground of the arena.

He was right. The main battle now raged between the two acolytes against Tali and Alasne. Tali held Nea'Ko's staff but had maintained a defensive stance to shield the unarmed Harrinari in the stadium, and Alasne had followed her lead. They were doing everything they could to shield the people around the arena from harm and to protect the structure itself.

Suddenly, a solid column of rock burst up from the ground and threw Alasne high into the air. The Oakol leader landed in a heap on a stone balcony above. Tali lost her mind. Her old scars glowed and radiated, and Tali slammed the staff on the surface of the main stage. A bright light burst to the sky, and the remaining flames were extinguished. Both the Sagean acolytes were blown off their feet and thrown against a side wall.

Ellaria struggled to look away, but Kovan grabbed her hand and pulled her to run for the interior, Echoryn following. The inner halls of the stadium were another sort of hell. The battle was harder to track among the many Harrinari fleeing for safety. Bonemen fired from cover, and arrows flew at unpredictable points in a crossfire.

Kovan stopped, his hand on his knees and sweat dripping to the floor. "We need to get the rest of the people out of the arena before everything is destroyed."

"We need to save Alasne, or the alliance, and possibly the war, will be lost," Ellaria said, pointing to where the woman still lay unmoving on the upper levels.

Kovan took a deep breath. "You're a frustrating person to be in love with, you know that," he said and ran back out into the arena.

The column of light had vanished now, and Tali was standing alone at the center of the amphitheater. She cried out for Alasne as she watched Kovan sprint in that direction. Kovan scrambled over different levels to reach Alasne. Nikki fell in beside him as they navigated through a swarm of people, Kovan yelling at them to go inside.

Some were still in combat with Bonemen soldiers as a second wave from outside the amphitheater had flooded the corridor.

In the chaos, Ellaria's ears were throbbing, but the cry from the sky was unmistakable and enough to freeze everyone in place. Ellaria's nerves could only tremble as her brain panicked, unable to cope with certain annihilation.

THIRTY-EIGHT
ARENA OF FIRE - KOVAN

A ROAR FROM A DRAGON PROMPTED A UNIVERSAL MOMENT OF silence. What began in a low rumbling octave finished in a high-pitched shriek. A yellow Dragon overwhelmed the sky each time it circled.

In the middle of the arena, the Luminaries had ceased their fight, waiting for the Dragon to land or attack. The Luminary wearing red looked crazed, and her hair was singed. She was mocking the yellow Dragon and daring it to shoot fire at her.

At the top of the stairs, the long shadow swooped overhead. Kovan waited for it to pass and vaulted over a short wall toward a huddle of people hiding on the stone floor and covering their heads. They were blocking his path to Alasne.

"Come on. Follow me. There's a large underground complex. It's safe, but you must move now!" he yelled at them.

The man closest to him looked at him like he didn't understand what Kovan was saying, but as Kovan waved him to stand up, the man shook his head no. Kovan moved on to the woman behind him —a dignitary, Kovan judged, by the jewels around her neck.

"Do you want to live? Come on!" Kovan yelled.

The Harrinari woman eyed the man she had crouched next to and stood up slowly. A small child was hidden under her robe. She tugged at the man's shirt, but he stayed low.

"Forget him, help your son out of here," Kovan said.

The Dragon swooped into the arena again. Kovan instinctually pointed his pulsator gun but otherwise stayed motionless. The Dragon ignored him and dove to the middle of the space, landing on the ground.

While his eyes were fixed on the Dragon, the woman took Kovan's outstretched hand. He snapped back and rushed her and her son toward the corridor. The group of Harrinari followed.

Kovan and Nikki stepped over the man and ran to Alasne. They were forced to dive to the floor as a huge fireball from the Dragon burned through the amphitheater, incinerating everything in its path. The stone of the stadium level was blackened, and anything that could catch on fire was on fire.

Nikki checked Alasne and looked for wounds. There was a severe gash on her head, and she was unconscious, but she moaned when Nikki began to inspect her.

Below, the yellow Dragon stood tall at the center of the arena. The Luminaries protected themselves and responded with attacks of their own.

The woman in red tried to wrap the Dragon with its own flames. For a moment Kovan thought it was going to work. The Dragon contorted its back and cried out, but the flames faded away, and the Dragon lunged its head to snap the woman with its jaw, but missed.

Kovan had seen enough; they needed to get out of there now. "Here," he said, shoving his pulsator gun into Nikki's hands. She stared at him, annoyed, but he didn't bother to argue. Kovan lifted Alasne over his shoulder and headed for the nearest archway back to the corridor.

Ellaria and Echoryn met them inside, running up a stairway toward them. The corridor on this level was almost completely deserted. Kovan laid Alasne down on the stone and looked back. Tali was trying to defend herself against the Dragon. Everything she tried seemed to fail.

"Don't even think about going back out there," Ellaria said.

Kovan picked Alasne up in his arms again. "We need to get to the lower levels. When this place starts to come down, we don't want to be up here."

They started toward the stairs, and Nikki handed Ellaria the gun.

Alasne was a slight woman, but Kovan's old arms ached from carrying her. They went down one flight of stairs after another until they reached the lower levels, where the Harrinari were still battling the Bonemen blocking the exit from outside the building and eliminating the possibility of escape into the wastes.

Alasne began to stir, and Kovan stood her slowly on her feet. She leaned against Nikki and looked up him.

"How are you?" he asked.

"I've been better," Alasne replied. She winced and looked around. "Where's Tali?"

Ellaria pointed. "Out there fighting a Dragon."

"What?" Alasne said.

"The battle is about to level this place. Is there anywhere we can go in case the level above begins to buckle?"

"The Ancients' passage. That's where Tali came from. It's deeper underground."

Kovan looked around. "How do we get there? We can't go back outside."

"At the end of this hall there's an entrance."

They made their way through the crowded corridor to the opposite end. A large archway opened onto a landing and a winding stairway. At first only Nikki and Alasne could pass through.

Alasne placed her hand on the stone arch and spoke. "All seeking refuge are welcome inside."

The archway lit up, and Kovan rushed to the stairs.

They wound down the stairs to the sublevel, the ground above them shaking and dust sifting over their heads like powdered sugar. They reached a huge room with two tall ornate doors on the opposite side, and a ramp to the main stage. To all their surprise, there was a woman waiting below.

Kovan didn't know her at first, but his eyes slowly widened with recognition and fury. Mia rushed over to Alasne with a bandage ready and a glass of water.

"Drink this, it will help with the headache," Mia said and turned to face Kovan and Ellaria.

"I know you," Ellaria said, unsure of herself. "Mia?"

The anger of betrayal pulsed through Kovan's body. He gripped the Elum blade tightly in his hand and placed the tip of the steel at Mia's neck.

"Kovan, what are you doing?"

"Tie her up," Kovan growled.

Ellaria seemed to snap out of a trance and walked closer to him. Screams from above carried all the way down to them, and something crashed and shook the foundation. A soft cry came from the ramp and they all turned their head to see Murphi the mystcat appear out from the ramp. Kovan smiled at seeing the cat, and he took a deep breath. He had to get back out there and help Tali.

"Tie her up," Kovan said again, and he took the gun from Ellaria. "Trust me and don't let her out of your sight."

Ellaria nose wrinkled in confusion, "Kovan, why?"

"I'll tell you when I get back."

"Where are you going?" Ellaria pleaded with him. "You're not going to fight the Dragon, you'll be killed."

"Let him go, Ellaria," Mia said.

"You shut up," Kovan said, pointing the sword at her again. "I won't let Tali die. I have to help her."

"Kovan?" Ellaria said, breathing fast. "Please..."

Kovan put his hands out to the sides and shrugged. "I'm going to help Tali. But if the Dragon wants to talk, I'm not going to pass up the opportunity to persuade it to leave. Seriously, keep an eye on her until I get back," he said, and he raced up the ramp.

THIRTY-NINE
DRAGON BLOOD - TALI

THE FIRE PULVERIZED THE GROUND AND RAMPARTS AND DEMOLISHED A path of charred rubble across the stone risers of the ancient arena. Tali held tightly to the Zenoch staff. Sweat was pooling at her back and brow and dripped away as she looked around for escape. The Dragon had not flown again since it started attacking, but it prowled around the arena with astounding dexterity and cast its fiery breath with impunity. The ground shook with each step as the yellow Dragon climbed the far-end wall. With its back turned, Tali sprinted for the archway to the underground passageways.

Her eyes were dead focused on the opening, and she missed the destruction of her surroundings, horrors that existed beyond her line of sight. The evidence was in the ash falling like snow all around. Scraps of purple sail-cloth, still burning, collected along her path and crumbled under her sprinting feet.

She reached the tunnel, and a hand grabbed her, pulling her to the wall out of the light. The blue skin of Tyzo's arm was streaked in charcoal and blood. His eyes went drowsy after they both settled against the wall. Tali immediately put her hands to his face.

"Ty, Tyzo!" she called as loudly as she dared.

With a shake of his head, as though clearing a fog, his eyes leveled on hers and he smiled.

"I thought you never smiled," she said, a jest to hide the worry about his appearance.

To hide it from him or herself, she couldn't say. Tyzo blinked and shook his head. She could tell he was having trouble staying awake. She checked the blood at his neck and traced it to a gash at the back of his head. She immediately looked around and found something to place against it to stop the bleeding.

"You're not going to die on me, you hear. Who will take care of Saphree if you die? Stay with me," she said to him.

Tyzo had helped her bring the Spirit Elders army through the gate and had promised to protect her back. During the fighting, she had seen him fighting with Bonemen, Zenoch warriors, and one of the automatons before the Dragon had melted it into a pool of bronze.

From the passage, she heard footsteps below and turned to unleash a bolt of kinetic energy, but it was Kovan running at full speed to her. She frantically waved for him to slow and back out of the light of the entrance. He crouched along the wall to her.

She looked at him and the black ash in his grey hair. He didn't seem to have a scratch on him, and she had seen him fighting nearly the entire time out in the arena. She couldn't help but laugh.

He pulled her close and squeezed her tightly. "Good to see you, Raven," he said with a broken voice.

Tali's eyes began to water, but she shook the emotion away as best she could. She had missed her friend.

When he let her go, he wiped tears from his own eyes. "Let's get you out of here," he said.

She nodded and pointed to Tyzo. "Him first," she said.

Kovan grumbled but pulled Tyzo to his feet and started to move back down the tunnel.

From the arena a massive roar broke through the chaos. The Dragon was irritated by something. Tali assumed something had attacked the beast. It looked frightened by something, if that was possible. Tali moved slowly to get a better look. The Dragon's thick pulsing neck twisted in agitation. The jagged and hard yellow scales shimmered in the dying light. It was frantically searching over the top of the structure to the upper cliff edge, where smoke coalesced before escaping into the atmosphere.

Below, one of the faction's armies was throwing spears at the

Dragon, but it didn't seem to care. Its attention was singularly focused on something else.

"Come on," Kovan called for her as he disappeared down the tunnel.

"Something's happening, hold on," she said, then she spotted what the Dragon was watching.

A shadow was moving along the top of the arena, where a cloud of dust lifted free, its form hidden in the faded rays of sunlight. She tried to focus on it, but the Dragon's tail swung overhead and slammed down. Tali couldn't see what new danger was approaching, and her ears were still ringing from the first ear-shattering roar when the Dragon had arrived. She wiped the stone dust out of her face and coughed.

The Dragon lifted in the air to attack the shadow. The smoke and ash in the air billowed in the wind of the Dragon's wings. The Dragon arched its back and unleashed a stream of fire, vaporizing everything in its path.

Smoke and flames filled the top lip of the ancient theater and a large chunk of rock crashed to the stage. *The threat had to be dead*, Tali thought, but the Dragon maintained its altitude, waiting to attack again.

Off the top edge, a blur in the charcoal-grey cloud vaulted through the air and landed on the Dragon's back.

Tali's heart sank when she realized who it was.

The Dragon soared higher, and Learon slipped from its back to its tail.

"No!" Tali cried aloud. She expected Learon to fall, but he held on and began to climb up the Dragon's back. His hair was cropped shorter, and he somehow appeared stronger, but it was him.

The Dragon turned in the air and tried to bite him. The act made the massive creature tumble back to the ground. It spun and sped toward Radmana again. Tali lost sight of Learon and moved around, anxiously trying to see. The Dragon entered the arena again, and Learon was there holding onto its wing.

Learon held a gleaming sword in his hands that sparkled in the light and looked like blue-green crystal. He sliced a gash into the creature's wing, and it sparked along the wound. A Dragon scale landed on the ground near Tali's feet. With the Dragon's blood, Tali could sense the Dragon's signature energy spewing free from the wound.

The Dragon went wild, and Learon was vaulted from the wing. He somehow oriented himself in air and landed on the top levels on his feet. Learon stood up facing the Dragon, with his chest heaving and the crystal sword held in both hands.

The Dragon flew up again and higher until it was like a small bird in the upper reaches of the atmosphere. As the Dragon escaped, Learon looked around, scanning the wreckage. Finally, their eyes met, and he smiled. The amphitheater shook again as the Luminary man was using his powers to fling debris toward Learon.

Learon ran toward the platform edge. Tali held her breath, afraid he was going to jump a hundred feet to the ground. At the last moment, he changed what surface he was running on, and his feet scampered across the side wall. He safely dove to the far side of the amphitheater. Tali snapped out of her trance and pulled the sunlight in and put it to work for her as kinetic energy. She threw the male Luminary off his feet and slammed him into the wall, but it was as though the man was made of rock. He crashed into the wall, leaving a depression in the stone, and then shrugged it off.

The man began another attack. This time his focus had diverted to a group of Harrinari in the stands trying to kill the last wolverack that had survived until now.

Tali felt exhausted from the battle. Shielding against the Dragon's fire had almost been too much. The Dragon's flames ate at her shield faster than she could form it with light. She rubbed her hands and pulled the heat energy from the fire around her to reenergize herself. She spotted Learon waving at her from the balcony. She didn't understand what he wanted, and she put her arms up to show she was confused. He kept showing her his fist slamming into his other hand and shaking his head no.

"What!" she screamed, and her voice carried further than she expected. Learon jumped off the platform toward the Luminary.

Is he crazy? Did he hear me say jump?

At the last second, she realized what he wanted, and she expelled energy to slow his momentum so he landed softly and quietly behind the Luminary. Before Learon could reach the man, the Luminary was warned by the woman in red. The Luminary stopped trying to attack the Harrinari and turned toward Learon, who was rushing toward him.

The Luminary moved his hands and made the dirt all around them lift free. The dirt plume obscured both of them, coalescing like a cloud in the air. When it crashed back to the ground, Learon stood above the Luminary, gasping for breath. The man lay dead at Learon's feet, blood on the blade of his sword.

The female Luminary shrieked, pulled her leg from some debris, and made her way toward Learon, screaming. A funnel of flames built around her. Learon backed his way toward the center of the arena and lifted the crystal sword above his head to shield himself from the Luminary's attack. But his stance wasn't to shield against the woman's flames, Tali realized. The Dragon was coming back.

The woman, still focused on Learon, didn't notice until the Dragon's shadow enveloped the arena. The woman Luminary looked up and pushed a wall of flames at the Dragon. It didn't slow the creature. Instead, the Dragon simply opened its huge jaws and swallowed the flames and the woman.

The Dragon landed at the last second, finding its feet like a cat. It looked back at Learon and roared as though trying to scare him away. Learon held the crystal sword with both hands before him. The muscles of his forearms flexed, and his arms and legs were streaked with blood and ash. The Dragon dropped its head low and mean in a posture Tali hadn't seen yet. It slowly progressed toward Learon.

"Kill it!" someone shouted from the stands.

The Harrinari lined the enclosed colonnade of the corridors and watched Learon face down the Dragon with a sword. More and more of them called out, but Learon didn't take his eyes off the Dragon. He stood motionless before it. The sword in his hands was gleaming in the sunlight and began to glow. The Dragon looked mesmerized by it.

Tali stopped breathing as she watched.

Learon's head tilted, and he brought the sword high above his head and slammed the blade into the ground a foot deep, then kneeled in front of the yellow Dragon.

He stared directly at the Dragon. For a moment Tali believed it would attack, but it made a movement of its head that Tali could have sworn was a bow in return. Then it lifted off into the sky and departed.

Learon got to his feet; his chest seemed to sag all at once as though he was finally breathing the air. Tali sprinted across the stone and slammed into him. Her eyes were full of tears.

He was different. She doubted those who didn't know him would have noticed. To Tali he simply was more himself than ever before.

"Hi, Tali. How about we stick together from now on?" Learon said, holding her.

She smiled but was still speechless. There's a magic in hearing someone special say your name. Up until that moment, she hadn't been sure what her feelings were, but in his arms, she was sure. She loved him. It went beyond the bond of their abilities. They belonged by each other's side.

Tali led him to the tunnel back to the depths of the arena. At the tunnel entrance she paused to look back at the wreckage. The amphitheater was in ruins. It was covered in ash and blood, and flames still raged among shards of stone and the dead. It was an image directly from an old dream she had once, when she was recovering from the illumination surge. Tali shrugged it off, clutched Learon's arm, and descended into the shadows of the arena.

Twenty feet down the ramparts, at the last reaches of the sunlight from the opening above, Learon stopped, and his calm blue eyes stared into hers. "Tali, wait. I have something to tell you," he said.

Tali bounced on her feet restlessly.

He smiled. "For most of my life, I've been lost. Sometimes my own face is foreign to me, or even the sound of my own name. But I'm not lost with you. I love you. I'm in love with you. I know what you're going to say, that it's just the bond…"

Tali put her finger to his lips to quiet him. His blue eyes sparkled with innocent impatience for being silenced. A silence that lingered. Tali was afraid to fill it. Her stomach fluttered and her heart was pounding fast.

"Oh, torque it," she said. Tipping up on her toes, she pulled him to her and kissed him.

INTERLUDES VI-VII

- Ronick -

- Meroha -

INTERLUDE VI
RONICK

RONICK WALKED ALONG THE HIGH WATCH OF THE FORTIFICATION, appraising the previous night's damage. The black Dragon and its ghost rider had attacked the battlements from sunset to midnight, leaving a ring of scorched territh around the city. In the end, the walls of Atava had held. There had been no warning and no time to prepare. The Dragon they had been used to seeing fly over the area was a dark green color, and this one had been black as ink. Everything the Renegades had thrown at it had done nothing but anger the giant creature.

There was a general surprise among the men, along with the sense of relief, when the Dragon finally departed to the west. Ronick's nerves were shot.

Darringer and Lady Orsen, the Atava ambassador, waited at the lower bastion for his report. Ronick took the winding steps down to them. They stood at the balustrade, looking out on the White Hawk Mountains.

"How bad is it?" Darringer asked.

"The lower walls had the most damage. The stone must be different, as it didn't hold up to the Dragon's breath like the upper walls did."

"I was afraid of that."

"The scorch marks on the facade are repairable. We will have to replace almost all the opening headers that burned."

"And the city?" Lady Orsen asked.

Ronick sighed.

"That bad?"

"We have finally contained all the fires, but the eastern quarter is in ruins. There were too many wood structures so close together. The buildings with heavier timber survived, but there were a lot of lives lost," Ronick said.

"Bigger question, will it comeback?" Darringer asked.

"By the Blue, I hope not. Our scouts are still reporting the Sagean's forces moving at us from the Fork. They'll take Jenovee in a month."

"You think this Dragon attack was a blow to weaken us for the Sagean."

"I think so. I hope so. The walls of this ancient city can withstand the Dragon, but the city itself is in danger."

Bells rang out from one of the high towers and then another, until all the bells were ringing a warning,

"Another attack?" Lady Orsen said.

"No," Darringer said. "Two means they've spotted someone coming."

They looked out over the mountains but saw nothing. They jogged around to the north, where the first bells still rang. Something was approaching from the plains out by the Dragon's Spine Mountain Range.

Near the lower wall at the edge of Ronick's vision, he could see a small company of people traveling toward the city. He climbed up to the high wall battlement and found a spyglass.

The watchman stepped away. "I can't tell who they are, sir. They're not Bonemen soldiers, that's for sure."

Ronick looked through the glass. There was roughly two hundred in their group, and they looked like no people he had ever seen. Their clothes were decorated with colorful patterns, and their skin was almost ashen. Some of their number rode horses, and others rode an animal that looked almost like a llama with antlers. At the head was an old woman with black paint over her eyes.

Somehow, he knew they were no threat. Ronick handed the glass back to the watchman and ordered the warning bells silenced.

He jogged back to Darringer and Lady Orsen. "We have guests."

"Guests?"

Ronick nodded, and they made their way to the north gate to greet the newcomers.

The tall wood doors creaked open, and the group of curious people slowly marched toward them. Lady Orsen went pale at seeing them, her eyes widening. Darringer and Ronick shared a look but moved out from the shadow of the gate to meet the leader.

"Hello," Darringer waved.

The people did not respond and continued to march until they were only a few feet from the entrance, and then they all stopped in unison, as though an unspoken signal Ronick had missed had told them to stop.

The leader stepped forward and was helped down from her horse.

She wore a high collar of fur and walked straight up to Darringer and spoke. "We are the One People, and our time to leave Wanvilaska has come. I am Unaharra. We're here to help defend the ancient city."

"Your late, the Dragon attacked last night."

"We're not late. And we're not here to defend against Dragons."

"Then why have you come? The Sagean's force is a month away."

"We are here to kill the Hellfiends."

"What?"

"The Hellfiends have risen."

INTERLUDE VII
MEROHA

MEROHA BOUNDED UP THE WOODEN STEPS FROM THE DARK CHAMBER to the main deck, gasping for breath. The sea air attacked her senses first. The blazing sun was such a stark contrast from the cellar space below where she had slept that she was momentarily blinded. But even blind and nauseated, she felt such a sense of relief, accompanied by her freedom from the small, cramped space, that it was a bath of serenity.

"Are you all right, miss?" the older deckhand said, extending his hand to help her to her feet.

She took the aid, stood, and straightened her clothes. "Thank you, I'm fine."

"Was it a rat or a nightmare?" he pried.

"I guess it was a nightmare," she lied. In reality it was simply a case of claustrophobia. An affliction that came as a surprise to her. She'd felt nothing of it inside the endless tunnels of the Tregorean Province. Though thinking back, she had found every excuse to go outside or to the elevated levels open to the sky.

Their destination was the walled island of Kotalla, Meroha's homeland, a place she once thought she would never see again. Somewhere along the line, in her course of rattling around with the rogues, she began to believe she would return home one day, and when she did, she would return with an army to liberate her people.

This was certainly not the army she had imagined, but four ships full of Tregorean rangers on a mission beset by the Quantum man was something equally magnificent.

Meroha's momentary lapse was extinguished by the sounds on deck, and she jumped into position and threw her muscles into repositioning the sail lines, the foresail in front of her thumping in the wind.

Aboard a ship, the whole world came alive for her. A world of lines, riggers, and knots; of waves, and wind, and open air. The Zulu Sea pitched, and the four-mast ships charged toward the walled island of Kotalla. All the Kihan ships were powered by steam turbines, their screw propellers aiding their speed.

Meroha stood up on the side rail, her hand holding the ratlines of the shroud near the main mast and the wind throwing her clothes and hair back. The peaks of the Avaleer Mountains had appeared on the horizon. The mountains she had made her midnight escape through.

She was going home, and a reckoning was coming with her.

PART FOUR

FORTY

AFTERMATH - LEARON

THEY ENTERED A LOWER ROOM FROM THE TUNNEL INTO AN ODD
scene. There were two Harrinari women, both covered with ash and
blood, and Tali ran to hug one of them. Ellaria was pacing in a room
beyond a set of ornate doors that stood ajar, and Kovan was nowhere
to be seen.

Echoryn was busy helping treat a wounded Zenoch man with
instructions from a woman who had her back to him, and she
appeared to be restrained.

The Harrinari women—Learon guessed that's who they were,
based on their clothes—headed for the exit.

"I have to go tend to my people, now," one of them announced,
and she and the warrior next to her left the room through a stairway
at the far end.

Echoryn looked up at him. Her typical feisty spirit was downcast,
and she gave him a subtle grin. "Good to see you, Squirrel. You look
confident, again," she said.

Learon hugged her, but Echoryn quickly let him go and walked
toward Tali, who was staring daggers at Echoryn.

Echoryn whispered something to her, and Tali's eyes narrowed,
but Echoryn kept nodding. Tali blinked rapidly. Learon had the sense
they were talking about him, and when they pointed to his hair, he
knew they were.

Ellaria waved them into the far room.

The three of them entered. It was a room very reminiscent of the room inside the temple in Marathal. It was vast, with tall columns all around and a Wave Gate at the far end.

Ellaria hugged him when he entered.

"Everything all right? Where's Kovan?" Learon asked.

"Everything's great. Tali found an obsidian pillar to activate the Tempest Stone. Kovan saw you coming back, and I sent him to get the stone from our room."

She embraced Tali next and beamed at them with pride. "Nice entrance, young lady," Ellaria said. "Alasne told us about the obsidian pillar on the Zenoch side. She said you were very excited to find it."

"Yes, the Spirit Elders have a Gate inside their temple in Darkanna. Everything there is still intact. They've known about the Gates forever but didn't know how they worked. I brought Alasne here a month ago and returned to help the Spirit Elders gather their army."

Kovan came running in with a bundled blanket in his arms.

"That's my blanket," Tali said.

"I know," Kovan said, and he unwrapped the Tempest Stone and gave it to Ellaria. The milky-white pyramid of crystal look as unblemished as the last time Learon saw it.

Ellaria stopped midsentence, eyeing the crystal sword at Learon's hip. "You found the Desolation blade?"

Kovan couldn't take his eyes off it, so Learon handed it to him to inspect.

"I knew you'd earn a sword. But not this," Kovan said in awe.

"Where did you find it? It was with the Shadowyn?" Ellaria asked.

"Sort of. It's a long story, but I found it on a sacred peak embedded in stone. I think Elias found it a long time ago and placed it there."

"Were you able to kill the Dragon, then?" Kovan asked.

"No. I could have, of that I'm certain. But no," Learon said.

"Why didn't you?" Tali asked.

Learon ran his hand through his hair, or what was left of it, and tried to figure out how to explain what had happened. "Her name is Luminaura. She's a protector of Radmana. When I have the sword in my hands, I can speak to her. I don't know why. I do know I'll never harm another innocent thing in my life. As soon as I cut its wing, I knew," Learon explained. The pain of having cut the Dragon made him shiver.

"The magic of the blade?" Ellaria asked.

"No. Just something that happened to me on my way here," Learon said.

Ellaria smiled the smile she gave when she was still curious for more but content for the moment. Looking at Tali, Ellaria held up the stone. "I guess it's time we find some answers, then. Shall we?" she said.

Tali walked over to the Gate and ignited the oculus pool, then stepped back to Learon. "Are you coming?"

"Go," Learon said. "I'll wait here."

"I'll be right back," she said and disappeared into the curtain of light.

Ellaria followed. Kovan sat on the dais with a look of exhaustion.

After a few minutes, the Gate closed, and Kovan glanced back into the main room and buried his head in his hands.

"You didn't want to go?" Learon asked, sitting next to him.

"And see another temple, no thanks. Besides, that stone doesn't have any answers for me," Kovan said, and he returned the sword. "Elias would be proud, you know?"

"I know."

"I guess we know why he wanted you to go to train with the Shadowyn."

"Yeah. How about you? Did you ever get that compass working?"

"Not really," Kovan said, then his eyes fixated on Learon's necklace. "I like the pendant. What kind of stone is that?"

Learon thought it was a surprising question, but answered, "It's a rose quartz, or heart-stone."

Kovan only nodded in response.

Learon stood up and paced around the room. Echoryn was talking with the prisoner in hushed tones and showing her a small blue book. Learon thought he heard his name. The woman who was tied up lifted her face at him entering the room, and she smiled. Learon couldn't help himself; he took a step back in shock. He did know this woman. It was his mother.

The step back obviously wounded her. He regretted the instant reaction. He had wondered how he would feel when he met her, but now that the moment was here, his feeling was clear. Echoryn backed away, and Learon kneeled at his mother's side.

"You're more perfect than I could have imagined," she whispered to him.

"Mother, I-I don't know what to say," Learon admitted.

"Nor should you. Just let me look at you," she said.

"Mother. I forgive you," he said, surprised by his own words, and he hugged her. She leaned into him and sobbed in his arms.

"You'll be the only one. But you're the only one that matters to me," she said.

"What do you mean?"

"Trust me," she said.

FORTY-ONE
OBSIDIAN - ELLARIA

INSIDE THE ZENOCH SPIRIT ELDERS TEMPLE, ELLARIA NEEDED A moment for her eyes to adjust. The brightness from the activated Gate strained her retinas. The violence of the instant journey almost made her throw up.

Tali stepped out of the Gate and showed Ellaria to the podium of obsidian. "I'm going to let the watchman know it's me. I'll be right back," she said.

Ellaria walked around the black pedestal with the triangular depression and looked at the slab of crystal just in front of it on the wall. Tali had told her, the Tempest Stone was the key to unlocking a library of information stored inside the crystal tablets. Ellaria only hoped the Zenoch's tablet contained the information she was looking for. She took the Tempest Stone and put it into place on the black plinth.

A beam of multicolored light poured out of it and projected into the tablet of crystal. A glow burst free and enveloped Ellaria in a ball of light. A collection of semi-translucent photos burst to life. She blinked, expecting it all to vanish, but it remained. She shuffled through images like they were a library of books at her fingertips. The translucent images floated in the air around her, an unimaginable amount of information contained in every inch of the crystal.

She picked a subject and began reading. She quickly realized she could die of old age, having never read everything in this one tablet.

She selected Karnika, and a large map appeared before her in greater detail than any map she had ever seen. It showed lands and cities long forgotten, cities equal to and surpassing Adalon or Orin in every way. Advanced cities, with machines they had only imagined.

It took her breath away, but it wasn't what she was looking for.

She struggled to navigate the images at first, but soon she was sifting through information and data as fast as her mind would allow. The first thing she discovered was that the New World was once considered the Old World, because all of it was part of the ancient world. Everything was hard to follow, so she searched until she found a timeline that explained it all. The world of civilized humans was nearly four thousand years old. The ones her fellow scholars referred to as the Ancients had gained great powers when they killed the Dragons, some two thousand years ago. However, without the Dragons, the world changed. The weather became unpredictable, and storms surged over the planet. Many species became extinct, and certain types of magic vanished overnight.

The Vygoths were a group of mages who, in order to solve the crisis, built a great machine in the city of Territhial in the Brovic Ocean. Their work was considered paramount to the survival of the species, and with the fate of the world on their shoulders, society began to call them the Fates. The timeline continued to list the names of the Fates.

What the machine was or how it worked she couldn't' find. She assumed it must be on another tablet, the same way the Sagean's sacred text was its own tablet. However, she found information that explained when the great rift was born and the world was cast in darkness, after an event at the site of the machine. *The Wrythen,* Ellaria wondered. *Did the Fates create the Wrythen or unleash it on our world?*

The Fates who survived found they no longer aged. They crafted amulets to defeat the darkness. When the Wrythen was finally imprisoned, the chaos mists of the Brovic grew, the light returned, and the era of the Luminaries was born. Five great Luminary factions ruled the corners of the world, and the Fates disappeared.

The Luminaries ruled for nearly three hundred years, rebuilding the world and the lost kingdoms. The factions were vastly different ideologically and were always at war. Soon, the world was again on the precipice of catastrophe. The Wrythen, now called the Old One, had begun to plague the world a second time. The Fates returned to help the Luminaries, this time using amulets crafted to defeat the being. Again, they lost, but the Wrythen was trapped again in the Brovic.

From this point in history, Ellaria knew more from the fragments they found after the Sagean Empire fell and the theory's described in the oldest books in Elias's collection. In the aftermath of the second battle with the Wrythen, the Sagean Order took control of the world. The history described in the tablet supported scholars' understanding that the Sagean Order began a twenty-year war that culminated in the destruction of many of the last ancient cities. Once in power, the Sagean Empire outlawed reading and writing, and sealed away any objects that remained from the Ancients.

The record in this tablet ended, and Ellaria assumed the rest from what she already knew of history. With this new information, her mind made further connections. The Fates were responsible for hiding the Gates from the Sagean, among other things.

She reluctantly closed the machine and stepped away from the stone. The ramifications of this historic account were staggering. She knew how impossibly old a lot of these relics were, but now she comprehended it on another level. The Tempest Stone was an archiving device almost two thousand years old. The Desolation blade was older, and as far as she knew, the only remaining weapon from the era of the Dragon Hunters. Ellaria took the Stone with her and found Tali leaning against the Gate, humming a song Ellaria hadn't heard in a very long time.

"Where did you hear that song?" Ellaria asked.

Tali looked at her, confused. "What song?"

"You were humming a song just now."

"Was I? I didn't realize. I think I heard it somewhere. What did you find?" Tali asked.

"The world is in trouble, and yet it's always been in trouble. But I can tell you I'm grateful Learon didn't kill that Dragon. Also, and more importantly, I know where the Wrythen is."

"Where?"

"The Brovic Ocean. Let's get back to the others. We must devise a path going forward."

"Definitely," Tali said, and ignited the Wave Gate again to return to Radmana.

FORTY-TWO

CONFRONTATION - KOVAN

KOVAN PACED AROUND THE ROOM. THE MYSTCAT MEPHI'S HEAD tracking him back and forth. He wanted answers from Mia but decided to wait for Ellaria.

From the outer room, Alasne and Nikki returned. Alasne's jaw was clenched, and her lips pursed.

"Where's Ellaria?" she demanded.

"Back in Darkanna with Tali. What's up?"

"I'm ready to march my people into Adara and wipe out the Sagean's army. We'll cross the ocean too and attack the Sagean himself after that."

"Is it that bad?" Kovan asked Nikki.

"Yes. More than half the Harrinari who came to the summit are dead. We've defeated all the Bonemen, and I sent a team to find the airship that landed last night," Nikki said.

"Make no mistake, my people want blood, and they will have it," Alasne said, her hands in fists at her side.

Kovan didn't want to argue that bows and spears would be a difficult match against the heavily armed Sagean army. They would lose more lives in future battles as well.

"Ellaria will be glad to have your alliance. We all are. And your friendship. Before we came here, Ellaria said she believed that the battle would be fought in the north and the south. Can you direct some of your forces to the south to wait for further orders in Logan?"

"Absolutely. The Eenod tribe suffered more than most. Their leader was killed, though his wife and child survived. She leads them now."

"We have reinforcement in the west near the river. They will go south with them."

Bolts of electricity flashed from the Gate to the ceiling, and the Gate's circles began to shift and move like waves. Everyone stepped back from the dais, and the oculus pool came alive with a bright light.

Ellaria stepped out and then Tali. They both froze on the platform, having walked into a crowded room.

Learon charged into the room with Mia. "Why was my mother tied up?"

He had cut her bindings, and Mia stepped to the platform. Kovan had the urge to grab her but thought about Learon and restrained himself.

"Because Mia can't be trusted," Kovan said.

"Why? Elias's letter spoke of something about this. What's going on?" Ellaria said.

"Because she has manipulated events in all of our lives. She took our daughter from us," Kovan said, finally telling her the truth. His body sagged, broken from the burden he had unloaded, the strength going out of him.

"What are you talking about, Kovan? Zoe is dead," Ellaria said.

"She's not," Kovan said adamantly. "I tried to find her, but I couldn't. Elias had me retrieve this torquing compass, but it didn't help."

Ellaria shook her head. Kovan knew she was angry speaking about Zoe, let alone at him suggesting she was alive.

"She took her from us, but I remembered. When I got back my memories, whatever spell Mia had done to make us think Zoe had died was gone. She did this to all of us. She even gave up Elias's son."

"No. That's impossible. That can't be the betrayal Elias spoke of."

"Everything's connected, but I couldn't leave the fate of the world to chance. I alone had the power to influence events in our favor," Mia said, the light of the Gate's pool behind her.

Mia and Tali had stayed on the dais, and Kovan discerned for the first time that as long as someone was standing on the platform, the Gate remained active.

"What?" Ellaria said.

"How did you convince us, and why? Why?" Kovan asked.

"The Unity Maze concerns all of you."

"What did you say?" Ellaria said.

"Including me?" Tali said.

"Even you, Tali. Ask yourself, if Kovan wasn't imprisoned in Ravenvyre, would you be here now?"

"But how did you know I would leave my mother and go with Kovan?" Tali asked.

"Because she's not your mother," Mia said flatly.

"What?" Tali said.

"And because I knew somewhere along the way the Fates who watched over you would intervene. They can't help themselves. The Fates have been doing what I did for centuries."

"What about my mother?" Tali said.

"Is Tali our daughter?" Kovan said. It was the conclusion he always came back to. From the moment he learned his daughter was alive, he felt it could be Tali.

"I don't know," Mia answered, but Kovan knew she was lying.

"What?" Ellaria snapped again, this time with half-mad eyes. "You stole my baby. You stole my chance to be a mother?"

She charged after Mia on the Gate's platform. When she caught her, she gripped Mia's hair in one hand and punched her twice in the face with the other before Tali pulled her off.

"Talk. I need to know everything," Ellaria said, her teeth gritted.

Mia wiped the blood off her face. "From the moment I met Elias, I had a vision of the end of the world. I knew he would fight multiple wars and battle against evil his entire life. After the Great War, he returned to the Kihan Province to be healed. He was losing control of his powers. They were growing stronger at a rate he couldn't handle, and he would black out from time to time. Sound familiar? Our healers helped him regain control, but he was weakened. We grew closer as he found his strength again, and I found my visions had changed. What I didn't know then was the effect the Sagean emperor inside of Elias was having on me.

"We fell in love, and when we thought Elias was fully healed, we moved to the New World and started a life. I continued to have my visions, but I had learned to cope with them. Then Zoe was born. You had waited so long to have children, fearing the war would return, and she was the light of all our lives. Elias and I were also afraid to have children. Zoe was special to us."

"Don't you dare," Ellaria growled.

"Keep going," Kovan said.

"Something about her had cracked through Elias's barrier. He realized that it was when he accessed his well of energy that the shield weakened, and he would see the Wrythen again. When that happened, my visions became far worse, and with all five of us there, I had my first sight of the Unity Maze—the vast connections of lives that all lead to the end of the world. All of us were integral, and Zoe was essential. I began to have dark visions of her future, yours, and ours. At the same time Elias wasn't sleeping. He was plagued far more than he told me by the Wrythen. We were all going mad.

"We came to you and told you of what was happening to us, and your suggestion was to hide. Soon after, your daughter fell off the cliff into the ocean, and Kovan had to save her. Both nearly drowned.

"But I had warned you both of it, days prior. When they were safely back home, both were lying up in bed for days, recovering. Ellaria, you came to me and said you trusted me, that Elias was scaring you, and you asked how I could use my abilities to keep you safe. A long time ago I discovered that to glimpse possible outcomes of the future, I only had to commit myself in my mind to an action and the changes to the maze would reveal themselves. So, I planned to hide her from you both. From all of us."

"You're crazy," Ellaria said.

"What about me?" Learon asked.

Mia looked at him with tears in her eyes, but she lowered her head and answered, "Visions are living entities that turn prophets mad. I had seen it with the previous prophet before me. No matter how hard you try to avoid it, that madness consumes you. It was never my intention to keep you from your father, Learon, or to abandon you. By the time I knew I was pregnant, I had hidden Zoe away and performed the Zosmos spell for all of us to forget. The drowning scare had provided the perfect trigger for the spell to work. Elias had left for the Old World and began to track down every piece of the Ancients he could. He had fought me not to take Zoe away, and in the end that anger carried over after the spell and he disappeared.

"Afterward, Elias had left believing he was partly responsible for Zoe's death because of the Wrythen, and I was stuck in the north with a child I couldn't take care of. By then my visions were out of my control. I would have visions that could enslave me and knock me out for hours. The madness worsened as my sleep became plagued with other lives, and one day I held you, Learon, and fell into a vision of your life. This had been happening in small increments, and I knew for a while how special you were, but this one was different. I saw the span of your life and intersections of good and evil. I woke up a day later to your screams. You were starving to death, and I couldn't take care of you. I couldn't do it.

"I started my search. But in my visions, you would often come in contact with Zoe, and you both would be hunted and killed. So, I began to believe you needed to be brought up far away from her. I started to listen for travelers, and I would introduce myself to them and shake their hands or kiss their cheeks just to glimpse their lives and see what kind of person they were. Time was running out as my health was worsening.

"At the same time, I began to research a little-known religion practiced by my people, the Kihan, as I had found out that the Zenoch and the Harrinari also practiced this belief in the Fates. I started to try and find out how their beliefs differed from my own. Somehow, I knew theses beings were connected to my ability, and I longed for understanding, but more than that, I longed for an end. For peace. In those days there weren't many places to go to find out this information. There was only one library in the north and very few experts on the other cultures. Even fewer doing research. That's how I met Rylan. We worked together. When I was younger, I knew your mother, Cara. She was a friend of mine in the city. Elias knew her too. She came over all the time, and I knew she could not have children. But she had a cloud to her, and it inhibited my ability to penetrate her future.

Later, I learned that this was because of her illness. People believe it's a confusion within the mind, but it's more like a wall. I discovered that this wall prevented me from seeing her future. Her friendship was a comfort, and I knew her to be a good person, so I decided that this wall could be another protection for you, Learon.

"I introduced her to Rylan, and I knew they would hit it off. I told them that I was dying, and they took you as their own. They suspected Elias was your father, and because of who he was, they agreed to never speak of it. Since that day I have dedicated my life to the completion of the Unity Maze, and now here we are."

"You stole everything from me," Ellaria screamed. Tears streamed down her face.

"You don't understand, being a mother is sacrifice. You sacrifice yourself for them and their happiness. For us that meant our children would be raised by other people. I'm sure they would not have lived otherwise, and they are needed to win the War of the Last Dawn," Mia said.

"You made that sacrifice for me. I didn't get to decide," Ellaria said.

"You did, only you can't remember. The threat to her now is the Sagean and the Wrythen. If the Sagean finds out you have a daughter, he will stop at nothing to take her from you."

"Fine, you've given us your mad excuses. Now, where is our daughter?" Kovan demanded.

"Where was I in your story?" Tali said.

Ellaria walked over to Kovan, grabbed the gun off his hip, and charged at Mia again. Mia backed up toward the still-active Gate.

"Please, Ellaria, don't kill her," Learon said. "I've already lost two fathers and another mother who can't remember me."

"I don't care!" Ellaria shouted, her eyes full of fury.

"Ellaria, I need answers," Tali said.

"I can bring Elias back," Mia said in a scramble.

"Elias is dead," Ellaria said.

"He's not. He's only waiting in the ether. He has Meroha working on how to bring him back."

Kovan's eyes darted back and forth to all of them, and he began judging the distance to Mia and whether he could reach her before she jumped through the Gate.

She looked at him then. "You can't reach me in time," she commented and then looked slyly at the rest of them. "Do all of you know about the Gates?"

"What about them?" Tali asked.

Mia smiled and stepped back into the light. Kovan dove for her but missed.

"Are you kidding me? What a psycho," Alasne said.

"She's not. Whether you believe her or not, she's not lying," Echoryn said.

"Why would she go back to the Zenoch Temple?" Tali asked.

"She didn't," Learon said.

"Of course she did. That's the symbol I selected." Tali pointed to the glowing symbol, but it had changed. "What symbol is that? How did it change on its own? How is that possible?"

"Elias told me in my letter that the Gates take the user where they want to go, regardless of the destination selected," Learon said.

"So where did she go?" Tali asked.

"I don't know. But the point is, when we walk through the Gate, we have to know what we want. If you go through wanting to be back home, it might take you to a Gate in Ravenvyre," Learon explained.

"I want blood," Ellaria said.

"No, wait," Kovan said, understanding the importance of their state of mind, but Ellaria stepped into the Gate after Mia and was gone.

"It's up to everyone here, but my goal is to defeat the Wrythen. If we need Elias to do it, then that's what I'm going to do," Learon said.

"We need to defeat the Sagean first," Alasne said, her own anger flashing.

"What are you saying, Learon?" Tali asked.

"I'm saying that I assume when I step through, I will be at the Gate in Nahadon. If Mia is there, great. If not, I'm going to help Meroha." Learon walked up to Tali and embraced her. "You go where you need to. I'll understand if I don't see you on the other side of this, but I hope I do."

Tali's body shook, and she wiped her eyes. "I want to follow you; I always want us to be together until the end."

"But you have to follow Mia," Learon said.

"Yes," Tali said.

"I understand," Learon said.

Tali kissed him on the cheek and stepped through the Gate.

"She'll be in Nahadon, Learon. All of them will be," Echoryn said.

"I will be, I know that," Learon said.

"I won't be going back there," Echoryn said.

"What?" Learon asked.

"I can feel the madness Mia spoke of. I've felt it for months. I want to find my own way now, Bohoja."

"But will you be all right?" Learon asked.

"I'll be fine, Squirrel. Now go."

Learon waved at them, and Kovan nodded, silently watching the young man disappear.

"I guess I'm going too," Alasne growled.

Nikki tugged at her shirt. "Don't leave me."

And Kovan suddenly saw their relationship in a different light.

"Organize our people and guard this place. I want to be ready to march our forces in two days. The time of the Sagean is over. I'll be back soon with help, I promise," Alasne said and stepped into the Gate.

Kovan was left with Echoryn, Nikki, and the Zenoch man who had just wandered into the room.

"What did I miss?" the Zenoch man asked, his voice hoarse and groggy.

"Too much," Nikki said.

Kovan motioned for Echoryn to go first.

"May you stay in the Blue, Kovan. I hope you find what you're looking for," she said, and she walked into the Gate.

Kovan rummaged through his bag and produced the communicator watch. He handed it to Nikki. "In case we need to contact you" —he slid the face to the side—"a message will appear here."

"Thank you. Protect her please," Nikki said.

Kovan nodded. He picked up the mystcat then stepped up to the shimmering pool, took a deep breath, and stepped into the light.

FORTY-THREE

HOMECOMING - KOVAN

KOVAN FELL FROM THE POOL OF LIGHT INTO A PIT OF BLACKNESS, HIS eyes burning. The cat leaped free from out his arms, as he stumbled to the ground. He gripped at the smooth rock surface until finding enough leverage to get to his feet. Picking himself up off the floor, he felt his lower back resist and radiate pain. *Traveling the Wave Gates is a young man's game*, he thought with the ground still moving at his feet.

"Ellaria! Learon!" Kovan called out, but no answer came except his own voice echoing back at him. "Tali!" he tried again, his eyes still not adjusting.

"Who's there?" a soft voice called down from a cavernous space, the echo distorting the person's voice enough that Kovan didn't recognize it.

Kovan climbed the stairs, where a young woman stood holding a lantern. Her face was obscured in the shadow.

The Gate had not taken him to the others. He was somewhere else.

"Where is everyone?" the woman asked.

Kovan knew the voice, and he slid back in the darkness of the steps. His shoulders slumped and he exhaled. He pulled the compass from his things as the woman approached. He had to check. He now knew that the red stone was heart-stone, and it didn't locate someone with abilities—it located the ones you loved. It located family.

He pressed his thumb to the red crystal, the dials of the compass spun, and the lights blazed in her direction.

The woman stepped down to him, and her appearance had finally shifted to show how young she truly was.

"You look different." He smiled as she helped him up.

Alasne felt her face and looked at a lock of her hair. "It must have been the Wave Gate. It effected my magic. The Harrinari perceive wisdom and age as the same thing. Without the spell, I would never have been able to bring the Harrinari together."

She held the lantern out, and Kovan's eyes filled with tears.

"What's wrong?" she asked.

"I was thinking."

"What?"

"That without it, you look like your mother."

She eyed him suspiciously and shook her head. "No."

"It's you."

"I wish people would stop saying that phrase to me. Now where are we, do you think?"

"I don't know, I went last so I could find you. Where did you intend to go?"

"To meet up with the rest of them, but they're not here."

"Is that really where you wanted to go?"

"No, I wanted to go after the Sagean."

"Then, my dear, I think we're somewhere in Tovillore."

FORTY-FOUR
THE NAHADON GATE - TALI

LEARON STUMBLED OUT LAST, AND TALI GRABBED HIM. SHE WAS slightly ashamed of herself to leave him, but she needed to know about her own parents. Learon wiped his eyes, and she led him off the platform into the darkness.

"Where are we?" Learon asked.

"We don't know. Mia doesn't either, but it's muggy in here," Tali said.

Learon's sight had come back, and he looked around as Ellaria lit a second torch and brought it over to them.

"I know where we are. I've been here before. We're in the jungles of Nahadon near the Temple of Ama, or what's left of it. This is where I found the letters," Learon said.

"What letters? Tali asked.

"The letters Elias left. I gave yours to Kovan. I'm sure he still has it…" he paused and scanned the room. "Do you hear that scratching?"

"No," Tali said. Learon ran to the far end of the room. "Where are you going?" she said.

She heard what sounded like a stone grinding on stone, and Learon came bounding back to her. He held her mystcat Remi in his hands.

"Remi!" Tali said, taking the sleek black cat into her arms. "What about Echoryn? she asked.

"She's not coming," Learon said.

"Where's Kovan?" Ellaria demanded and charged toward Mia.

"He made his choice," Mia said.

"What do you mean?" Ellaria said, her voice raised. She was so frantic now, her hands were shaking.

"He knew what was important to him, and it wasn't revenge," Mia said.

"You mean…?" Ellaria replied. Her body sagged.

Mia nodded and Ellaria fell to her knees and wept. Tali went to comfort her. While Kovan was intent on finding his daughter, Ellaria's focus had been on her anger, and the realization was too much for her to bear. Her body spasmed as she sobbed in Tali's arms.

Tali looked up to Learon. "Where's Alasne?"

"I don't know," Learon shook his head. "Are we sure she was coming through?" he asked.

"I'm sure," Tali said.

Ellaria wiped her eyes and looked over at Mia. "Are they together?"

"They are," Mia said.

"Is Alasne my daughter?" Ellaria asked softly.

"I believe she is," Mia said.

"Why? Why play a trick on us? Why not just tell us?"

"It wasn't a trick. For one, I wasn't sure. I don't remember where I hid her. I recalled meeting an old woman who knew something of alchemy and spells and a way of hiding her. Though I knew Alasne's face from my visions, she has used her mage's ability to hide her face from her own people. To appear older and more like the woman she was raised by. Mostly, I didn't say because it was a kindness for Kovan. He suffered for so long with the idea that he had failed to save your daughter. He needed to find her for himself."

Ellaria nodded.

"I think Kovan has believed it was Tali for a long time now," Learon said.

"I did too when I heard you humming that song. It was a song Kovan used to sing to Zoe," Ellaria said.

"I remember now. I heard Alasne whistling it." Tali took a deep breath. "I guess maybe I was starting to believe it too. I have had a connection to Kovan since I first met him," she said.

"Sometimes bonds are connections through energies we don't understand. That's what your connection is to Kovan. Blood is often overrated and insignificant," Mia said.

"Who are my real parents?" Tali asked.

"I honestly don't know. I've known about you for some time, and I know a Fate has watched over you your entire life," Mia said.

"Who?" Tali asked.

"The Fate goes by the name of Morrowmaki Drevoren."

"Maki?" Tali said. She put a hand over her own mouth in shock.

"All I know is you were found on the islands of the Dire by the man you came to call your father. He brought you back to Ravenvyre. I'm not sure when Maki became aware of you. He could have been with the soldiers that found you, or it's possible he put you on the island. I don't know."

Tali sat down on the cold stone floor, her world having been turned upside down.

"So where are they? Where is Kovan now?" Ellaria asked.

"I don't know," Mia said.

"Lie," Ellaria snapped.

"If Alasne went through first, then Kovan simply followed her," Tali surmised. "So where would Alasne go, if not here?"

Learon snapped his fingers. "When she came back from seeing to her people, she was furious. She wanted to go after and kill the Sagean."

"So where would that take them?" Tali said.

Ellaria stood up and wiped her eyes clean, and Tali could see a new calmness had come over her. "Tali, will you activate the Gate again? I would like to go meet my daughter."

"How?" Learon said.

"Because to be reunited with my family is all that I want in this world. The Gate will take me there. Wherever that is. I intend on taking the fight to the Sagean. I'm tired, and I want this war over with."

"We'll follow you," Tali said.

"What about Elias?" Learon said.

Ellaria still held Kovan's gun, and she again pointed it at Mia. "Was that all bullshit, or can Elias be brought back? And talk fast because your theory is the only thing keeping you alive anymore."

"Yes. Elias is partly in the realm of the dead and part of him remains in this world. Meroha, with the help of the Kihan, is trying to liberate Kotalla from their dictator so they can access a sacred site on the walled island."

"What site?" Tali asked.

"The Crystal Cave," Ellaria answered. "The same place Edward researched. It's a massive cave of crystals and probably a powerful place to harness energy."

"There's something else, isn't there? There always is," Tali said.

"Tali's right. In my letter, Elias said there were a few ways for him to come back. What are they?" Ellaria asked Mia.

"I can only think of one possible way, and it definitely requires the Crystal Cave," Mia said.

"Have you seen it? You know how it plays out, don't you?" Ellaria said.

"No. I've seen it both ways. One in which you are successful, and he returns to fight by the side of the Trinity Guard—and another where you fail."

"So how do we do it? What's the way you know of?"

"As I said, his spirit is partly in the realm of the dead and part of him remains with the living. That part that remains with the living would need to be strong enough to bring him back," Mia said.

"Where is it?" Learon asked.

"The part of him that I know of that remains with the living is inside of Kovan," Mia said.

"What?" Ellaria said, her eyes wide.

"His scar," Tali said, the answer coming to her. "The scar on Kovan's chest, what's that from?" she asked Ellaria.

"In the Great War, Kovan was wounded by a spear while fighting the Viper Lords and freeing their slaves. I don't know how bad it was, I wasn't there."

"I was," Mia said. "I was there in the Kihan palace when Elias brought him in, a shard of steel sticking out of Kovan's chest. Our healers said they could do nothing for him. Elias went crazy, and he became light itself. He poured part of himself into Kovan and passed out. Whatever he did, he saved Kovan's life, and I've always believed that he left part of himself in Kovan for it to have worked."

"That feels like the method Elias referred to in his letter that he didn't want me to pursue, and it also explains why Elias's mystcat wouldn't leave Kovan's side," Ellaria said.

"So, we find Kovan, and go from there," Learon said.

Ellaria nodded and signaled Tali to turn the Gate on. She placed her hand on the cold components and pulled the heat out of her torch and channeled it into the Gate. The ancient device came alive. With the path clear, a sense of finality settled inside her mind. She turned back to the others.

"Any idea where we are going?" Tali asked.

Ellaria handed the torch to Mia and stepped toward the glowing light, Kovan's gun tapping at her hip. "My guess, the lost city of Ashalon. It doesn't matter."

Learon jumped up beside Tali on the platform. Staring into her eyes, he opened his hand and held it out for her. "She's right. What matters is that whatever we do from here, we do together."

Tali took Learon's hand, the spark of his touch flooding through her, and she echoed his words, "Together."

THE END OF BOOK THREE

Epilogue

"Just you and me, Morrowmaki?" Poe asked, looking out over the clouds.

"Haven't you heard, Shadin or Moria the Mistress of Merinde, as she goes by now, has gone crazy. She's forgotten about all of it and us," Maki said.

"How was the Wrythen able to get to her?" Poe asked.

"I don't know, but now she works for him," Maki said.

"Is Caleb coming?" Poe asked.

"He should be," Maki said.

An old man climbed the hill ahead of them, the guitar on his back appearing before he did.

"You bastard, Caleb, that's mine," Poe said.

"It was yours, you minstrel. But you lost it," Caleb said.

Maki rolled his eyes. Poe and Caleb always fought like brothers. "Give him back the torquing guitar."

"Fine. You're welcome for keeping it safe all these years." Caleb took the strap off and handed the old wooden instrument to Poe. Poe shook it and tipped it over. Sand fell out of the sound hole. He looked back, furious at Caleb.

Poe had always possessed an ability to play and sing ballads like no other person Maki had ever heard. Whether Poe was bestowed the gift at the Energy Meridian or if he had always had it, Maki didn't know.

"Maybe now you can write a good song again," Caleb said.

"I sing a great ballad about you now," Poe said.

"I'm sure you do. Anything is better than those legendary Lore Tales you wrote," Caleb said.

"What's wrong with those? Have you even read them?" Poe asked.

"I've read them. There's not a speck of truth in them," Caleb said.

"They're exaggerations, sure, but they've lasted a long time. I tried to write books about truth. Real truth. People hated them. In the face of truth, the people hid themselves in their blankets of religion, remember?"

"Not really. I chose to be drunk for those four hundred years. So, now what? You sing ballads as some minstrel named Lamdryn?" Caleb said.

"Yeah. I don't see you helping the humans fight what we unleashed," Poe said.

"I saved Kovan Rainer from dying of dehydration in the wastes. How about you?"

"I gave him his memories back," Poe said.

"Maybe you two should branch out and help the others. Did Kovan at least unite the Trinity?" Maki asked.

"I believe so. There was a battle at Radmana. The Nimbus showed up with my sword," Caleb said.

"Did he kill the Dragon?" Maki asked.

Caleb shook his head no.

"Good. That's good, but they're running out of time. Soon the Brovic mists will clear, and the Wrythen will be free," Maki said.

"And once again we'll have to fight it," Caleb said.

"We will, but first we have another problem to deal with," Maki said.

"What?" Caleb asked.

"Maki says, we have a problem with Shadin," Poe replied.

"We do, and our pact says we have to deal with her," Maki said.

Caleb shook his head and turned away from them to look out on the horizon.

"There's not many of us left, is there?" Poe said, strumming his guitar. "Alaina Darrowin died in birth. Tazrus died, and we all know what happened to Cyrus,"

"Why now? Why these humans?" Caleb asked.

"It's their time, their turn to put right what we wrought upon the world," Maki said.

"In other words, it is as fate would have it," Poe said with a grin.

"Very funny, Poe. You've always been witty," Caleb said.

"Poe is right, we are the creators of fate. It's time we bent it in our favor," Asher Morales said from behind them.

They all turned to look at him. The old ship captain walked closer to them, his intense copper eyes, scanning each of them. Morales always maintained an air of command, even around powerful beings. He stopped in front of them with his arms crossed.

"The end of ends is upon us brothers," Morales said in a cold foreboding tone. "The Wrythen has brought Hellfiends out of hibernation, they will reach civilization soon. This is the third war and the last."

"How do you know that, Asher?" Caleb asked.

"I found out while returning from Hazon," Morales said.

"You took Mayzanna Buroga back to Hazon?" Poe asked.

"Yes. He has promised that the Hazon people will be ready."

"If the end is near, what do you suggest we do? How do we help the Trinity Guard?" Caleb asked.

"We need to split up to help who we can. However, one of us must kill Shadin. She is the Wrythen's now,"

"I'll do it," Maki volunteered.

One of Morales's eyebrows raised at Maki's offer. Confrontation was not Maki's style, but he didn't want Caleb to have to do it.

"No. It should be me," Caleb said.

"Fine. We will sail for Manashera this evening. Shadin has already led her army out of Merinde," Morales said.

"Is she looking for the Menodarins?" Maki asked.

"She must be, or what's left of them," Poe answered.

Maki looked at all of them and wondered if all their scheming had been enough to turn the tide and give them a chance to defeat the evil they had released on the world centuries ago. Then maybe, finally, they would have some peace for their winter's heart.

GLOSSARY

Note: The current date is the 25th of Savon in the 54th year of the 23rd epoch.

Acarite: A bright blue crystal, also called the soul crystal. Prized for its blue color, which many nations see as sacred.

Afterblue (The afterblue, the blue hours, blue sun): The atmosphere of Territhmina is clear and thin enough that when the sun reaches the highest point in the sky the sun turns a blue color. For the Sagean faith this time is spent in worship. Afterblue refers to the moment the sun leaves the apex of the sky and the color of the sun returns to normal. The thin atmosphere contributes to a high volume of water vapor in the air. More rain and colder temperatures.

Age of Eckwyn (ek-win): The time before the Sagean Empire, spanning the 2nd to the 6th epoch, when the people of Territhmina were unified. See also **Ancients**

Alchemist's Codex, the: Written by Xand Zosimus. It is the oldest and most extensive book on alchemy ever found.

Ammadon: The name for the Tregorean Province

Amadazumi (ah-ma-daz-ew-me): The name of the God of the northern region, near the Gray Sea.

Amatori Market: The great market in Ravenvyre. The market established a wider notoriety because of the large contingent of crafters, tinkers and alchemists found in Ravenvyre, who sell their gadgets and potions there.

Amber Coins: The common currency of the world is stamped amber coins. The amber has an odd bluish tint from pyrite inclusions. Each coin is marked with a symbol denoting the location of its origin.

Anamnesis Vase, the (aka the Eyes of Deja Maru): An ancient vase, with eyes at the top. The vase can extract memories in the form of liquid that pools inside the vase into cubes.

Ancients, the: The common term for the forgotten Age of Eckwyn. A time lost to history. All that is known is that the civilization that existed before the Sagean Empire was advanced and divided. See also **Eckwyn Age.**

Anthracite: A black stone used in fires to ward off the beasts. It burns blue.

Artificer: A machine maker of small lifelike devices, such as mechanical butterflies, bats, spiders and owls.

Ascendency Tower: The main government seat and headquarters for the Coalition of Nations and the Councils Court.

Atlas tablet: A Soft crystal used in the Whisper Chains Melodicure Machine that empowers the machine. An ancient relic believed to possess the ability to find anyone in the world.

Band of the Black Sails: A crime syndicate that mostly operates out of Aquom. They plunder and pirate the Mainsolis Sea and the Zulu Sea.

Band of Redeemers aka the Renegades of Tovillore: A small force of people from the west of Tovillore banded together to protect the country and fight the Scree and the beasts and the Lionized, in order to free the country.

Bards of Renown: Poe Lamdryn, Marcus Shayval, and Antara Ronvia. The three authors are the most well known throughout the world. Creators of the oldest tales, plays and poetry in the world. Including the Lore Tales of *Caleb Reaver and the Gaurdian of the Beyond*, *The Tin City of Telatheior*, *The Queen Of Ravens*; the tales of *Avari Nova*, and *the Radmana Crown*. And famous plays, *Echo of Silence*, *The Twilight of Nevermore*

Barium star-powder: A black powder used for fireworks and explosives.

Barrel Mosaic Theatre: A large round theatre in Midway, with arch filled columns wrapping around the entire structure, and colored glass in alternating openings.

Bogdrin: A swamp creature with a tentacled face. They are a rare creature known to exist in the blood marshes off the western coast of Nahadon. They have been seen as far north as the swamps of Aquom.

Bonelark: A large, featherless flying beast. Fully grown they can reach the size of an adult human. Though rare, these creatures eat human flesh and bone. They first appeared during the Great War and are one of the beasts controlled by the Sagean Emperor. Not much is known about their physiology, but it is believed they don't hunt in numbers and stay close to their nests.

Bonemen, The (The Bloodless, the Bone Army): The Sagean's personal army. The bonemen or also known as the bloodless or the bone army. They derived their name as a representation of last servitude beyond death. For even bones remain after the blood is gone and the flesh has decayed.

Branch Spider: Large poisonous spider with thick brown hair. Typically, found in the forests throughout Tovillore, non-deadly to humans:

Cadowa: A slender boat with a very tall single sail. Used predominantly in Aquam to navigate the shallow and thin canals and waterways.

Calendar Year: The Territhmina year is 396 days long and divided into 12 months. Summer (Jovost, Savon, Shadal), Fall (Dcluarch, Harven, Faden), Winter (Emberheart, Hazune, Souludal), Spring (Anander, Thawrich, Reesee). The New Year begins on the first day of summer and is the longest day of the year.

Capacitor gems: Any stone or crystal capable of energy.

Carriage Houses (Circus Caravan): Large moving houses, using a combination of steam power and pull horses. The wood housing structures are built on long wagon flatbeds and coming in a variety of shapes and sizes. Typically, with small sleeping compartments and a main sitting room. Various window sizes are all around the house, with exteriors of wood trim and framing.

Cloaked Knife: An elite group of mercenaries trained at the Citadel. This special military unit grew from the remnants of the Ultrarians.

Cloudparter: Enormous metal airships that transport people and supplies across the mountains and throughout Tovillore.

Confidence chairs: Attendees at the council's court in support of the ambassador who called them there.

Craftcore, The: The center for scientific development in Adalon.

Craftsmith: A crafter of objects not associated with a blacksmith.

Crime Syndicates: There are six known crime syndicates around the world. Most of them originated after the fall of the Sagean Empire. They are: The Deviants Core, The Supremacists, The Guard, The Shield, The Reckers, The Broken Flame, The Devisors and **The Band of the Black Sails**.

Crystals, Jewels & Gems: Crystals are categorized into five groups based on their use: Energy stones, Power stones, Protection stones, Healing stones and Lore stones. Lore stones are rare or considered myth in some cases.

Energy Stones:
Quantum Stone: a capacitor gem that recharges continually until the stone's integrity eventually degrades, (Extremely Rare).
Caliber stones: orb stones used as lights by luminaries, (Extremely Rare).
Joulestone: crystals that can hold electrical charges. Fragments are used throughout the world to power small gadgets, guns, (Common).

Power Stones:
Turquoise: strength and stamina.
Blue acarite: Spirit, energy and clarity.
Ruby: added skill and movement and agility.
Topaz: inspiration.
Emerald: luck and reflexes.

Protection Stones:
Obsidian: protection and clarity of mind.

Blood stone: protection and cleansing.

Healing Stones:
Jade: healing and wisdom.
Clear Quartz: healing and memory.
Rose Quartz (love stone or heart stone): love bond and blood cleansing.
Amethyst: calms the spirit, dispels anger and fear, grief and stress.
Sun Stone: healing of wounds and internal aliments.
Bismuth crystal: stomach aches and headaches.

Lore Stones: Considered myth and legend.
The Elder Stone: ultimate protection stone and stone of wisdom.
The Dream stone: provides a connection to dreams.
Mistinite Crystal: crystal prisms with a glittering milk like luster, reveals hidden realms.
Gemstar Stone: asteroid fragment used to power the wave gates.

Corridon: A system of canals inside the Tregorean Province, many running inside the mountains. The three main canals arc called: the Lagrin, the Loren, and the Veerin.

Court of Dragons: The counsel of acolytes in service to the Sagean Lord. Typically, an order consisting of Seven members as the emperor's counsel.

Daraku (dare-ah-kew): The dark lord's son.

Darkhawks: Elite group of fighters located to the New World.

Dawning gale: A mysterious songbird with camouflaging feathers. The bird is known to be heard singing in the Mountains at dawn, but because of its spectral feathers it is rarely ever seen. It's considered by many as a bad omen to see a Dawning Gale.

Day of Light: The New Year begins on the first day of summer, and the longest day of the year. It is the most celebrated holy day in the Empire.

Desolation Blade: The only weapon known that can kill a

dragon. The sword is a mages creation. Te crystal blade is bonded with Dragon blood and ash.

Dire, the: A small grouping of islands in the Brovic Ocean, seven leagues off the Coast of Rodaire, beyond which no one dares travel. It marks a point of no return in the Brovic Ocean. All who have sailed beyond it have died or never returned.

Dragon Ring: A ring used by Luminaries to train and protect apprentices

Dragon's Well: A large underground structure on the island of Denmee used by the Court of Dragons. Housing meeting room, study chambers and a Library. The Well has an expansive open circular center full of arching openings where the winding stone steps descend from the surface.

Dreamer's smoke: An alchemist's dry potion that produces a cloud of white mist and renders all who inhale it asleep.

Drizar: Large reptiles that live in the deadlands.

Drooping pine bark: A common tree in Tovillore, its bark is used in fires and wards off the Sagean's beasts. It burns blue.

Dust Room: A sacred room inside the Tregorean Palace containing a magical dust that is attracted to the spirit of things; blood, objects, substances, and people.

Efferial-rock salt: Alchemists salt, used in healing spells and potions

Egregore mind: An ability of the One people of Wanvilaska to share each other's thoughts.

Elegan Language: An ancient undecipherable language of the Eckwyn Age. Its use predates the Territhian language instituted by the Sagean Empire.

Elum Blade: A sacred sword of the Shadowyn. With a short thin blade, it is holstered upside down and is only 2 and half feet long, including the long hilt. The technique and material used to make the blade are unknown.

Encumbrance, the: People's term for the Coalition of Nations. Referring to both the corruption and game of politics.

Emberbroth: A spicy burning alcoholic drink, served both hot and cold.

Eruptor: A power charged rifle, that fires electrical bolts. It is nearly three times stronger than a pulsator.

Firespark: A thick red liquid, an alchemist's potion created during the Great War. It explodes in a burst of fire once in contact with air.

Furies: A term used by alchemists to describe the known and unknown forces of nature. All alchemy, sigils and spell work derive their power from the Furies.

Fusion Mage: A master of the furies that govern the world. The fusion mage is said to be able to manipulate the elements of the world and make connections to transform the forces of nature to their will.

Gas discharge lamps: Sealed airless glass tubes, with a local capacitor, producing an electrical current that charges a chemical inside, producing light. Oxygen is white, sodium vapor is bright yellow, or orange and krypton is blueish white or green when low.

Genesis Chamber: The main chamber inside the Temple of Ama where the Sintering Fountain resides.

Goreadoom Ant: Giant yellow stripped ants that burrow in the Jungles of Nahadon at the base of trees. Their bit is known to be so painful their victims pass out.

Great War, the: The Great War spanned for 990 days. It began on the 1st of Emberheart in the 15th year of the 23rd epoch and ended on the 1st of Jovost year 18 of the 23rd epoch.

Greencoats: The organized policing force of protectors and law enforcement throughout the world. Also known as peacekeepers.

Green Leopard: A fierce predator found in the Jungles of Nahadon that hunts by body heat and breath, It lives in trees and hunts at night.

Guardian amulets: The amulets said to be constructed by the ancient Luminaries to protect the world. The number of amulets made, and their individual powers are unknown.

Guardians of Illumination, the: A book written by Orin Ioka. It is the oldest account of the Luminaries in existence.

Hammer blast rifle: A powder ignited projectile gun for long range accuracy. Discontinued manufacture and use following the Great War and the invention of charged ammunition.

Hellfiend: A mutation of the bear family. This beast is very rare, seen only once during the Great War. Tracks have been found in both the Sun Mountains and the Soaring Mountains.

Horse types:

Cold blooded horse: a larger horse used to pull carts. These horses are harder to scare and used by military forces.

Hot blooded horse: a fast and slim horse used for speed. They are known to scare easily.

Light horse: a racing breed

Warm blood: a mix of cold and hot blooded horses. They are athletic and strong and the most commonly used for travel.

Nyrogen: a rare breed of horse from the southern regions of Rodaire. They are temperamental, but considered the fastest horse in the world.

Hyperion Compass: A magical compass used by the Sagean Empire to track down the gifted.

Illumination surge: The moment a luminary's powers are truly born inside them. It is the point when the luminary's ability to store energy that they've unconsciously gathered is released. This may occur at any time, but the later in life it takes to occur, the stronger and deeper the luminaries well for energy will be.

Imperial Road: A white stone road arrayed throughout Tovillore, connecting the major cities. The stone road has four grooved tracks to allow wagon wheels to stay in position. Most major settlements and cities are along the track. Also known as the stone track.

The Jaws: The road between the Howling Forest and the Leaving Forrest. Both known to be home to wolveracks and Bonelarks.

Joulestone: *See crystals.*

Joybird: A performer in a showman's traveling circus.

Kihan: What the Tregoreans call themselves.

Lark of the Dead: The act of dueling or gunfighting between two people.

Legion of Light: A group of zealots and believers in the teachings of the Sagean faith. Disbanded after the Great War and the fall of the Sagean Empire.

Linage Book: A book on the Accounts of Talents of Sagean Luminaries.

Lionized, the: Contemporary zealots of the Sagean faith. A radical organization rising up with fall of the Coalition and the appointment of the Prime Commander. They long for the return of a Sagean Emperor.

Longneck Cawacons: A large herbivore with towering necks and wide base bodies that are low to the ground. A rare but gentle animal often seen in the circus menagerie.

Luminaries: A special race of humans with the ability to sense, control, and manipulate energy. This process is referred to as binding. The flows of energies they sense are referred to as the tempests. Once, they were common and collectively ruled the world under separate factions. The separate factions were divided based on their world views, and beliefs. Each faction was its own religion. For reasons lost to history, the Sagean faction took control in the 6th epoch. Most of the other factions were killed or died off. During the reign of the Sagean Empire, their own numbers of luminaries also dwindled.

Luminance Squad: A squad appointed by the Prime Commander to hunt down and capture Qudin Lightweaver.

Magnetometer: A device that measures magnetism—the direction, strength, or relative change of a magnetic field at a particular location.

Magnotype: A typewriter machine with intricate gears and an ink well. It uses magnetic displacements of a needles and gears they are used to communicate messages across the world.

Manus Zabel: The master showman, illusionist and show runner for the *Show of the Magnificent*. A traveling circus throughout the Mainland of Tovillore and Rodaire that Ellaria traveled with as a teenager.

Melodicure machine: A gem powered machine of unknown origin and construction, in use by the Whisper Chain. It aids the Chain in finding people throughout the world.

Menodarians: A race of beings that once existed mostly in Merinde. They are known for their slender, tall forms and their intellect. They have flat faces and were known to be closely guarded and distrustful of other races.

Meiyoma blade: The common sword in Rodaire. Characterized by its long gentle arching blade with two hand length handles. Handles range from plain wood to decorated jade. The hilt is commonly in the shape of a crescent moon.

Miner's Collective: The headquarters for the Moonstalkers, the Bounty Hunters Guild in Amera.

Mirthless: A tall monstrous humanoid being with a face structure that looks like exposed bone. And thin skin pulled tight over muscles that the creature looks almost bloodless.

Monarch trees: Extremely large trees that grew to incredible heights. Only known grove exists on the island of Hazon.

Moonstalkers: A guild of organized bounty hunters.

Moonstone dust: An alchemist's dry potion. A fine powder that protects against evil spirits.

Moorlon: The high plateaus and farming plateaus of the Tregoreans.

Mudfoot: A slang term or derogatory reference to river folk who live along the banks of the Uhanni River. They are known to attack or rob small ships and vessels.

Mystcat: A special breed of cat that is unusually attracted to the gifted. They search out and bond to luminaries and other gifted beings. They are quizzical, sneaky, and very loyal. They love heights and their fur is usually white and gray, all gray, or black. With black being the most rare. Their eyes can be green, blue & yellow and they produce a low harmonic purr. They also bend their ears in patterns of anthropomorphic communication. Additional powers remain unknown.

Ovardyn (O-var-din): The lord of darkness and ruler of The Nothing and the realm of Evil Spirits.

Pathfinder: A experienced traveler or woods guide, with extensive knowledge of the world

Nil Wasp: Giant poisonous wasps that nest in the Jungles of Nahadon

Nothing, the: The domain of Evil Spirits. It is the realm where the demon Ovardyn dwells.

Nowarin Basilisk: Large sand snakes in the Nowarin dessert. They can grow to be the size of whales, but are mostly unseen, as the desserts are uninhabited.

Paravin Schools: Small schools of higher learning in some of the cities. An alternative to the larger Guild run universities. With the aim to teach trade crafts.

Peace King: The Free Cities of The New World were instrumental in the Resistance's success in the Great War. Lead by Arno Danehin, the fourteen-year-old son of Bara Danehin who was killed in the battle of Axern. Arno Danehin railed the troops to win the battle and for the rest of the war assumed the leadership of the armies of the New World. After the war, he was named the Peace King of the Free New World.

Phifer cloth: A cloth of scientifically engineered material that is microscopically fused metal with alchemic symbols sometimes engraved into the weaving. It is impact resistant, highly conductive and so light of weight that it floats on water or even would fail to crush a dandelion. The lithium mesh coat is typically worn by soldiers. Gold colored or black, depending on the rank. Its nickel phosphorus alloy lattice acts as a thermal insulator, acoustic and vibration dampening.

Prolaten: A government official in Kotalla that is the voice of the people.

Protagen force: An eternal fury of bound elements more powerful than the opposite pulls of magnetic energy.

Pulsator: A handheld, charged gun or projectile weapon that fires charged tungsten rounds or bolts. It replaced the less powerful and inaccurate powder firing guns. They are notoriously expensive, and the many components are sought after for various modifications and customizations.

Quandinium: A metal found in abundance across the world. It is most often used in building construction for its strength and lack of conductivity. Other characteristics include: corrosion resistant, a high melting point, ferromagnetic.

Quarter Day Festivals: There are four festivals at the quarter marks of the year. One in each season; Brighden (spring), Alustra (summer), Harven (fall), and Solstar (winter).

Ravenhawk: The nickname of war hero Ellaria Moonstone. A general of the Resistance in the Great War. The name was derived from her service as both a general and a spy during the war.

Raven's breath: An alchemist's potion, truth serum.

Ravinors: The most feared of all the Sagean's beasts. These rare monsters retreated mostly to the south swamps of Tovillore and into the jungles of Nahadon after the war. They are the most intelligent and dangerous of all the beasts. They are lizard like humanoids, walk on two legs and have long snouts with exposed sharp teeth. Sharp claws on their hands and short spiked tails. They are presumed to be reptilian but have many anthropomorphic traits and social behaviors.

Reckoner: A card game played in the major cities. The deck of cards is housed in an action turner that counts down the individual turn meter. Starting after the third turn the reckoning can appear on the turner — ending the game. Anywhere from 2 to 8 people can play, but rules vary. The cards have individual strengths and weaknesses, represented by figures and objects throughout Territhmina history. The object is to field the strongest set of cards to defeat your opponent. The game evolved from the Eckwyn Age and was outlawed for eighteen hundred years until the Empire issued a new and revised deck of cards featuring Sagean Lords. As a way to quell the prominent families forming an uprising in the 19th epoch. A reprint of the original pre-Empire deck was made during the Great War, but an actual fully intact set of original cards has never been found.

Red Spear (aka The Red Dune): A massive rock spire of red clay in the Echo Canyons, used as a prison by the Sagean Empire. The prison was discovered during the Great War and shut down.

Rendered: Automaton beings or machine hunters built by the Sagean.

Religions of Territhmina:
The Sagelight Faith: The Great One, The Light,
The Faith of the Fates: The Entwiner
The Great Creator Amazuie: Hazon
The Great Diviner: Harrinari

Rhuskero Bull: a large grey skinned bull with a single horn. The bull is famous in Adavan and was once used for sport.

Risen World, the: The realm of souls ascended to a plane of existence of pure energy. Where they reside in peace and harmony until they are called upon for a new life.

Rune Book of the Sintering Fountain aka The Dragons Awakening: An ancient book on the sintering fountain and the Scepter used to activate the machine.

Sagean (Saw-Gee-in): The luminary leader of the Sagean faith and Emperor. According to believers of the faith, the Sagean is the living manifestation of the God of Light. The Sagean Empire ruled the world uncontested from the 6th epoch until the 23rd epoch, when the empire was overthrown during the Great War. The last Sagean Emperor, Mayock Kovall, the ninth line of the Sagean progression was defeated by Qudin Lightweaver in the battle of Dragon Spine. The Sagean luminaries can control energy, and were known to manipulate the minds of others, control animals, and alter their appearance.

Sagean's Consortium, the: The name for the remaining army that continued to wage war for the Emperor after the Sagean's death at the Battle of Dragon's Spine. The Consortium waged war and continued to cause conflicts until they were defeated, almost three years later, at the Black Spire of the Citadel.

Sagean Testament: A book guarded by the Sagean ruler passed down to each in line. Its contents are unknown to anyone outside of the lineage of Sageans and their closest acolytes.

Sagelight, the: Can refer to the Sagean faith or the sacred religious text itself.

Sagemitter gauntlet: A glove. It is light as a feather, and only partially covers the fingers. Made of phifer cloth, it allows a luminary who wears it to easily harness and form the energy they sense and bind it into solidified objects.

Scepter of Corinsure: A large black scepter with a dragon wrapping around the staff and engraved alchemist's sigils. The top houses a brilliant blue gem. Named after the 2nd Sagean Empress.

Scholar's Guild, the: An organization entrusted with control over education, curation of history, all publications and select institutes of higher knowledge. Including supervision over alchemists, machine patents, inventions, civil planning and architecture.

Scree: People who were abducted by the Sagean and his agents and whose soul were taken for the Soul Gem to power the Sintering Fountain. There are many names for people suffering from this affliction throughout the Mainland.

Sea-rippers: Giant scorpion crustacean creatures that appeared out of the Brovic ocean on the shores of Rodaire, destroying cities until the Rodairean Legion killed all of them.

Shadow dust: A fine powder that blooms into a cloud of black mist. Created by alchemists during the Great War.

The Shadow Field: A forbidden are of the jungle south of the Tregorean Province beyond the Wall of Nagari.

Shadowyn, the: A small province hidden in the mountains. They train a group of elite warriors for protection from the outside world. Known for their stealth and ability with swords.

Shodders: A common term for cheats, cheaters, grifters, halfwits and anyone who tries to swindle someone with faulty goods, false claims or bad products.

Silver six gun: An old powder fired handgun. The predecessor to the pulsator. These, like all powder powered guns, were discontinued after the Great War.

Sintering: The pressing, molding or binding of elements together.

Sintering Fountain: An ancient machine found in the Temple of Ama. The machine rests inside the Genesis Chamber. Powered by a large crystal of trapped human souls, the fountain is said to have been created to transform humans into Luminaries.

Spirit Elder: The oldest Zenoch leaders. They are considered the wisest of all the Zenoch society. The Spirit Elders guide the Twilight elders in decisions, but do not lead the Zenoch people.

Spotted Shadow Cat: A large feline native to Karnika, the wasteland savanna of The New World. It is usually dark red fir and spotted. They are slim and extremely fast.

Soul Gem or Soul Crystal: A large crystal ball used to contain deposited souls. Protected by metal bands.

Stonebank, the: The affluent section of the city of Aquom.

Sualden: The name for the heart of the Tregorean Province. A massive city carved into the mountains facing Lake Azeerall.

Tazrus Shroud: During the luminary wars, the ancient luminary Tazrus produced a spell so powerful it concealed the great advancements of the Eckwyn Age from all who lived. Including the wave gates.

Tempest Stone: An ancient artifact said to contain the collective knowledge of the ancients.

Temple of Ama: Also called the Temple of Souls, the ancient structure is a complex of jagged spires and ruins in the jungles south of the Tregorean Province in a forbidden are known as the Shadow Field. The towering center spire contains the main temple and the Genesis chamber.

Territh: The name for the land or below the surface of the ground. Interchangeable with soil, dirt or ground.

Territhamy: Scientific study of the land.

Territhian language: The common language throughout Territhmina. Instituted by the Sagean Empire in the 9th epoch. It is the universal language.

Territhmina: The name of the world. The origins of the name predate the Age of Eckwyn.

Territh Driver: Pyramid constructed ground hammer or pile driver used to excavate the ground.

Tinkersmith: A skilled technician with small machine parts, gears, gadgets and workings.

Trancing sand or Ghost sand: Alchemist powder used in sigil spells.

The Traveling Show of Wonders: The current traveling circus of the Mainland of Tovillore and Rodaire, run by Archibald Zabel. It Includes a Menagerie tent for animals and attractions, a Mystics tents for magic shows and elixirs, and fortune tellers, and seance rituals, The Joybirds tent contains the spirits bar and a stage for live local acts, & the Grand Spectacles tent for jugglers, acrobats and large stage shows.

Tregoreans: A race of beings who are known to live in the mountains and jungles of Nahadon, a providence they have lived in untouched throughout the Sagean Empire. They are recognized by their pointed ears and pristine facial appearances. They have been reported to commonly wear tight clothing that camouflages into the surrounding forests and jungles. Very little is known about them, as they do not let outsiders in and are very protective of their lands. It is believed that they live twice the length of time of humans.

Trinity Guard: An ancient order of three bonded specially empowered people to protect the world; consisting of a Luminary, a Nimbus Warrior, and a Fusion Mage.

Torakuma: A mythical large mammal that once lived in the northern snow filled regions Sharing a classification origin of both felines and bears, the large panther like animal, has thick white fir with black stripes at its face. The females have twisted dark grey antlers that angle backward. Also called an Ice Panther or Tigerbear.

Tune of the Redeamer: A famous song.

Tungsten Carbide: Metal used in military weapons due to its extremely high melting point.

Turquoise Flats: A cavernous expanse blanketed by a bright colored lichen. The lichen softens in the sun and hardens at night.

Twilight Elder: The leaders of the Zenoch People

Ultrarians: An elite special forces unit established by Kovan Rainer, the war hero, near the end of the Great War. This force tracked and defeated the final remnants of the Sagean supporters called the Consortium.

Underdeath: A slang term meaning worse than death. Meaning something as horrible or revolting as a corpse.

United Coalition of Nations: The collective governing body of Territhmina. Established, following the Great War, a pact for peace, unity, law and order was signed by all the nations of the known world. While every nation signed the treaty, only a select number of ambassador seats were granted for inclusion on the Coalition Council based on population and land size. At the time the New World was given only one chair represented by their King.

Unity Maze: A term used by prophets to explain the chaotic web of life, time, and the entangled world of the living. The Maze is how prophets understand fate.

Varium Crystal: A small, hollow, delicate crystalline glass jewel that can be filled with an alchemist's concoction, like firespark.

Vazey: Aloof or evasive.

Viper Eye or yellow gem: A yellow crystal gem that captures energy of those who contact it.

Viper Lords: The five coastal cities of Nahadon are controlled by individual rulers.

Wall of Nagari: A ancient stone wall bordering the Shadow Field jungle.

Warbird: Small mechanical hummingbird used by the Sagean and his Court to send messages.

Wave Gate or Acuber magnetic wave gate: Ancient stone and metal gates, constructed with gemstone stars. They were once used by the luminaries to travel instantaneously around the world. Their locations are unknown. Texts suggest they utilize special matter to warp space, allowing objects to pass at speeds faster than light on a gravitational wave to another gate through a unique magnetic connection.

Wavelifers: Term used to describe people who make their living sailing the Anamic Ocean or Zulu Sea.

Way of the Wind: The Rodairean style of sword fighting.

The Western Wall: A Tregorean battlement wall that snakes along the eastern slope of the Shade Mountains in Nahadon, over-looking the Dry Coast. The Wall extends eight hundred leagues from north to south and protects the Tregorean Lands from invaders from the West.

Winddrifter: A smaller airship typically built from a modified sailboat. It uses a steam powered engine and a large air balloon along with large sails to navigate the skies. Sizes, styles and colors vary.

Whisper Chain, the: An organization for the delivery of secret messages, started during the Great War as a secret courier service. They have since expanded their organization to every major city. Their offices are often indistinguishable and hard to locate. Access to the organization and their services is exclusive to its members.

Wolveracks: A beast from the great war once controlled by the Sagean. They are a solitary animal with the size and features of a very large wolf. They have pointed ears and long fang-like teeth. Their upper mane is very full and wiry, but their hind legs are muscular and shorthaired. They have a tough hide and strong tails that grow up to five feet in length. Their eyes can glow yellow when they are aggressive. They don't live in packs, but sometimes hunt in them. Considered very dangerous and aggressive, they become ravenous by the smell of blood.

Wraith or The Night Wraith: A mystical spirit believed to be the hand of death and the messenger and guide to the Nothing.

Wrythen, the: A dark spirit entity that appeared to Qudin on the Dragon's Spine just before he vanquished the Sagean Lord. It seems to be drawn to luminary powers.

Xand Zosmos: The author of the greatest book of alchemy that the Scholar's Guild owns. It surfaced sometime before the Great War.

Zacaren language: A thick dialect spoken throughout Nahadon, but mostly in Zawarin. The language includes a lot of words considered non-territhian.

Zenithal: The summer season is commonly referred to as the zenithal season. In reference to the sun.

Zenoch: A race of beings in the northern mountains of the New World. They are recognized by their blue skin. They are very secretive and considered extremely dangerous. The government of the New World has not tried to expand into their lands. Instead choosing to section off various points as border stops to prevent people from wondering too far.

Zenoch Hierarchy Name: The Zenoch use a system of names, to delineate the ranking of every member of their society, example "Tree-Spear". Each word is associated with a ranking.

About the Author

Steven Rudy is an emerging author of Fantasy and Science Fiction. He studied architecture and creative writing at the University of Colorado at Boulder. Currently he lives with his wife and three children in Colorado and works as an architectural designer.

This is Steven's third book.

You can find him at https://stevenrudybooks.com/ or on social media…

 facebook.com/EpicFantasySeries

 x.com/MysticPeddler

 instagram.com/stevenrudyauthor

www.ingramcontent.com/pod-product-compliance
Lightning Source LLC
Chambersburg PA
CBHW011806200726
48289CB00016B/2865